FRONTAL ASSAULT

Leaping at the Death Merchant, the Russian came at him with an empty AKS-74 assault rifle, the bayonet attached to the barrel glinting its 12-inch blade. Camellion's last 10mm round in the Bren-Ten caught the young Russian while he was still in mid-air, the big bullet boring into the pit of his stomach and half-doubling him over.

Before the dying soldier could fall all the way to the floor, Camellion grabbed the AKS-74 from the man's hands, spun the weapon around and impaled another Russian leaping from the parapet of corpses, the momentum of the flying body driving the blade so far in that it was the muzzle of the barrel that called a halt to the quick entry. The man gave a loud gurgle. Blood poured from his mouth and his eyes jumped out as if attached to invisible stalks—

Don't feel bad, pig-man. Dying of cancer could be worse!

Other titles in the **DEATH MERCHANT** series from Pinnacle Books:

#1 THE DEATH MERCHANT
#2 OPERATION OVERKILL
#3 THE PSYCHOTRON PLOT
#4 CHINESE CONSPIRACY
#5 SATAN STRIKE
#6 ALBANIAN CONNECTION
#7 THE CASTRO FILE
#8 BILLIONAIRE MISSION
#9 LASER WAR
#10 THE MAINLINE PLOT
#11 MANHATTAN WIPEOUT
#12 THE KGB FRAME
#13 MATO GROSSO HORROR
#14 VENGEANCE: GOLDEN HAWK
#15 THE IRON SWASTIKA PLOT
#16 INVASION OF THE CLONES
#17 ZEMLYA EXPEDITION
#18 NIGHTMARE IN ALGERIA
#19 ARMAGEDDON, USA!
#20 HELL IN HINDU LAND
#21 THE POLE STAR SECRET
#22 THE KONDRASHEV CHASE
#23 THE BUDAPEST ACTION
#24 THE KRONOS PLOT
#25 THE ENIGMA PROJECT
#26 THE MEXICAN HIT
#27 THE SURINAM AFFAIR
#28 NIPPONESE NIGHTMARE
#29 FATAL FORMULA
#30 THE SHAMBHALA STRIKE
#31 OPERATION THUNDERBOLT
#32 DEADLY MANHUNT
#33 ALASKA CONSPIRACY
#34 OPERATION MIND-MURDER
#35 MASSACRE IN ROME
#36 THE COSMIC REALITY KILL
#37 THE BERMUDA TRIANGLE ACTION
#38 THE BURNING BLUE DEATH
#39 THE FOURTH REICH
#40 BLUEPRINT INVISIBILITY
#41 THE SHAMROCK SMASH
#42 HIGH COMMAND MURDER
#43 THE DEVIL'S TRASHCAN
#44 ISLAND OF THE DAMNED
#45 THE RIM OF FIRE CONSPIRACY
#46 BLOOD BATH
#47 OPERATION SKYHOOK
#48 THE PSIONICS WAR
#49 NIGHT OF THE PEACOCK
#50 THE HELLBOMB THEFT
#51 THE INCA FILE
#52 THE FLIGHT OF THE PHOENIX
#53 THE JUDAS SCROLLS
#54 APOCALYPSE, U.S.A.
#55 SLAUGHTER IN EL SALVADOR
#56 AFGHANISTAN CRASHOUT
#57 THE ROMANIAN OPERATION
#58 SILICON VALLEY CONNECTION
#59 BURMA PROBE
#60 THE METHUSELAH FACTOR
#61 THE BULGARIAN TERMINATION
#62 THE SOUL SEARCH PROJECT

#63

DEATH MERCHANT

THE PAKISTAN MISSION

Joseph Rosenberger

PINNACLE BOOKS NEW YORK

DEATH MERCHANT #63: THE PAKISTAN MISSION

An original Pinnacle Books edition, published for the first time anywhere.

First printing/June 1985

ISBN: 0-523-42091-9
Can. ISBN: 0-523-43256-9

Printed in the United States of America

PINNACLE BOOKS, INC.
1430 Broadway
New York, New York 10018

9 8 7 6 5 4 3 2 1

While much is too strange to be believed,
nothing is too strange to have happened.

—Thomas Hardy

The strange, the fantastic and the impossible exist only because we do not understand the laws of nature, including the world of the invisible around us. I include Death. It means nothing to us, since when we are, Death has not come, and when Death has come—we are not. . . .

—Richard J. Camellion

THE PAKISTAN MISSION

BOOK ONE

CHAPTER ONE

Modern Pakistan is a cesspool of confusion, barbarism and backwardness, and we're in the middle of it. Richard Camellion walked slowly along the twisting stone path, his right hand in the pocket of his navy-blue wool Cutter coat, his fingers around the butt of a .380 Sig Sauer P-230 pistol. This winter in northern Pakistan was cold, the nighttime temperature dropping as low as fifteen degrees above zero.

To the Death Merchant's right, Michael "Mad Mike" Quinlan was also watching the black shadows of the two Pathan guides in front of him and Camellion and wishing he were somewhere else instead of on his way to the Shrine of Abdul Bu-I-Zum, a Moslem saint. Situated in a rocky area dotted with stunted bayberry bushes and small maples, the shrine was only a few kilometers south of the town of Murree, or thirty-two klicks northeast of Islamabad, the capital of Pakistan.

This was the eighteenth day since Camellion and Quinlan had landed at Karachi's International Civil Airport and had then taken a train to Islamabad. To date, there had not been any serious difficulties, only minor annoyances, the first of which had occurred at the airport. Customs officials had confiscated Mad Mike's four bottles of Scotch. This had been a major catastrophe, for Quinlan loved the joys of Bacchus.

Reflecting now on Mike's consternation at the airport, the Death Merchant thought of how General Mohammad Zia ul-Haq, the president of Pakistan, had tightened government control over the morals and manners of the people.

Public flogging was now permitted, with a microphone placed

before the criminal so that his shrieks of pain could be heard by the assembled crowd.

Gory penalties for serious crimes were now lawful. This meant multilation, the severing of fingers, hands, ears and noses.

Yet President Zia is a mouse when it comes to standing up to the Soviet Union. He's only a tiger with the defenseless, with his own people.

Certain farsighted men in the United States considered President Zia a weakling, whose timidity was inviting the Russians to invade his country.

For that reason, Mohammed Zia ul-Haq had to be removed.

President Mohammed Zia ul-Haq had to die. . . .

After a week in Islamabad, doing what two "historians" from the University of Kansas were supposed to do—asking pertinent questions and visiting ancient sites—Camellion and Quinlan had made contact with the "cutout" from the CIA station at the United States embassy. Yes, the arrangements had been made. The cutout agent had more good news: the airdrop from Bikarner, India, had been made.

A short time later, they had met the same two fierce-looking Pathans who were now leading them to the tomb of the Moslem saint—Wanja Likstom and Punji Sorhib—and were on their way to Peshawar, once the frontier headquarters for the British. Peshawar appeared to be two cities. The cantonment that the British had built was a gracious tract of wide avenues and, in summer, flaming bougainvillea. The other section, called the City, was a bazaar, a place of winding alleys and noise and intense aromas, dense with shops, cyclists, horse-drawn tongas, carts pulled by water buffalo, and putt-putting three-wheeled taxis.

Likstom and Sorhib, as mean-looking as king cobras at mating time, had taken the Death Merchant and Colonel Quinlan to the City. They had gone past the Namakmandi, the salt market and the home of the false-teeth-makers, and on to Qissa Khawani, the Street of the Knifemakers. In a small house at the end of the Qissa Khawani, they had found Iskander Chaudhriy and four other men waiting. Chaudhriy was the chief lieutenant of Mujibur Ali Mirza-Khan, the Pathan leader of the revolutionary Quiddin Azi-Hulam'ki, the "Circle of Pure Blood" party. Strangely enough, the good-looking, friendly Chaudhriy[1] was from the Bugi tribe, which hated the even more warlike Pathans.

[1].Pronounced *Chawed-ri-e*.

At once, the small party had started for the stronghold of Mujibur Ali Mirza-Khan in the Safed Koh mountains in the northwest frontier.

The meeting with Mirza-Khan had gone well—almost. The seventy-nine-year-old leader, who looked sixty, was especially pleased with the ordnance the CIA had flown in from India and dropped on his base—300 Galil automatic rifles, 200 9mm Beretta 92SB autopistols and ammunition for both, plus various kinds of grenades and plenty of medical supplies. The airdrop had also included several large cylinders of goodies for Camellion, Quinlan and Mad Mike's two men who had flown in to Karachi from West Germany while the Death Merchant and Colonel Quinlan had been on their way to the Safed Koh. "German businessmen" on a vacation, Karl Wilhelm "Willy" Bruckner and James Victorio O'Malley—the Peppermint Kid—would also take a train from Karachi to Islamabad.

There had been a setback. Mirza-Khan had bluntly refused to help the Death Merchant, Colonel Quinlan and his two Thunderbolt Unit Omega mercs assassinate President Zia and other high officials of the Pakistan government, his unwillingness not based on any moral consideration. Although a Moslem fanatic, Mirza-Khan despised President Mohammed Zia for his conciliatory attitude toward the Russians. Mirza-Khan would have liked to see President Zia and every member of the federal parliament dead ten times over and buried in unmarked graves. He had refused for a reason that was purely practical: any assassination attempt would almost certainly be doomed to failure. President Zia and other key men in the government were too well guarded, especially Zia, who seldom left the presidential palace and feared not only killers from the various tribes but assassins from the Soviet Union.

To the Death Merchant, Mirza-Khan's rejection was another "minor annoyance." He had known all along that the CIA had wanted the impossible. It would take a small army even to get close to President Zia. But . . . keep trying to persuade Mirza-Khan. He could change his mind . . . *when icebergs float in hell*.

The cake may have been hollow, but it had a thick frosting. Mirza-Khan had been only too anxious to have his men help in a surprise attack on the new Soviet base outside of Narang, just across the Pakistan-Afghanistan border and less than a hundred kilometers from Mirza-Khan's stronghold in the Safed Koh. But

Mirza-Khan had one condition: more weapons, including mortars and heavy machine guns, as well as flame throwers and recoilless antitank rifles.

Mujibur Ali Mirza-Khan had said to the Death Merchant, "We will discuss the attack against the Russian dogs after you and Kir[2] Quinlan return with your two friends. I caution you: do not underestimate the talents of General Saha I'Zada and his Chanwiri-lu-Shabudar. His secret police are as sly as hungry foxes. Go now. May Allah guide your steps."

Wanja Likstom and Punji Sorhib, the two guides, had taken the Death Merchant and Colonel Quinlan back to Peshawar, this time all four using the caution of wanted criminals. All visitors from the West were watched by the "Protectors of the People," the secret police, and it was almost a certainty that agents of General Saha I'Zada had followed the two American "historians" everywhere in Peshawar. By now, Camellion and Quinlan would be missed, and the secret police would be quietly looking for them. When they didn't find them—and they wouldn't—they would immediately suspect that the two were foreign agents.

Camellion and Quinlan did have one consolation. They were no longer "naked." They were well armed, due to the airdrop from India that had also included various handy devices and a Satcom transceiver, an AN/URC-101 with 5 kHz spacing.

There had been only one course of action to take: hide out in a house that belonged to a member of the Circle of Pure Blood and wait until contact could be made with Willy Bruckner and the Kid, a task that could be very dangerous. With two American "historians" having already disappeared from Peshawar, the secret police would keep a very sharp eye on the two "West Germans," Bruckner and O'Malley.

Apparently, the secret police had done just that. It was five days before the information—carried along the twisted chain of contacts, from Company Cutout to messengers of the Circle of Blood—reached Camellion, Quinlan, and the two guides holed up in a house on Pur'ku'I-Kunarq, the Street of the Sky. They were to meet Willy and the Kid at 01,00 hours of the next day, in front of the shrine of Abdul Bu-I-Zum. To be precise, fifty feet in front of the tomb.

The cold wind raced over the rocks, swept through the bare trees and did its best to pluck the blue corduroy Cragsmere hat

[2]. The same as the English "Mister."

from the Death Merchant's head. He looked up at the sky, at the half-moon playing tag with thick patches of high clouds. He and Quinlan and the two Pathans could see as well as any four men whose eyes had adapted to darkness. Still, their vision was limited to a radius of ten feet, a big minus in case of trouble, especially with an enemy who might be lying in wait with night-vision devices.

"It's about time you say stop," Mike Quinlan said in a low voice. At six-foot-one and 200 pounds, he was an inch taller and twenty pounds heavier than the Death Merchant. He edged closer to Camellion. "We both know we're not going to walk right up to that tomb and yell, 'Hey guys! Where are you?' "

"We would have to be morons to do that, wouldn't we?" Camellion replied. He then called out to the two guides. "Sorhib, Likstom. We stop here."

Wearing *chudkis,* heavy woolen thigh-length coats, and *kobasas,* the tall black woolen Cossack-like hats of the Pathans, the two guides stopped and turned to Camellion and Quinlan, puzzlement in their dark eyes.

"Why we stop here?" asked Punji Sorhib in fractured English. "We only halfway to sacred place." A good four inches taller than Quinlan, he was a very thin man with stained, broken teeth and a Fu Manchu mustache that hung down past his chin. At one time he had been a gunsmith in Darra, in the northwest frontier, the stronghold of the warlike Pathan tribe.

"How much farther do we have to go?" Camellion inquired. "Would you say another kilometer? I also notice that we seem to be moving slightly upward."

Sorhib spat on the ground. "Another kilometer we must go. Certain I am of the distance, Kir Camellion."

"We are on a very long slope," explained Wanja Likstom, who was as fierce looking as Sorhib, only a head shorter and much heavier. The Death Merchant sensed he was also more intelligent than Sorhib. "The shrine is at the top of this slope."

"Make your point, Richard," Quinlan said impatiently. He let the Condura nylon utility satchel in his right hand settle to the ground and wished he had a drink.

"My point is the approach to the tomb." Camellion turned back to Sorhib and Likstom. "Is this the only way to the tomb, or can we take another route?"

"This way is the ordinary route from the south," Likstom said, shifting to his other foot. "There is another approach from the east, from the old caravan road. This is the only way from Murree."

"What about the approaches from the west and the north?"

The Death Merchant watched the two Pathans exchange quick glances.

"One cannot reach the shrine from the north and the west." Likstom took a few steps toward Camellion. "As I told you, the shrine is at the top of this long rise. To the north and west are rocky slopes. They are steep, Kir Camellion."

"We think same as you," appended Punji Sorhib. "Up there could be Chanwiri-lu-Shabudar wait for us, maybe, huh?"

"Maybe—*ched!*"[3] Camellion said. "We're not going to walk up there blind. Could we climb the slopes on the west and the north side without making a lot of noise?"

"Could we get to the bottom from here, my *baya-darkas?*"[4] asked Quinlan, pushing up on his wool cap.

"Very difficult to do in the dark," Likstom said. "Impossible in the dark without making a lot of noise. It would be difficult to even get to the slopes in the dark."

"But could we do it if we could 'see' in the dark?" posed Camellion.

Likstom shook his head. "Allah no longer works miracles. That is only for the storytellers around nighttime fires."

"Maybe Allah doesn't, but modern technology does. Show them, Mike."

Quinlan picked up the Cordura satchel, unzipped it and took out one of the Cyclops night-vision devices that had been air-dropped to Mirza-Khan's base. The instrument appeared to be four-inch-long goggles mounted on a metal housing from which dangled rubber head straps. A product of LEA,[5] the Cyclops utilized an infrared intensifier that amplified background light—starlight and cloud reflection—18,000X, the images viewed through binocular eyepieces.

Quinlan set each eyepiece to six diopters and handed the night-vision device to Wanja Likstom. "Look through the eyepieces, my friend. You will see a great change."

Hesitantly, Likstom placed the Cyclops NVD against his face

3. "Yes."

4. "Blood-brothers."

5. Law Enforcement Associates, 700 Plaza Drive, Secaucus, New Jersey 07094.

and looked through the eyepieces. "*Chuvarki!*"[6] he exclaimed, not believing what he knew had to be true. The darkness had disappeared. Now there was only a soft twilight. Clearly he could see the rocks, the trees, the entire countryside. So be it! These infidels were clever.

Excitedly, Likstom handed the device to Punji Sorhib, who put it to his eyes and turned toward the faint, dull glow that was the lights of Murree. "By the power of Allah," he muttered, "I can see even the trees and the rocks that are a hundred meters from this very spot." Amazed, he looked dumbly at Camellion and handed the Cyclops device back to Colonel Quinlan.

"We have two of these machines that can see in the dark," Camellion told the two guides. "I will wear one and one of you will wear the other. Now, do you think we can reach the slopes from here and, after we get there, climb the slopes to the tomb?"

Both Likstom and Sorhib nodded quickly.

"We do it easy with see-in-dark things," Sorhib said confidently. "If secret police they wait for us up there, we see and kill them." He tapped his chest. "I wear the see-in-dark thing."

"*Yibo.*[7] I will." Likstom looked angrily at his countryman.

"But I am the senior guide. It was Malik[8] Mirza-Khan who said that it was so," protested Sorhib.

"I am older than you," pointed out Likstom. "So it is I who will wear the see-in-the-dark thing."

Sorhib declined to argue. According to *Pukhtunwali,*[9] age took precedence over seniority (and ugliness).

Colonel Quinlan handed the device to Likstom and showed him how to adjust the rubber straps over and around his head, while the Death Merchant reached into the bag, took out the second Cyclops, adjusted the mechanism, then slipped the device over his face and secured the holding bands.

Soon, with the Death Merchant and Likstom in front, the four had begun a careful walk down the side of the pathway. At this point the inclines on both sides were not steep. By digging in the heels first and leaning slightly backward, one could descend the 200-meter slope without too much difficulty.

A short time later, after they had reached the bottom, the

6. The closest English equivalent would be "Amazing!"

7. "No."

8. "Chief."

9. The Pathan code of conduct.

Death Merchant said to Wanja Likstom, "Tell me, my *baya-darkas*, you are familiar with this area, is that not so?"

"*Ched*, that is true; I know it well," replied Likstom.

"When we are 125 meters from the shrine, let me know. We'll then go in very slowly."

"If the secret police are waiting, there could be several waiting down on this level," Quinlan offered. "They're not stupid. We have to assume that they've assumed we'd smell a trap, sneak in below, then scramble up the slope to the shrine."

"Let's say they are down here." Camellion sniffed the air. "More likely than not, they won't make any moves until we're halfway up the slope—and we could be wrong. It's possible that they're not up ahead." He unbuttoned his coat, reached in and pulled out a Bren Ten autopistol.

"If they are down here, more will be above us," said Quinlan, "which means that Willy and the Kid and their two guides will be on their own." He looked worriedly at the Death Merchant, who, with the Cyclops NVD over his face, could have been a being from Planet X. "The hell of it is, only their guides will be armed."

Camellion pulled the Bren Ten from the holster. "Let's not dig any graves before we have to. We can't be positive that the Kid and Bruckner were even followed. For that matter, we don't even know that the Kid and Bruckner and their guides got here; something unforseen could have delayed them."

Growled Punji Sorhib, "We stand on this spot. We do nothing. We lose time."

Quinlan gave a low, knowing laugh. "Don't deal me any phony hands of hope, Richard. We've been through too much fire and ice together. We both think that Willy and the Kid were tailed by the secret police. The odds are that they were."

Wanja Likstom reached out with both hands and patted Quinlan and Camellion on the shoulders. "The guides will take good care of your friends—you see."

He patted Camellion and Quinlan again, his heavy hand a source of annoyance to Camellion who disliked being touched. There wasn't anything he could do about it. The men of Pakistan (except for the Kalash people), like the Arabs, were great touchers.

The Death Merchant turned to go. "Let's get moving," was all he said.

They forged ahead as rapidly as was possible under prevailing conditions, stepping carefully on pebbly rocks and moving around fair-sized boulders and *choppi* thorn bushes. Quinlan and Sorhib kept directly behind the Death Merchant and Wanja Likstom. There was only silence, a heavy sense of desolation and the acute awareness of danger. At length, Likstom touched Camellion on the arm.

"We are close," he whispered. "About a hundred meters. How do we continue? If agents of the Chanwiri-lu-Shabudar are waiting on top . . ."

Camellion paused. "How wide is the area above, the area close to the tomb?"

Likstom scratched his right cheek. "I can't be sure. Not more than sixty meters. What difference does it make? We are down here."

The Death Merchant studied the slope. A long, uneven slant! From the bottom to the top—eighty feet. Camellion shifted his think machine into high gear. Sixty meters was practically 200 feet. *That means the secret police will have a lot of room to hide in.*

"Proceed like the turtle," Camellion ordered Likstom. "You watch the ridge."

"They cannot see us from above," responded Likstom. "The distance is too great."

"They could—and will—if they have see-in-the-dark devices."

The four men crept forward. Now it was step by step, second by second. By now, Colonel Quinlan and the two Pathans had pulled handguns, Mad Mike armed with a 9mm Glock-17 Austrian military pistol, the hands of Sorhib and Likstom filled with 9mm Beretta 92-SB autoloaders.

They covered a distance of seventy-five feet. Then a hundred feet was behind them. The threatening silence continued, broken only by the rise and fall of the wind.

They stopped among a group of boulders and Likstom whispered, "I see nothing on the ridge. . . no one." He continued to stare at the area above and to the right.

"Of course you don't see them," Quinlan said brusquely, annoyed by Likstom's illogic. "They won't show themselves until we are halfway up the ridge."

He was proved half wrong a few moments later.

The Death Merchant, the Cyclops NVD imprisoning his face, at first saw only boulders, the bleakness of scrub grass and *choppi* bushes and weather-worn limestone that projected upward in grotesque forms and shapes. He drew back slightly in surprise when he saw, eighty feet in front of him, a man step from behind a wide slab of limestone. Some kind of instrument was in one of the man's hands.

As though the Pak government's secret police had orchestrated the moves, a second man stepped out from behind a diminutive pinnacle of limestone thirty feet to the left of the first agent, who was now raising the hand-held night-vision scope to his eyes. While Hassan Uganki, the second agent, was raising his NVS, the Death Merchant calculated some harsh realities, instantly reached a conclusion, and said, "All of you—down!" in a loud voice and raised the big Bren Ten[10] pistol. He snap-aimed at the first man and squeezed the trigger, the shot shattering the silence and causing Mike Quinlan to let out a stream of purple prose that would have horrified an Algiers prostitute.

The first agent, Puli Bagalan, never had a chance to get a good look through his West German Buerger nightscope and see who it was who was killing him. He didn't have time to feel any pain either. The 10mm FMJ bullet, with its truncated cone tip, stabbed him high in the left chest, buzzed through his body, zipped out his back and spun him around with such force that his legs almost tied themselves together in a bow.

Hassan Uganki, the second secret police agent, was rattled to the point of pure panic. He didn't get even a glimpse of the Death Merchant. All he heard was the sky-shattering shot and the sound of his own pounding heart. All he had time to do was throw himself behind the limestone, jerk out his Browning, take a transceiver from his leather coat and turn it on. *Dukow-i'kotil Allah ka-mak!* Something was very wrong. . . .

Quinlan, Sorhib and Likstom had dropped and rolled behind the boulders. Now down beside them, the Death Merchant pulled his other Bren Ten pistol.

Mad Mike was furious with Camellion. "Buffalo balls! Why

[10].The Bren Ten is a brand-new double-action autopistol that is manufactured in the United States by Dornaus & Dixon. In a sense, the Bren Ten is tied in with the famous Bren of WW II—the British light machine gun. The Bren LMG was developed from a Czech design built at the Brno (Czechoslovakia) factory and finalized at the British Enfield arsenal. The two names, Brno and Enfield were combined to form "Bren."

Brno is still a leader in firearms production and now produces the famed CZ-75 pistol in 9mm Parabellum. The Bren Ten is a slight improvement over the CZ-75 design. Not only does it fire a more powerful cartridge, but the safety features have been improved. It holds eleven 10mm cartridges. Price: $500.

did you waste that turkey up ahead? That shot alerted all of them. Damn it, you should have ignored him!''

''Ignore him? Then do what?'' demanded Camellion, his tone mild and patient. ''There were two of them up there. That means more are upstairs, and maybe on this level, on the other side. We can't go forward and we can't climb upward until we settle their hash. The way I did it, there's one less we have to deal with. Now we'll let them make the next move.''

The blast-boom of the Bren Ten had alerted the other Pak government agents, as well as Wilhelm Bruckner, James O'Malley and their guide, Alfu Krod, all three of whom had been impatiently waiting among some white cedars in front of the ten-foot-high granite tomb of Abdul Bu-I-Zum. Instantly the three men were on full alert, Alfu Krod pulling an old Colt Model 1917 .45 revolver.

''*Donnerwetter!* We were followed!'' muttered Bruckner. ''You were right, Kid. Well, we fight to the finish, *ja!*''

''We will wait here!'' Alfu Krod whispered nervously. ''We not move!''

''You wait if you want,'' whispered the Peppermint Kid. ''But you're making a mistake if you do. They trailed us here—right? So they know where we are—right? We're going out after them.'' He pulled an exact copy of a British .38 Webley Mark IV revolver from inside his coat. The weapon had been made by a Pathan gunsmith and O'Malley had bought it in one of the bazaars in Peshawar.

''I'll go south,'' grunted Bruckner. He had pulled two weapons he had bought in Peshawar, a perfect replica of a French 9mm MAB autopistol and a black-handled dagger with a seven-inch double-edged blade.

Neither O'Malley, Bruckner nor Krod had seen any of the nine secret police agents who had trailed them to the shrine. Two of the agents were to the side of the west slope, only now one was a corpse. Five were on top, within the area of the tomb—one behind the mammoth tombstone, two on the west side and two on the east ridge. The last two agents of the Chanwiri-lu-Shabudar—the CLS—were below on the east side. In response to the warning from Hassan Uganki, the eight agents now put a contingency plan into effect.

Abdul Takmir and Faiz Parwan started up the east slope,

Parwan carrying a Buerger nightscope and a Czech Vz-25 submachine gun. He and Takmir would join the two agents on the east ridge, then the four of them would close in on the three suspected revolutionaries, who might even be Soviet agents!

Paka Ghorm and the two agents on the west ridge would help the two men by the west slope deal with the enemy on that side. Behind the tomb, Ghorm also carried a Vz-25 SMG. So did Logar Kunarq, whose position was northwest on the ridge; he also had a nightscope.

Sayed Faizabad was a hundred feet south of Kunarq. He had a nightscope but was armed with only a Browning P-35 autoloader.

We'll let them make the next move, Camellion had said. The agents of the CLS did just that. Logar Kunarq, who hated Russians and Westerners with equal passion, looked through the Buerger nightscope and opened fire with his SMG, sending a stream of slugs toward the Death Merchant and his men below. A few moments later, Faizabad studied the terrain below through his night-sight viewer and carefully fired three shots with his Browning. Paka Ghorm began to creep toward the west side.

A hail of Vz-25 SMG 9mm projectiles rained down, stinging the tops of the boulders protecting Quinlan, Likstom and Sorhib. Chips of granite splattered over Quinlan and the two Pathans, but none of the slugs even came close to the Death Merchant, who, in an effort to trick the single enemy to the north, had ringed himself with boulders. Because of the long slope, Kunarq could not fire directly down at Camellion and the other men; he could only fire at a steep, sideways angle.

However, two of Faizabad's 9mm projectiles had come closer to the target than Kunarq's. They had because it was usually easier to fire a pistol while looking through a nightscope than it was to fire a submachine gun. One of Faizabad's 9mm slugs actually zipped through the brim of Camellion's hat.

"Mike, do it when you can," Camellion called out. "Likstom, Sorhib! Concentrate on that machine gunner up there."

Once more there were two sharp cracks from Faizabad's Browning, one slug ricocheting from a rock close to Camellion's head, followed by the lower, more furious sounds of Kunarq's SMG and more howling of metal glancing off granite.

Mike Quinlan wouldn't have any trouble seeing the slab of limestone protecting Uganki. Wanja Likstom had relinquished his "see-in-the-dark thing" to Quinlan, protesting all the while.

"Fire when you see the flashes of their weapons," Quinlan whispered to Sorhib and Likstom. Then, during the lag time in the firing from above, he got off five quick shots at the side of the limestone ahead, yelled, "Let's charge him! He's only one man!" and quickly ducked down, hoping the Pak agent behind the slab to the north could understand English.

Hassan Uganki could. At one time, Pakistan had been under British rule and English was a second language to most Paks.

Thinking that the enemy was about to rush him, Uganki leaned out from behind the limestone and fired a half-dozen slugs from his Browning. He didn't bother to aim. He only wanted to keep his position from being overrun. He only wanted to stay alive.

He didn't get what he wanted. He was careful and exposed as little of himself as he could. But that little was enough for the Death Merchant. Three times he pulled the trigger of one Bren Ten pistol. One 10mm smashed into Uganki's right shoulder and almost tore off his arm. The second hit him low in the waist area and tore through the ascending colon. The last slug sliced into his right front thigh and broke the femur. As good as dead and bleeding like a butchered hog, he fell back, the Big Sleep beginning to close in on him.

Kunarq again cut loose with his submachine gun and Faizabad got off four more rounds with his Browning, and again every slug, while coming far too close for any measure of comfort, missed Camellion and the three other men. This time, however, the Death Merchant, taking a chance by raising himself slightly, had been able to detect the rapid flashes from the muzzle of Logar Kunarq's Vz-25 SMG. This time he used the Bren Ten that still had a full magazine, firing cop style, with both hands, nine times. Only two of the big slugs struck Kunarq, and the first one didn't do much damage. It grazed his left rib cage. It was the second slug that did the damage. It stabbed into his abdomen, twisted him around, slammed him to the ground and started him on the road to Forever.

Paka Ghorm, by now getting closer to Kunarq's position, saw his fellow agent fall and heard four loud shots to the southeast, toward the east ridge. Assuming that the four other agents on that side were closing in on the two spies and their guide, Ghorm rushed to the dying Kunarq, picked up the infrared viewer and checked his SMG.

To the south, Sayed Faizabad snapped off a few more rounds with his Browning.

* * *

The Death Merchant, Colonel Quinlan and the two Pak guides didn't dare move, although by now Sorhib and Likstom had managed to spot the very brief but bright flashes from Faizabad's Browning. None of them could be sure that Camellion had whacked out the machine gunner.

"We must move," Quinlan said harshly. "For all we know, one of them could have radioed for help. And those four shots we heard. Either it was the Kid and Willy firing at the police or vice versa."

"I'm almost positive I got the joker with the chatterbox," Camellion said slowly. "Once we snuff the slob with the pistol, we can either go up this side, or go around to the north and climb that slope. We—"

It was then that Paka Ghorm began raking the boulders with his Czech SMG, the 9mm slugs tap-dancing on the rocks furiously.

"Tell me again, buddy. What did you say about being positive?" remarked Quinlan, whose nose was so close to the ground he could smell the soil,

"I was saying that we have a Lazarus up on that ridge," Camellion said with mock seriousness. "I'll bury him for good once I know his position."

As suddenly as it had begun firing, the SMG stopped. Ghorm had exhausted the ammo in the magazine. As if taking his cue, Sayed Faizabad got off six rounds with his Browning P-35. One came close to Mike Quinlan; another skimmed across the Death Merchant's back.

This time, however, Sorhib and Likstom were ready. The instant Faizabad stopped firing, they both reared up and fired their Berettas, round after round, three of their 9mm hollowpoints finding a surprised Sayed Faizabad—one low in the chest, one high in the stomach, one high in the forehead. He died with the swiftness of a light being turned off.

Punji Sorhib was just as unfortunate. Before he and Wanja Likstom could flatten themselves completely to the ground, another hail of 9mm projectiles rained down from Paka Ghorm, all missing flesh, save one. It caught Sorhib in the left temple, tunneled through his head at a downward angle and came out underneath his lower right jaw. He dropped without a sound—stone dead in the Pakistan countryside.

Ghorm's last shot was still bouncing back and forth between sky and earth as Camellion raised both Bren Ten autopistols and began pulling the wide triggers. Two of the big bullets found Ghorm. One struck him just below the left knee; the other one hit him very high in the forehead, opened his skull and sprinkled the ground with part of his brain. The slug that hit the leg sent the limb backward, which meant that the rest of the corpse toppled forward toward the edge of the ridge. The dead man went over the edge, leaving a spray of blood and gray matter behind him. The corpse rolled twenty feet and came to a stop.

"Zig it and zag it!" said a happy Camellion, who jumped to his feet and tore toward the west slope. Quinlan and Likstom didn't lose any time in getting up and racing in the same direction and toward the same goal—the corpse on the slope.

James Victorio O'Malley, who was called the Peppermint Kid because of his fondness for sweet peppermint schnapps, had learned his trade in the British commandos. One of his specialties was infiltration—and he was good. The wiry Briton could almost slither over eggshells and not make a sound—or break one either. He proved it now by creeping to within twenty feet of Balak Chikra, one of the agents on the east ridge. Chikra had decided to stay put and wait for Faiz Parwan and Abdul Takmir. For that reason, he had turned from the south and was now watching the northeast section of the ridge. It was when he shifted to a more comfortable position and his feet raked through the underbrush that O'Malley heard the sound—in front of him. As slow as a stalking tiger, O'Malley crept forward, inch by inch, testing the ground and the dead leaves and fallen branches before moving over them. At length, he found Balak Chikra. In the darkness, he could barely see him, but at least he had located him. He was debating how to waste the damned bloody blighter when he heard sounds from the northeast. The only thing that really worried O'Malley was whether the imitation .38 Webley would fire. If it didn't . . .

In only seconds he heard Abdul Takmir and Faiz Parwan and very soon could see the dim forms of the two men. He couldn't be sure, but he thought one of them was carrying a submachine gun and what could be an infrared nightscope.

O'Malley fired, the sound of the exploding cartridge screaming into the night. Abdul Takmir let out a loud groan, dropped the nightscope and the music box and fell. Faiz Parwan was the next man to go down, a .38 bullet only half an inch from his heart.

Balak Chikra had started to get up at the approach of Takmir and Parwan, and the Peppermint Kid's slug hit him in the middle of the back, striking one of the buckles of a strap that crossed his back and chest. At the ends of the strap was an olive-drab canvas case filled with a West German Forgeister transceiver.

In spite of the pain from the bullet, which had pushed a small portion of the buckle into his back, Chikra tried to turn around and fire. He failed. O'Malley's fourth bullet hit him in the left side of the neck and sent him to the ground, drowning to death in his own blood. Still very cautious, O'Malley crept forward, wondering how Willy was doing. . . .

Appearances seldom tell the whole story. Wilhelm Bruckner looked like the Hollywood version of a German army sergeant—big, slow-moving and stupid. Willy Bruckner was big, and there the resemblance ended. Willy's 240 pounds never interfered with his moving with all the speed and grace of a ballet dancer—when he had to. He was also a survivor, and because he had the natural-born instincts of a predator and a stone killer, he didn't crawl due south. He knew that if he did, he would probably bump into the secret police agents who had been behind him, Alfu Krod and the Kid.

Willy crawled east for an estimated hundred feet, stopping when we was only ten feet from the ridge. He then turned and began a due-south course. All he had to do was get behind the agent or agents. He finally did, succeeding at about the time the Death Merchant was pumping 10mm projectiles into Paka Ghorm.

There was Jokbi Sariq, not more than twenty feet in front of Willy, lying prone on the ground, facing the north. *Jawohl,* this would be easy. But not with the *Französisch* MAB. He would use the dagger. The pistol might misfire. A dagger couldn't miss—not when he threw it. All he had to do was get the *schweinhund* to stand up.

A wolfish grin spread over Bruckner's large face as he reached down and picked up a fair-sized rock. He measured the distance. Carefully then he threw the rock and pulled the dagger.

Colonel Quinlan and Wanja Likstom didn't even slow down when they caught up with the Death Merchant, who was searching the corpse of Paka Ghorm. They rushed straight to the top of the slope, took a prone position six feet from the ridge and waited for Camellion to join them. Some minutes later, he came up the slope. He had holstered his two Bren Ten pistols and was carrying a Vz-25 submachine gun and a hand-held nightscope. He crawled over the ridge and got down between Quinlan and Likstom, the former of whom whispered, "We can't move out. We can see in the dark but Willy and the Kid can't. And they seldom miss when they shoot."

"I thought they did not have weapons?" Likstom screwed up his weather-pounded face and turned to look at Quinlan, who was searching the area ahead through the Cyclops NVD over his face.

"It's like this, my *baya-darka*"—Quinlan grinned—"there are, or were, enemy agents up here, and they were armed. We can count on O'Malley and Willy to have killed a few by now and to have some of their weapons."

"We can't call out to them either," the Death Merchant said. "We'd give away our position, and there could be secret police lying in wait up here, or on the east slope. On the other hand . . ." He reached into a side pocket of his Cutter coat and pulled out the UHF/VHF FM walkie-talkie he had taken from the corpse of Paka Ghorm. "We can try this WT and see who we get."

"What good will that do?" Clearly puzzled, Likstom rolled over on his right side, looked at the Death Merchant and pulled his *chudki* closer around his chest. "Only the enemy will answer, if they answer at all!"

Quinlan gave a little laugh. "You don't know our two friends. By now they've killed some of the enemy and have their weapons. They'll have searched the bodies, have found other walkie-talkies and be thinking along the same lines as us. They know they can't look for us anymore than we can look for them."

Camellion switched on the walkie-talkie and spoke into the mouthpiece. "This is the Easter bunny. Come in somebody, anybody."

A long, low and cynical laugh came from the speaker, then, "If you 'ave to use stupid names, why not Funkledunkle? I say, this wouldn't be that creep from the Colonies, Richard Camellion, would it?"

"It would, Kid," Camellion replied, feeling a great relief. "What's your situation—and don't give your position."

"We're safe, we are. I killed three of the blokes. Willy got one. How about you chaps? By the way, one of them had a long-range West German radio with him. Do you think we might make use of it."

"You smoked three. But we heard four shots."

"The last guy must 'ave been wearin' a concrete vest. I had to shoot him twice. How do we play it?"

"You and Willy and your guides move—"

"We only 'ave one guide."

"OK. You three move to the rear of the tomb. We'll meet you in back of the tombstone. And Kid, bring that German radio."

"Good enough," said the Peppermint Kid. "We'll see you chaps there. Don't get trigger happy. We won't. Out and ten-four and all the rest of that bloody nonsense."

The Death Merchant shut off the walkie-talkie, dropped it in his pocket, pulled out his Bren Ten pistols and proceeded to shove fresh magazines into the butts.

"Why do we need the German radio?" Quinlan asked.

Camellion pulled back the slide of one Bren Ten. However, he didn't let the slide snap back into place with a clang as it pulled a cartridge into the breech. He eased the slide back into place.

"We'll have Wanja here call in to the base headquarters of the goons we killed and report that we've been captured. Likstom, you do speak Urdu,[11] don't you?"

"Of course, but your scheme will not work," replied Likstom. "We don't know the names of one agent, and suppose there is some kind of special code they use. They had to come from Peshawar. Murree is too small a settlement to have a unit of the Chanwiri-lu-Shabudar."

"We'll give it a try anyhow," Camellion insisted. "We do have one name. I took the identification folder from the cold cut on the slope."

"It's too bad we don't know where those agents parked their cars," Quinlan said forlornly. "We could use one of their vehicles. That 1965 Ford we have could break down anytime."

"Oh, no! The Ford will not break down." Likstom sounded surprised. "Pokik keeps all his machines in wonderful condition. Why he controls all the taxi business on the Khyber road. He could not do that with automobiles that did not run properly."

"I don't suppose it makes all that much difference," said Quinlan, who had gotten up and, in a low crouch, was moving with Camellion and Likstom in the direction of the tomb. "We've been doing the impossible for the ungrateful for so long with so little that we are now qualified to do almost anything with nothing."

[11]. The official language of Pakistan.

He suddenly started to laugh.

"Yeah, it's the truth, but it wasn't the least bit funny," Camellion said, his voice metallic. To the northeast, all he could see were rocks, dead grass and dead leaves, and the grim, granite tomb of the Moslem saint who had blown up himself and sixty-eight British soldiers.

"I was thinking of something else," Quinlan explained, still chuckling. "I'll tell you about it sometime. . . ."

CHAPTER TWO

Pakistan has never been a favorite with tourists. Even before President Zia's regime turned the nation into a strict Islamic society and moved the capital from Karachi to Islamabad, the country held little interest for Westerners. The exception was professional mountain climbers who often attacked K2, one of the world's tallest mountains, in the Hindu Kush range. K2 itself is right on the border of northern Pakistan and southwestern China.

About half the size of Mexico, Pakistan never did have Western-type entertainment. Never were there any nightclubs; however, the larger hotels did have bars and cabarets, with dancing nightly, except Friday, the Moslem day of worship. President Zia and his military regime changed all that. All bars and cabarets were closed, movie houses locked. Censorship fell over the press. Foreign books and magazines were banned.

The new section of Islamabad was built around the small village of Anzebkiz, a settlement of Christian Pakistanis, who had as their center a Methodist church made of stone. There had always been religious freedom in Pakistan, ever since the nation, formerly a part of India, had gained independence in 1947. In theory, there is still freedom of religion under President Zia's administration. In practice, the dominant faith is the Islamic religion. Government restrictions and subtle harassment have made it impossible for other religions to continue.

The Methodist church is still standing, but it is no longer used for any kind of Christian service. Instead, it is a kind of second office for General Saha I'Zada, the chief of the Chanwiri-lu-Shabudar.

Swarthy-skinned, with high cheekbones and the face of a peasant (which he had been at one time), I'Zada spent a lot of time in the Methodist church building which he had renovated, a comparatively easy task. The pews had been removed, as well as crosses and other objects used by believers in Jesus Christ. The walls had then been painted green, a sacred Moslem color, and covered with inscriptions praising Allah and Mohammed, his prophet (in white). The bell had been removed from the steeple and the foundation of the steeple used to construct a thirty-foot-high watchtower and observation post.

General I'Zada liked open spaces. With the pews removed, I'Zada, who always sat behind a table in the front of the building—not far from where the pulpit had stood—could look out over a 47x82-foot area that was empty. During the hot months the interior was cool, due to the thick stone walls.

Lieutenant Mohammed Kusan Moukarim had always considered General Saha I'Zada an oddball with a dual personality, who could choose the best from two totally different worlds and never have any emotional conflict over it. He was a paradox. For example, while I'Zada was a fanatical Moslem who believed that Western culture could contaminate Pakistan society, he was convinced that Western technology could benefit Pakistan.

The evidence of I'Zada's double-think was all around Moukarim as he sat with the general and with Lieutenant General Yahya Si'Quetta, I'Zada's aide, in the front of the building that had been a church. At one end of the long table, the top of which was covered with lamb's wool, was a French Alpha-X Electronic Telephone that revolutionized memory dialing. Not only could the phone automatically dial an incredible 255 numbers, but there were no memory codes to look up. Names were typed in and a button pressed; that's all there was to it. At the other end of the table was a portable Grundig Satellite 3400 short-wave radio and a Bionaire 2001 air purifier.

Even the chair I'Zada was using was a product of Western technology. It was the oddest-looking chair that Mohammed Moukarim had ever seen. A Tripos Balans lounge chair, it had a frame of twenty-four layers of laminated beechwood that was locked into shape by an electronic heating process. What made the chair unique was that due to its shape one could relax in a full rearward lounge position or in an ordinary seating position. Or one could lean forward and work in an upright, yet kneeling position—and comfortably—this due to the thick pads on the front ends.

General I'Zada was in an ordinary seating position. He was dressed in traditional long white *shalwar*, over which was a *sherwani*, a long frock coat with a high closed collar. Moukarim could see that underneath the *sherwani* the general was wearing a shoulder holster filled with either a pistol or a revolver.

Inshallah. . . General Saha I'Zada was indeed a paradox.

"An excellent job you did in the South Waziristan district, Lieutenant." I'Zada congratulated the young secret police operative. "It is only unfortunate that those Shi'ite death squads[1] of Khomeini's had to be our religious brethren. Tch, tch, tch . . . Moslem should not kill Moslem."

"That is true, my general." Moukarim was quick to agree. "My unit and I gave them every chance to surrender. We even called out and told them they would not be harmed, that we would only send them back to Iran. They would not surrender. They were determined to blow up the arms depot and blame it on the Pathans. We had to kill all twenty of them when they charged us."

Lieutenant General Yahya Si'Quetta said cynically, "That's one time we did Ali Mirza-Khan a favor without meaning to. He's the most dangerous of all the *Maliks* in the northwest frontier and the most influential among the Pathans. The other *Maliks* listen to his advice."

"Collectively, as a tribe, all of them hate the central government here in Islamabad." General I'Zada was heavily ironic. "Mirza-Khan and the other chiefs would like to see us and President Zia hanging from poles. Worse for government, the Pathans control the Khyber Pass and are really the boss of the Aza Khel refugee camp."

"The Afghan refugees are not a problem," Si'Quetta said. A tall but not bulky man, he had curly black hair, even and angular features and sleepy-looking eyes, the latter giving the impression that he was a lazy thinker—always a fatal mistake to his enemies. A calculating man, he never acted on impulse and was always very careful to give at least the appearance of agreeing with General Saha I'Zada. But the sun would not always shine on General I'Zada, or on President Zia either. . . .

[1].These fanatics are trained in methods of subversive and suicidal struggle, their mission to assassinate. Their reward is the assurance of paradise. They are the Pazdarans, the revolutionary guards, and have fought in El Salvador and Nicaragua.

"They are not a problem now," I'Zada said, "but they could be if the Pathans excited them against us. And how would it look to the world if we forced the refugees to return to Afghanistan? At present, the Pathans are a bulwark against the Russians should the Soviet Union ever decide to move from Afghanistan, through the Khyber, into our nation. Naturally, the good Christians of the West would not help us any more than they helped the Afghans."

"We know the Christians for what they are," Lieutenant General Si'Quetta said venomously. "They have always murdered in the name of God. During the Middle Ages, the Roman church tortured and killed millions for 'witchcraft,' even small children—and all of it in the name of God. That same church today is equally sadistic and stupid. Imagine! That pope telling the savages of Africa and the fools of Central and South America to have all the children 'God sends'! Already those nations are vastly overpopulated, and millions of their people are starving. Yet they should 'trust in the Lord'! Somehow, bread never falls from heaven."

"The Roman church has always been a cancer on the body of humanity," I'Zada said. A thin smile stole over his pale lips. "But before this century is over, the Roman church shall be no more."

He paused, then gave his full attention to Lieutenant Moukarim, who was twenty-eight, solemn-eyed and dressed in the grass-green uniform of a Chanwiri-lu-Shabudar officer. "We have an important mission for you, Lieutenant, one that is of two parts. You will pick a dozen agents and then proceed to find the exact location of Chief Mujibur Ali Mirza-Khan and his clan of Pathans."

"May I ask why, General?" inquired Moukarim.

"Ali Mirza-Khan always has his best fighters with him. Once we pinpoint his camp, or the village in which he and his people are quartered, our army and air force will wipe them out to the last man, woman and child. Our president has decided that it is time we rid ourselves of those troublesome Pathans, once and for all—at least Mirza-Khan and his group. Once he and his people are destroyed, the other Pathan chiefs will not give us any trouble, or rather none that we won't be able to handle."

Seeing the confusion on the face of Mohammed Moukarim, I'Zada leaned forward so that the chair tilted and he had the weight of his body resting on his knees against the thick pads of the Tripos Balans lounge chair. "You have a problem over what I have said, Lieutenant Moukarim?"

Moukarim slowly nodded. "My general, you have said that the Pathans are a protection against the Russian animals. Why then, if we kill large amounts of their numbers, should they fight for us, if and when the Soviet Union decides to invade our glorious country?"

General I'Zada often told himself that life was constantly surprising him with ridiculous inconsistencies. Here was another one—Lieutenant Moukarim and his inability to see one single tree because of the vast forest.

He said in a patient tone, "Lieutenant, should the Soviet Union ever send men and armor through the Khyber Pass, the Pathans would not fight for us. They would fight with the fury of the demented. They would fight for *themselves* and for the Islamic Republic of Pakistan."

He extended his right arm and put his hand flat on the tabletop. Moukarim could see that his boss was wearing a large, foreign-looking wristwatch. It was a Polaris II Compass watch. "Always keep in mind that the Pathans are convinced it is we who are traitors, we who are the enemy of their nation, 'their' Pakistan. Now do you understand?"

"*Ched*, it is now clear," Moukarim said quickly. Nonetheless, he remained troubled. Basically a decent man, his instincts silently screamed in protest at President Zia and General I'Zada's scheme to destroy Ali Mirza-Khan and weaken the Pathans. Moukarim was convinced that the plan was not only morally wrong—Allah never condoned murder!—but extremely dangerous to the basic security of the nation.

Relations between Pakistan and India were at an all-time low. Not only was India accusing President Zia of sending arms to Sikh extremists, which Zia was doing, but Indian Hawks, with Soviet KGB support, were seeking a "Greater India" at Pakistan's expense. This meant—first—destabilizing President Zia ul-Haq's government, then the conquering of Pakistan, a task that would be extremely difficult.

Inshallah . . . Moukarim realized it was not up to him to decide policy for Pakistan. *Yibo* . . . not his decision . . . "And the second part of the mission, General?" he asked, his voice tight.

I'Zada smiled. "We feel the second part of the mission will be more difficult. Weeks ago, a pair of foreign agents entered the country. Americans, they landed at the airport in Karachi. They were supposed to be historians."

Speaking in a steady voice, I'Zada explained that CLS counterintelligence had not been suspicious of the two Americans, not at first, but, since they were foreigners, had watched them as a matter of routine.

From Karachi, the two had journeyed to Peshawar.

It was in Peshawar that the two Americans vanished.

Lieutenant General Si'Quetta interjected, "It was after the Americans disappeared from Peshawar that we realized they were most probably agents of a foreign power. We still could not be positive. There was the possibility that the two had met with foul play, though there wasn't any evidence that they had been murdered by bandits."

Resuming the briefing, General I'Zada spoke crisply, a trace of anger in his voice. It was then he told Lieutenant Moukarim about the two West Germans who had also flown into Karachi. On a vacation . . . they had told Customs. They too had traveled to Peshawar. However they did not disappear from the frontier city. They had made contact with a Pathan who had proceeded to show them the sights and to take them to the local bazaars.

"We worked on the theory that the two West Germans might try to make contact with the Americans," I'Zada said, his eyes never leaving Moukarim. "We were correct. At least we think we were. We won't know until you and your unit find and capture the two Americans and the two West Germans." He gave a dry laugh. "I realize that is confusing, Lieutenant. Let me tell you what happened.

"Nine CLS agents had managed to trail the two West Germans and the Pathan from Peshawar to the Shrine of Abdul Bu-I-Zum, near the small town of Murree. The plan was to wait and see if the three would meet the two Americans, then take all of them into custody.

"The nine-man unit, having come from Peshawar, had reported to its base command. The last report was that the nine had established themselves around the three suspects and were waiting to see what might happen. Hassan Uganki, the control agent, did report that the two West Germans and the Pathan were involved in something illegal. Snuggled down, not far from the tomb, they were obviously hiding and lying in wait for someone."

"That's the last we heard from the unit," Si'Quetta cut in bitterly.

Moukarim's eyes widened. "All nine disappeared?"

"They were found murdered—shot!" I'Zada said sharply.

"That is why I said we'll not have a true picture until you find the West Germans and the two Americans."

"Or the four Russians!" inserted Si'Quetta. "We don't feel that they were Germans and Americans. They could even be Israelis."

Feeling uncomfortable, Moukarim thought for a moment. "There isn't any hard evidence that the West Germans—if they were from that country—met the Americans, or whoever they really are?"

I'Zada said carefully, "We are operating on the assumption that the four made contact at the shrine. Our belief is that the four came to Pakistan to offer foreign aid to Malik Ali Mirza-Khan. We think the mission of these foreign agents is to incite all the Pathans to revolt against our government. Should that revolt take place, should we have another civil war, it would be exactly what the Indians and the Soviet Union would want. The Indians would move in on us from the east. The Soviet Union would invade from the west."

Lieutenant Moukarim felt a chill ski down his spine. With the feeling that he was being given an impossible task, he shifted uneasily in his chair. "But, General, let's assume that I do find the main camp of Chief Mirza-Khan. After—"

"We will not assume!" I'Zada said coldly. "You must find his base."

"I will find the camp, General! I will!" Moukarim said nervously. "But after our forces wipe out the camp, won't that trigger a revolt by the entire Pathan tribe? There are 75,000 of them!"

"It's a possibility that they could unite against us," admitted I'Zada. "We doubt it. When the other chiefs see how easily we crush Chief Ali Mirza-Khan, it isn't likely that they will revolt. They aren't stupid."

"And by wiping out Mirza-Khan and his people, we'll smash the foreign plot to arm him," added Lieutenant General Si'Quetta. He recrossed his legs and leaned forward in the armchair. "You see, we are confident you will find the four agents in the camp of Mirza-Khan. That camp is either in the Safed Koh or in or around one of the villages in the northwest frontier. How you and your men will infiltrate the area is your concern. We can work out the details of radio contact as soon as you choose your men."

General I'Zada said softly, "We have to take the chance that the Pathans will not rise in rebellion. The chance that they might is the lesser of two evils. Better that they revolt now, with only the weapons they have, than later, when they are well supplied with weapons—perhaps even heavy ordnance—from India."

"Could the four be working for the Indians?" asked Moukarim.

"We don't know, but we don't think so," answered I'Zada. "We believe it's the Americans—the CIA."

"The new Soviet base outside of Narang, in Afghanistan, is another reason why the Pathans won't start an insurrection." Si'Quetta smirked. "That base is only forty-eight kilometers from the Khyber Pass."

General I'Zada nodded smugly in agreement and said to Moukarim, "As I told you, the Pathans love Pakistan more than they hate us. They realize that a civil war at this time would only tempt the Soviets to move through the Khyber. The Soviets know they must have an entrance to the Persian Gulf." He cleared his throat. "Go now, Lieutenant, and choose your men. Pick them carefully, then report back to us. You have two days in which to gather your men."

As soon as Lieutenant Mohammed Moukarim had left the building, I'Zada remarked, "If only we could have told him that we know every move the Russians are making. Such information would have given him confidence. Of course we couldn't. He could be captured."

"I don't think so," Si'Quetta said. "He has an excellent record and is known for his daring and initiative."

General I'Zada looked out over the open space in front of the table. There was only the stone floor (and the two guards at the double doors). Although the interior of the church was cool during the hot months, it was difficult to heat during winter. "*Yahya*, we are going to have to have more electric heaters in here. The building is too chilly. Attend to it."

"We'll have to install another power line," Si'Quetta said. "The present circuits won't take the surge of power needed for more heaters."

"Then do it. Have another line run into the building."

Lieutenant General Si'Quetta felt a surge of self-satisfaction. I'Zada was a fool. He only thought he knew every move of the Russians. Si'Quetta wished he could shout the truth: *Idiot! When your flesh is feeding the worms of the grave, I'll be the supreme administrator of Baluchistan!*

CHAPTER THREE

"It would be unwise for one to expect Allah to smile constantly in his direction," Mujibur Ali Mirza-Khan said to Richard Camellion. "To be sure, your killing of the secret police dogs at the tomb can only mean that General I'Zada will intensify his search for you and your friends. May Allah protect you."

Iskander Chaudhriy frowned, his black eyes focused on the Death Merchant. "It could be that the Protectors of the People will deduce that the four of you have sought refuge with us, Kir Camellion," he said tightly. "That is not good."

Remaining silent for the moment, Camellion detected the accusatory note in Chaudhriy's low voice, and he knew that the hint of complaint had not gone by Mike Quinlan, and Bruckner and O'Malley, all three of whom were sitting cross-legged on Camellion's side of the thick rug on the stone floor of Mirza-Khan's house.

Mirza-Khan, sitting in a *bodza*, a chair with foot-long legs and a leather seat and back, looked solemnly at Chaudhriy, who was seated to his left on the rug. "Iskander, you should choose your words more carefully. We must not make our guests feel that they are not welcome."

"I did not mean my words to be offensive," Chaudhriy said mildly. He smiled at the Death Merchant and the three other men. "All of you are welcome to stay with us as long as you wish. We have a common enemy—President Zia ul-Haq, a disgrace to our nation and an insult to Allah."

"We thank you, Kir Chaudhriy, and we thank you, Malik-Sahib Mirza-Khan," Camellion said politely. And to himself:

You're not fooling anyone, Chaudhriy. You hate our guts and we're not fond of yours. . . .

Even at the first meeting, weeks earlier in the City, in the house on the Street of the Knifemakers, the Death Merchant had sensed that the fierce-eyed, good-looking Iskander Chaudhriy was intensely resentful, although the man had been friendly enough and had done an excellent job of concealing his antipathy. *This joker will bear watching,* Camellion had thought at the time.

However, Camellion was thankful that he and Quinlan and Quinlan's two men, as well as Wanja Likstom and Alfu Krod, had reached the Dera Ismail Khan mountains without mishap. The journey had taken twelve days, and there had been those times when they had suspected danger was very close. On the morning of the thirteenth day, the party of six had reached Gubukil, the small village that was Mirza-Khan's winter headquarters—a mountain village of several hundred stone huts that was in a dangerous location, only twenty-five kilometers from the famed Khyber Pass and only seventy-three kilometers from the Afghan town of Narang and the Soviet Spetsnaz base. The base contained the largest concentration of Soviet Special Forces in Afghanistan. Why the Spetsnaz were there was no secret, not to the CIA. An invasion of Pakistan was not in the distant future . . .

The Khyber Pass was the key. One of the world's most fabled mountain gateways, the Khyber was not a high pass. It climbed only to 3,370 feet and enveloped more than twenty miles of road on a harsh, rocky almost treeless landscape, with gravelly, often dry streambeds below and sun-blistered peaks above.

The Death Merchant had seen the Khyber on two other occasions, and he had found nothing exciting about it. To him, the Khyber was the most brutal stretch of country he had ever laid eyes on, a hell that was as inhospitable as the Great Empty Quarter in Arabia.[1] It bristled with reminders of hate, of violence, of death. There were forts and the ruins of forts and picket posts on top of every dominating crag. There were even concrete dragon's teeth, planted to stop Nazi tanks when Britain feared a strike into India during World War II.

The Pathans in the villages and towns in the pass went about armed to the teeth. Why? If one had been foolish enough to ask any of the Pathans, the man would probably have replied, "Why

[1].See Death Merchant number 49, *Night of the Peacock.*

do you Americans have a nuclear bomb? You have the bomb to keep peace in the world. I carry a weapon so no one will bother me."

"No one" could also mean another Pathan or a member of another tribe. Feuds were common, feuds that usually started over women, land boundaries or water rights. Revenge was absolutely essential. Unless a man took revenge, he would be considered weak and would soon find others taking advantage of him.

Wanja Likstom had told Camellion about one blood feud that had continued for 102 years. One hundred and nine people had been killed.

"Some years ago, the *jirga*[2] forced the two families to declare a *tigah,* or truce," he had explained. "Of course, some hothead can always start it up again."

Likstom had explained that the revenge system, the eye-for an-eye code upheld by the *jirga* system, actually served to discourage violence. "A dispute outside the tribal area would lead to the courts," he had said. "With the feud system, it can only lead to the graveyard. This means that a man will not act hastily."

There was a general *tigah* on the Khyber road. "Should any tribesmen commit a crime on the road, the fine will be very high, perhaps the sum of 50,000 rupees.[3] You see, Kir Camellion, the *tigah* makes it possible for the Khyber Road and the pass to remain an international link. At the same time it enables a man involved in a blood feud to walk in safety, knowing that while he is on the Khyber Road his enemy will not shoot him. Ah, yes . . . it is a good system in these troublesome times."

For thousands of years, the Pathans, with a handful of other tribes, had controlled the Khyber Pass, and they had held it! Even great armies had been destroyed in and around Peshawar at the hands of the terrible tribesmen whom Herodotus, the Greek historian, called "the most warlike of all."

For countless generations the Pathans in and around the Khyber had derived income extracted from passing caravans. Those days of easy living had ended. Now the tribesmen were haulers, plying the road in trucks painted in vivid colors. Other Pathans, such as Pokik Lumardfik, a member of Mirza-Khan's clan, had

[2].A council of elders that settles disputes.

[3].$5,000.

fleets of automobiles to carry passengers and various kinds of contraband. The Pathans were smugglers on a grand scale. Landlocked Afghanistan received a good deal of the goods that tribesmen's trucks picked up at Karachi, Pakistan's seaport. As it often happened, a lot of the merchandise trucked into Afghanistan often found its way back into Pakistan, such items as cigarettes, radios, perfume, bolts of cloth, etc. President Zia's government banned such foreign imports to protect local Pak industries or to hold down the deficit in the balance of payments.

There was a darker side to Pathan smuggling, one that affected thousands of drug addicts even in the United States. The Pathans derived the lion's share of their income from the smuggling of opium. During the growing season, a traveler in the northwest frontier could find scores of villages that seemed to rise from a vast, weaving carpet of red and pink poppies . . . poppies that were far far more than long-stemmed flowers.

A Pathan who might smuggle liquor would be severely warned to discontinue such dealings. There would not be a second warning. Should the man continue to smuggle liquor, the *jirga* would order his execution. It was different with the growing and smuggling of opium. This was not against the Koran, and thus not a sin against Allah. Nor did it bother the Pathans that the heroin, derived from the opium gum, would be distributed all over the world.[4] To their way of thinking, they were not responsible for what the Russians might do with the opium. It bothered the Pathas even less that it was the Russians who were buying the raw opium. After all, the Russians had hard cash. Another reason was that some of the heroin always made its way into the bodies of Soviet soldiers. That was good. Inshallah . . .

President Zia was well aware of the illegal poppy trade but refrained from moving against it with either the secret police or regular army troops. He couldn't, not without risking a bloody revolt by the Pathans.

Ironically, Mujibur Ali Mirza-Khan was one of the largest poppy farmers in the North-West Frontier. He and his clan produced at least a ton of raw opium a year. Just as ironically, Mirza-Khan and the goodwill of all the Pathans were just as valuable to President Zia as they were to the United States. In any Soviet invasion from Afghanistan, it was the Pathans who

[4].See Death Merchant number 61, *The Bulgarian Termination*, and future Death Merchant number 65, *Operation Nose-Candy*, this latter dealing with cocaine.

would fight the initial battles. *Unless the Soviet Union succeeds into talking President Zia into establishing an autonomous Baluchistani state.*

With their usual hypocrisy, the Soviets swore to Zia that they would "guarantee" the Baluchistani state in return for access from Afghanistan to the Pakistan seaport of Karachi. Not only would such a one-sided arrangement give the Soviet Union access to a warm-water port, it would also give the Russians access, through the Gulf of Oman, to the Persian Gulf, and via the Gulf of Aden, to the Red Sea.

Oil-rich Arabia would be surrounded.

U.S. oil would be endangered.

But there was far more to the diabolical Soviet plot . . . far far more.

President Zia was caught between a great big boulder and a very hard place. For two years he had given a firm no to the Soviet proposal of an autonomous Baluchistani state. He had also given a blunt *yibo* to the Soviet proposal that he permit the Russians access through Pakistan to the nation's south coast and/or the Arabian Sea.

General, then President Mohammed Zia ul-Haq was a complex character. In the words of Courtland Grojean, "Our assessment of him is that he's not a coward. His military record reveals he's a very brave man. He's flatly told the Soviets to butt out. Yet he's completely ignored Soviet air-force incursion into Pakistan's airspace. We know for a fact that Soviet aircraft has flown nine different times over the northwest frontier. Four flights bored in east as much as eighty miles—one flight was ninety-six miles—and at no time were the planes challenged by the Pak air force. Analysis indicates that the Russians are keeping up a constant surveillance of all the Pathans. Do I have to tell you why, Death Merchant?"

"Don't call me the Death Merchant!"

"Sorry, Camellion. It's just that the tag the KGB gave you, years ago, seems to fit."

Sitting on the rug, Camellion now reflected on his conversation with the chief of the CIA's covert section. Sure, he knew why. In any invasion, Soviet troops would first have to knock out the savage Pathans guarding the Khyber Pass.

Which is one of the reasons why Quinlan and his two boys and I are here—to knock out the Spetsnaz force at Narang and forestall an invasion. . . .

Forestall would be all that Camellion and the Pathans could do. In the end, the Soviet Union would win. Willpower alone could not defeat Russian armor. The guerrilla war would go on for years, just as it was going on in Afghanistan, but the blood and misery would be worth it to the Soviet Union. Success would mean that Russia would have almost 400 miles of southern Baluchistani coastline . . . every inch washed by the warm waters of the Arabian.

The Soviet Union would gain something else: one of the world's leading drug distribution centers. At one time, it was the Golden Triangle of Southeast Asia that was the leading producer of opium. That distinction now belonged to the Iran-Afghanistan-Pakistan region. But with all the trouble in Iran and Afghanistan, those two nations had fallen behind in the production of opium. The Russians had tried growing opium in Afghanistan and had failed miserably. The Afghan *Mujahideen*[5] destroyed the fields at night. That made Pakistan the top grower of opium in the world, producing on an average of 400 metric tons of opium gum per year and exporting much of it into Afghanistan, most of it on the black market.

President Zia's government was helpless in another way. While the government called it smuggling, the Pathans call it a trade. Zia and his government knew that if they didn't provide the tribes with a source of living, they would become criminals. There was only one ground rule: opium could not be hauled on main roads, including the Khyber Road.

The tribes, especially the Pathans, ignored the rule, and so caravans of camels and donkeys were constantly moving across the border, each animal carrying so much opium; and of course there were cars and trucks, some of the latter so lavishly decorated with sparkling gimcrackery that they resembled circus calliopes.

''Kir Camellion, have you and your friends constructed a plan for attacking the dogs of the north at their base in Narang?'' As Mirza-Khan spoke, his long fingers fished about the almonds in the tray in front of him, selecting those with soft shells that could be easily cracked.

''*Yibo*, we have not, Malik-Sahib Mirza-Khan,'' the Death Merchant said matter-of-factly. ''We felt it would be best to start

[5].Afghan guerrillas.

fresh, by first consulting with you and getting your valued opinion. The task will be monumental, right up to the brink of possible impossibility.'' From the corner of his eye, he saw Wilhelm Bruckner reach for the pot of tea on the low table within the circle. It seemed ridiculous—the big, brutal-looking German drinking tea, his thick fingers holding the cup with all the delicacy of a brain surgeon. The tea and sweet cakes also brought to mind Pathan hospitality. No sooner had he and Quinlan and the other men arrived in Gubukil than five *badragga*, or bodyguards, had escorted them to the house of Mirza-Khan where women, wrapped in dark-green- and blue-striped blankets, had prepared a meal of *jaou*, a thick, dark bread filled with goat cheese, crushed walnuts and bits of white yak meat. Surprisingly, there had also been green beans, tomatoes and asparagus, all out of cans. And lots of canned meat that could have been Spam! Camellion presumed that the canned goods had come from truck caravans, from imports that had arrived at Karachi.

Michael Quinlan said. ''It's a matter of men, proper weapons and proper tactics, Malik-Sahib Mirza-Khan. Pistols and rifles against automatic weapons, against Russian tanks, would be asking Allah to perform miracles.''

He mentioned Allah! A good touch that. ''It's also a matter of approach,'' Camellion said. ''The attack would require at least several thousand men. The problem would be moving them from the northwest frontier to a position from which they could launch a surprise attack on the Soviet base outside of Narang. The distance is from fifty to eighty kilometers. It would be quite an undertaking.''

The calm expression on Mirza-Khan's nut-brown face didn't change. ''Such movements would be very difficult, but not impossible. We would travel at night and hide in the light of the sun.''

''We do have machine pistols, machine guns and assault rifles,'' said Jiko Krim-Lizak. ''We would not dare attack the Russian dogs with only ordinary rifles and handguns.''

Heavily bearded and wearing a black *toba*, a sheepskin jacket and gray baggy pants, Krim-Lizak acted as liaison between Mirza-Khan and Iskander Chaudhriy, when the latter was out in the field on a ''trading''—smuggling—expedition. In his early forties, Krim-Lizak, who had a limp, wore two autopistols in open holsters around his waist—expensive 9mm Sig Sauer automatics. ''It is obvious, I think, that the key element is total surprise.''

Seeing how the Death Merchant and the other men were startled by Jiko Krim-Lizak's mention of machine guns and automatic weapons, Mirza-Khan smiled. "My good friends, let me ease your surprise. We have accumulated the modern weapons over a period of years, obtaining them from the Afghans and from India. The Afghan *Mujahideen*[6] often take weapons in raids on Russian outposts or when they ambush a Soviet column.[6] We buy weapons from them, paying with the gum of the poppy."

"I say, that's something to curl your knickers—the Afghans selling Soviet weapons!" exclaimed James O'Malley. "I should think that the Afghan guerrillas would want the guns for their own use, all they could get their hands on."

"They do, Kir O'Malley," said Mirza-Khan. "But any man can only use one weapon at a time. There are enough weapons for the Afghans and for us. There is another reason why they sell us captured Soviet arms. We pay for them in opium gum. The Afghans return the gum to us so that we can act as their agents in the purchase of weapons from black-market arms dealers in Bharat, that nation you call India. Our commission is twenty percent. We take the twenty percent in weapons for ourselves. And so we have not only automatic weapons, but also grenades, mortars and antitank missiles."

Iskander Chaudhriy's dark eyes were frosty as they bored into the Death Merchant. "Those weapons were for our revoltion, to be used against President Zia and his corrupt government. We had not planned to use them in some wild scheme against the Russians in Afghanistan." His voice was filled with anger and frustration.

The Death Merchant had had his fill of Chaudhriy. "*Bayadarka* Chaudhriy, do you not mind the Soviets using reconnaissance planes to spy on Pathan settlements? Such aerial surveys are not the acts of friendly people. Then again, it could be that Soviet violation of Pathan skies does not concern you because the blood in your veins is not Pathan but Baluch blood!"

Chaudhriy drew back in anger, the direct, unexpected insult freezing his vocal chords. Colonel Quinlan moved his tongue slowly over his lower lip, his gaze glued to Chaudhriy while Jiko Krim-Lizak busied himself with cracking walnuts. In contrast, Ali Mirza-Khan watched Camellion and the enraged Chaudhriy.

Chaudhriy was of the Baluch tribe. He was also well-educated. After his education was completed, he had returned to Pakistan

[6].See Death Merchant number 56, *Afghanistan Crashout*.

and joined his father in the family business. During the next nine years, he was arrested six times for "activity counter to the wishes and goals of the state." Finally, in 1981, he left Karachi, made his way to the northwest frontier and joined Mirza-Khan's group, maintaining that the Baluchs were too subservient to President Zia.

Chaudhriy didn't lose his temper as Camellion had hoped he would.

"Kir Camellion, I won't return your unkind words with an insult," he said craftily. "You are a guest. I will overlook your ignorance and say that I am here because I love my country and because I believe in freedom."

"We also believe in freedom," Camellion said in an easy manner. "That is why we are here."

"Come come, Kir Camellion." Chaudhriy laughed. "You're here because you're doing a job. You don't give a damn what happens to the Pakistani people."

He's a lot smarter than I thought! "That's right. We are here doing a job, and we're risking our lives doing it. So far, Colonel Quinlan and his two men and I have taken far more risks than you."

Colonel Quinlan joined in, his voice calm and low-pitched. "You know, Kir Chaudhriy, you remind me of a timid farmer who sits and does nothing while the weasels invade his chicken coops. Why do you think the Russians have that base at Narang? Why do you think there are only Spetsnaz stationed there?"

Chaudhriy, his mouth a tight line, considered Quinlan with a skeptical eye, "There isn't any direct evidence that the Russians at Narang intend to move through the Khyber, much less invade our nation—unless we're to believe what the American CIA would have us believe."

"I dislike being called a liar, even when I am a guest in another man's house!" Low but sharp, the Death Merchant's voice carried a warning, and as he spoke, he scrutinized Mujibur Ali Mirza-Khan. He was satisfied when he saw faint traces of admiration on the Pathan's deeply lined face. *Good! The old warrior admires nerve and bravery. The CIA report was right.*

If the rest of the evaluation-assessment profile was correct, Mirza-Khan was part philosopher and part barbarian. Although a true believer in Mohammedanism—Allah is God and Mohammed is His prophet; period!—Mirza-Khan was still a man who felt that God manifested Himself through many beliefs and creeds.

There were no infidels in his eyes; there were only human beings faithful to different creeds. In his philosophy, what mattered was how an individual lived up to his belief. This alone made Mirza-Khan suspect in the eyes of the ever-suspicious Courtland Grojean. A Moslem who didn't consider any non-Moslem an infidel! Impossible. The old boy must have an angle.

But the old boy doesn't have an angle. Or does he?

"The CIA could have lied to you, Kir Camellion," Iskander Chaudhriy said quickly, yet there was uncertainty in his voice. "I think it's well known that all intelligence services refrain from telling their operatives the full truth. That the Russians have built the base at Narang as a hopping-off place to attack us could only be rumor, misinformation."

Mirza-Khan said sagely, "There are two ways to be fooled: one is to believe what isn't so. The other is to refuse to believe what is so."

"I don't feel that we can refuse to believe that there are Indian troops massed along certain areas of Pakistan's eastern border," the Death Merchant said. "India is enraged over President Zia's helping Sikh extremists with arms."

Chaudhriy reluctantly agreed; he had no choice. "The Indian government's displeasure with Zia over his shipping weapons to the Sikhs doesn't have anything to do with the Soviet base at Narang—and don't tell us that the Soviet KGB can 'force' the Indian army to attack. The Indian government always plays both ends against the middle, but the Indians are not a fool."

Mike Quinlan said in a positive tone, "They're underestimating the Soviets and overestimating their own ability."

"You Americans have always been know-it-alls." Chaudhriy sneered. "It's that pop-electronics culture of the instant that colors your thinking in regard to world situations."

"The *Russischs* are very clever," murmured Willy Bruckner, as if thinking aloud. "They want to conquer the world."

"They don't want to *conquer* the world," Camellion said, thinking that it always required an unusual mind to undertake an analysis of the obvious. "The Soviet Union wants to dominate the world. A vital part of that goal is to cut off oil from the United States. All of it is part of a Russian scheme to destroy freedom in all noncommunist countries. Make no mistake about it, Pakistan is right in the middle of it—whether you like it or not, Kir Chaudhriy!"

"I think you're overemphasizing Soviet intentions," Chaudhriy said smugly. "Not that I don't feel that the Soviets are a threat, but I can't see them starting a war they know they can't win."

The damn fool is walking right into it! "The overall evidence says otherwise, and if you were an observer of world events and military developments, you'd know it."

Another insult! An angry Chaudhriy could only say, "What evidence?"

The Death Merchant told him, beginning with the premise that the only world power blocking Soviet aims was the United States. The second factor was oil, the lifeblood of any military power. Oil meant Arabia, which, while a peninsula, was essentially an island, a large body of land that could be reached only through two narrow waterways, the Strait of Hormuz, which joins the Persian Gulf with the Arabian Sea and the Indian Ocean, and the Bab al Mandab, which joins the Red Sea with the Gulf of Aden and the Indian Ocean. These two straits were the most important waterways in the world.

"Whoever has control of these two choke points controls the economic destinies of Western Europe and Japan and, to a certain extent, the destiny of the United States."

Chaudhriy uttered a little derogatory laugh. "I think Kir Camellion that—"

"Stop interrupting, Iskander!" For the first time, Mirza-Khan's voice was authoritarian. "Kir Camellion's analysis is most logical. Let him continue."

The Death Merchant did. He went on to say that the Strait of Hormuz is dominated by Iran on the east and by one of the Trucial States, Oman, on the west. The Bab al Mandab is dominated by South Yemen on the east and by Ethiopia and Somalia, which constitute the Horn of Africa, on the west. In recent years, either directly or through stooge nations, the Soviet Union has moved to establish itself as the dominant military and political force on both sides of these critical waterways. On the Persian Gulf's western shore Cuban troops have positioned themselves in Yemen for possible invasions into Saudia Arabia, Oman, and Aden. Furthermore, on the Bab al Mandab, Russian-led Cuban troops have already turned Ethiopia into one vast military camp and a Soviet naval base has been built at Massawa on the Red Sea. These Soviet moves indicate a strategy aimed not merely at shutting off the flow of oil from the Arabian Peninsula, but at neutralizing Western Europe, a strategy not of conquest but of envelopment and dislocation.

"Apparently," Camellion finished, "the Soviet Union believes that oil is the lever with which they can move the Western European nations right out of NATO. It is certainly easy to imagine what the Russians would do if they were in a position to control the Arabian waterways. In exchange for a declaration of neutrality, including a withdrawl from NATO and the closing of all U.S. bases, the Soviet Union would guarantee unlimited access to Middle Eastern oil and, as a bonus, immunity from any East-West war. The Europeans would find that offer hard to refuse. Ninety-five percent of their oil comes from the Middle East. Nothing is absolutely certain until it happens, but the evidence speaks all too clearly for itself. We'd be fools to ignore it."

"Man has two days in this world, his own and his son's," Mirza-Khan said meditatively. "If you are right, Kir Camellion, the days of our sons are numbered."

"Allah has numbered to the second the days of all men," the Death Merchant said, "but it is not Allah who brings hatred and death and war. That is the work of evil men."

Jiko Krim-Lizak hooked his fat hands on the collar of his *toba* and blinked rapidly at the Death Merchant. He had a very large nose that resembled a two-car garage when he looked up. "We believe you are speaking the truth, *Baya-darka* Richard Camellion. For many years, the black forces of Iblis[7] having been roaming unchecked throughout the world. However—"

"*La ilāh illa Allāh!*"[8] intoned Mirza-Khan at the mention of the Evil One.

"However, Kir Camellion, the opinion of our brother, Chaudhriy must be considered. An attack by us on the Soviet base at Narang is a serious matter. It would deplete our manpower and our weapons. And would such an attack even be worth it?"

"We would lose far more than we would gain," offered Chaudhriy, speaking with greater confidence now that he felt he had an ally. "The Russians aren't bothering us. Why should we bother them? Why should we deliberately provoke them?"

Now for the knockout punch. If it doesn't work, Mike and I and Willy and the Kid might as well grab the midnight camel and head for home. "There's a difference between provoking an

[7]. The Islamic devil. Also called *Shaitin*, from the Zoroastrian Satan. *Iblis* is a contraction of *Diabolos*.

[8]. "There is no God but Allah."

attack and getting in the first blow,'' Camellion responded. ''Self-preservation should be the first consideration of any people.''

''Fine words, but what is your point?'' Chaudhriy sounded worried.

''Suppose I could prove that the Soviet base at Narang exists for only one reason: to spearhead an attack into Pakistan through the Khyber. It's the Pathans who will be the first target.''

As Camellion spoke, he studied the interior of the large room. A Pathan dwelling is a simple affair, consisting of only two rooms, the large room being the main room of the house—the living room, the family room, the room where guests are received and entertained, all rolled into one. In the second room, food is prepared. This room is partitioned off, with the other half serving as the sleeping quarters.

In an open hearth a fire burned, the smoke drifting up to a round hole in the ceiling. It was this fire that supplied the heat, such as it was. The only other light came through the two windows and the small *kotik* candle, the candle and flame of the ancestors. If the season had been spring or summer, the party would have been sitting on the *hurja,* the ''sitting and talking place'' of a shaded porch in front of the house.

Mirza-Khan became very alert. ''Proof, Kir Camellion! Such proof you can give us?''

''Malik-Sahib Mirza-Khan, you are familiar with the nation of Afghanistan?'' Camellion said. ''Its mountains and plains. You know where they are.''

''*Ched.* Well do I know the land of the Afghan,'' answered the Pathan chief. ''It is the land now controlled by the evil Iblis, just as the Soviet Union is ruled by that monster enemy of Allah.''

''*Muhammed rasul Allah,*''[9] Jiko Krim-Lizak said with reverence.

Willy Bruckner chuckled faintly. ''*Ach! Der gute dumme Teufel!*''[10] Everyone blames him—''

''*Sein sorgfalt!*'' Quinlan warned Bruckner, thankful that the Pathans did not understand High German. He then smiled politely at Mirza-Khan. ''It's a Christian expression we use when Satan is mentioned. It means 'Begone Satan.' ''

The Death Merchant didn't mince words. ''Ask yourself Malik-Sahib Mirza-Khan—and you too, Kir Krim-Lizak! Why would

9. ''Muhammed is the messenger (or prophet) of God.''

10. ''The good stupid devil.''

the Russians build a large base in northeast Afghanistan, and so close to the border of Pakistan? Surely, the dogs of the north don't need the base to protect Kabul, the capital. Kabul is 150 kilometers to the west. And certainly not as protection or a base to strike against the *Mujahideen*. The rebels are in the Paropamisus mountains in western Afghanistan and in the Pusht-I-Rud region in southern Afghanistan. What purpose then does the base at Narang serve?"

"And why," added Quinlan, "is the base staffed with only Spetsnaz?"

Mirza-Khan sat silent . . . thinking.

"All of you are free to believe what you want," the Death Merchant ground out with an I-don't-give-a-damn tone. "But I say this: the Soviet base was built for only one reason: to attack Pakistan through the Khyber. Your people, Malik-Sahib Mirza-Khan, will be the number-one target. Your reputation as fierce fighters is well known to the Soviets."

Stroking his long white beard, Mirza-Khan squinted at the Death Merchant. "These Spetsnaz you keep mentioning. Tell us about them. They are man. They can bleed. They can die."

"The Spetsnaz are Soviet Special Forces," Camellion said. "One might describe them as very special commandos, and they're very good."

Camellion didn't bother to give the nitty-gritty information about the Spetsnaz, which were called diversionary troops in the West, and were tasked with hunting down and assassinating enemy political and military leaders, seeking out and destroying the enemy's nuclear facilities, destroying important targets and disrupting the enemy's power systems. Strangely, however, Spetsnaz units were not trained to engage in guerrilla warfare. Why should they be? The Soviet Union didn't intend to lose any war.

An independent Spetsnaz company consisted of a headquarters element, three parachute platoons, a communications platoon and supporting subunits. A company had 115 men, including nine officers and eleven *praporschiki*, or warrant officers. When conducting sabotage operations in the enemy's rear areas, the company operated as a single unit or would be divided into smaller groups, although the maximum number of groups was fifteen. A Spetsnaz brigade comprised a headquarters element, a headquarters company, four or five parachute battalions and supporting units. The strength of a brigade's fighting units was between 1000 and 1500 men.

The base at Narang will have at least 1500 men, probably closer to 2000. Defeating them will take a miracle, no matter how good the Pathans are. . . .

Iskander Chaudhriy said brusquely, "I don't see why we have a problem. If and when the Russians come through the Khyber, they'll be spotted before they even cross the border into our country. We would have more than enough time to prepare our defense."

"Wrong!" Camellion snorted. "Hours before you would even see Soviet armor, troop carriers and self-propelled guns, Soviet planes would bomb every village in sight in the northwest frontier. You'd never get organized."

Quinlan's voice was funereal. "By the time you got organized, the Russians would be on your doorstep. It wouldn't be a battle. It would be a slaughter. Your women would be raped and small children would have their throats cut."

Mirza-Khan's old eyes narrowed. "You are saying that if we attack the Soviet Special Forces base, we can prevent such terrible destruction to our people?"

The Death Merchant was very careful with his reply. "By attacking the Russians first, we probably will postpone an invasion. We'll be doing the unexpected, so it's possible that we might force the planners in Moscow to think twice about fighting not only the Pathans but the rest of Pakistan. They might call off the invasion. To be honest, I doubt if they will. They will probably try to make the Indians attack and then move in from the west during the confusion."

The Pathan chief spoke the words that the Death Merchant wanted to hear. "So be it. We will attack the Russians at Narang. With the help of Allah, we will destroy the dogs from the north."

Michael Quinlan laughed. "Pardon me, Malik-Sahib Mirza-Khan, for laughing. But I'm under the impression that the Pathans do not even consider the Russians human."

An enigmatic smile formed on Mirza-Khan's thin lips. "We are all made of the same clay, but a jug is not a vase," he said slyly.

Iskander Chaudhriy lost his temper. "What about our own revolution?" he stormed at Mirza-Khan. "Overthrowing Zia has been our dream for years! We'll be throwing all that away."

"Your dream is like heaven without a choir," Camellion said. "Your revolution could never succeed."

Chaudhriy turned savagely on Camellion. "What do you know about it?" he spat out. "You Americans stir up trouble all over the world. You come to this country and expect us to do the dying for you, just to save your precious oil in Saudi Arabia. Why should we become involved in your power plays with the damned Russians?"

"A fight to preserve freedom is everybody's business," Camellion snapped right back. One of our U.S. senators, Barry Goldwater, said it like it is: 'Extremism in defense of liberty is never a vice.' "

"Juisis mi-kof qi'hakas, Camellion, gokmo s'lin!"[11] Mirza-Khan said sharply to Chaudhriy. "Kir Camellion is right. A small child plays with his toys and his fantasies. The child grows into a man and his fantasies vanish. It is time we stop our dreaming. We could not defeat President Zia's tanks and big guns and airplanes. It would be a revolution in name only, a revolt we could not win."

Completely frustrated, Chaudhriy blurted out, "B-but we don't even know how many Russian dogs are at Narang! We know nothing about the base, how it might be guarded—nothing!"

The Death Merchant jumped into the conversation. "We would have all the information we needed after we reconnoiter the base. By we, I mean Kirs Quinlan, Bruckner and the Pepper—and Kir O'Malley. After we returned to Pakistan, we could then plot our approach and the sneak attack."

"We would need dependable guides," Quinlan said, business-like. "Pathan guides who are familiar with the area around Narang."

Jiko Krim-Lizak said unexpectedly, looking straight at the Death Merchant, "We will have to have more weapons, more machine pistols and explosives."

"You'll get them," Camellion answered promptly, half lying since he didn't know whether the CIA could deliver more weapons. It was a matter of red tape and Yale and Harvard halfwits making decisions. It wasn't up to Grojean.

"The guides you will require are not a problem," Mirza-Khan said to Camellion and Quinlan, then to Chaudhriy, "Iskander, find four men who are very familiar with the area around Narang.

[11]. "You are insulting Camellion who is our honored guest."

They must be very brave, determined and willing to die. They must be men who know that the dead are buried in the earth and never in the heart."

"It will take a few days, maybe longer," Chaudhriy said sullenly. "Not all our people are familiar with that section of Afghanistan."

The Death Merchant was uneasy. Even if he and Quinlan killed every pig farmer in Afghanistan, the Soviet Union would remain intact and, eventually, slaughter all the dreams of mankind and turn the world into a planet of pallbearers.

The four of us are doing a delicate balancing act, and there is only room for so many on the high wire. One slip and we're dead. . . .

CHAPTER FOUR

Pleased with what he saw, Lieutenant General Gregor Kerchenko of the *Glavnoye Razvedyvatelnoye Upravleniye* (Soviet Military Intelligence)—better known to intelligence agencies the world over as the GRU—ground the cigarette under his heel and placed his gloved hands on his hips in a satisfied manner. "You and your people have done well, Comrade Colonel Arbikochek," he said, "and in such a short time. Excellent."

"Thank you, Comrade Kerchenko," replied Josef Arbikochek, who was the commander of the 1800-man Spetsnaz force quartered in the thirteen wooden barracks over which was camouflaged netting. Only low-flying aircraft, or satellite photography, would be able to detect that the area contained barracks, ammunition dumps, food stores and other buildings and was not as barren as the rest of the region around the town of Narang.

"The operations building is just ahead of us, sir," Colonel Arbikochek said, "if you are finished with your inspection." He turned up the wide collar of his greatcoat as protection against the chilling wind blowing in from the plain. "I might add that every building is guarded day and night. The entire perimeter is protected with electric eyes and is mined. It's impossible for anyone to slip into the base."

"I have seen enough." Kerchenko slapped his left leg with his swagger stick. "Let's go to operations." The swagger stick was made of a bull's pizzle and had been given to him by his wife on his fiftieth birthday.

A tall, broad-shouldered man with iron-gray hair worn very short, Kerchenko had spent eighteen years in the GRU, was trusted by the all-powerful Central Committee, was considered politically reliable and had been posted in various countries in Europe and in the Middle East. He despised Afghanistan even more than he hated Holland, which he considered a nation of lazy parasites and often referred to as a "country of bad back benefits."

In operations, Kerchenko, Arbikochek and Major Petyr Ukormidev, Colonel Arbikochek's adjutant, removed their coats, caps and gloves and got down to business.

Lieutenant General Kerchenko had flown straight from Moscova to Kabul. From Kabul, a Mi-6 helicopter, escorted by two Hind-A gunships, had taken Kerchenko and his baggage to *Mogilki*[1]—the code name of the Spetsnaz base outside of Narang. The first thing he had said to Colonel Arbikochek and Major Ukormidev was that he would be staying several months at the base, a fact he reinterated after he had sat down in operations with a glass hot *charkoi* tea in his hand.

"My orders are to fly straight back to Moscova and give a detailed report to the general staff on the success of the operation." He regarded Arbikochek quizzically. "The operation will be a success, Colonel Arbikochek."

Kerchenko's words were half statement and half question, and Josef Arbikochek knew the GRU officer was seeking reassurance. He didn't blame him. So much depended on the strike that would test Pathan fighting ability. If it went as planned, the full-scale invasion of Pakistan would take place six weeks later.

Only twenty nine years old, Josef Vadim Arbikochek was not the usual Russian fighting man. Of superior intelligence, his physical and intellectual abilities had placed him in the top one percent of Soviet military recruits. The recruits in the highest category (those who had done well scholastically) could go to the Kremlin Guards, the KGB government communications troops, the KGB frontier troops or to the Spetsnaz. Josef Arbikochek, then only eighteen, had chosen the Spetsnaz. He had risen rapidly and had been among the top ten of his graduating class at the reconnaissance faculty of the Kiev Higher Combined Arms School. He had been number six at the Spetsnaz officer training academy, the special faculty of the Ryazan Higher Airborne School.

Three years ago he had been sent to Afghanistan, with the rank of captain. Within a year and seven months he had been promoted to major. After his last operation against the Afghan *Mujahideen* in the Paropamisus mountains—his unit had slaugh-

[1]."Little graves."

tered 406 Afghans—he had been promoted to colonel. That had been in July of 1984. The GRU command in Kabul had then ordered him to oversee the building of *Mogilki*.

"The strike will be successful; I am sure of it. But we must have the correct information," Colonel Arbikochek said evenly. "I do not mean that as a reflection on the *Geh Eh Ru*."[2]

He walked over to a wooden filing cabinet, took out a map and spread it out on a table in the center of the room. It was a topographic map of the northwest frontier of Pakistan, scaled one inch to four miles.

Lieutenant General Gregor Kerchenko and Major Ukormidev took positions on either side of him.

"Comrade General, we have been given very little information about the operation," Arbikochek said. "All we know is that we're to strike against a group of Pak tribesmen called Pathans. It would help if we had the particulars, if that information can be given without compromising security." He took a mechanical pencil from his uniform pocket and placed the tip on a small dot, next to which was Russian lettering. "This is the village of Gubukil in the Ismail Khan Mountains. It is our understanding that this insignificant settlement is the target."

"*Da*, Gubukil is the target," replied General Kerchenko, loosening his collar. The large oil burner, not far from the table, was throwing out a lot of heat. "And you and Comrade Major Ukormidev are wondering why we are using such force against an out-of-the-way village of *ne kul'turno Chernozhopy*."[3]

Major Petyr Ukormidev chuckled. "It did occur to us, Comrade General."

Two years younger than Colonel Arbikochek, Ukormidev was also built like a well-conditioned athlete. His hair was glossy black, his dark eyes intense and intelligent, his features even. However, he did have an unsightly scar at the bottom of his left cheek, the result of a training exercise during which a BTR troop carrier had overturned.

Lieutenant General Gregor Kerchenko explained that the village of Gubukil was being used as the winter headquarters of Mujibur Ali Mirza-Khan, the chief of the largest Pathan clan. Of far greater importance, the other *Maliks*, or chiefs, listened to Mirza-Khan's advice and always took their lead from him.

[2].GRU in Russian.

[3]."Uncultured asses."

"This old son of a bitch has only a tiny group of people with him," explained Kerchenko. "We couldn't possibly destroy his entire clan which numbers around 20,000. The point is that once he and the core of his clan are neutralized, the other Pathan chiefs will put up only token resistance when we move through the Khyber Pass."

Major Ukormidev lit a cigarette, his brow furrowed in thought.

Colonel Arbikochek turned to General Kerchenko. "The Pakistanis will not be an easy people to conquer. It's my understanding that they are every bit as fierce—I should say stupid—as these damned Afghans who haven't the sense to know when they're beaten."

But the Afghans weren't beaten. Colonel Arbikochek knew that the Russian army was bogged down in Afghanistan; and the fact that the war had gone on so long ensured that Afghanistan remained an international issue, thus damaging the Soviet Union politically.

Kerchenko nodded. "Intelligence—both ours and the findings of the *Kah Gay Beh*—indicates that President Zia won't put up any resistance once he has assurance from Moscova that we only want access to the southern coast of Baluchistan. There is also some indication that the Pakistani army will even help us clear the Khyber region of the Pathans."

"Then we're actually doing President Zia a favor when we invade his nation!" Ukormidev laughed.

General Kerchenko put down the empty glass. "*Da*, in a sense. The Pathans have been a sore boil on Zia's butt for years. Those savages consider themselves a law unto themselves and do as they please. Zia would love nothing better than to smash them for all time."

Ukormidev flicked an ash from his cigarette. "I don't understand why he hasn't already moved against them. After all, he has half a million men in his armed forces, and they're well trained."

"Zia's afraid that any action he might take against the Pathans will incite other tribes to revolt," Kerchenko said, "especially the Baluch, who hate his insides. Remember how Zia's army slaughtered the Baluch when they revolted, years ago. Zia's government is unpopular, and like most fools who have little daring, he wants to play it safe all the way around."

"Our Intelligence must be very certain to instill that kind of confidence in our leaders," Arbikochek said politely, and hoped that General Kerchenko didn't suspect that he was on a fishing expedition, "particularly since the *Geh Eh Ru* was able to pinpoint Chief Mirza-Khan's winter headquarters."

General Gregor Kerchenko crossed his legs and smiled in self-satisfaction. "It wasn't that difficult. We have an agent in Chief Mujibur Ali Mirza-Khan's camp." When he saw Arbikochek and Ukormidev register surprise, he added, "The man is not one of our professionals. He's a Pak traitor, as is the other informant we have. He's very close to President Zia himself. The instant Zia makes a decision, we know about it." He laughed heartily. "We have promised both filthy traitors that we'll make them the 'president' of Baluchistan after we conquer Pakistan and secure the nation. Naturally the two traitors are not aware of each other's existence. I caution you both. What I have told you about the two traitors is most secret. I was, however, given permission by the First Directorate to reveal the information to you. But that information cannot leave this room."

"We understand, Comrade General Kerchenko," replied Arbikochek.

General Kerchenko nodded, thankful that Colonel Arbikochek and Major Ukormidev were not regular Red Army officers. Red Army officers were so damned stupid. He recalled the time he had been sent to the Sinai in 1978, after the Israeli-Egyptian war, and had been attached to UNEF, the United Nations Emergency Force. U.S. and Soviet observers had always worked together in patrolling the LFA/MRZ[4] zone, and invariably the Red Army officers always revealed their stupidity—not to mention often showing up drunk. The Red Army officers had learned their English through a system of correspondence courses and were ill prepared to handle the complex radio jargon of a multinational military force. As a result, when quick decisions had to be made, the Soviet army officer always deferred to his U.S. partner's judgment rather than risk public or private rebuke for a wrong decision.

There was the problem of alcohol. When Red Army officers were invited to dinner, they always arrived with a bottle of vodka and insisted it had to be finished before dinner was served. Worse was their gullibility. General Kerchenko recalled one occasion when he and a Red Army officer and a U.S. Army officer had spent the night in the desert. When it came time to

[4].Limited Forces Area/Missile Restricted Zone.

retire, the *Amerikanski* had prepared his sleeping bag. The Soviet Union did not issue sleeping bags and the Red Army officer, having never seen a sleeping bag, asked the American officer about the piece of strange-looking equipment.

"It's my dream bag," the American officer had told him with a straight face, not realizing that Gregor Kerchenko, who, at the time was under the guise of a Red Army captain, knew better. Out of necessity, Kerchenko had remained silent as the Red Army officer had whipped out his notebook and had written, *American sleep in the open in beds they call dream bags*. As soon as the Red Army officer had returned the notebook to his pocket, the American had said, "It's only called a dream bag after sunset. After dawn, we call it a sunshine bag."

Out had come the notebook again!

Years later, Gregor Kerchenko still felt embarrassed when he remembered the incident.

General Kerchenko said, "Comrade Colonel, you do realize that your force of thirty will not jump to the target. The strike force will be ferried to Gubukil in Mi-6 helicopters. Four Hind-B gunships will accompany the force. They'll strike first, but—" He stopped short and laughed. "There I go! Trying to tell you your job. You'll have to pardon me, Comrade Colonel Arbikochek."

"Three hundred men will require six choppers," Arbikochek said, "and the map indicates there is more than ample room in which to land. We'll strike just before dawn. There shouldn't be any problems. The enemy will be awakened by the sound of the rotors, but they won't have time to organize before the gunships strike."

"It will be nothing more than a practice exercise." Major Ukormidev shrugged. "Like shooting geese with shotguns."

Colonel Arbikochek moved the fingers of his left hand slowly through his blond hair. Well, no doubt Petyr was right. Yet there were other factors to be considered. The strike against Mujibur Ali Mirza-Khan was nothing. It was the full-scale invasion of Pakistan that troubled Arbikochek. The Soviet Union was in enough trouble without invading Pakistan in an effort to isolate the United States from its oil in Saudi Arabia. *It was a mistake. The Americans would fight.*

Josef Arbikochek didn't like to admit it, but down deep in his heart he knew that the Soviet Union could not win a prolonged war against the United States, not a conventional war. A nuclear war meant the end of everything, of civilization everywhere.

Morale was already so low in the Red Army that General Yuri Yepishev[5] was in danger of being replaced. There was that very weak spot in the armed services that no one wanted to talk about: the unfortunate fact that the Soviet Union was comprised of many nationalities and ethnic groups. The talk of a "unified people" was nonsense. There were the Baltic, Trans-Caucasian, Central Asian peoples, etc., all of them strangers to each other but united in opposing Moscova.

Arbikochek suddenly remembered a remark his father had made years ago. Josef had only been thirteen at the time. His father had been drinking when he had said that it was easy to know the Soviet view of the world.

"Just stand truth on its head and you get the twisted perspective from Moscow. . . ."

[5].General Yuri Yepishev's official title is Chief of the Soviet Army and Navy Main Political Directorate. In short, he is the chief political commissar of the Soviet Union.

CHAPTER FIVE

Over the crawl of crazy years, Richard Camellion had learned that it is never stress that kills. It is the effective adaptation to stress that permits one to live. It was this knowledge that was the main reason why he considered all his missons ninety-five percent boredom and five percent panic, unlike living which he considered one hundred percent dullness. Even so he was not mentally weary when he and Mad Mike Quinlan, after the meeting with Mirza-Khan was over, set up the AN/URC 101 Satcom tactical transceiver on one of the high hills not far from the village.

The UHF/VHF radio was the latest in technology, having continuous coverage from 116-150 MHz and 225-400 MHz in AM and FM modes of operation. The 5 kHz spacing permitted more than 6,800 VHF channels and had twenty watts of power for satellite communication. It wasn't possible for the Death Merchant to know whether a U.S. NSA satellite might be overhead, so while Mad Mike held the portable "dish," Camellion contacted the CIA station in Tel Aviv, Israel. The Y Station then patched him in directly to the Center in the U.S. There wasn't the slightest danger that the Soviet KGB in Kabul, Afghanistan, or the Soviet Embassy in Islamabad, Pakistan, could pick up the transmissions. The KGB couldn't because the two-way voice communications would be "hopped" over 6,800 channels, all in a microsecond.

A disgruntled Michael Quinlan said, while he and Camellion were waiting for the patch-in, "We know that Grojean is going to demand that we make another attempt to talk Mirza-Khan into helping us wang out President Zia and General Saha I'Zada. The Fox never lets up."

The Death Merchant carefully adjusted the AN/URC's power selector.

"He can demand all he wants. He's there. We're here. Besides, we have other things to worry about."

Quinlan shifted the pickup and dispatch dish to his other hand. "Yeah, like staying alive."

"Haven't you wondered why it was so easy for the secret police to trail Willy and the Kid and Alfu Krod to the Shrine of Abdul Bu-I-Zum? The Invisible Man would have had a hard time trailing Bruckner and O'Malley, especially with Krod along and with all three practically paranoid about a tail."

Dismay flashed over Quinlan's face. "I can't feature a leak among these people. It is possible that the secret police just got lucky."

"Croc crap! You don't believe the Chanwiri-lu-Shabudar got lucky any more than I do. Hold it. Langley's coming in. Keep the dish steady."

Quinlan had been right. After the Death Merchant had given his report, Grojean began a long sermon on how "our framework of surreptitious manipulation for that area of conflict requires the termination of President Zia" and insisted that Camellion "use all your persuasive powers to convince Chief Mirza-Khan of the necessity of removing President Zia from the Pakistan government."

The Death Merchant didn't bother to tell Grojean that what the CIA considered necessity wasn't necessity to Mirza-Khan. Camellion, however, did use the subject of killing Zia as a psychological foreword in requesting more weapons for Mirza-Khan.

"A thousand automatic rifles and whatever else you might send might make him more receptive to the idea of terminating Zia. Anyhow, he and his men can't attack the Russian base at Narang without the weapons."

The Fox did not put up an argument. He did say that such a large amount of firepower could not be shipped—airdropped—from India. "We're going to have to close that route," Grojean explained. "The Indian intelligence service is becoming suspicious. We'll use the navy. Or maybe fly the shipment in from Israel. I'll give the details later. Make contact again in a few days."

The Death Merchant said, "The Indian route is our escape out of this mountain 'paradise.' We can't jump off a mountain, flap our arms and fly out. So how about it?"

Not to worry, Grojean reassured Camellion. The Bikarner, India, escape route was secure as far as four persons were concerned. Fifty large crates was a different matter. Anything else?

Camellion and Quinlan resumed their discussion of a possible spy among the Pathans as they were putting away the AN/URC.

"The Peppermint Kid did tell me that there was another guide other than Krod," Quinlan said. Carrying the case that contained the "dish," he carefully picked his way among the loose stones of the uneven slope. "His name was Lukriz Au-mumin. They left him in Peshawar. You could be right, but we're safe enough here in Gubukil."

"Maybe and maybe not," Camellion said thoughtfully. "Mirza-Khan and the Pathans now with him moved from the Safed Koh range to the Dera Ismail Khan mountains only nine days ago."

"Meaning what?" Quinlan glanced curiously at him.

"You heard Mirza-Khan. The Russians have already made two recon flights over this village. How did the pig farmers know the location of this little speck of a village unless someone gave them the information? And who's to say that someone hasn't informed the KGB or the GRU about us?"

Quinlan, too much of a realist and a survivor to discount any possibility, found interest and suspicion mounting. "The bottom line could be the Spetsnaz dropping in on us to wreck any plans we and the Pathans might have—right?"

"We would, if we were in their place."

"Well, we know the answer," said Quinlan without enthusiasm. "Mirza-Khan might not be at all receptive to the suggestion that the entire village move. On the other hand, such a move would be comparatively easy. There are numerous caves we could hole up in, and they'd be warmer than those stone houses."

"Let's go talk to the old boy," said Camellion. "That fart head Chaudhriy will be the first to veto any move."

Walking against the wind, they continued toward the village where the houses climbed the steep hillsides like stairs. Seldom were two houses on the same level. On some earthen roofs goats were grazing on grass shoots; other animals were hopping from hillside rocks to other roofs that were covered with patches of snow, as were the rocks and the ground around the dwellings.

Even with the best of weather, the northwest frontier was never hospitable to the Pathans who called the area home and accepted nature's harsh conditions. Here it was the bubbling of water that was the sound of life, water that, during spring and summer, would nourish yellow carpets of mustard and sugarcane in the valleys, plus emerald slivers of wheat on the hillsides.

And acres of deadly poppies . . .

The valleys of the northwest frontier had been cultivated for almost five thousand years. The Gandhara civilization thrived at the time of Alexander the Great's invasion in 327 B.C. and much later dotted the valleys with thousands of stupas, shrines and Buddhist monasteries, and yet, reflected the Death Merchant, Pakistan was a nation of stark contrasts. While life on the northwest frontier had remained unchanged—*Except that now they have modern weapons and modern transportation!*—Islamabad, the splendid new capital, contained buildings that were ultramodern. In and around Karachi were steel mills more up to date than some found even in the United States. There was even a nuclear power plant outside of Karachi, and for years the CIA and other intelligence services had been wondering if Pakistan could be building an atom bomb.

Mike Quinlan lit a Green Circle cigarette—a Pakistani brand—as they neared the village. "I get the feeling that we've stepped back in time, farther back than if we were in Africa."

His mind on Malik Mujibur Ali Mirza-Khan, the Death Merchant didn't answer. The old Pathan chief was surprisingly well informed about a lot of subjects, especially the international situation, and believed that a nuclear war between the United States and the Soviet Union would destroy civilization. He was also convinced that Iblis—the Christian Satan—was responsible for all the evil in the world. It was only then that Camellion and his company of three had learned that Mirza-Khan was more than a *Malik*. He was also a *Mullah*,[1] hence his pronouncements about Satan:

"Any name we use is meaningless. It would only be a name given to a totally evil spirit that is basically nameless.

"Iblis cannot do evil except through a human body. He does not have the power to kill or to do physical harm. He must use human beings to do his work of evil."

[1].A Moslem "priest." Technically, a title of respect for one who is learned in or teaches, or expounds the sacred law of the Koran.

Mirza-Khan was also dogmatic about the operation of Allah's office:

"Allah always answers prayers. The trouble is that most people regard prayer as a list of requests. True prayer is not talking to Allah; it is listening to Allah.

"Allah permits evil because He did not make us puppets. He gave us free will. We can choose either good or evil."

No doubt about it, thought Camellion, *the old boy is the Jerry Falwell of Pakistan.*

By the time Camellion and Quinlan were almost to the first house, they could see people in the bright afternoon sun. Many of the women were baking *shishaou,* ordinary bread, over open fires. All were wearing the female version of the *chudki* (longer than the men's *chudkis*), and underneath the warm coats the *cheo,* or plain black dress. While most of the older women were veiled, wearing the traditional *chador,* the majority of younger women, many of whom were quite pretty, had their faces uncovered. And weren't quite a few of them pregnant? So be it. Man was a manure-making machine—*Mount Everests of crap all over the world!*—but to the Pathans a man was fire and a woman fuel. And the average male Pathan was always hot. . . .

Just before Camellion and Mad Mike reached the two-room stone dwelling they shared with O'Malley and Bruckner, they passed a small group of men sitting around a large fire watching a *tum puchawao* or "bow shaker," a fortune-teller who could consult the lesser spirits always grouped around Allah. How the bow quivered determined the good or bad of anyone's future fortune.

The Merchant of quick Death and Mad Mike, who had been a free-lance merc since leaving the French Foreign Legion, found Bruckner and the Peppermint Kid sitting on crates of Galil assault rifles playing poker.

Putting away the AN/URC, Camellion apprised the Kid and Bruckner of his plan to talk Mirza-Khan into moving his people into the caves above the village.

O'Malley got to his feet and hooked a thumb through a brass ring on his leather jacket. "What did Washington 'ave to say about another shipment?"

"It's coming but not from India," Camellion said. "Indian intelligence is getting wise. I'll get the details later. The guns will probably be flown in from Israel. I'm hoping that news of the shipment will put Mirza-Khan into a receptive frame of mind."

"*Ja, das ist gut!*" Bruckner, who had gotten to his feet, began buckling on his gun belt. Each holster was filled with a 9mm Steyr GB autoloader. "If der *Russisch* attack, they could only land the helicopters below the village. Then they would have to climb upward to attack. We would be above in the caves and could slaughter der *schweinerei* and turn this village into a *Todesborn*!"

"We wouldn't have to turn the village into a death fountain," Mike Quinlan said grimly. "The Russians would do that with gunships before the choppers would put down."

"Let's hope the Spetsnaz don't attack," Camellion said in a bored voice. "Firefights are not conducive to one's longevity."

"We might even catch a cold." Quinlan chuckled.

"Well chaps, should we have a go at it?" O'Malley suggested. "The old fuddy can't do more than say no to the move. . . ."

Two of Mirza-Khan's *badragga* met Camellion and his men at the door of Mirza-Khan's house and informed them that the *Malik* was in conference with Iskander Chaudhriy and Jiko Krim-Lizak.

"Tell Malik-Sahib Mujibur Ali Mirza-Khan that I have very important information for him," insisted the Death Merchant, his voice a firm command.

A minute later and Camellion and his three men were seating themselves on the rug, facing Mirza-Khan, whose inscrutability always irked Quinlan. Jiko Krim-Lizak's narrow face was as calm as well water while Iskander Chaudhriy was his old scowling self.

"Kir Camellion, you have valuable information," said Mirza-Khan. "I trust you received this good news from your *Malik* in America?"

The Death Merchant explained that a thousand assault rifles and other kill equipment would be airdropped in a short while. As Camellion explained the situation, he could see a pleased expression spreading over the Pathan chief's face, and he hoped the old *Mullah* would remain in a happy frame of mind after he suggested that the whole village pack up and move into the caves.

Surprise! Surprise! Not only did the delighted expression remain on Mirza-Khan's face, but he actually laughed when

Camellion said that in his opinion the people of the village should move into the caves in case of an attack by the Russians.

"My *baya-darkas* and I were discussing such an evacuation," said Mirza-Khan, evidentally enjoying the slightly astonished looks on the faces of the Death Merchant, Quinlan, Bruckner and O'Malley. "Tell us. Why do you suggest we leave this place? What are your reasons?"

"You and your people have been in Gubukil only a bit over a week," Camellion said. "During that short time Soviet aircraft have flown over twice. Each time, you said, they passed over at less than 300 meters. Such low altitude indicates very close scrutiny. That kind of observation indicates that a strike is imminent. To remain in this village is to fall into a trap, perhaps one set by Iblis himself. Hell is in charge of all Soviet policy."

"Hell might be in charge, but the Russians bleed and die like other men," Chaudhriy said gruffly, his English almost without accent. "I for one can't see them parachuting into these mountains. And why should they attack us? We are not a threat to the Russians in Afghanistan."

"Malik Mirza-Khan's clan is not a threat, not in itself," Camellion said. "But he's the hub around which the rest of the clans would organize. By killing Mirza-Khan, the Soviets would hope to crush any Pathan resistance before it could even begin."

Mirza-Khan stroked his beard. "The dogs of the north overestimate my importance. But our conclusions are the same as yours, Kir Camellion. The Russians have flown over this village twice. We cannot ignore that fact. To remain here would be foolish. We will begin to move to the caves this very day." He paused, then added, "I do agree with some of the things Iskander said. I do not believe the Russians will drop from the sky at the end of parachutes."

Krim-Lizak folded his hands in his lap, his steady gaze searching the Death Merchant's face. "Kir Camellion, did you not say that the Spetsnaz dogs always use parachutes?"

"I said that the Spetsnaz were highly trained as paratroopers." The Death Merchant wondered if Mirza-Khan also suspected an informer. *If he does, is he deliberately refraining from mentioning it?* "I also said that the Spetsnaz were trained to fight either on land or sea. There's only one way they could attack this settlement. First, helicopter gunships would reduce the houses to rubble with missiles and incendiaries. Troop-carrying choppers would then land south of here, in the old riverbed, and discharge troops."

Mad Mike Quinlan furthered the Death Merchant's analysis. "The caves are only sixty meters north of the village. From the caves we could kill the invaders—should they come—with the ease that wheat is cut in the fields."

"To remain in the village would be suicide," ventured the Peppermint Kid, taking off his black beret.

"We are in agreement, Kir O'Malley." Mirza-Khan nodded vigorously. "And as Jiko said before the four of you arrived, the dogs from the north might attack all the sooner if they have learned that the four of you are among us. The Russians would realize that intelligence agents from America would be working against the Soviet Union."

The Death Merchant tossed out the line. But would Mirza-Khan take the bait? "But how could the Russians know that you and your people are here in the Dera Ismail Khan, much less that four Westerners are with you?"

"Four Western intelligence agents?" added Quinlan. "Even if none of us are . . . anyhow, not technically."

Mirza-Khan frowned at Camellion and Quinlan. "I am troubled that you should not have guessed the answer. The Russians have their agents in the Zia government. We do not have any proof, but it is reasonable to believe it is so."

"General I'Zada often sends his Chanwiri-lu-Shabudar agents among the tribes and clans of the northwest region of our nation. We discovered two such traitors in our midst during the frosty months of last fall."

"You killed the two traitors?" Bruckner said loudly.

"*Yibo*. It is against the Koran to kill under such conditions," said Iskander Chaudhriy. "We did punish them and extract our revenge. We put out the eyes of the two traitors and turned them loose. This was in keeping with our code of *Punkhtunwali*." From his tone, it was evident that Chaudhriy was relishing the memory.

Quinlan cleared his throat in a particular manner that was a silent message of warning to the Death Merchant.

Camellion addressed Chaudhriy very politely and very formally "*Baya-darka* Chaudhriy, have you sent a messenger to find guides who can lead us to the Soviet base at Narang?"

Willy Bruckner said, "Why are there no men here in the village who would know the way to the pig base in Narang?"

"There are no men who know the safe route," Chaudhriy said coldly, emphasizing the word *safe*. "Even with guides who are familiar with that area of Afghanistan, the risk will still be enormous. I tell you that I think you are fools to undertake such a mission. You will be discovered by the Russians. They will torture and execute you."

"They will try; they will fail," Camellion said, the extreme iciness in his voice making even Chaudhriy regard him perplexedly. *It will be the Cosmic Lord of Death who will decide. . . .*

"We sent a messenger an hour ago," Krim-Lizak said tenderly, as if trying to reassure frightened children. "Be at ease, our American friends. It could be as long as a week before suitable guides are found and brought to Gubukil."

"I am sure the guides can be found among friends of mine in other villages," said Chaudhriy. "The guides, whoever they may be, must be very brave and dependable. I might also say, very foolish. They too will be risking their lives."

Mirza-Khan got wearily to his feet and looked at the Death Merchant and his men. "We have talked enough and the day grows short. Come, let us begin the move to the caves."

The evacuation of Gubukil required two and a half days, all of them filled with the complaints of wives and daughters who did not want to have to bake *shishaou* and *jaou* over fires in the caves, much less carry blankets, bedding and other household items, as few as they were. The problem was not solved by any firmness of the Pathan males, but by the Death Merchant, who pointed out to Mirza-Khan that it would be a serious mistake in tactics to desert the village entirely.

"Should the Russians fly over and see that the village is deserted, or if they would see smoke coming from the mouths of the caves, they would know at once we have moved, and they would probably guess that we were expecting an attack."

Chaudhriy attempted to make light of Camellion's analysis. "There are openings in the tops of the caves. Our women could cook inside. The smoke would escape through the top openings."

"And Soviet electronic detectors would instantly detect the smoke," Camellion said savagely. "Cooking in the caves is out of the question."

For days, Camellion had been trying to decide whether it was strictly on a personal basis that Chaudhriy disliked him and the three mercs . . . *or is there another reason? It's almost as if he fears us. . . .*

The Death Merchant then suggested that a score of women and an equal number of men remain in the village during the day, during which time the women would bake and the men keep the fires burning, not only outside but in the dwellings. At night, several men would feed the fires inside the houses.

"Ah . . . but Allah has not provided heat inside the caves," Mirza-Khan said with irony. "Kir Camellion, how do you propose that we keep warm?"

"Blankets and plenty of warm clothing. There isn't any other way."

Iskander Chaudhriy was furious and made no secret of his feelings.

"And how long will this kind of living continue?" he demanded angrily. "Sleeping in the caves and cooking in the village—it is madness!"

"For several weeks," Camellion was quick to reply. "Some discomfort with safety is preferable to comfort with death hanging over our heads." Deliberately then he tossed the insult at Chaudhriy. "Or do you prefer comfort and risking the lives of all these men, women and children?"

"*Inshallah!*" Mirza-Khan spoke rapidly, the word clipped off. "Kir Camellion is right. We will do as he says. I feel that is what Allah wants."

Some smoke was necessary in the caves. Illumination was necessary, light provided by sheep's-fat lamps. The caves themselves were a twisting maze, as hospitable as the inside of a tomb, with walls and ceilings that dripped moisture and floors that were only smooth and/or level in small areas. Yet the discomfort was not as intense as had been expected. The human body gives off a lot of heat. At night, the men huddled closely together in groups, under tents made of blankets. The women huddled in other groups, small children in the center.

Four days passed, with three Soviet Antonov-14[2] aircraft flying over during the afternoon of the fourth day. Altitude: less than 1000 feet.

[2].A braced high-wing monoplane with two nine-cyclinder radial cooled engines. A small utility and observation craft with a tricycle landing gear. NATO designation: CLOD. The Soviets call the AN-14 *Pchelka*—"Little Bee."

"They didn't fly over for the fun of it," Quinlan said slowly, watching the aircraft disappear in the west. "But we don't have time to be in a hurry. We'll have to sit tight and wait to see what happens, and without much fun while we're doing it."

"Quit your complaining," Camellion said jovially. "Fun is like insurance. The older you get, the more it costs. What are you griping about? There were three quarts of Scotch in the airdrop of a few weeks ago."

"Don't remind me, Richard. The hell of it is, if I drank any of it, it would be an insult to these people. You know how they feel about alcohol."

The Peppermint Kid laughed. "Usually we're where there's cheap booze and loose women. Here there's no booze, and if we looked twice at one of the women, we'd get our bloomin throats cut."

The big Bruckner, to whom humor was as alien as rollar skates to a bedbug, glared out over the desolate, snow-smudged landscape. He growled in German, "We won't be bored once the guides get here and we start for Afghanistan. Frankly, I don't trust any of these damned people. They're too primitive, too weird, too superstitious."

"Meaning they believe in God, eh Willy?" joked the Peppermint Kid, who was always teasing Bruckner about his atheism. Along with the Death Merchant and Mike Quinlan, O'Malley spoke German and half a dozen other languages.

"Willy has a point, even if maybe for the wrong reasons," Camellion said in a voice that had a strong trace of honest concern. "We can't afford to trust any guides, not after what happened back at the Shrine of Abdul Bu-I-Zum."

"Yeah, so what do we do?" A twisted grin started to crawl across Mike Quinlan's mouth. "The Pathans don't know we have a map, but we don't know how accurate the map is."

"More importantly is what we're not going to do," Camellion said. "We're not going to eat or drink anything prepared by the guides—if Chaudhriy ever finds any, and I don't think he's looking too hard. There were plenty of MREs[3] in that last air drop. We'll use them and fill our own canteens, and two of us will remain awake while the rest of us sleep."

"Come to think of it, there were half a dozen noise suppres-

[3]. "Meal: Ready to Eat"—a meat entree, cracker pack, cheese spread, mixed fruit, beverage powder, sugar, candy, etc.

sors in the airdrop,'' Quinlan said. ''They're in with the crates marked for us. They'll come in handy.''

''I say, there's really nothing to worry about, except staying alive,'' quipped the Peppermint Kid.

The Death Merchant's laugh was scornful. ''Don't kid yourself, O'Malley. Nothing is something that isn't. It's a nice subject to discuss when you have nothing to say. We're going to have plenty to say before this mission's over. . . .''

CHAPTER SIX

It was a feeling of pure pleasure, knowing that you were on the way to the target and that the enemy had little chance to defend himself. At the same time, Colonel Josef Arbikochek felt guilty. Always brutally honest with himself, Arbikochek knew that wiping out Gubukil and its pathetic inhabitants would not prove the superiority of the Spetsnaz. Only once had the Spetsnaz fought trained, seasoned veterans of an enemy force. Disguised as Syrians, thirty-one Spetsnaz had fought the Israelis in Lebanon—and had gotten their Red asses beaten! Thirteen had been killed, seven badly wounded. The remaining eleven had retreated in wild confusion.

Even though the unit had not been under his command, the thought of its defeat was still a black thought in Arbikochek's mind. Those *yobanyy Yevrei*![1]

Sitting in the command chopper, Arbikochek reassured himself that nothing could go wrong with this operation. Why it would amount to little more than target practice for the men in the six Mi-6 troop-carrying helicopters. Each large craft had an enormous five-bladed rotor, was powered by two 5500 s.h.p. Soloviev D-25V turboshaft engines and, fully loaded, could cruise at 155 mph.

"How many more minutes until we reach the target?" Arbikochek inquired of Major Petyr Ukormidev, who was sitting next to him and, like the other men, was wearing black combat fatigues, a black helmet and black paratrooper boots.

Major Ukormidev consulted his wristwatch. "The gunships

[1]."Damned Jews."

will go in in approximately thirteen minutes. Their attack has been estimated at only two minutes.''

A fanatic for perfection, Arbikochek asked for the second time since the liftoff from the base outside of Narang, ''Petyr, you are positive that there is ample room south of the village for our six carriers and the four gunships? Comrade, we must be certain!''

''Josef, quit your worrying,'' Ukormidev did his best to reassure the neurotic Colonel Arbikochek. ''Only yesterday afternoon we double-checked the figures derived from the photographs taken not only from previous recon aircraft but also by the slower flying *Pchelki*. There is no mistake. We will land on a riverbed that is always dry in winter. Our aerial survey experts estimate the bed to be twenty-seven meters wide, and they have assured us and General Kerchenko that there will not be any problems with the touchdown.''

''And with little else,'' remarked Arbikochek. ''The gunships will attack with such speed that most of the trash in the village will be killed during the first pass. Why they will die peacefully, without even knowing what killed them. At 0400 hours, the entire village will be asleep.

''Including the four enemy agents,'' Major Petyr Ukormidev said very thoughtfully. ''If you don't mind my saying so, Comrade General Kerchenko's orders to capture and return the four to the base is ridiculous. If they are hiding with Chief Mirza-Khan and his people, they will no doubt be killed by the Mi-6s. Should they survive, the men will shoot them down. How can we tell the men to look twice before they fire? How are they supposed to recognize four Israelis or four Americans?''

''We will ignore Comrade General Kerchenko's order,'' Arbikochek said with uncharacteristic bluntness. ''He really doesn't expect us to find the foreign agents.''

Listening to the steady sound of the rotor and the roaring of the turboshafts, Arbikochek lapsed into silence, thinking of how Kerchenko had informed him and Major Ukormidev of the four agents the previous morning.

''Two were posing as Americans,'' Comrade Gregor Kerchenko had said. ''Very possibly they are. I doubt it. The other two—they arrived in Pakistan after the first team—carried West German passports. Our informant is positive that the two teams made contact with each other. In fact, with the help of revolutionaries, they murdered nine agents of the Pakistani security service. It's possible the four could have sought refuge with Mujibur Ali Mirza-Khan."

"Comrade General Kerchenko, if the four are with that murderous old son of a bitch," Colonel Arbikochek had said, "they are there for only one reason: to stir up trouble, to try to get the Pathans to revolt against President Zia."

"Which is another reason why Mujibur Ali Mirza-Khan and his clan must be eliminated from the sphere of political activity," General Kerchenko had said. "A revolt at this time would conflict with Moscova's plans."

An uneasy feeling began to creep through Colonel Josef Arbikochek, a sensation of black dread he tried to drive from his mind. But the feeling persisted. Nonsense! he told himself. What could possibly go wrong? They were only ignorant tribesmen armed with rifles. How could they fight gunships and the Spetsnaz? Impossible!

Colonel Josef V. Arbikochek had been dead right. At 4:00 A.M. the people of Gubukil were fast asleep, but not in the village. They were in the caves north of it. Included within the realm of Morpheus were the two men who had been keeping the home fires burning in the settlement. They had put enough wood on the fires inside the houses to keep smoke pouring through the ceilings until past dawn. Why should they not take their rest also?

In spite of the black night—there was no moon—and the silence—except for the low whispering of the mountain wind—the two men in the village and the people in the caves were warned minutes in advance of the attack, five minutes before the four gunships could swoop down on the dwellings of Gubukil and make their kill run. The noise from the four Mi-8s and the six Mi-6s was terrific—ten rotors furiously chopping at the sky and telegraphing the approach of the ten big birds.

When the Soviet eggbeaters were still eleven klicks away, the thunderous *thub-thub-thub-thub* awakened Chinbur Vik-Mokok, who was a light sleeper and one of the two men in the village. Instantly, he was wide-awake, shaking Ghulam Liaquitzi, and hissing, "They're coming. We must flee and warn the others."

By the time that Vik-Mokok and Liaquitzi had rushed outside, fired off shots with their .38 British Webley revolvers and were running toward the caves, the Soviet air armada had covered more klicks and the four gunships—designated Hind-D by NATO—were preparing for their attack.

One of the world's most heavily armed helicopters, the Hind-D[2] is a deadly killer, equipped with night and all-weather sensors and weapon-aiming devices and instrumentation. In its nose is a four-barrel gatling gun (14.5 or 23mm caliber), and its two stubby wings carry racks for a total of twelve "Spiral" missiles and rocket pods for a total of eight 551-pound bombs, gun pods or other stores.

With their infrared night-vision viewers, the Soviet pilots weren't troubled by the darkness. They enjoyed their work. Killing people was fun, especially when there was almost no danger of the victims fighting back. While the six troop-carrying Mi-6s hung back and hovered motionless, the first Hind dove in from the northwest, the automatic electronic aiming and firing mechanisms shooting off the Spiral missiles and, seconds later, space-dropping eight *palazhyl* bombs—cluster bombs of thermite that first separate, then bounce for several meters before exploding.

Twelve violent explosions, only micromoments apart, rocked the area, enormous flashes of bright red and orange fire that made the jagged mountains stand out starkly. Almost immediately after the explosions there were eight intense white-bright blossoms of the exploding *palazhyl* bombs as molten thermite shot out in long, beautiful streamers and splattered over the rubble of demolished houses.

It took only sixteen seconds. Then the first Hind was roaring upward and the second bird was revving down and streaking in toward what was left of the village.

The warning shots of Chinbur Vik-Mokok and Ghulam Liaquitzi did what they were supposed to do: they warned Mirza-Khan and his people and the Death Merchant, Mad Mike Quinlan and his two top mercs. Many of them now watched in rage and horror as the Hinds crushed the village like an elephant stepping on a cockroach.

It was a typical example of Russian overkill. The first two Hinds completely destroyed every single house in Gubukil. Ninety-six goats were burned to death by the thermite that now bathed

[2].It was because of the deadliness of the Hind-D, Hind-A, and Hind-E that the U.S. Hughes AH-64, or Apache, was designed, to counter Soviet threats, not only in Cuba but in Europe.

the mountains with flickering blue-white light, creating huge shadows that glided over hillsides and fluttered over the openings of the caves.

The Death Merchant and his three helpers and a dozen Pathans kept down and watched the last of the Hinds roar up and away.

"Those bloody stupid ivans." The Peppermint Kid sneered. "Two of their birds could 'ave done the job. Instead they used four and wasted all those missiles and fire bombs."

Camellion and Quinlan, watching the hell below them through Cyclops night-vision viewers, could see that three kilometers to the south the six Mi-6 "Hook" transports were descending to the riverbed.

The Hooks were among the largest transport helicopters in the world. The length of the fuselage was slightly over 108 feet, with the diameter of the main rotor being 114 feet. There wasn't any armament, but each Hook could carry fifty fully equipped troops. The first Hook sat down, then the second, then the third and so on—all with precision. The Soviet pilots were good.

"Burn my butt on a broken broomstick," Quinlan said in disgust, staring through the Cyclops NVD. "Six of those Hook babies. That means 300 men if each one is fully loaded. The pig boys from Slut-Mama Russia must be scared stiff of the Pathans. Hell, they didn't need any men. Two gunships could have done the job—and did. Gubukil 'ain't' no more."

"Right on, Mike! But we suckered them," Camellion said. "We're up here and not down there or we'd be burnt toast. And you'd better believe the Russians are afraid of the Pathans. In any hand-to-hand confrontation, one Afghan can kick the crap out of two average pig farmers. The Pakistanis are rated to be even more fierce than the Afghans. The Pathans are supposed to make the other Pak tribes look like cub scouts."

"You keep talking and you're going to have me feeling sorry for those Slavic saps down there!"

"Somebody had better feel sorry for them, if they come this way. It'll be a pigshoot."

We can do no more. Now we wait. Camellion mentally reviewed the "defense program." Mirza-Khan and his group were armed with Galil assault rifles and Egyptian- and Chinese-made 7.63 mm Kalashnikov ARs and plenty of ammunition. For sidearms, they had 9mm Berettas, any number of Egyptian 9mm

Helwan[3] and Soviet 7.62mm Tokarev autoloaders. Hundreds of grenades, many American-made, others Soviet-manufactured and traded from the Afghans. There were also fifty British Sterling SMGs, four RPG Soviet antitank launchers and fourteen ATGMs[4] for the RPGS.

Why do I get myself into these messes? To watch that Swiss bank account grow, that's why! If only the Pathans follow Mike's instructions and mine!

The Death Merchant and Mike Quinlan had insisted for several days, that if the Russians attacked, the Pathans should not fire a single shot until the pig farmers came up the slope and were well within range.

If the Russians came up the slope. *If* the Russians attempted to charge the caves—*And they will!*—to which there were twenty-six openings, some very large, others so small one had to stoop to get in. The Death Merchant and Colonel Quinlan had warned that under no circumstances were the Pathans to leave the caves and charge down the slopes. Sheer bravery could not compensate for Soviet training and discipline.

Iskander Chaudhriy, carrying a Gilil, a canvas bag full of magazines for the assault rifle and a holstered Beretta pistol strapped around his waist over his *chudki,* wriggled in between the Death Merchant and Colonel Quinlan.

"Let me look through one of the see-in-the-dark instruments," he requested. For a change, he wasn't sullen and the implied "or else" was absent from his voice. "The fires are burning low in what was once our village and I cannot see what is going on in the distance."

"Sure." The Death Merchant pulled the Cyclops NVD from his face and held it out to Chaudhriy. "Kir Chaudhriy, the men have their orders. I want assurance that they will obey those orders. And keep your head down. There're two gunships still hovering to the south and you can be positive that they're looking over the entire area with infrared viewers. I'll roll out of the way and you look between the rocks."

Chaudhriy had placed the NVD over his face and had begun to adjust the straps. "The men will obey, but they do not like it. It is not our way to wait like trapped animals in holes. It is particularly so when our land is invaded by filth."

[3].Similar to a Beretta and made by the same Italian company.

[4].Antitank guided missiles.

"Dead men don't need pride," Camellion said. "In this case, brainpower equals life."

"Are the stuffed figures ready to be put into position?" Quinlan's voice was mechanical, his entire being centered on strategy—only one of the main reasons why he and his Thunderbolt Unit: Omega mercenaries were in such demand throughout the world.

The Death Merchant had moved out of the way, and Chaudhriy answered Quinlan as he squirmed into Camellion's former position. "The figures are ready, twenty of them. They will be put into position with weapons the moment one of the gunships comes in this direction. But I do not think that any of the birds without wings will do that. The dogs will see how their missiles and fire bombs have destroyed our homes and will think we are dead. They will then return to their base in *Doulat i Jumhouri ye Afghanistan*."[5]

Camellion felt sorry for Chaudhriy. *But how could he be expected to know about modern slaughter tactics?*

"I'll tell you what's going to happen," Camellion said, lying on his left side. "Thermite never destroys completely. When the Russians don't find any charred bones, they'll guess the village was deserted. The pig farmers don't like being outsmarted. They'll guess we're up here, and that's when the fun will begin."

"You are sure of that, Kir Camellion," Chaudhriy said in an odd voice. Can you know what is in the mind of the enemy?"

"Experience, lots of experience. I've been through it before." *In a lot of places and in different times . . . a cycle of Death that never seems to end.*

"*Tiorariz! Fu'iq quet-utoiz*—Amazing! All is daytime," exclaimed Chaudhriy, astonished at how the NVD turned black night into early twilight. "I can see the enemy dogs far in the distance, even the two birds without wings that are hovering about the other machines on the ground. I also see those devils from the north. They are dressed in black and getting out of the larger machines without wings. Each man is carrying a weapon."

"Spetsnaz," Quinlan said without rancor. Like the Death Merchant, he considered the Russians nonpeople without hopes or dreams, love or desires. He began to edge back, squirming on his stomach, at the same time taking off the Cyclops and, reaching across Chaudhriy, handing the device to Camellion. "I'm

[5].The real name of Afghanistan.

going to join Willy and the Kid. They can use some help with those RPGs."

"They could use an observer." Camellion slipped the NVD over his face. As it is, Willy and O'Malley will have to fire damned fast. Another thing is that—"

"They've done it before, under more adverse conditions than these," remarked Quinlan, a lilt to his voice. He was enjoying every minute of the danger. A normal life would have driven him to suicide. *Even an abnormal life has driven him to drink, the crazy bastard!*

"I was going to say that the effective range of those eighty-five-mil projectiles is only 328 yards, or 300 meters."

"That's almost a thousand feet—but so what?" said Quinlan, who was now back far enough from the opening of the cave to get to his feet. "Even the gunships are out of range; once they run out of chain-gun ammo, they'll be as useless as an armless man trying to play basketball. It's still the Spetsnaz who have to do the leg work. There's no way they're going to get this high, not up those slopes." He grinned mockingly. "See you both later. Give my regards to Mr. Death if you see him. . . ."

Quinlan disappeared into the darkness of the cave, and the Death Merchant, once more watching through the NVD, and Chaudhriy saw that the Spetsnaz force was moving very quickly, fanning out in five-man squads toward the smoking rubble of the village, each man carry an ARK assault rifle, in which there was a banana-shaped magazine filled with 40 5.45x38mm rounds.

"Kir Camellion," began Chaudhriy in a pleasant voice. "On the long slopes are rocks large enough to conceal even three and four men. Why would it not be proper to position our men behind those rocks and have them wait for the Russian dogs, if the filth from the north comes this far?"

"It would not be proper because your people would be going to their deaths," the Death Merchant said patiently. "Take a good look, my *baya-darka*. See those three weapons that the Russians are removing from one transport, the ones with tripods? Those are AGS-17s, or what the pig farmers call *Avtomaticeski Granatomojot Stankovi*, or 'grenade machine gun.'[6] See them?"

[6].This is the *Plamya*—"flame"—that fires grenades of three types. The first is an antitank round with a HEAT warhead. The second is an antipersonnel round with a warhead containing iron and plastic needles which are fatal over a radius of 4.4 to 5.5 yards. The third is a phosphorus round.

"*Ched,* I do."

"They're automatic grenade launchers that fire 30mm grenades at the rate of fifty to a hundred rounds per minute. When the Russians discover that the village was deserted, they'll use the three grenade machine guns to saturate the slopes with antipersonnel rounds. It would be a bloodbath, and the blood would be Pathan blood."

"I see Chinbur Vik-Mokok and Ghulam Liaquitzi," Chaudhriy said excitedly. "They were fortunate to have escaped the bombing and to have reached rocks on the lower slopes. See them? They are coming up a slope."

The Death Merchant, studying the Spetsnaz coming in from the south, did not answer. He only hoped that spotters in the two hovering gunships wouldn't detect Vik-Mokok and Liaquitzi. Then again, it was possible that if the pig farmers did see the two men, they would think they were only survivors of what the Spetsnaz had intended to be a massacre.

"Those dogs move fast, like the wind," Chaudhriy said. "They are almost to where the village was. All we can do is wait and hope that Allah favors us."

"*Inshallah.*"

In full battle gear, Colonel Josef Arbikochek was a happy man. The attack had gone exactly as planned. The village of Gubukil had been wiped off the face of the earth—in this case blown off the face of the mountain—and all of its inhabitants killed. No doubt, Mujibur Ali Mirza-Khan was dead, and the four foreign agents, should they have been in the village.

Captain Stefan Belous flicked his cigarette to the ground. "I doubt if the men will have to fire a single shot, Comrades," he said heartily.

"But they will, Comrade Belous," Major Petyr Ukormidev said with a mocking sneer. "There will be some survivors. We already know that two escaped. One of the choppers saw them going into one of the caves to the north."

Standing ramrod straight, Colonel Arbikochek shrugged. "Two or half a dozen. What does it matter. They're not worth going after. We must stay on schedule. There's always the risk we could meet Pak air-force planes on the return trip. They would have to challenge us or look like cowards."

"Well, Comrade Colonel, aren't they?" Belous snickered, fingering his small black mustache.

"*Nyet*, Comrade, they are not cowards," Arbikochek said in a frank voice. "It's President Zia who is playing the Soviet Union against India, Israel and the United States. Don't confuse him and his government with the people, especially with the Pathan tribes."

Major Petyr Ukormidev raised a hand-held Chonna infrared viewer to his face and looked toward the north. "Lieutenant Diakanov and the men are in the village. We should get his report shortly."

The report from Lieutenant Yuli Diakanov came in twelve minutes later. Colonel Arbikochek turned up the volume of the walkie-talkie for the benefit of Major Ukormidev and Captain Belous.

All three Spetsnazki were stunned to learn from a disgusted Leiutenant Diakanov that there was not a single burnt bone to be found in the village, not one piece of burnt cloth, not a single fragment or parts of a weapon or tools or household goods. Nothing.

"Comrades, all we have accomplished is to roast a number of goats," Diakanov reported. "The people of the village were not here. What are your orders, Comrade Colonel Arbikochek?"

"Remain in position. Do nothing until you hear from me," Arbikochek said, and switched off the transceiver, trying very hard to control the anger in his voice.

Captain Belous appeared stupified. "It's impossible to believe. There were hundreds of people in the village, and he tells us we killed only—only goats!"

Major Petyr Ukormidev, who didn't look happy, was more realistic. "That son of a bitch, Chief Mirza-Khan anticipated our attack and relocated his people."

"They're in the caves, up there waiting for us," Colonel Arbikochek said through clenched teeth, frustration and fury making him tremble. "We'll blow apart that whole damn mountain if we have to!"

He turned on the walkie-talkie.

The instant the two hovering Mi-8 gunships revved up and started to move north the Pathans inside the cave with the largest opening—which made it appear to be the cave with the biggest interior—moved a dozen figures into position, placing them behind and to either sides of rocks and placing weapons in their "hands." The figures were clothes packed with straw and held together with cords. But would the Russians take the bait?

They know we've outwitted them! Watching the two gunships approach, the Death Merchant, Iskander Chaudhriy and the other men got to their feet and moved back, knowing that the two helicopters would soon start firing. They could see the black-clad Spetsnaz zigging and zagging it toward the slopes.

The Death Merchant, turning to Chaudhriy, didn't bother with formality. "Iskander, have the men here spread the word that everyone is to remain at least thirty meters behind the openings of the caves. The Russians will first bombard the slopes with grenades. They will then use the grenade machine guns to saturate the mouths of the caves while the special forces rush the slopes. Our men are not to move forward to the openings until the grenades stop exploding."

"*Chopdi!* But by then those dogs will be almost on top of us!" Chaudhriy said in alarm. "They will be only a few meters in front of us."

"A few meters is all we need. Go! Do it!"

The caves were similar to the mazes that prairie dogs call home: numerous rooms, situated every which way and of all sizes, connected by narrow corridors. Wilhelm Bruckner, James O'Malley and five Pathans, armed with Galil assault rifles and Sterling submachine guns, were just inside the mouth of a cave whose low, narrow entrance was 400 feet east of the opening containing the stuffed straw figures. Willy and the Kid intended to destroy the two Hind-D gunships, their confidence increasing when Mike Quinlan joined them.

The two Hind-D helicopters did what the Death Merchant had predicted—and if the straw men fooled the pilots, no one would ever know. Parallel to each other, they opened fire from an altitude of only 150 feet. Their four barrel cannons roaring, thousands of 23mm projectiles rained into seven openings.

The irritating noise didn't bother Quinlan, Bruckner and the Peppermint Kid, who crawled through the opening, Willy and the Kid dragging RPG launchers, Quinlan lugging a canvas bag filled with four 85mm projectiles.

"It's so bloody dark we'd drown if we had to take a pee!" grumbled O'Malley after they were past the entrance and belly-crawling to a line of boulders the size of 100-gallon oil drums. In the immediate vicinity the rocks and scree were piled and scattered haphazardly, and while there was ample cover for Quinlan and his two mercs, their chances for survival would decrease to zero if they were detected by the two gunships.

"I hope to Christ they don't send the other two kill choppers," Quinlan said, opening the canvas bag and pulling out a projectile. "But first we have to scratch these two." Expertly he shoved an 85mm projectile into the firing end of the RPG launcher that Bruckner was holding toward him.

"I say, lads. It's going to be touch and go," O'Malley said as Quinlan loaded his launcher. "We can get one of the bloody bastards, but the other bird might be out of range."

Bruckner switched to German. "They're moving back and forth from east to west. We can fire when both swing east and are closest to us."

Quinlan smiled. "This sort of reminds me of South Africa."[7]

"*Ja*, that *toten-maschine*[8] Camellion, was with us then." Bruckner raised his RPG and started to sight in on one of the Hinds, using the constant flashes from its cannon as a focal point and centering the crosshairs a few feet back from the FP.

"You fire first, Willy," O'Malley said. "I'll fire before the other bird can swing away."

"Don't miss," Quinlan warned. "We have to cancel their tickets with the first rounds."

"I say, when do we ever miss?" O'Malley sounded hurt as he raised his launcher. He didn't fool Quinlan, who knew he had all the sensitivity of a crocodile.

"You jokers," Quinlan said, "those two Hinds are swinging this way. Like I said, don't miss."

Bruckner didn't. He pulled the trigger of the RPG. There was a loud whoosh and the 85mm projectile was on its way, striking the Hind-D four seconds later—right behind the pilot's compartment. Exploding with a fairly loud *MEROOOMMMMM*, projectile and gunship disappeared in a big ball of fire, and then there were only thousands of pieces of burning junk falling earthward.

Before Gaik Vanovsky, the pilot of the second Hind-D, could recover from the shock and horror of the first bird's being blasted from the sky and pull out of range, the Peppermint Kid pulled the trigger. Only God, His Angels and the Cosmic Lord of Death knew it, but if the gunship had been twenty more feet to the

[7].See Death Merchant number 46, *Blood Bath*.

[8].''Death machine.''

west, it would have been out of range. Instead, there was another *MEROOOMMMMM*, another ball of fire and more burning debris falling to the rocks, along with Vanovsky and the other two crew members who had been transformed into bloody mush.

"Now let's get the hell out of here," Quinlan said. He and Willy and the Kid were doing a fast belly-gut shuffle toward the cave when the three *Plamya* grenade machine guns opened up. In only seconds, the lower slopes erupted with scores of explosions, each 30mm grenade a bright flash of flame that sent rocks flying with the force of shrapnel.

There was a tactical purpose to the bombardment by the *Avtomaticeski Granatomojot Stankovi*. As 30mm grenades exploded on the lower slopes, the Spetsnaz, who had been nestled down in the ruins of Gubukil, began to move north toward the caves. The farther north they proceeded, and the crews of the grenade machine guns moved with them, the farther north exploded the grenades, so that by the time the first wave of Spetsnaz reached the bottom of the slopes, the grenades were exploding in the middle and at the top of the slopes, a defensive tactic that prevented any kind of ambush.

In a very short time, grenades were falling within the entrances of the caves. In an instant, the darkness was changed to brief fire, concussion and flying rock. The Death Merchant, Quinlan and his two men waited, surprised by the fierce Pathans' patience.

Every man knew what to expect. Iskander Chaudhriy had done as the Death Merchant had instructed: he had told the men to spread the word—stay away from the entrances until the grenades had stopped exploding. When the grenades stopped falling, charge forward and kill, kill, kill.

It required only eight minutes for the Spetsnaz to charge three-fourths of the way up the slopes. By this time the three granade machine guns had stopped firing. The coice had not been up to the crews. To have continued tossing grenades would have meant to risk killing their own comrades. The Spetsnaz charged up the remainder of the slopes, straight toward the darkened entrances of the larger caves.

It was only a matter of fifteen feet. It was that distance that caught the Russians short of the openings. By the time the Russians gained several more steps, the Pathans were firing with a variety of weapons. The Spetsnaz had only succeeded in rushing into what amounted to a wall of steel-cored slugs. Forty-six died instantly, in spite of their bulletproof vests. But there wasn't any magic protecting the Pathans; they too died from bursts of 5.45x39mm AKR and AKS-74 assault rifle projectiles.

Lag time never plays favorites. While desperate men of both sides paused and tried to reload, the living pushed aside the dead and the dying and stumbled forward. Well trained and well disciplined, the Russians finally reached the entrances where the Pathans were waiting to kill every dog from the north they could get their hands on.

The fighting now became eyeball to eyeball, with Russians and Pathans killing each other at point-blank range. When the hot and hungry weapons had eaten all the ammo, both sides closed in on each other with empty weapons, with knives and, in some cases, with bare hands. There was only one rule: kill or be killed.

Thinking that the one thing the world needed was a popular government at popular prices, the Death Merchant lay next to Iskander Chaudhriy, next to whom were ten Pathans. The twelve opened fire within micromoments of each other, the Death Merchant and Chaudhriy triggering Galil assault rifles, the other seven using two Sterling SMG and five Egyptian Kalashnikov ARs, the furious roaring deafening. For the moment, it was a one-sided battle, the Spetsanz dying with such rapidity that their corpses crashed into each other and hindered the progress of the living coming in behind them.

It was not, however, a pig-farmer turkey shoot. Turkeys could never shoot back. The Spetsnaz did. They dropped and fired short bursts, then got up and, still firing, stormed forward, gaining a few more yards . . . that is, those who didn't die; and when the Russians ran out of ammo in their assault rifles, they pulled their Vitmorkin machine pistols. As determined as the Pathans, the Russians intended to reach the caves.

Dozens of projectiles zipped very close to the Death Merchant, Chaudhriy and the other men. Some of the men took time to reload; the more experienced, knowing the value of each second, pulled pistols and revolvers, the Death Merchant first emptying his Sig Sauer P-230, calmly spacing each .380 bullet, always aiming for a leg, knowing that a .380-caliber slug would never penetrate the bulletproof vests of the Russians. Iskander Chaudhriy, constantly cursing the Russians, used a Beretta and a Hi-Power Browning, firing first one pistol and then the other. Having the time of his life and ignoring the high vel projectiles buzzing around him, Camellion holstered the Sig Sauer, pulled the two big Bren Ten autopistols and began firing with deadly accuracy.

Having succeeded in reaching their objective, the Spetsnaz fought like maniacs. None were over twenty-five. All were in prime physical condition and were experts in one-on-one combat.

The Russian leaping at the Death Merchant came at him with an empty AKS-74 assault rifle, an attack that didn't trouble Camellion. He had had slop-slobs come at him with everything but the kitchen sink. Nonetheless, the bayonet, with its twelve-inch blade attached to the barrel of the AKS-74, didn't give him any great feeling of security.

It was the last 10mm round in the right Bren Ten that caught the young Russian while he was still in midair, the big bullet boring into the pit of his stomach and half doubling him over before he started to crash to the stone floor of the cave. Faster than the Cosmic Lord of Death could give a fatal coronary to a businessman, Camellion dropped the Bren Ten, stuck out his left foot, and, before the dying pig farmer could fall all the way to the floor, grabbed the AKS-74 from the man's hands, spun the weapon around and impaled another Spetsnazki leaping from the parapet of corpses in the mouth of the wide cave, the momentum of the Russian's body driving the blade as far as its muzzle. The man gave a loud gurgle. Blood poured form his mouth and his eyes jumped out as if attached to invisible stalks. *Don't feel bad, pig man! Dying of cancer could be worse!*

Because of the man's weight against the blade, Camellion didn't have time to jerk out the bayonet. Instead he used the AKS-74 the way a farmer would use a pitchfork. With a tremendous effort, he swung the corpse in front of another Russian, who was trying to get Iskander Chaudhriy, the corpse and the other soon to be dead Spetsnazki crashing together and falling to the ground in a pinwheel of flying arms and legs and hoarse grunts and frantic curses.

Iskander Chaudhriy and all the rest of the Pathans were giving far more than a good account of themselves. In spite of their strenuous training, the Russians were not a match for the Pakistanis who, from babyhood, had been nourished on rugged living and violence. When defending their homeland they were particularly vicious.

Using empty pistols, rifles and *kaurangs*, Pathan knives with fifteen-inch-long double-edged blades, the Pathans might as well have been butchers on a killing floor.

The big Chaudhriy, his good looks marred by a twisted sneer, stabbed two Russians so fast that they hardly had time to feel the sharp blades slicing into their viscera. They both hit the rocky deck, trying to keep their intestines from spilling out like unrolled sausages.

Somehow, two Russians had managed to get to the rear of Chaudhriy, their intention to bury their *pastavilki*—trench combat knives—in Chaudhriy's back. They would have succeeded if it had not been for Richard Camellion and another Pathan, Nunur Seif-Bualy, who had the longest chin that Camellion had ever seen.

Vladimir Turayev, the Russian closest to Camellion, was rushing at Chaudhriy's lowerback with a *pastavilka* in his left hand. Dmitri Preinivech, the other pig farmer, had picked the center of Chaudhriy's back as his target. The plan of the two pig farmers fell apart when the Death Merchant jumped in, grabbed Turayev's left wrist and forearm with both hands, jerked the man's arm sideways and upward and slammed his foot into Turayev's rib cage. The jackass kick was so powerful that some of the Russian's ribs snapped, three of the jagged ends spearing into the left lung.

Dmitri Preinivech's luck was as bad. Nunur Seif-Bualy rained all over the Russian's parade by chopping him across the throat with his *kaurang*, the force of the heavy blade half decapitating the Soviet soldier, blood spurting in waves as soon as Seif-Bualy pulled back the blade.

The Spetsnaz were very well trained in *sambo*,[9] and it was this art of killing that resulted in the death of many of the Pathans, who depended on speed and brute strength. One pig farmer tried a high front snap kick to the Death Merchant's chin, a blow that would have broken his jaw had the heel connected. However, the Death Merchant detected the move at about the same time he sensed another man rushing at him from the rear. He and Chaudhriy did have the edge on the Russians and the other Pathans in that they were still wearing the NVD over their faces.

Camellion first whacked out the Spetsnazki to the rear, surprising the joker with a right back kick to the solar plexus, the smash throwing the Russian into instant shock. He went down with internal bleeding in his stomach and his liver, a look of petrified horror on his face.

Moving very fast, Camellion had ducked the high foot-to-chin

[9].*Sarvilskya at'yib mikazal balupi o'nasrat:* "To sustain life with the open hand."

snap kick that Albert Visko had been positive would land on target. While Visko was still off balance and trying to regroup, Camellion chopped him down with a left-legged snap kick to the testicles, the shock so great that the Russian couldn't even scream. He did slobber all over himself and, with all the fluidity of a wet rag, wilt to the floor, his body jerking.

Albert Visko wasn't any worse off than scores of other Spetsnaz who had succeeding in charging through the larger cave openings, especially Mama Russia's "best" who had been unlucky enough to reach Mad Mike Quinlan, Willy Bruckner and the Peppermint Kid.

After the Russians crawled over their own dead and finally reached Quinlan and his two men, they did not find an easy victory. They found only that the Cosmic Lord of Death had postponed their agony for last.

Sergeant Yevgeny Pripolhodov received the last shock of his life when he tried to run Bruckner through with the bayonet on the end of his AKS-74, not for a moment believing that the huge, ponderous-looking German could move with such speed. He found out otherwise.

"*Du kannst mir mal an den Sack fassen!*" snarled Bruckner, who stepped aside, let the blade slip by, jerked the assault rifle from Pripolhodov's hands, backhanded the stunned Russian, then picked him up the way a wrestler would pick up an opponent in preparation for a back body slam. Only Bruckner, holding the squirming man at waist level, shoved his back into the bayonet with which Vladilen Raina was trying to tickle Mike Quinlan's colon. Bruckner's shove had been so powerful that an inch of the bayonet protruded from Pripolhodov's stomach, much to the rage and astonishment of Raina, who, in a flash, thought of a giant worm squirming on a giant pin. Pripolhodov's weight forced Raina to lower the AKS assault rifle, yet he didn't have time to pull the weapon and its bloody bayonet from Pripolhodov's body. It wouldn't have made any difference. The Peppermint Kid, using a British Frogman's diving knife, stabbed Raina in the left side, just below the waist. Almost all in the same motion, he let another Russian have a TNT side kick in the back of the head. Under ordinary circumstances, such a kick would have snapped the victim's neck, but the Kid had been an inch off. All the blow did was rattle Galilik Alferin's brain and knock him toward Mike Quinlan, who promptly smashed in his left temple with a steel spring kosh.

Quinlan chuckled and muttered, "You shall not gather at the river, sucker."

Neither would three other Spetsnaz—two rushing at the Peppermint Kid, one tearing toward Willy Bruckner while a third had zeroed in on Quinlan as his target.

Sergei Kolenikov was positive that he could gut Bruckner with his bayonet. Intuition suddenly told him he was sitting in Death's lap when Bruckner, a big, ugly grin on his big, ugly face, jumped eighteen inches into the air and let the sharp blade cut air between his legs—four inches below his testicles. Kolenikov didn't have time to jerk back the AKS and its bayonet. He could only feel the assault rifle being forced downward by Bruckner's right hand. An eyeblink! Then a big blackness exploded in his head, the result of Willy's left fist pounding him in the forehead directly above the nose.

Robert Andifev and Stanislav Tavigun, the two nitwits rushing the Peppermint Kid, were next in line for a surprise. A flip of the Kid's right arm and Tavigun stopped as if hit by a Soviet tank. The blade of British Frogman knife was buried in his chest, all the way to the handle.

Andifev, intent on burying his bayonet in the Kid's belly, couldn't call a halt to his own action, his own momentum carrying him forward. Seeing Tavigun killed hadn't done anything for Andifev's confidence. His positive attitude took another nose dive when the Kid easily sidestepped the bayonet, half turned to his left and slammed his right elbow into Andifev's solar plexus. Andifev let out a choked, gagging cry, dropped the assault rifle and started to double over. But he wasn't conscious when he hit the ground; he wasn't because, when he was going down, the Kid put out his lights with a *Shuto* chop to the side of the neck. Andifev dropped unconscious only four feet from Gregor Ipziv, whom Mike Quinlan had killed with a well-placed kosh blow to the side of the neck.

All the Pathans had fought the Spetsnaz, with the exception of the forty-two men who had guarded the women, children, Malik Mujibur Ali Mirza-Khan, Jiko Krim-Lizak and other men too old and infirm to fight.

The beginning of the battle had not been unexpected, but it had ended faster than rain running down a gopher hole. There came a time when in the caves there were only dead Spetsnaz and dead Pathans, and wounded and/or unconscious Russians and Pathans.

There were many Spetsnaz still alive and in good health. They were in full retreat, stumbling frantically down the slopes, terrified for their lives.

Watching the frenzied exodus through Chonna night-vision viewers, Colonel Josef Arbikochek, Major Petyr Ukormidev and Captain Stefan Belous could only stare in disbelief and fury. It had been an emotional crucifixion for all three when they had seen the two Hind-D gunships destroyed. Belous and Ukormidev had urged Arbikochek to send in the two remaining gunships, but he had refused on the grounds that the first two Hinds had done their job: they had peppered the openings of the caves with thousands of rounds. The second reason was that Arbikochek didn't want to risk having the last two Hinds shot down. Damn it! Who could say how many ground-to-air missiles those savages had!

Reality could not be ignored. The Spetsnaz, now in full retreat, had lost and were racing back to the helicopters.

A stunned look on his square face, Captain Belous lowered the night-vision device. Even the sound of his own voice sounded alien and unreal to him. "Comrades, we have failed to secure our objective."

"We've lost, you idiot!" said Colonel Arbikochek, who sounded like a biblical prophet, his hoarse voice barely above a whisper. "Those savages whipped our ass!"

"Comrade Colonel, how are we going to explain this to Comrade Lieutenant General Gregor Kerchenko?" asked Major Ukormidev in a choked tone.

"How?" Arbikochek almost screamed the word. "We tell him the truth, that's how! There isn't any other way. Every man coming back will be interrogated by political commissars. So will we once Comrade General Kerchenko makes his report to the High Command in Kabul and Moscova learns of our defeat."

"Comrade Colonel, w-what do we do about our dead out there?" said Captain Belous timidly. "To leave them . . . they're evidence that we invaded Pakistan. Should President Zia . . ." He let his voice trail off.

Unscrewing the handle from the night-vision device, Colonel Arbikochek thought of Lieutenant Yuli Diakanov. He was also dead. One of Diakanov's sergeants had submitted the last two reports on the walkie-talkie.

He turned and looked at Belous. The man had always been a dunce. "Those are not Spetsnaz who died on those slopes,"

Arbikochek said evenly. "They are not even Russian. They're Pakistanis dressed in Soviet uniforms. Moscova will say it's the work of the American CIA, American intelligence working with President Zia and General I'Zada. Our leaders will turn it all around into a disinformation campaign. Besides, we have other worries."

Neither Major Ukormidev nor Captain Belous asked him what those concerns might be. They too wondered how it would feel to be demoted to the rank of private and stationed in Siberia or on the Russo-Sino border. . . .

BOOK TWO

CHAPTER SEVEN

14.00 hours.
The Street of Allah's Gate, Peshawar.
Four days after the Spetsnaz attack on Gubukil.

Lieutenant Mohammed Kusan Moukarim and Hawaji Gulaka, wearing old Western-type clothes under their *chudkis*, waited as Banwad Girnayl sold a replica of a German P08 Luger to a customer. Unlike Moukarim and Gulaka, Banwad Girnayl was not a career member of the infamous Chanwiri-lu-Shabudar. He was a trusted informer who often fed valuable information to the "Protectors of the People."

The fat, bearded Girnayl was also a master gunsmith, one of the best, if not the best, in Peshawar. Moukarim and Gulaka admired his work as they waited. The ceiling and walls of the eighteen-by-thirty-foot room were filled with the most fantastic assemblage of weapons one could imagine. On the rear wall were Walther P-38s, Browning Hi-Powers, 9mm and .32-caliber Star and Llama pistols, American .45 Colts, German Lugers, TT-33 Tokarevs, Stechkin MPs and 9mm Makarovs, plus an assortment of American-designed revolvers.

From the ceiling hung all makes and models of assault rifles. There were M-16s, AR-18s, Colt CAR-15s and dozens of British Stens. There were Russian PPSh-41 submachine guns, plus Egyptian Maadis, Czech Vz-58s and plenty of Soviet AKs. And there were old style weapons—hundreds of handmade .303 British Enfields in every configuration possible; Mark 1 "Jungle Carbines," complete with British proof marks. There were even Mauser-type bolt-action rifles in 7.62x39mm ComBloc using

Kalashnikov magazines and fitted with pistol-grip wooden stocks. And ammunition. Boxes and boxes and boxes of ammo in twenty different calibers.

The customer finally left the shop and Banwad Girnayl, hurrying toward Lieutenant Moukarim and Hawaji Gulaka, apologized for the delay, a worried look on his leathery face. Constantly, he lived with the dread that the Pathans and the Garukals (the next-largest tribe of the northwest frontier) would learn that he was a spy for the Pakistani secret police, whom the tribes hated as much as they hated the Russians. Discovery would mean death—a sharp knife across the throat. It was the code of *Punkhtunwali*.

Girnayl's eyes darted to the front door, then back at Moukarim and Gulaka. "You were not followed," he whispered. "You are sure it is safe?"

"You have no need to worry," replied Moukarim. "It's important that we talk with you."

"Wait." Girnayl went to the front door, reached up and attached one end of a spring through a metal eye. Now, when the door opened a bell would tinkle loudly. He turned and led Moukarim and Gulaka past the heavy blue cotton curtain into the rear room, which smelled of charcoal, heavily spiced lamb kabob and peppermint tea.

Since the two Pakistani intelligence agents and Banwad Girnayl were not friends—he worked strickly for money—the master gunsmith did not bother with formality. He didn't even ask them to sit down.

"I turned in my last report several weeks ago, through the usual contact," Girnayl whispered anxiously, moving his hands up and down and eyeing Moukarim and Gulaka suspiciously. "Why are you here now in my place of business?"

He stared again, very suspiciously, at the heavily mustached Hawaji Gulaka, whose deeply pockmarked face made him appear sinister. Very efficient with firearms, knives and fists, the tall Gulaka, who held the rank of third sergeant lieutenant in the Chanwiri-lu-Shabudar, often assisted Lieutenant Moukarim in dangerous undertakings.

"Banwad Girnayl, we want you to tell us of the rumors you have heard about Malik Mujibur Ali Mirza-Khan and his people." Lieutenant Moukarim opened his *chudki* and took off his Western-style felt hat. The room was very warm.

"We are seeking the location of Mirza-Khan's winter headquarters," said Hawaji Gulaka, who made Girnayl think of an embalmer.

A natural coward whose greed was twice as strong as the wide yellow streak down his back, Girnayl shook his head and began squeezing his hands together. "It is bad business," he said. "It is rumored that Malik Mirza-Khan is the leader of the Circle of Pure Blood. It is said that he sends assassins who murder tax collectors and other officials of our glorious President Zia's government and—"

"We're not interested in propaganda," Moukarim said wearily, disgusted with Girnayl's boot licking. "Tell us what you know—now."

Girnayl looked even more worried. "Chief Mirza-Khan was in Gubukil, in the Dera Ismail Khan—so it was told to me by certain smugglers of the poppy gum."

"Men who bought weapons from you?" said Hawaji Gulaka.

Girnayl glanced at Lieutenant Moukarim for reassurance.

"Answer him," ordered Moukarim.

"*Ched*. These smugglers often pass through Peshawar. They buy weapons from me and give me information in return for low prices for the firearms. That is how I know that four days ago the village of Gubukil was attacked by Russians who came from Afghanistan. The Russians came in with aircraft without wings and attacked very early in the morning. I was told that the Russians were slaughtered by Malik Mirza-Khan and his fighters."

Lieutenant Moukarim and Hawaji Gulaka exchanged glances of mutual incredulity. Secret informants of the Chanwiri-lu-Shabudar had reported a small armada of helicopters flying in from Afghanistantan, and there were any number of conflicting stories in circulation: Mirza-Khan and his people had been wiped out; the Soviets had been massacred; a battle had never taken place.

"Banwad Girnayl, you sound very positive. How did the smugglers obtain this information?" asked Moukarim, casually lighting an American More Ultralights cigarette. "They must have given you concrete facts with strong threads of proof."

"Only yesterday afternoon two were in here." Girnayl continued to squeeze his hands. "They were only a few kilometers from Gubukil, sleeping in their *ti'rus*,[1] when the Russians attacked. The two were on their way to Gubukil to buy gum of the poppy from Chief Mirza-Khan."

[1].A type of Pak sleeping bag made of leather, wool and sheepskin.

"Then they did not see the attack?" said Gulaka.

"*Yibo*, they did not. They told me that by the time they arrived in the vicinity dawn had been born. They remained in the mountains and surveyed the entire area. They told me that Gubukil had been destroyed, that every house had been destroyed. They told me that the slopes north of the village were carpeted with the corpses of the Russian invaders. They said they watched Chief Mirza-Khan's men strip the black uniforms from the corpses and—"

"Black uniforms!" Moukarim said in a low voice. "You did say black uniforms?"

"They said black uniforms. Is that important?"

"Continue."

"The two smugglers kept themselves concealed and watched Mirza-Khan's men strip the Russian corpses of black uniforms and weapons. And they removed the clothes of their own dead. They said many Pathans had also been killed. And they said that there was the wreckage of two birds without wings on the slopes."

Hawaji Gulaka turned to Lieutenant Mohammed Moukarim. "If the two smugglers were telling the truth, Malik Mirza-Khan and his men were warned in advance of the Russian attack. How could that even be possible? Where could they and his people have hidden before the Russians attacked?"

"The caves," said Banwad Girnayl. "Mirza-Khan and his people had to have been warned, as you say. What they did was take refuge in the caves in the mountain north of Gubukil. I have more information."

Lieutenant Moukarim's expression became apprehensive. Black uniforms meant Soviet Spetsnaz. This alone meant that the two smugglers had told Girnayl the truth. But how could Mirza-Khan have defeated them?

Lieutenant Moukarim's eyes ordered Girnayl to continue.

"They said that—"

"You keep saying *they*," Gulaka said morosely. "What are the names of these men? Don't worry. We won't arrest them for smuggling."

"Answer his question," said Moukarim.

"Their names are Elahu Zaffarad and Ayub Kiswagar." Girnayl spoke hesitantly. "I have known them for six years. I assure you they are reliable and did not speak untruths to me."

"What else did they tell you?" demanded Moukarim.

"They said that they stayed in the mountains and watched most of the day. What you should know is that Chief Mirza-Khan and his people did not return to the caves. They moved west."

Sensing that Girnayl was leading up to something, Moukarim snapped impatiently, "Get to the point."

"You asked where Chief Mirza-Khan and his people were," Girnayl said hurriedly. "They have to be in Sirzihil. Sirzihil is the closest village to where Gubukil once stood."

"You have no proof," Hawaji Gulaka said.

"What proof is needed, Kir Moukarim? There is no other settlement within sixty kilometers of Gubukil. Where else could Chief Mirza-Khan and his people go? Even during the hot season, Sirzihil is the closest refuge, the closest source of water."

Lieutenant Moukarim nodded and eye-signaled to Sergeant Gulaka that it was time to go; they had learned enough.

Once they had left Banwar Girnayl's gun shop and were on the Street of Allah's Gate, Lieutenant Moukarim whispered, "Come, we'll make contact with Lukriz Au-mumin."

CHAPTER EIGHT

The pale, yellow sun was low between snow-covered peaks and the night wind was becoming chillier when the Death Merchant and the seven other men stopped for the night on a huge ledge protected by a large slab of granite overhang. There were plenty of boulders on the ledge to serve as wind-breaks—but only when Camellion and his three men and the four guides were lying down, that is, at rest for the night.

The past six days had been crammed with tension, physical hardship and movement through the rugged, unfriendly Dera Ismail Khan mountains, and filled with mourning for the ninety-six men who had died in repelling the Spetsnaz. The only consolation was that 164 Russians had died and dropped straight into hell.

To have remained in the caves would have been foolhardy. It was always possible that the Russians would return with an even greater force. Weighed down with household goods, clothing and enough Soviet weapons and ammunition to start a mini-war, Malik Mirza-Khan and his people had begun the journey to Sirzihil, nineteen miles to the west. There was no other refuge.

To add extra weight to the already heavy problems of the Death Mechant, the CIA had still not decided to air drop more weapons to Chief Mirza-Khan.

Camellion had done all he could. Immediately after the move from Gubukil to the cold, damp caves, he had again contacted Courtland Grojean on the AN/URC 101 Satcom Tactical Transceiver. The Fox was sorry, but the NIC[1] was still debating the pros and cons of another airdrop.

"Richard, I am going to say it the way it really is," Mike Quinlan had said. "This mission has fallen flat on its face."

The Death Merchant did not vehemently disagree. "Not necessarily," he had said. "After all, every exit is an entry to somewhere else."

"Possum poop! I tell you, we're stretching our luck." Mad Mike was convinced that they were on an endless road to nowhere.

Camellion again made radio contact with Courtland Grojean before the arduous journey to Sirzihil to inform the chief of the Company's covert section of the Russian attack and of the Pathan victory. He had also apprised the Fox of his scheme to scout the Spetsnaz base in preparation for an attack by the Pathan and the Garukal tribes.

The news from Grojean was encouraging. The "Wise Ones" of the NIC had made their decision: the airdrop would be made. "But," Grojean had said, "we'll have to go over the details after Mirza-Khan and his people get to—where did you say—Sirzihil?"

As soon as Camellion had relayed this news to Mirza-Khan, the old chief and *Mullah* of the Pathans said that he would send messengers to the chiefs of the other clans and arrange a meeting to map out the plan of attack against the hated Spetsnaz base.

The Kremlin and the Soviet High Command in Kabul, Afghanistan, had made a very serious mistake in judgment. The valued Spetsnaz had been badly beaten by the Pathans, and a sneak attack had backfired, serving to unite the Pak tribes and make them thirst for blood.

At the time—it had been four days ago—it didn't seem possible for the Death Merchant and his three men to reconnoiter the Spetsnaz complex. The guides would be coming to Gubukil, which no longer existed. How would they know that everyone had moved to Sirzihil? Willy Bruckner had suggested that several men be left behind to inform the guides of the attack and to tell them where the people of Gubukil had gone.

A sympathetic look had crossed Mirza-Khan's wrinkled face. "It is a plan that would not work, Kir Bruckner. The guides

[1]National Intelligence Council, a special group with the Central Intelligence Agency that advises and offers suggestions to the various departments within the Agency, as well as to the President and to NSA. Its members are nicknamed "The Wise Ones."

would see from the mountains that our village had been destroyed. They would not come down to the ruins. The men we would leave behind would never see them."

"It is *chawdup*!"[2] Iskander Chaudhriy had insisted. "We should forget the attack on the Russian base."

Jiko Krim-Lizak had addressed the Death Merchant and his group of three. "Gentlemen, you are worrying needlessly. The guides will use common sense and know we have gone to Sirzihil. It is the closest village."

As it turned out, the guides did not have to guess anything. Only one day away from reaching Sirzihil, the Pathans, the Death Merchant and his three men, all bone-weary, had met the guides, all four of whom had stopped to rest at Sirzihil before moving on to Gubukil. They had heard rumors of an attack but had not been certain; they had to see for themselves.

It had been decided. The Death Merchant and his group of three and the four guides would leave Chief Mirza-Khan and his people and cross the border into Afghanistan. The four guides, from the clan of Malik Soltiz Khahol Shadhidi, maintained firmly that they knew every inch of the route to Narang.

Asad Dizakan (who could have been an "old" Richard Nixon with a beard), the eldest of the guides, and Syed Serneabiz were still smuggling the gum of the poppy into Afghanastan, into the area around Narang.

Dizakan had explained. "We sell the drug to the Afghans who trade it to the homesick Russian dogs for weapons."

Mean-looking Abdus Powidi and Tamil Digarh—the latter slightly hunchbacked and as bald as a shiny white doorknob—had been drivers on the "Khyber Route" for several years, now and then going into Afghanastan and trading radioes, watches, Western-made cooking utensils and, strange as it might seem, old-fashioned, portable porcelain commodes—chamber pots with loose handles.

"The Russians only regard us as ignorant savages from Pakistan," explained Tamil Digarh. His long hair was parted in the middle. He had rosy cheeks and had an aura of brisk efficiency. "But now, my *baya-darkas*, since they attacked Gubukil and were killed in our land, it would be most unwise for us to meet any of the jackals from the land of the Red Star."

[2]."Ridiculous."

* * *

Survival is identical to a contest: one must work as if there were, to the very last second, a chance of losing one's life. Even if there had not been an ambush by the Pakistani secret police at the Shrine of Abdul Bu-I-Zum, the Death Merchant and Quinlan would have trusted the four guides only so far—as far as they could see their hands. It was a matter of policy.

More than ordinary precautions were taken. Camellion and his men had their own water and their own food, packs of Meals: Ready to Eat. They made it a habit that always, on the trail, one of them was behind the last guide in line, and they had protection that only they knew about. One had to sleep. One had to be protected while one slept. To sleep in shifts was not possible, not without conveying to the Pathans that they weren't trusted.

In the cases parachuted to Chief Mirza-Khan's camp in the first airdrop had been a half-dozen devices known in the trade as PPA—Personal Protection Alarms, ultrasmall motion detectors. Disguised as a three-celled flashlight (the flashlight section worked), each PPA had a M-DR[3] of four feet. Should man or animal get within four feet, the device would send out a piercing shriek that would jangle the nerves of God and make the long-forgotten dead sit up and look around in dismay. A special rf pentagrid oscillator prevented the PPA from being triggered by the person using it.

During that first gloomy day—the clouds were low and snow threatened—all went well with Camellion & Co. and the four guides, who, while not exactly bubbling with friendliness, were not exactly unsociable. But this was understandable. Moving along over narrow mountain trails and climbing laboriously over boulders was not conducive to conversation.

The four guides were well armed, two carrying Egyptian Maadi AKMs and, concealed under their heavy *chudkis*, Walther P-38 autos. Tamil Digarh was armed with a Czech Vz-58[4] assault rifle and a .45 American Colt. Syed Serneabiz had an American M-16 and a 9mm Spanish Star.

The four Pathans carried knives. Three had *kaurangs* in leather holsters stuck in their outer belts. Asad Dizakan, however, carried a highly ornamented *jambiya* dagger in an engraved metal

[3].Motion-detector range.

[4].A copy of the Soviet AK. The Soviet Kalashnikov is the most popular, the most copied and the most used assault rifle in the world. It is an excellent, dependable weapon.

sheath—the kind of wide-bladed knife popular with Moslems in dispatching "infidels" in bygone days (and even today, depending on the place, the time and the circumstances).

A fanatical collector of knives, the Death Merchant would have given six hours, seven minutes and one second of his life for the *jambiya*.

At the end of the first day, Abdus Powidi, the "boss" guide, chose to spend the night on top of a large hill, pointing out to the Death Merchant and the others that since the sides of the hill were filled ankle-deep with scree, an enemy could not approach without being heard. "There isn't any way they could climb the sides without the loose rocks making a lot of noise," Powidi said, "and there are numerous large rocks on the top that will serve as windbreaks."

And plenty of room for Mike, Willy, the Kid and me to spread out with our PPAs. . . .

After a cold supper, the four Pathans spread out their *ti'rusis*,[5] placing the sleeping bags side by side, in a group. If they wondered why the Death Merchant and his people spread their *ti'rusis* ten feet from eath other—and on the other side of the hilltop—they never voiced what they may have been thinking.

By dawn, the entire group had eaten a cold breakfast and was on its way, at times moving through deep snow that threatened to pour over the tops of their *lebidows*, the high Pathan over-the-knees leather boots.

The day itself was pure misery, the twisting route so treacherous it would have worried a mountain goat. By the time the sun was low and the infant night was beginning to grow over the mountains, all eight men felt as if they had carried sacks of anvils all day; and this time, camped on a high ledge, they risked a fire. There were certainly not any Russians in the area and they were still well within Pathan territory.

Again, the Death Merchant and his mean ate Meals: Ready to Eat, only this time with hot coffee made in a collapsible, telescoping pot. The Pathans ate strips of dried mutton and a kind of vegetable soup, having their meal some distance from Camellion and his group and acting as though the Westerners didn't exist.

The Death Merchant and his group spoke in German, a language they were sure the four guides did not understand. The conversation became philosophical after supper, Willy Bruckner

[5]. *Ti'rusis* is plural. *Ti'rus* is singular.

maintaining that wars caused by differences in religious beliefs had killed more human beings than Hitler and Stalin combined.

"India is a good example," he said gruffly. "For centuries, the Hindus and the Moslems have been killing each other. Or the war between Iran and Iraq. More than half a million have already died. That crazy son of a bitch Khomeini is sending ten-year-old children into battle. The little fools go into battle thinking that they'll go straight to heaven when they're shot down—with Khomeini's permission! It does prove how stupid Moslems are. At least Jews and Christians have more common sense."

The Death Merchant said, "One has to go back in history to see why Christian belief conquered the ancient world. Christianity spread from the Middle East because it offered something that the Jewish and Roman and Greek religions didn't have: eternal life. Poor, deluded people still believe it. Life might be a hell on earth, but after death—provided one is a good little 'slave' and has more faith than reason—one can have a king's palace. This formula-promise of 'glory in the sky' still works and expresses itself through nationalism. That's one of the reasons why good old Ron Wilson Reagan acts like a celestial chairman who has the backing of God."

"Reagan may believe he's right, but he sure as hell is not keeping within Jeffersonian principles, is he?" Quinlan said with a lighthearted reflectiveness. He had brought a quart of Scotch along on the journey and now, carefully—his back to the Pathans—poured some of the liquor into his small, stainless-steel cup. "But what the hell! The world has never learned anything from history. It never will. Religious wars are still a part of our so-called civilization. Willy said it right. Look at Iran and Iraq."

"The war between Iran and Iraq is identical to the Forty Years War following the Reformation in Europe," Camellion said with a big sigh. "Identical in every way."

Mad Mike had taken a big sip and now licked his lips. "Ah, you are so correct, Richard. The Catholics versus the Protestants! The Shi'ites versus the Sunnis! And right smack bang in the Middle East is little Israel screaming that God gave it the right to kick hell out of the Arabs, who just happen to be Moslems!"

"Nationalism is always an expression of religious belief," Bruckner annuced dogmatically. Then, as a afterthought: "There are exceptions. Hitler, the damned Russians and the Red Chinese. They're pure materialists."

O'Malley, wiping his fingers, looked at Camellion and Quinlan.

"I say, chaps. I never did understand the difference between the Sunnis and the Shi'ites. I 'ave the theory that members of both sects 'ave hollow heads filled with 'ot air."

Mad Mike licked his lips again. God! The Scotch tasted good!

The Death Merchant, who was fond of the little Brit, explained. "It's not at all complicated. The 'good' Christians in Europe slaughtered each other because the Catholics were convinced there had to be an intermediary between God and the common people. That's where the pope came in. He had a spiritual hotline straight to heaven.

"The Protestants said, 'Nonsense!' They were equally adamant in their belief that anyone could have personal contact with God. They said to hell with the pope.

The same difference prevails between the Sunnis and the Shi'ites. We can call the Sunnis the Protestants. The Sunnis believe that one can have a direct relationship with God, with Allah. The Shi'ites—the 'Catholics'—maintain that this is pure heresy and conflicts with the Koran. The Shi'ites insist that Muhammed is the Prophet of Islam and that Ali, his cousin and son-in-law, the Immam, or the divinely designated 'leader' of the faithful—or the pope.

"It so happens that maniac Khomeini and the Iranians are Shi'ites. The Iraqis are Sunnis. So you see, that old bastard Khomeini—"

"Colonel al-Qaddafy is my favorite lunatic!" interposed Quinlan.

"Khomeini believes he is the modern Immam and knows what Allah wants. It follows that Allah wants all the Sunnis of Islam killed because they're heretics. Collectively, the Sunnis and the Shi'ites hate the Jews. Sprinkle Christianity into this stew of superstition and you know why Jerusalem, throughout the centuries, has been destroyed thirty-seven times in the name of three different gods."

Wilhelm Bruckner stared solemnly into his stainless-steel cup half filled with coffee. As a young man in West Germany, he had been clumsy at sports and tongue-tied around the *fräuleins*; yet he had not always been a professional mercenary. An educated man, he had been forced to flee West Germany after accidentally killing a man who had been mistreating his dog. Bruckner had fled to France and had joined the French Foreign Legion, in which he had met Mike Quinlan.

"I remember when I was six years old in Nazi Germany," Bruckner recalled. "Now and then I still dream about that little lying son of a bitch Goebbels, giving speeches and saying how God was on the side of the Third Reich. Well, the Americans, the British, the French and the Poles—they all said God was on *their* side. For years, I have always thought of God as an old general who is constantly changing uniforms because all nations invoke him."

Quinlan filled his cup with Scotch, put down the cup on a flat rock and almost tenderly screwed the cap on the quart bottle. "There is a basic difference between Christianity and Mohammedanism. The Moslems never went in for colonization. The Christians did. That could have a bearing on why Christianity spread so rapidly to the New World and why Islam, to this day, is anticolonial."

"They never colonized because the Arabs never 'ave been a sea people," O'Malley said. "It was the Spanish who 'spread the faith.' "

"And the English and French and Dutch," Camellion said in agreement. He looked at Bruckner. "Willy, you're only half right about nationalism being an outward expression of a religious belief. Often it is, but not always. Sometimes there's even a gray area. The Afghans and the Pakistanis hate the Soviet Union, but not only because they're Moslems and the pig farmers are atheists. The Paks and the Afghans also have a fierce pride in their lands. With both it's also love of country. Or we can use El Salvador as an example of pure nationalism without religious expression."

"*Ja*, you do have a point," Bruckner said, nodding his big head. "Ninety percent of the Salvadorans are Catholic. Even most of the Marxists are Catholic."

"I 'ave the feeling that the end of our civilization is shaping up in the Middle East," O'Malley said, "and that when it's all over with only the cockroaches will inherit the earth. Something 'as to give. There's more medicine than ever in the world, yet more sickness. More religion, yet more evil. All the talk about universal brotherhood, yet 'alf the population of the world is hungry." He uttered a small laugh. "It must be Mirza-Khan's Iblis! He's the bloody blighter responsible for all the misery in this world, all the pain and suffering this world 'as."

The Peppermint Kid had intended his remark about Iblis to be a joke. He hadn't expected Mad Mike to comment. He had expected die-hard atheist Willy to grin and Willy had. But he was surprised when Camellion didn't so much as smile. He was almost shocked when Camellion said, "Iblis, Ahriman, Set, Loki, Mahadeva, or Satan—whatever one wishes to call the supreme spirit of evil, it's only a human term. Another thing is that the idea might not be as superstitious as we might think. Truth is often implausible. Forty years ago, many scientists laughed at the atomic theory. They are no longer laughing. Today we have proof that the entire external world is made up of electrical charges, or points of energy which in themselves have no color or taste or smell or shape. Everything, including our own bodies, is merely the mind's interpretation of electrical excitement. What then is reality? For that matter, who are we, what are we?"

"*Mein Gott*!" gasped Bruckner. "Next, you'll be telling us that you believe in Satan himself."

It was then that Camellion smiled. "Not at all, Willy. I am only suggesting that we might be wise to reevaluate the possibilities in other continuums of so-called gods and devils."

"Gods? With an S?" O'Malley was clearly puzzled. "I say, I was under the impression there was only one god."

"The creation of the world is attributed to 'gods' in the original Hebrew of the Bible. The word was *Elohim*. It's usually translated as God. The fact is, *Elohim* is plural and means gods."

Michael Quinlan never pried into an associate's business. For one thing, he didn't give a damn. For another, he considered it none of his business. Now, however, he had just enough Scotch in him to be more than slightly curious. Although he and Richard Camellion had been friends for years, Mike didn't even know where Camellion had been born or if Camellion was even his real name, much less what god the tall Texan—if he was from Texas—might believe in. "Tell me, Richard," Quinlan began, "what do you personally think? What do you believe about the afterlife condition?"

The Death Merchant laughed and leaned forward as if to stand up. "You wouldn't believe it, Mike, if I told you. It would be too implausible. Right now, I suggest we all grab some shut-eye. How juiced are you, Mike?"

"People who can't handle their booze get juicee," Quinlan said imperiously—and they all knew he didn't mean it. "I become intoxicated."

"So how intoxicated are you, Mike?"

"Let's put it this way. If one of those guides tries anything, you can believe I'll hear the son of a bitch."

"I believe it. Now, let's get to bed. Make sure your PPAs are turned on and placed in the right direction."

"*Ja, mutter*—yes, Mother," mocked Bruckner.

The Death Merchant reached for the rolled *ti'rus* and stood up. He wasn't concerned about the guides sneaking up on him. Even without the PPA, no one would have been able to approach him. Camellion dabbled in a lot of arts and practices, one of which was self-hypnosis. Anytime he slept under dangerous conditions, he used autohypnosis. The smallest sound would awaken him.

There is never absolute certainty in any operation. If the guides were enemies, suppose they reared up in the middle of the night and cut loose with weapons? The Death Merchant didn't like to think of that possibility. Neither did Quinlan, or Willy, or the Kid.

O'Malley had said it: "If we got killed in the middle of the night, here in Pakistan, no one in the West would even know we were missing. If they didn't know we were missing, they wouldn't know we were dead—would they?"

CHAPTER NINE

"Did Lieutenant Moukarim estimate when he expected Malik Mirza-Khan and his people to reach Sirzihil?" asked General Saha I'Zada, who disliked this office in the Government Security Building. It was too small, the architecture too Western.

"He did not," answered Lieutenant General Yahya Si'Quetta. Sitting in a leather chair in front of I'Zada's desk, he gave I'Zada a long, cynical look.

"General, Moukarim emphasized that he could not even be certain that Mirza-Khan would go to Sirzihil. My advice is to wait until Moukarim and Gulaka develop more accurate information."

"Where else could Mirza-Khan go but Sirzihil?" I'Zada, dressed in the light brown uniform of a Pakistani army general, left his desk, went across the room and studied a large map on the wall. "See for yourself, Yahya. Sirzihil is the closest village to Gubukil. The unknown for us is whether Mirza-Khan might have a place of safety we don't know about. We can be safe in assuming that he and his people anticipated the Soviet attack, or he would have not survived. We do know that Gubukil was destroyed. Our own reconnaissance aircraft have verified its destruction."

"One of our concerns should be why our agents have detected any Soviet reconnaissance planes," Si'Quetta said in a quiet tone. "Another factor we have to consider is that Sirzihil—if we do obtain proof that Mirza-Khan has gone there—is not accessible from the air. We could not send in helicopters, at least not close to Sirzihil."

I'Zada's deepening frown automatically made Si'Quetta explain. "The racket of approaching helicopters would not only warn

Mirza-Khan, but Sirzihil is located high up in the mountains. I have already discussed the matter with General Muddin-Quaidy. He said the closest approach by helicopters would be eight kilometers east of Sirzihil. From there, the troops would have to proceed on foot over rough terrain."

"But Sirzihil could be bombed from the air?"

"*Ched*, but that's not the point. At the present time, we can't even be sure that Mirza-Khan is there. Frankly, we don't know where he is. Being a former military man, I'm sure President Zia will understand our position."

"Hmmmmmmm." General I'Zada nodded, sat down close to the map and crossed his legs. For a moment he studied a large picture on the far wall. An abstract painting. More of President Zia's nonsense about being "modern."

He suddenly turned his head and looked at Si'Quetta. "President Zia will also want to know how and why Mirza-Khan suspected that the Soviets would attack his winter headquarters. Granted, he's a clever old fox, but *that* clever! Why, I ask you, should Soviet Special Forces—the Spetsnaz—attack only Mirza-Khan's camp? Why was it imperative that the Russians destroy him?" I'Zada paused, then answered his own questions. "Unless Mirza-Khan was planning to do something that would interfere with Soviet plans and intentions!"

Lieutenant General Si'Quetta knew he was on tricky ground. "There isn't anything to indicate that the Pathans or the Garukals are interfering in Afghan affairs. If anything, the Soviets should be angry with us for keeping open the refugee camps in the Khyber."

"President Zia would like to close the camps," I'Zada said. "We know why he can't. How would it look to the West—and not only from the standpoint of mercy? It would appear as though we were caving in to the demands of the Soviets."

"So far President Zia has been a master chess player," said Si'Quetta. "He's keeping both the Soviets and the West off balance."

General I'Zada consulted his Polaris II compass wristwatch. "It's time for our meeting with President Zia," he said, standing. "I'm going to recommend to him that we postpone the attack and wait until we have positive intelligence. I don't suppose there's anything on the four foreigners?"

"Nothing," answered Si'Quetta. "They seem to have vanished." Putting on his heavy greatcoat, he stopped, turned and stared at

I'Zada, who was carefully adjusting his visored cap. "I can't shake the feeling that somehow those four are with Mirza-Khan and that they had something to do with saving his ass from the Russians."

"Nonsense," I'Zada said with a slight laugh. "It was probably the other way around. He saved them!"

CHAPTER TEN

Richard Camellion was instantly awake and on full alert. Yet, as his right hand tightened around the butt of the Bren Ten pistol, he didn't move. He didn't rear up. He did know that something was very wrong, and he did blink very rapidly, adjusting his eyes to the darkness. Within seconds he knew he had been right. He could barely see the outline of the Pathans. But there they were, all four on their hands and knees, crawling very slowly toward him and Quinlan and Bruckner and O'Malley. He couldn't tell whether they were packing handguns or knives; they were still too far away.

Dumbbells! Don't feel bad. A lot of people don't have any talent for "wet-work." This wasn't the first time—or the tenth—that would-be assassins had tried to whack him out. It wouldn't be the last. Automatically, he could almost time to the second the approach and the deaths of the Pathans.

Kill all four? Wound all four? Kill three and save one for intensive questioning? Well, well . . . Camellion debated while he watched the four guides creep closer. With each second, he could see them more clearly. He had decided to waste three and save one for interrogation when he saw that all four Pathans, pulling themselves along on their elbows, were packing iron in their hands.

Well, fudge! Guns put a different light on the entire situation.

Camellion sized up the situation. He wasn't concerned about any of the Pathan guides putting a slug into him. The danger in wasting three of the guides and saving the fourth was that the fourth might get off a lucky shot and kill, or wound, either

Quinlan or Bruckner or O'Malley when they were knocked awake by the roaring of the Bren Ten and reared up.

Or—I could wait until the first two guides are close enough to Bruckner and the Kid to trigger their PPAs.

The trouble with that plan was the lag time, the few seconds it would take Bruckner and the Peppermint Kid to fire. By then . . . *it might be too late.*

Flaw number two. In the darkness, Camellion couldn't be sure that he would only wound one Pak.

What bothered the Death Merchant was why the four guides were creeping in. *If they only wanted to kill us, why not make a try during the day? Why crawl over in the middle of the night? Why not just smear us with one of their assault rifles? One little bitty burst would do it.*

Ah well . . . blast all four. Camellion pulled his hand from inside the *ti'rus*, and with it the big Bren Ten autopistol. To one side of his mind was the realization that the Pathans were creatures of flesh and blood and bone . . . individuals, no doubt with plans and hopes for their families. Pathetic little human beings, creatures so imprisoned in emotions.

Bye-bye, dummies. You're dead! The Death Merchant reared up and started firing, the explosions of the Bren Ten sounding like bombs going off in the quiet night. One-two-three-four. It took only 4.099 seconds to turn the four guides into dead men. To be on the safe side, because of the blackness, Camellion pumped four more 10m projectiles into the four cadavers, none of whom felt the second slugs. Three had died so fast they hadn't even felt the first projectiles. Tamil Digarh had been the exception. He had felt only a lightning stab as the bullet tore into the top of his body four inches to the left side of his neck. The slug missed the clavicle, bored all the way down the length of his body and stopped when it hit the top of the ilium or hipbone. The second 10mm bullet popped him in the lower back, zipping in at a very steep angle. It broke his spine, shot through his lower bowel, tore away his testicles and buried itself ten inches in the hard ground.

"Well, good gravy!" said Quinlan in a loud voice. By then, while the eight Bren Ten explosions echoed across the mountains, Mad Mike sat up, a Glock autoloader in each hand.

Bruckner and the Peppermint Kid, pistols in their hands, soon scrambled out of their *ti'rusis* and turned on flashlights. As the Death Merchant moved toward them, they shone the bright beams over the four corpses.

"How did they try it?" asked O'Malley, turning toward Camellion. "What 'appened?"

"It came time for them to go," Camellion said, his tone amused. *Medicine tries to postpone it. Religion tries to soften it. But in the end, the Cosmic Lord of Death drums his bony fingers on all of us. Hah, hah, hah! That silent conspiracy of Nature that prevents terrified humans from knowing Reality*!

Briefly then, he explained what had taken place.

"This is one fine friggin' mess!" raged Quinlan, who had walked over to Camellion and, by means of a flashlight, was looking down at the four corpses. "And it proves that Chaudhriy set us up for a hit. I'm going to break every bone in his body, starting with his fingers!" Furiously, he kicked the dead Asad Dizakan in the head. "Now all we have is a map and our own resources!"

"Our situation would seem to be a bit muddy at the moment," offered O'Malley, holstering his Glock. "Between the four of us, all we can say in the Pak language is hello, good-bye, and Praise Allah."

The Death Merchant's grin was from earlobe to earlobe. "I don't think that if we run into any tribesmen in these mountains, we'll have to carry on a conversation about stereophonic subcarriers or unijunction diodes." He shoved a full magazine into the Bren Ten he had used, pulled back the slide, sent a cartridge into the breech and switched on the safety. He became dead serious. "We can go back. It's up to the three of you."

"Nuts to that noise," Quinlan said brutally. "I don't like unfinished business. Neither do Willy and Jimmy. Neither do you, Camellion."

"We do what we came to do," Bruckner said in his brand of fractured English. "We scout the base of der Spetsnaz *Kadavergehorsam*."[1]

O'Malley was casual. "I concur with Willy. We 'ave the map. We know we 'ave to reach Sylhet Pass. Rather simple, eh?"

"Yeah, like pushing toothpaste back into the tube," Quinlan said. He was cold sober, his alertness a surprise to Bruckner and O'Malley but not to Camellion, who had seen Mad Mike "intoxicated" on half a dozen missions: no matter how drunk he became, he always became instantly sober whenever Death got close.

[1]. "Obedience of corpses." A term used by the Nazis to indicate how Russian soldiers blindly obeyed the orders of their officers.

Mike continued, looking at the Death Merchant. "First we have to sort out what's going on. Those Pak creeps could have tried to snuff us on the trail. Why didn't they? Why all this sneaking around in the night?"

"I was wondering when you'd get around to that?" joked Camellion.

"Cut the bullshit. I'm serious. This is a worse mess than being in the middle of Mexico City!"

"Theory is all we have," Camellion gave his opinion. "Maybe they were cowards, but I doubt it. Considering who and what we are, Iskander Chaudhriy warned them to be very careful. But I agree with you, Mike. They didn't have to crawl on their hands and knees to waste us."

"But they did!"

"Maybe they didn't want to use guns for some reason," suggested O'Malley. "Perhaps those chaps wanted to do us in with knives."

"I think they wanted us alive," Camellion said. "To make us prisoners. I think they wanted to turn us over to the Russians."

"Now that makes sense." Quinlan was enthusiastic. O'Malley and Bruckner nodded vigorously. "If you're right, then the ivans are expecting them—and us. But in a different manner than how we'll arrive. Man, we have a lot of planning to do." Quinlan stared at Camellion, who was moving toward the bloody corpse of Asad Dizakan. "What are you going to do?"

The Death Merchant bent down. "I want the *jambiya* he's carrying. Search the other three and see if they have anything that might give us some kind of clue."

The planning mentioned by Quinlan had to be predicated on the device that the Peppermint Kid found on the corpse of Syed Serneabiz. As large as a cigarette case, the transmitter was of East German manufacture, was powered by a small, round Vokkner battery and had only one function: to send out a steady but spaced signal on the HF band. Camellion could not be sure, but he estimated its range to be between twenty-four and thirty-two klicks, or between fifteen and twenty miles. Well built, the transmitter could only have been detected by sophisticated bug equipment, such as a spectrum analyzer or an IPMS[2] and/or other equipment built by such experts as Law Enforcement Associates.

[2]. In-Place Monitoring System.

The reason that Syed Serneabiz was carrying the "tracer"—the transmitter—was as obvious as why one sees jolly fat men with fake white beards and red suits several weeks before December 25.

The Russians were tracking them.

"Or soon would be," Camellion said. "We're still out of range—I think. I estimate the border is still about thirty-five klicks away."

"All we 'ave to do is smash the bloody thing," O'Malley said happily. Instantly he caught the fatal flaw in his line of reasoning. "But if we did, the ivans would know we found it."

"Exactly, precisely and you're right!" Camellion sounded as sly as a Bedouin trader. "Let the slop from the land of pigs think all is well. We'll use the transmitter to turn the tables on them." He called out after Quinlan, who was headed toward his *ti'rus*. "Mike, you have the map the CIA airdropped. Get it out, old buddy."

"Thank God for the Ear," O'Malley said, looking very serious and reaching for his cigarettes. "I never did trust those Pathan chaps. Why, damn it all. They're almost as uncivilized as you Americans."

Quinlan reached down and pulled a plastic map case from his canvas kit bag. He also reached into his sleeping bag, took out the half-empty bottle of Scotch, uncapped it and took several very long swallows. Only then did he turn to Camellion and Bruckner and O'Malley and say in a deceptively mild voice, "I'd like to know why the four of us agreed to this crazy mission in the first place! God damn it! We must have sawdust for brains!"

They studied the map for only five minutes, Camellion not wanting to remain on the hilltop any longer than necessary. There wasn't any way of knowing who was in the mountains and might have heard the shots from the Bren Ten.

Taking the P-38s, the .45 Colt and the Spanish Star from the four dead men, plus the canteens and the food that had belonged to the guides, Camellion and his tiny force covered the four cold cuts with rocks, Bruckner commenting as he covered the corpse of Abdus Powidi, "If I was a Hindu, I would say this *schwein*'s soul left the body through the mouth!"

O'Malley dropped a pile of rocks over Tamil Digarh. "Why, because his mouth is open?"

"*Ja*, those *dumm* Hindus think the soul leaves the body either through the mouth or the eyes or the nose. They're crazy and stupid."

By the time Camellion and his men were moving carefully down one side of the hill—the Death Merchant and Quinlan wearing Cyclops NVDs—the time was 04.22 hours.

They did have some special, unusual protection: "the Ear," which was the result of American technology, especially the microchip industry of "Silicon Valley," California.[3] Technically, the Ear was called a pulse interdigital sound-alternator sensor, although (and unofficially) Company men in the Technical Division referred to the device as PISS. In simple language, PISS detected far-away sounds in much the same manner that the "Ears" used by hunters magnified the sounds of game animals.[4] Only PISS didn't cost from $50 to $200. It did cost $19,500 and magnified sound so well that one could hear human voices (normally spoken speech) within a mile and a half in open flat country. In mountain terrain, PISS had an estimated effective range of 1,219.2 meters, or 4,000 feet.

PISS was not used in the ordinary manner. One did not have to walk around holding a microphone and wearing heavy headphones. Another nice feature was the size of PISS—only slightly larger than a box of cigars. The difference was that inside the "box," there wasn't any rolled tobacco leaves. There was only very complex circuitry and room for three LDC batteries. Another difference was that there wasn't any microphone, not a conventional one, anyhow. There was an antenna that, telescoping, could be extended from six inches to four feet. And there were straps by means of which the operator could wear the device on his back—the only sensible way to carry it because of the long antenna. A wire from the single earplug ran to the box, which had an on/off switch, volume control and battery-power meter.

A Galil assault rifle in his hands, PISS on his back with the antenna fully extended, the Death Merchant led the way down the hillside.

The Peppermint Kid carried the small transmitter that had been found on the corpse of Syed Serneabiz; it continued to give off its spaced signal on an HF frequency.

By sunrise, the Death Merchant and his crew were several miles from the hilltop four-body cemetery.

[3]. See Death Merchant number 58, *Silicon Valley Connection*.

[4]. Most of these devices, while magnifying sound a little, are not worth the money.

All went well the first day, that night and the second day. But even under normal conditions, the Death Merchant and the three men of Thunderbolt Unit Omega would not have enjoyed the raw beauty around them. They had seen it before in many places, in other times, and always Death was with them. The Man in the Satin Sandals was with them now, waiting patiently.

Camellion and his men were in the heart of the Dera Ismail Khan which were a part of the much larger Hindu Kush[5] range far to the north, where Tirich Mir, at a height of 25,230 feet, reigned supreme. All around the four men were jagged peaks, snowclad and magnificent.

At the present time, the mountains of the Dera Ismail Khan were far more dangerous than the Russians, even to highly experienced men such as Camellion and his three associates. There were times when, for miles, the trail was only narrow shelves of rock held in place by God and, when He was too busy, by luck. No matter, because for centuries, yaks, donkeys, horses and men had traveled over them.

During the middle of the afternoon, the four men crossed a narrow ridge that was so rocky and cratered it looked like a battlefield. It had taken them four hours to climb the slope and reach the ridge. A quick meal, a half hour's rest, and they started down the opposite side, which was very short and steep. By 17.00 hours, they had crossed a small plateau that ended at the cut-up edge of a 2000-foot precipice. Beyond and far below was a valley, but by then darkness had such a grip on the wide-open spaces that visibility had dropped ninety-five percent. There wasn't anything for the men to do but settle down for the night.

The next morning they could see that below was a valley, nestled like a small cup on a mammoth rocky hand, a valley whose poplars, orchards and pockes of fields were frosted with snow. A picture postcard! In months to come there would be a drastic change. The spring would melt the snow, and with summer would come the *Siah bad*, the scorching "black wind" that would blow over much of Pakistan and Afghanistan. The orchards would be heavy with lemons, oranges, apricots, tangerines and pomegranates. Properly irrigated fields would be productive and golden wheat would wave in the breeze.

Lying on their stomachs close to the edge of the cutoff and studying the valley through powerful binoculars, Camellion and

[5]. "Killer of Hindus" in Hindi.

his men could see a village on the side of the valley closest to them, some of the houses close together, others high up, resting alone on rocky projections. All the houses were built of squared logs chinked with stones and mud. In another five months, corn, beans, walnuts and mulberries would be spread out to dry on the flat roofs.

By the sides of some of the houses and on some of the even roofs were short clay pots that reminded him of a *huaca*, a container used by the Indians in Peru, and he thought of the time he had been on an archeological dig close to the Xingu River. Indian workers had found a very old *huaca* that had contained some clear liquid. One of the Indians had accidentally dropped and broken it. Later it had been noticed that where the *huaca* had been broken and the liquid spilled, the rock had become soft and malleable, before subsequently hardening.[6]

"We could save five or six klicks by going through the valley down there," muttered O'Malley, who was lying between Quinlan and Bruckner. He didn't remove the binoculars from his eyes. "Unless the map is wrong. So far, it 'as been accurate. The CIA chaps did a fine job."

"Going down there would be too much of a risk." Camellion leaned over on his left side, shoved his binoculars into the leather case and vaguely wondered how the Company had obtained the information for the map. No doubt from some deep-cover agent in the Department of the Interior of the Pak government.

"You're right," agreed Quinlan. "We can't risk a confrontation with the people down there. Not all Paks take kindly to foreigners, and the Paks down there are certainly in what could be called the backwoods."

"The map says that the route we want is to the northwest," Bruckner said. "Well, that way will take longer—*ja!* But it will be safer."

Camellion turned his back to Quinlan. "Pull up PISS's antenna and we'll get going. We should reach Sylhet Pass by late tomorrow afternoon."

For the past few days, the pulse interdigital sound-alternator sensor had picked up only the sounds of animals—wild yaks, *durrna* birds and, at one time, what could have been several bears. But by 14.00 hours of this day the situation changed for

[6]. See future Death Merchant number 64, *The Atlantean Horror*.

the force of four. They were on a trail that was only ten feet wide (at the maximum), as uneven as ocean waves during a typhoon and that twisted dangerously around the side of a mountain. They were moving single-file when the Death Merchant, behind Quinlan, detected human voices coming through the single earphone of PISS, voices that were merely whispers.

"Hold it! I hear voices!" he said, a look of alarm on his face. He pulled out the earphone, moved closer to Mad Mike, who had turned around, and handed it to him. Mike put the earplug into his ear, listened for several long moments, then pulled it out and handed it back to Camellion. The Death Merchant inserted the earphone into his ear and resumed listening.

Quinlan made an angry face. "They're speaking Pak gobbledegook. Hell, they have to be within a mile of us."

"We can't go back," O'Malley said tightly. "We'd lose too much time, and we'd 'ave to go down the long slope we just climbed. They'd see us."

Willy Bruckner flicked away his cigarette and said in German, "There's only one trail in this section of the mountains. They're either coming toward us or moving away from us." He studied Camellion severely for a moment. "Which is it?"

"Five minutes ago, I could barely hear the voices." Camellion also switched to German. "Now they're loud whispers. The Paks are coming toward us. I'm certain."

"Well, we can't fly," said Quinlan, looking all around. "We either go ahead or turn back. It has to be one or the other."

"But we can *climb*," Bruckner said. He stuck out his big chin, then jerked his head toward the side of the mountain, which, at this point, was almost perpendicular. Worse, large and snow-splattered rocks that did not appear to be anchored too solidly covered it.

"Would we have the time?" Quinlan looked at the Death Merchant, then turned to gaze at the side of the mountain. A man would have to have wings to climb a side that steep!

"We'd have the time, but that's not the issue," said the Death Merchant, holding a finger on the earphone. "See for yourself. One slip and we'd end up a big bloody spot on the trail."

"Or get carried down the side of the entire mountain if we started a landslide," O'Malley said quickly.

"Why don't I climb it and have a look around when I reach the top?" suggested Bruckner, whom they knew to be very good at such climbing. Among the four, he was the best. "I might be able to see how far away the Paks are."

The Death Merchant made the decision. "*Nein*, Willy. It's too dangerous even for you. We'll move ahead and hope for the best. Judging from what's coming in through PISS, I don't think there's more than a dozen of them."

Quinlan's eyes became flinty with disagreement. "Since when do we make any move based on 'hope for the best,' Richard?" His firm tone was an outright demand for an explanation. "Those odds are fifty-fifty, with nothing in our favor."

"You're right, but the odds would be even more against us if we tried to shinny up the side," Camellion replied, a cunning look flashing in his deep blue eyes. "It's not as bad as it would appear. There are four of us and maybe a dozen or so of them—or can't we outshoot them, should it come to that?"

"We would have to," Quinlan answered with a half smile. "Huh! We couldn't outtalk them, not in their own language."

"At least we're *dressed* like Pathans," said O'Malley, looking down at himself. "*Chudkis, kobasas, lebidows*, the works. The trouble is, we don't *look* like Pathans, though I'm told that some of the Kalash people have blue eyes."

The Peppermint Kid suddenly had the impression he was talking to himself. The other three had already started to move forward.

Three hundred and eighty-four feet later, all four received a pleasant shock. The trail had turned around the side of the mountain and widened considerably, to almost fifty feet. However, the best part was what lay to the right. No longer was the side of the mountain almost vertical. Instead it sloped upward at a forty-five-degree angle, one that could easily be climbed. Even better, it was littered with boulders large enough to conceal fifty men.

"Well, well, it only proves what faith and patience will do." Camellion smirked "Now, lads, all the odds are on our side."

"Faith, patience—and don't forget good breath," Quinlan said, amused. "All we have to do is 'walk' up the side and wait until the Paks go by."

"You mean the three of you will go up the slope," Camellion corrected, giving the full explanation when they stared at him, but not in disbelief. They had learned to expect anything from the Death Merchant. "Mirza-Khan is supposed to be respected by all the tribes in this land. I'll wait down here and—"

"OK, so he's almost a saint!" O'Malley said. "What does that 'ave to do with being a damm fool and making a target of yourself?"

"I'll wait down here, meet the Paks and give them the facts. I'll tell them I'm a good friend of Mirza-Khan's and am on my way to check on the Spetsnaz base across the border. Let's see what their response will be."

"You're not playing with a full deck!" Quinlan was adamant. "There are Pathan bandits who don't give a fuck about the ivans. These guys might just say 'Screw Mirza-Khan' and, like Jimmy said, try to blow you away. Naturally, they won't because you'll be depending on us to whack 'em out first. Scratch it, Richard. It's too much of a gamble."

"Why not just kill them and be done with it?" proposed Bruckner.

That was one reason why Camellion liked Bruckner. Willy was a firm believer in simplicity. He was always wanting to terminate somebody.

"Men, let's be practical," Camellion said seriously. "We need all the help we can get. If the Pak group is friendly, who knows? Maybe they'll help us."

"Oh sure! And maybe I'll become a farmer in the middle of Kansas!"

Quinlan spit on the ground and hooked his thumbs over the buckle of his gun belt.

"Suppose none of them speaks English?" said a grumpy Bruckner.

Camellion made light of the entire situation. "Pish-tush, it won't be all that risky. The Paks will be so surprised to see me out here in the mountains, all alone, that they won't be gawking around on the slope. You three will have ample time to get up there into position. Why you yo-yos can shoot the eyelashes off a fly at a hundred feet and not even make him blink! I won't be in that much danger."

The Death Merchant (minus PISS, which Quinlan was now carrying) waited not far from the left side of the trail, leaning against a large boulder, the Galil held loosely in his gloved hands. Mike, Willy and the Kid worried too much.

The odds are on my side—I think! And I sure as hell hope I'm right!

He thought again of the valley they had surveyed that morning.

Again he recalled the *huaca* that had been broken in Peru. He had thought about it all these years. If it had been the liquid that had softened the rock, why hadn't the liquid eaten through the *huaca*? Or had the interior of the *huaca* been coated with a special substance?

Eleven minutes later the Pathans came around the curve of the trail. They spotted Camellion, stopped and began talking excitedly among themselves, their eyes on the Galil which, although Camellion held loosely, could be brought up and fired in a split second—and the Paks knew it.

"*Har kala Allah rashi*—Welcome in the name of Allah," called out Camellion, who knew at once that the fifteen Pathans were not bandits. Six were women. Another indication was the weapons they carried. Most of their long arms were old-style British Enfield rifles. However, he did spot three World War II German MP-38/40[7] submachine guns and a French MAT-49 SMG.

Carrying various parcels of luggage, besides their *ti'rusis* (the women loaded down with more than the men), the group moved toward Camellion, looking at him curiously and continuing to jabber among themselves. Camellion, relieved but still cautious, was intrigued by the old man he sensed was the leader. The old boy had a long henna-colored beard and a face as solemn as a mortician trying to sell the grieving widow his most expensive casket. He was not wearing a *chudki* or a *kobasa*. His outer garment was a long gray overcoat—Western style—and around his neck and over his red turban was a long white woolen scarf. It was the weapon the old man carried that fascinated Camellion the most. It was an ancient flintlock, very long and with an enormously curved stock. Camellion also noticed that as the band approached, their speed determined by four of the donkeys the women were leading, the younger men kept their rifles at the ready.

"*Staray ma Allah rashi kuchi*—I return your greeting in the name of Allah," the old man called out in a surprisingly strong voice when he was still thirty paces from Camellion.

Positive the group members weren't bandits but still tempting the Cosmic Lord of Death, Camellion leaned his Galil against the

[7]. This is the famed Schmeisser, which uses 9 × 19mm Parabellum. With excellent controlability, the SMG is rugged, reliable and accurate. It is still in use throughout the world, particularly in South America and Asia.

side of the large boulder. *Wouldn't I feel stupid if they shot me down*? "Do any of you speak English? he inquired, noticing that the old gentleman had a monocle screwed in his right eye, not a genuine monocle but one rounded side of a pair of eyeglasses, a string attached to that part of the outside frame where the front end of the earpiece would have been attached.

The patriarch frowned and turned to the young man next to him, a husky dude who was in his late twenties. While wearing the traditional *kobasa*, the cossack-like hat, he had on a Russian private's dirty green great coat and leather gloves and boots that appeared to be of Western manufacture. Hearing Camellion, his eyes widened slightly and an amazed look dropped over his face.

"I speak English," he said with a thick accent. "I am Jaiiah Talequn. The old one is Nelkik Farah-Rinrooz. He is my grandfather. Who are you? What are you doing here alone in this wilderness."

"My name is Richard Joseph Camellion." Camellion tried to sound serious, yet authoritarian. "I am on a most important mission for Malik Mujibur Ali Mirza-Khan, who is a good friend of mine."

Nelkik Farah-Rinrooz's eyes lit up, and the other Pathans looked at the Death Merchant with renewed interest. Neither they nor Farah-Rinrooz understood English, but they did know Mirza-Khan's name when they heard it. And a magic name it was. For now they regarded Camellion with more than interest. There was also respect and friendship on their faces.

Jaiiah Talequn turned to his grandfather and rattled off an explanation in Urdu. The Death Merchant caught Mirza-Khan's name half a dozen times, especially when the grandfather replied. Finally the nephew returned his attention to Camellion, his voice more friendly. Camellion also saw his hands relax on the MAT-49 SMG.

"Kir Camellion. My grandfather said to tell you that Chief Mujibur Ali Mirza-Khan is a good friend of his, that they have known each other since they were boys." A cautious note crept into Jaiiah Talequn's voice. "My grandfather said that since you are a friend of Chief Mujibur Ali Mirza-Khan, you perhaps are a friend of Cuhib Narlashka?"

Camellion retained a straight face. *They're testing me. I would do the same under similar conditions.*

"I have never heard of Cuhib Narlashka," Camellion said

truthfully. "I am a good friend of Jiko Krim-Lizak and Iskander Chaudhriy. I am sure you know those two fine men."

Again Camellion saw recognition on the faces of Nelkik Farah-Rinrooz and Jaiiah Talequn, as well as on the curious faces of other men, and the women too. Some of the women were pretty, their eyes outlined in red mascara. Camellion, who never missed anything, saw that when one woman removed her bulky gazelle-skin gloves, her hands were stained purple from dye.

Once more there was a hurried conversation between Nelkik Farah-Rinrooz and his grandson. At length, Jaiiah Talequn said to the Death Merchant, "Kir Camellion, my grandfather said to tell you that you are most welcome to share our evening meal with us. He said to tell you also that while he does not wish to place himself on the path of your business for Chief Mujibur Ali Mirza-Khan, he remains mystified as to why you are alone in these mountains and why Chief Mujibur Ali Mirza-Khan should send only one individual on a mission which must be important."

Ah . . . still testing, still probing. OK, go for broke!

The Death Merchant carefully watched for a reaction as he spoke.

"I am not alone. My friends and I—they are also friends of Chief Mujibur Ali Mirza-Khan—heard your approach. We accomplished this by means of a special listening device we use in the West. We could not know whether you were friends or enemies. My companions are on the slope." Seeing fear and mistrust leap into the eyes of the Pathans, he added quickly, "Now that we know you are blessed in the eyes of Allah and are friends, I will tell my friends to reveal themselves and to join us. We would feel honored to have tea with you and to share our food."

There was another hurried conversation between Jaiiah Talequn and Nelkik Farah-Rinrooz, the latter of whom smiled, nodded vigorously and looked toward the slope.

Jaiiah Talequn's words were friendly. "My grandfather said it was not our business to ask you of the mission that you and your friends will perform for Chief Mujibur Ali Mirza-Khan. He said he would be happy for all of us to drink tea together and to share a meal with you and your companions."

Not letting the matter rest or calling out to Quinlan and the two other mercs, Camellion came right to the point. "Chief Mirza-Khan intends to deal a serious blow to the dogs that come from the giant country to the north and have been murdering your religious brothers in Afghanistan. Chief Mirza-Khan will destroy a special Russian base east of the town of Narang in Afghanistan. It is the mission of my friends and myself to scout this nest of vipers and report back to Malik Mujibur Ali Mirza-Khan. Even as I stand here and give you this good news, runners of Chief Mirza-Khan are talking to the other *Maliks* organizing them for an attack against the Russians."

Only then did the Death Merchant turn to his right and yell in English, "Come on down. They are friends and under the protection of Allah."

He had not failed to notice the astonishment and the quick look of fear on the faces of Jaiiah Talequn and some of the other men as he had explained the mission; and as Quinlan and O'Malley and Bruckner stood up and started to move down the slope, Nelkik Farah-Rinrooz and his nephew began to carry on a fast and furious conversation. By the time Mad Mike and the other two mercs were halfway down the slope, two other Paks had joined in and were moving their hands in every direction as they jabbered in Urdu.

By the time Quinlan and his two men had walked up, doing their best to look friendly, Jaiiah Talequn had turned to Camellion. "We are on our way to Tigmal, a village to the east. What you have revealed has made some of us want to change our minds. I and four of my blood brothers"—he motioned with his hand toward four other Pathans—"would like to go with you. We can be of help. We are very familiar with this section of our nation."

"Who said there ain't no Santa Claus?" muttered Quinlan.

Another member of the Pathan band spoke up excitedly, "We are from Pindiwal. It is a village that is only a few *serais* from the border that divides our land from the country of the Afghans." Shorter but heavier than Jaiiah Talequn, Nemattulah i-Nan was in his early twenties. He had a very large mustache, a wide face and a nose that was short for a Pathan.

Shotit Pushko-Mialat also had a big mustache. It was he who said in very poor English to the Death Merchant and his group, "We have our own dye works in Pindiwal. We left only yesterday morning. We had heard rumors of a Russian attack many *serais* to the southeast. We realized if it was true, it would only be a short time before the slime from the north would attack us and all the villages close to the border."

"You did not hear a rumor. It was fact," Camellion said plainly. "The Russian dogs came from the very base we will scout. They came in birds with revolving wings and attacked

Gubukil, the village that Malik Mujibur Ali Mirza-Khan was using for his winter headquarters. My friends and I were there. We helped Malik Mirza-Khan beat back the Russians. By now, Malik Mirza-Khan and his clan are in Sirzihil."

First hearing the word *Gubukil* and then *Sirzihil*, Nelkik Farah-Rinrooz began to tug at his nephew's arm and speak rapidly. Jaiiah Talequn explained just as rapidly, confirming the Spetsnaz attack. Immediately, the old man became furious. He began shouting and waving his old flintlock.

As Farah-Rinrooz ranted and raved, Camellion did some hard thinking. The Pathans always gave distances in *serais*. *So! Since a* serai *is slightly more than a klick, Pindiwal is only three to five miles from the border*.

Jonhor Gonsuf, another member of the group, explained to Camellion what had angered Nelkik Farah-Rinrooz. "He is cursing the Russians in the name of Allah. He said he would like to join us and your group, but that he knows he is too old. Time has made his bones stiff."

"Kir Richard Camellion, you will let us join you?" asked Nemattulah i-Nan anxiously. "We will die for our land. This is the land of our fathers and their fathers. It is not the land of that jackal, Zia, who rules from Islamabad."

"You and the others are welcome," Camellion said evenly. "But I want to warn the five of you. Going into Afghanistan will be very dangerous. We could get killed, or worse, fall into the hands of the Russians. My friends and I would not. We would kill ourselves."

"We would also die by our own hand," i-Nan said fiercely. "To kill ourselves under such conditions would not be a sin in the eyes of Allah."

Jaiiah Talequn, having calmed down his grandfather who was still muttering under his breath, said to Camellion, "We will first have to reach Sylhet Pass. From the pass, we can sneak into the land of the Afghans. You are correct in every way, Kir Camellion. It will be very dangerous. But we have done it before, many times."

"Before—many times?" Now Mad Mike was interested. "I thought you operated a dye works in Pindiwal?"

The Paks grinned. Jaiiah Telequn laughed. "That is true. We did have a dye works. But we also carried the gum of the poppy into Afghanistan." He spread his hands. "How else could we live decently?"

Nelkik Farah-Rinrooz said something to Talequn, who translated for Camellion and his three men. "He said we will go back to the wide place in the trail and have tea and share a meal."

Camellion nodded agreeably. "Tell me, Kir Talequn, how far are we from Sylhet Pass. When will we get there?"

"If all goes well, by late afternoon tomorrow. . . ."

17.11 hours. The Death Merchant's force had now increased to nine, including himself, and the men were on their way toward the deadly Sylhet Pass, deadly because it was closely watched by both the Russians and the border guards of the Pakistani army. Under ordinary circumstances, when the Pathans were smuggling the gum of the poppy from Pakistan into Afghanistan, the Pak army guards could be bribed. Not this time . . .

Noticing that the wind was stronger and more chilly, Camellion thought of Nelkik Farah-Rinrooz and his whittled-down-by-five group that had disappeared in the distance, the women leading the donkeys and *jukfi* carts piled high with bolts of colored cloth and household goods. While drinking tea and eating dired goat meat, dried figs and *shishaou*, he had been able to inspect the flintlock that Farah-Rinrooz carried. The weapon was 167 years old and had belonged to Farah-Rinrooz's great-great-great-grandfather, the lock plate bearing the date 1818 and the initials VEIC, Venerable East India Company. At the time, the Death Merchant had wondered if Nelkik Farah-Rinrooz realized he was carrying an antique for which collectors would have paid—at minimum—$25,000? Probably not.

That flintlock is worth one-fourth of what I'm worth to the KGB.

The last Camellion had heard, the KGB was offering—no questions asked—$100,000 American for the exact identity of the *Cempt Tobtocpam*: the Death Merchant.

CHAPTER ELEVEN

The Death Merchant and the other three mercs were proving that nothing splendid is ever achieved except by those who dare to believe that something within them is far superior to circumstances. That the Death Merchant and Quinlan and his two men had even gone to Pakistan proved they were a cut above average mortals (or were Grade-A candidates for a Laughing Academy).

The five Pathans deserved their share of credit. They didn't have to be going into Afghanistan and sticking their necks into the mouth of the Russian bear. The fact that they were made the Death Merchant and his three men admire them. They were brave men . . . and they had been truthful.

Jaiiah Talequn and the four other Pathans knew this area of the Dera Ismail Khan the way the Death Merchant knew the Big Thicket in the southeast section of Texas. Able to climb like mountain goats (Quinlan compared them to Himalayan *tahrs*, goatlike creatures that seemed to defy gravity), the five Pathans took several shortcuts, both involving the ascent of very steep slopes and passage through deep gorges often filled with rocks the size of automobiles and hip-deep snow. In spite of the furious pace, it was deep twilight by the time the party reached the vicinity of Sylhet Pass, and they were still a mile short of the high rocks north of the mouth of the pass.

Make camp and wait. It was their only recourse. A further setback was that they would have to hide out all the next day. Jaiiah Talequn said that the single mile was fairly open and offered no place to hide from Russian or Pak recon planes or from the binoculars of Pakistani border guards.

Jaiiah Talequn explained: "Neither our own border guards nor the Russians, on their side of the border, go into the mountains at night. They are out in force—the Russian dogs and Zia's border guards—during the daytime. But aircraft do fly a lot at night. We will make the final approach tomorrow night. We—"

"What's wrong with tonight?" said Quinlan. "Darkness is darkness, and won't planes be flying tomorrow night?"

"Kir Quinlan, we are too tired; we must rest," Talequn said practically. "Even with the see-in-the-dark things you possess and the 'magical ear,' the way would be very difficult. *Ched*, the planes will be there. The way will be difficult. The wind has kept the area free of snow, but there are numerous deep—you would call then gullies—we could fall into. We must wait. Our bodies must be rested."

Mad Mike frowned but didn't argue. Camellion sensed that O'Malley and Bruckner were dissatisfied with the wait. Custom demanded that the Paks share their food, and Bruckner hated certain dishes, comparing them to what "you find in the bottom of a hamster's cage."

"Our *baya-darka* is right," Camellion said, stepping in. "We all need rest. There's a limit to how far we can push ourselves." He then proceeded to tell the five Pathans about the signal transmitter they had found on the body of Syed Serneabiz and the attack of the "guides."

"Not every tree bears sweet fruit." Talequn tugged at his *toba*. "It is a disgrace that some Pathans should shame their brothers by being traitors."

Biho Tozmo'qu, who was one of the five Pathans who had come along, was more down-to-earth. "The past cannot be changed. "Did you not hear what Kir Camellion said? The tracking radio has a range of thirty-six *serais*. That means the Russian eaters of dung know we are here in these very mountains." He stared at Camellion in the flickering light of the small fire within the cave. "How can we cross into the land of the Afghans without the Russian enemy knowing we are there and following our every move?"

Time for truth. The Death Merchant told Biho Tozmo'qu and the other Pathans that one man would remain behind with the transmitter. That man would move in a southerly direction, then turn around and go back north, making the Soviet enemy think that the force was still in Pakistan. "The man who will remain behind will be one of you."

The five members of Nelkik Farah-Rinrooz's band did not like the arrangement, yet they were practical and saw the necessity of one man's remaining behind, and they had given their word to follow Camellion's orders.

"The man with the transmitter will return to this cave," Camellion said. "We will meet him here on the return trip."

Although not famous like the Khyber, the Sylhet Pass was of vital importance to both the Pakistanis and the Afghans. Stretching from east to west, the Sylhet was five miles wide at its east end, in Pakistan, and three miles wide on the western end. To the north and the south were high mountains of the Dera Ismail Khan. In the west end of the Sylhet were two Pak villages, Aimangent and Chagasar. Of the two, Chagasar was the larger. It was built close to the actual border so that much of the west section of the community spilled over onto the soil of Afghanistan.

The Death Merchant and his band wouldn't be able to keep to the mountains on the north side of the pass when they crossed into Afghanistan because of a mile-and-a-half gap in the mountains at the border. On the western side, in Afghanistan, the breach was one mile. The other half mile was on the eastern side, in Pakistan.

"Crossing that small space on this side of the border will be filled with danger," said Talequn. "It lies just beyond the stretch of openness we will cross tomorrow night."

Nemattulah i-Nan said, "We will have to go through Chagasar. You men from the West can cover the bottom portions of your faces with the collars of your *chudkis*. No one will notice you, or us. We will not be bothered."

Michael Quinlan wasn't as philosophical as the Death Merchant. "And what happens when we get to the Afghan side of Chagasar? I suppose the Russians are going to ignore us and let us wander around as we please? Maybe you believe in miracles. We don't."

Talequn's answer was a surprise even to the Death Merchant. "Russian soldiers do not interfere with Pakistanis moving into Afghanistan. We have learned that the Russians also want a certain amount of the gum of the poppy to pass into Afghanistan. The Russians also realize that to close the borders in this area would prevent refugees from Afghanistan from crossing into Pakistan. Those nonbelievers from the giant nation to the north are not fools. They realize that for untold centuries the Sylhet has been an open door of commerce between us and the Afghans. They do not want to incite the tribes in the northwest frontier region of this land. They know too that Afghan fighters are hundreds and hundreds of *serais* west of the Sylhet."

The bare-bones details were that Narang was only thirteen *serais* or seven miles west of Chagasar. The Spetsnaz base was five *serais* or two miles east of Narang. On the Afghan side, from Chagasar to the beginning of the mountains was one mile.

Said Jonhor Gonsuf, "We will go west through the mountains, which end two *serais* from where the Russians are gathered in their special place—the Spetsnaz, as you refer to them.

Only three miles through the mountains! Not too bad. With the Death Merchant it was still a matter of double-think. He had already broken the prime rule of never revealing to a friend what you would conceal from an enemy. He had deemed it necessary with Nelkik Farah-Rinrooz's band. In that case his instincts had been correct. However, getting to Chagasar, to the mountains a mile west of Chagasar, then through the mountains to scout the Spetsnaz base—and then getting back into Pakistan—would require more than skill. Why bother? How could any force of Pathans and Garukals even get close to the Spetsnaz base without the Russians seeing them, when the Paks were still miles from the target. It would be a slaughter. . . .

Spenser called Luck "heedless hap," Milton "a nickname of Providence." Whatever it was, the four Pathans and four mercs from the West did succeed in crossing the entire open area the next night and, the next morning, in getting to Chagasar, a very old town whose buildings were a hodgepodge of wood, stone and mud, although the design of some of the structures revealed British influence.

There wasn't any indication that the people of Chagasar were worried about a Soviet invasion. At 1:30 in the afternoon, Fagul Ju-ki'-iszihar, the "main street" of the town, was packed with people—Paks (some in Western overcoats, hats and suits) mingling with Afghans, turbaned Takiks and Uzbeks and Turkomans from the north, both of the latter in high black boots and heavy long robes of many colors. There were numerous Hazaras, Garukals, tall Pathans, Baluchis and Nuristanis, most carrying automatic rifles. Now and then there was the stink of human waste in the air or a the pleasant aroma of incense, the clatter of horsedrawn wagons, horse- or donkey-pulled *jukfis*, and Russian taxis and jeeps honking their way through the throng. From tea shops came the tangy, inviting smell-flavor of roasting lamb and goat, at times the blare of Islamic music from scratchy loudspeakers.

They passed shops where bolts of cloth were sold, or firewood or handguns or herbs and medicines. Other shops displayed knives and scissors and Turkoman carpets or karakul-fur coats. Taking their time, as if they were not in any hurry, they moved west on Fagul Ju-ki-'iszihar and soon were in the Afghanistan section of Chagasar—the Russian sector!

"I still don't believe we got this far," whispered O'Malley.

Jaiiah Talequn replied in a soft voice, "When you ride a good horse, do not worry about the country in which he was born."

With one part of his *chudki* collar covering the lower part of his face, the Death Merchant shoved aside that intense feeling of *déjà vu*, dwelt for a moment on Talequn's reply to the Peppermint Kid, then thought of Shotit Pushko-Mialat, the man who had remained in the mountains with the transmitter. This whole damn mission was like a fixed deck in five-card draw, dealer's choice. *So much dealing from the bottom that the cards are dog-eared. In this Pakistan deal, it's difficult to tell the friends from the enemies.* Or who was or wasn't reliable. Would Shotit Pushko-Mialat merely sit in the cave with the transmitter and wait, or do as Camellion had directed him? He had given Camellion his word that he would first move south, then turn around and head back north.

That transmitter is our ace against the Russians. What's done is done. . . .

In another hour and fifteen minutes they were on the road out of town, and Biho Tozmo'qu was saying in a low voice, "Do not worry, men of the West. The Russians do not ask for identification until one is five or six *serais* west of Narang. The killers of Allah's children suspect any person going past Narang. They do because very few of us ever go as far as even Narang itself, not in these troublesome times."

In the distance were the mountains that would take the party of eight to within one mile of the Spetsnaz base. Something else was also in front of the group, coming toward them and other people on the road—a Soviet BTR-40—the standard recon vehicle of the Soviet army, followed by two Zolak trucks. Another BTR-40 was behind the two trucks. In only a few minutes the four vehicles had passed and were gone.

"Those dogs very seldom go into the shops in Chagasar,"

Jonhor Gonsuf said with a sneer. "Even in groups they are afraid of a knife in the back. Only too well do they know how they are hated."

The Death Merchant studied the countryside. It was rocky and unfriendly, the tops of the larger rocks, from which the wind had blown snow, tiny islands of desolation. As they neared the foothills, he could see hardwood trees and a confusion of boulders, monoliths and cliffs of crumbling granite—a mess, as if kicked by giants.

There wouldn't be any difficulty getting from the road into the mountains. No one would be suspicious. Not only did the road meander close to the mountains, but there were also Afghans living in the jumble of rocks, poor tribesmen, most of whom were *kuchis*, Afghan nomads, huddled in black goat's-hair tents. Caught in their own emotional trap. Hating the Russians, but not able to bring themselves to leave their native land.

The Death Merchant and his group, looking as poor and as miserable as the other people who were carrying bundles, merely followed some of the Afghans when they left the road and took a narrow trail that moved upward into the mountains, the highest of which appeared to be about 3000 feet.

"It won't be that simple," Mike Quinlan had said when, the previous night, Jaiiah Talequn had explained that it would not be difficult to get to the west end of the mountains, photograph the Spetsnaz base and survey it through binoculars. "The Russians aren't the least bit dumb. They know that the west side of the mountains offers a good vantage point of their base. They'll either have some of their own people, or turncoat Afghans, on the west rim."

"Will not your 'magic ear' warn us of them in time?" asked Talequn.

It took several hours to reach the top of the short line of mountains. No one gave them a second glance. Only once were they addressed, by an old Afghan in a tattered red robe: "*Staray ma-shi*—may you not be tired."

"*Har kiri shi*—you also, friend," replied Biho Tozmo'qu.

The plan was uncomplicated but dangerous. The eight men would set up camp in the middle of the mountains, wait until 01.00 hours and then proceed west and do what had to be done.

Time seemed to pass with extraordinary slowness. Finally, however, one o'clock in the morning arrived. Leaving their *ti'rusis* behind, the Death Merchant wearing PISS, the "magic ear," they crept west. Jaiiah Talequn had been right: the "magic ear" was their salvation. At this point-blank range, it was easy for PISS to detect sleeping groups of Afghans, the least sound of snoring greatly amplified. Only once did the Death Merchant hear voices engaged in conversation. Nemattulah i-Nan, who understood the Afghan language better than the three other Pathans, listened in and reported that the conversation was between two old men, worried about finding food the next day.

Without incident, they closed in on the west rim of the mountains, and with extreme care made their way to the farthest edge of a straight-down very high cliff to a section with boulders large enough to offer concealment. Camellion had firmly cautioned the four Pathans to keep close to the ground, warning them that the Spetsnaz, far below, were sure to have powerful night-vision scopes constantly scanning the west rim and west sides of the mountains.

The Death Merchant found what he desired: a line of boulders between which they could crawl and get a clear view of the Spetsnaz complex. Grojean had insisted that Camellion photograph the base. *Which won't help us a bit with any attack by the Pathans. The film won't be developed until I get it out of Afghanistan and Pakistan.*

Camellion had asked Grojean: "Couldn't one of COMOR's[1] satellites do the job?"

"COMOR doesn't have any spy eyes that fly over that area," Grojean had explained. "If we diverted a satellite to photograph the base, we'd tip off the Other Side that we're aware of the base. You have to do it. It's your job."

The Death Merchant now did just that as Quinlan and his two mercs, using binoculars, surveyed the base below and a mile away. After Camellion put away the camera, safely stashed the roll of 35mm film and surveyed the base, his happiness (such as it was) took a nose dive. The vast area was surrounded by a double chain-link fence, a twenty-foot space between the fences, both of which were topped with rolls of concertina wire. Within the fences were barracks and buildings that had to be ammo and supply depots. Plenty of vehicles—rows of T-10 heavy tanks, T-54/55 main battle tanks, reconnaissance vehicles, BTR ar-

[1]. Committee on Overhead Reconnaissance.

mored cars, BTR carriers, supply trucks, APCs and command vehicles.

Fudge! Look at all those damned guns! There were rows and rows of self-propelled artillery, such as 152mm self-propelled guns, 122mm SP howitzers, 180mm S-23 field guns, 152mm D-20s, 122 D-30s and hundreds of 100mm T-12 and 85mm D-44s and SD-44 antitank guns.

"Look at all that steel!" whispered Quinlan tightly. "Only a man with the mind of a President Carter would say that the Soviets weren't preparing for an invasion of Pakistan!"

In spite of the seriousness of the situation, Camellion found himself almost smiling over Mad Mike's remark, then his face became grim. *Well, Carter was a worker. He put in a twelve-hour day. It's a good thing he didn't work fifteen or sixteen hours a day. He would have really wrecked the country!*

There was an airfield below, south of the Spetsnaz base. Unfenced, it had long runways, more than ample to accomodate the Ilyushin IL-76 (Candid) and the even larger IL-83.

There were plenty of choppers—Mi-8s, Mi-14s, Mi-6s and even a few Mi-10s—giant choppers designed to carry outside loads beneath, rather than in, the fuselage (NATO designation: Harke).

Willy Bruckner whispered, "There's no way that the Pakistanis will get within twenty kilometers of that base. To even think of attacking those swine below is madness."

The Death Merchant, more than anxious to get to Sirzihil and contact Grojean on the AN/URC 101 Satcom transceiver, lowered his binoculars. Covert acts were always an implementation of a specific foreign policy, but Bruckner had slammed the hammerhead squarely on the nail. What was needed, if any attack on the base was to succeed, was planes. *Strike bombers and ten gunship choppers, plus troop carriers. We don't even have a Piper Cub!* "Lets get out of here before we get our Christmases canceled," Camellion said. "We've seen enough."

"Too much, if you ask me," muttered Quinlan.

Carefully they started to retrace the route, once more going around groups of sleeping Afghans. They were halfway back to their own *ti'rusis* when they heard helicopters approaching from the west, the *thub-thub-thubs* of rotors growing louder with each second.

"Those pig-farmer birds are headed straight toward us!" Quinlan said grimly.

CHAPTER TWELVE

It was somewhat more than ironic that when the Death Merchant was getting a glimmer of an idea of how the Russian base could be attacked successfully, the *thub-thub-thub* of enemy rotors made him think of something else: survival!

"Down!" he snapped in a hoarse whisper. "Get under anything—rocks, whatever you can find."

At the time, the group was under cloudy sky in an area filled with huge outcroppings of stratified rock, some with long flanges that could conceal a man. A geologist would have called the region "a wave-cut terrace that had undergone shearing." Either the mountaintops had been raised, scores of millions of years ago, or the sea level had sunk.

With only seconds to spare, the Death Merchant and the other men managed to squeeze under a crooked shelf, the Peppermint Kid first pushing down the antenna of PISS while calling the Spetsnaz a "bunch of bloody vodka-drinking grandmother fuckers!"

Just in time! An Mi-6 Hook troop-carrying chopper roared over, heading east, the sound of its giant rotor thunderous. Behind it, but at a much slower pace, came an Mi-8, only a hundred feet above the ground, its blinding searchlight moving slowly back and forth.

"Those pig-farmer sons of bitches!" snarled Mike Quinlan, who had squeezed himself in next to the Death Merchant. "They know! They're searching!"

"Listen!" hissed Camellion. "There are more of them."

As the Mi-6 and Mi-8 choppers headed east, the Death Merchant and his men could hear the rotors of three more birds—and these were revving down, landing, to the west.

"They have to be coming down in that small area around 150

meters from here," Quinlan said coolly. "There isn't any other place they could land."

The plan of the Spetsnaz was clear in the minds of Camellion and Quinlan, as well as Willy Bruckner and the Peppermint Kid. Even the four Pathans could deduce that one Hook and the gunship would land on the east end of the mountains while the second Hook troop carrier and its escort of two Mi-8s would sit down on the west end. Two separate forces—fifty Spetsnaz at each end, if each Hook was carrying a full load of men—that could approach from each end and close the trap in the middle. Was it a general sweep . . . *with us here at the wrong time, or is it possible they are after us in particular?*

Since the Death Merchant and his men were far closer to the west end, it was the Russian troops from the west they would have to deal with first. Eight against fifty! *Now is the time to say, "Mercy, Mercy, Mother Percy!"*

He nudged Quinlan in the back. "Move out. I've an idea that might work. Tell Willy and the Kid and the Paks to get rid of their hats and heavy coats. We'll carry nothing but weapons and ammo, plus PISS and the two Cyclops."

"I'll bet the pig farmers grabbed Pushko-Mialat and made him talk," Quinlan said coolly, edging out from underneath the ledge. "We'll probably never know." He didn't bother to ask Camellion about his idea. There wasn't time. Anyhow, he suspected what Camellion had in mind. Total escape was possibly only by flying.

It took only a few minutes for the men to remove their *chudkis* and *kobasas* and quickly pull magazines of spare ammo and take loose pistol and revolver ammunition from leather compartments in their *ti'rusis*.

The Death Merchant and Quinlan, already wearing NVDs over their faces, had more than their Bren Tens and Glock autopistols in the way of sidearms. They also had two AWC suppressed Ruger RST-4 .22-caliber assassination pistols.[1]

[1]. Suppressor and "silencer" are one and the same. Silencer is actually a British term—the blokes called automobile *mufflers* "silencers" in Britain. It's the Americans who came up with "Suppressor."

Silencers work because of metal baffels and "wipes," round rubber or plastic material. Silencers do wear out. Rubber wipes are good for only 50 to 250 rounds. Aluminum baffels are subject to erosion, a problem that is rapidly being solved by the use of stainless-steel.

Suppressors/silencers are never totally silent, although a lab-built special assassination weapon—for example the AWC Ruger RST-4—can be made so quiet that the shot cannot be heard in the next room with the door closed or, if the door is open, during conversation. Factory-built military silencers will erase only half the report.

"I say, those two silenced Rugers should give us a bit of an edge," O'Malley whispered. With Bruckner, he began creeping after Quinlan and Camellion. The Pathans followed, all four exhibiting the calm efficiency of men who had been under fire. However, the four were confused over Camellion's order to shoot ("if and when you have to shoot!") the Russian dogs in the head or below the belt.

"They will be wearing soft body armor,"[2] he had said.

Well, then, how did Kir Camellion and Kir Quinlan expect their little bullets from their little make-no-sound pistols to find the stinking flesh of those killers of infants from the north? *Chawdup!* The Pathans felt that Camellion and Quinlan and the other two knew what they were doing. They were brave and resourceful men.

Scanning every rock, Camellion led the way north. He wasn't particularly worried. This present mess was like cancer: either they would live or they would die. Time for action. *Let me see . . .* There had only been a single camp of Afghans west of where he and his men had been when the two Soviet choppers had roared over. That camp was now between him and his bunch and where the three Soviet choppers had put down. *We'll know when the Russians reach them when we hear the firing. The Spetsnaz can't know precisely who we are, so they'll kill everyone in sight. The Afghans will fight back!*

There could be more Afghans to the north. He estimated that it was 1500 feet to the north rim of the mountains, and there was no way of knowing how many Afghans had been sleeping between the rim and where his force was now. The ear-smashing racket of the "birds-without-wings" had most certainly awakened all the Afghans in the mountains and all of them would first hide and await developments, then fight it out. The only thing that Camellion could do was to depend on NVDs and the "magic ear" to warn him of any Afghans to the north. Against him and his group was that he didn't want any of his people firing weapons at any Afghans, who wouldn't take time to inquire who they were. The Afghans would see the two NVDs and instantly deduce *that we're either Russians in disguise or turncoat Afghans. Damn fudge three times over!*

And he knew that if he and his men did have to knock off some Afghans, the Spetsnaz wouldn't be fooled. They knew how

[2]. Cloth material as opposed to metal—hard armor.

long it would take their men from the east end to move west and kill everyone in their path. Should the west-end Spetsnaz hear firing too close to them and "off schedule," they could reason why and, very possibly, head northeast and make escape impossible.

It happened. Camellion heard low voices coming through the earphone of PISS. He got down on one knee, motioned for the others to get down and whispered to Mad Mike, "Give your NVD to Willy or the Kid and get back with Talequn and his boys—and if you want to know why, it's too keep you safe. You can fly a chopper better than I can."

In spite of being as close to hell as he wanted to get, Quinlan wanted to laugh. "You can say that again. I'd rather face the whole Red Army than fly out of here with you at the controls of a chopper. Man, you could scare even God!"

"And send i-Nan up here to decipher what I'm picking up," Camellion said, more than a little amused. It was the truth. He did fly a chopper the way myopic old ladies drive cars.

Shortly, Nemattulah i-Nan had shoved in the earphone and, an expression of amazement on his face, was whispering, "They are moving to the east. One man is saying that it might be possible to escape the Russians. Another man does not think so. He is saying that he thinks they will all die, all the men and all the women. A third man is saying that Allah wants them to kill as many of the unbelievers as can be done. Another man is now saying that the women will also fight the devils from the north. They too will be in heaven in a very short time. I think it is safe for us to proceed."

The Death Merchant took the earphone from i-Nan and did some hard listening on PISS. There wasn't any direction finder on the "magic ear," and he could only judge distance by the volume of the voices. The volume control was automatic: the closer the subjects, the louder the voices. Camellion decided that i-Nan had been right. The voices were receding toward the east.

The group moved over terrain as cut up as a battlefield, around and over rocks that had been ancient when human beings were still more ape than man. There wasn't any moon and vision was limited to ten feet at the most, except for Camellion and Bruckner. Wearing NVDs, they had unlimited "twilight" vision.

Moving in pairs, they heard automatic weapons firing from the southwest, almost fifteen minutes after they had first detected the sounds of the five Soviet helicopters. The roaring of AKMs and

AKRs and other weapons was proof that the Spetsnaz had caught up with the Afghans in the single camp to the west. Camellion sensed that the Afghans must have deliberately waited for the Russians, feeling that indefinite flight was impossible. How else could the Spetsnaz have found the Afghans so rapidly?

Either way, the Death Merchant and his men—not 300 feet from the north sides of the mountains—had gained time. Even if the Russians to the west hadn't been momentarily halted by the Afghans, the pig farmers would have proceeded very slowly. They had to. A Hook could carry only fifty fight men, plus the crew of three. Therefore, only fifty men could cover the width of the mountains, a difficult task even with Chonna infrared viewers. From north to south the distance of the width varied from 1000 to 2000 feet. Each ivan would have to have a lot of space between himself and his nearest "comrade." Then again, maybe not. *Since I know the danger of a force spread thin, the Spetsnaz know the danger of a force spread too thin.*

By the time they reached the edge of the north side and were only a long spit from the rim, they heard more firing, only this time from the east—faintly, over a mile away. And above the snarling of SMGs and ARs there was another sound everyone dreaded: the increasingly loud *thub-thub-thub* of a Mi-8 gunship—the same gun chopper that had passed over and had flown east. The bird was now returning.

"*Donnerwetter nochmal!*" snarled Bruckner. "We will all be dead men if that swine flies over us and uses his searchlight. Look around. Nothing but chimney rocks. Nothing to hide under."

Jaiiah Talequn had hurried up to the Death Merchant. "Kir Camellion, why do we not go down the north side of these mountains? With the see-in-the-dark thing, it—"

"No way, it wouldn't work," Camellion said. "I don't intend for us to die. We're going to grab several of the birds-without-wings and fly off these mountains right back to Pakistan—or die trying!"

Talequn's eyes widened with anticipation. He had always wanted to ride in a bird-without-wings.

Quinlan gave Camellion an odd look, then said to a delighted Talequn, "Where would we go, even if we succeeded in climbing down to the flatlands?"

All of them soon saw why a climb-down would have resulted in certain annihilation. The Mi-8 Hind-D did not fly over. It didn't even come in their direction. It did center itself over the northside slopes and go from port to starboard as it moved slowly west, its searchlight probing.

The Hind found what it was seeking, its searchlight trapping a frantic group of Afghans seeking escape down the north slopes.

BRRRRRrrrrrrrrrreeerrrr. The electric four-barrel gatling in its nose roared, ending the hopes and dreams of the Afghans.

"See what we meant," Quinlan said. He looked at Camellion and spoke in German. "You told him 'several' choppers. Another thing, who's to say the three gunships won't knock us out of the sky?"

"Oh, didn't I tell you?" Camellion said with mock innocence. "You're going to fly the Hook. I'll fly one of the Hinds. The Kid can ride shotgun."

"A gunship could hold four men," Quinlan said evenly. "I was thinking—"

"I know what you were thinking, Mike. But we're not leaving the Paks. We're not leaving any of our people behind. As for the two other Hinds blasting us, we take our chances."

"I always take care of my people," Quinlan said offensively, emphasizing the *my*, his voice icy. "These Paks are expendable."

The Death Merchant's voice was frigid. "I'm in charge, Mike. We're going to do it my way, or you can take Willy and the Kid and thumb a ride. But we are not going to abandon deliberately people who risked their lives for us. That's final. Period. *Kaput!*"

Sensing that an argument was developing between Camellion and Quinlan, Bruckner, who respected and admired both his *Standartenführer* and the Death Merchant, stepped in. "We might all die before we reach the chopper to the west. Let's follow the plan and see what happens."

Quinlan gave Camellion a dirty look and remained silent.

The plan was to move west along the rim and then angle in toward the southwest, a route that would take them to the area where the three choppers had landed. By the time they reached the three Soviet birds-without-wings, the Spetsnaz that had come from the west would be far to the east, and the Russians who had landed on the east end of the mountains would still be far enough away.

Camellion and his men lost several points after they had moved an estimated 280 feet west. One of the Hinds to the west had lifted off and was patrolling the south slopes. In the meanwhile, the other Mi-8 had finished its patrol of the north side and was searching for victims on the east slope. Evidently, the Mi-8 that had been parked to the west was supposed to survey the west slopes.

More firing far to the east!

Blam-blam-blam-blam. A series of grenades exploded close by, 200 feet *behind* the Death Merchant and his group. The Russians from the west had passed them. The way to the choppers was open.

Nonetheless, Camellion and his bunch took each step with extreme caution. The pig farmers had a lot in common with high blood pressure: what you didn't know about it could kill you.

One hundred feet. Two hundred feet. Then 350 feet. And that's when the Death Merchant heard voices on PISS, the "magic ear." He put out a hand and stopped Bruckner. "The pig boys are coming this way. Pass the word. Everyone down and stay down."

Bruckner, a Galil AR in his left hand and the suppressed Ruger RST-4 assassination pistol in his right hand, turned quickly to O'Malley behind him.

At the time, the area in which the force found itself was not ideal for concealment, boulders being too small. It stood to reason that the Russians would be carrying night-viewing devices.

Camellion, who spoke and wrote Russian like a native, soon heard what the two men were saying. One was telling his companion to move more slowly "or we'll be shipped home in a box."

"If we go any slower, we'll be crawling. What we are doing is foolish. There is no one this far to the north. And why should we kill these innocent people? They are not a threat to our base."

"Careful, Oleg," said the other man. "Don't let anyone hear you talking like that, or it will go into your record."

Ahhhh . . . a pig farmer with a sense of decency. You're still a corpse.

"They're definitely coming our way—straight at us," Camellion whispered to Bruckner, "a bit to our right. There are only two of them. You zap the one on the left."

It took four more minutes for the two Russians to come close enough for Bruckner and the Death Merchant to see them clearly through the night vision devices strapped over their faces. The two Spetsnaz wore heavy black uniforms and equipment belts, with pouches that resembled American LC-2s. Equipment suspenders, spare ammo magazines on one side of the belt, holstered Vitmorkin machine pistols on the other side. Black ballistic helmets. Both men carried AKR Shinkov submachine guns. The Russian on the left was also carrying a handheld Chonna infrared night-sight scope. Every now and then he would hold it up and survey the entire region, forward and flanks

"Let 'em have it once they're within thirty meters," Camellion whispered. "Any closer and they might see us."

The two Russians crept closer, creeping slowly to their own executions and not knowing it.

Sssstt. Sssstt. Camellion and Bruckner fired. The man to the Death Merchant's right stopped, dropped his AKR assault rifle and toppled backward like a fallen tree. He lay there on his back, his body jerking. The Death Merchant's .22 bullet had caught him just below the nose, bored through the roof of his mouth and cut out through the back of his neck. Oleg Shipkinov was choking to death on his own blood.

The other Spetsnaz had stopped Bruckner's bullet with his throat. He spun to the ground like a giant top, blood spurting from his mouth.

"Tell the men we got 'em," Camellion said to Bruckner. "I'll go on ahead and make sure those two are coldcuts. Watch for my signal."

Camellion shoved the silenced Ruger into a makeshift holster underneath his *toba* jacket. On the run he wouldn't have time to aim the Ruger. Should he meet more ruskies, he wanted something with a lot of firepower, such as the Israeli Galil assault rifle.

The Galil in his hands, ready to fire, he got up, hurried over to the two bodies, saw that what had been men were now corpses, turned and motioned with a hand to Bruckner. He was pulling the Vitmorkin machine pistols from the holsters of the dead men by the time the others reached him.

"Get those ammo pouches with spare Vitmorkin and AKR magazines," he ordered. "We have got to make tracks."

Making sure that the weapons were on safe, Camellion reached up and handed the two Vitmorkins to Jaiiah Talequn and Jonhor Gonsuf. "They work like regular pistols. Don't move the firing levers. I've set both pistols to fire three-round bursts. On full automatics, you'd be out of ammo in a few seconds." He handed them each a pouch containing four magazines. Eighteen 9mm cartridges were in each clip.

The Peppermint Kid handed the AKR submachine guns to Biho Tozmo'qu and Nemattulah i-Nan. "I'll tell you chaps how—"

"We know how to use these fine weapons," Tozmo'qu said with a broad grin. "They work the same as the old AK-47s. We have traded AK-47s and AKRs with the Afghans."

Quinlan held up a Ladko[3] transceiver he had pulled from one dead man's equipment belt. "You never know, Camellion. This walkie-talkie might come in handy."

The Death Merchant, who had already taken a Ladko walkie-talkie from the other corpse, got to his feet and handed the Chonna NVD to Jonhor Gonsuf, the Pathan closest to him. "I've turned it on," he said to the delighted Gonsuf. "All you have to do is look through it. Darkness will be daylight."

Quinlan stood up and looked at Camellion, who was preparing to move out. "Something is not kosher. What were these two jokers doing here? By this time, the ivans who landed to the west should be half a mile, if not more, east of us."

"I know," Camellion said softly. "To me, it's evidence that the Spetsnaz are not killing indiscriminately. Yeah, they're killing anything that moves, but for a reason. They're after us. They know that with all the Afghans up here, there's little chance of taking us alive. They're doing the next best thing—killing everyone in sight. Hear all that gunfire to the east? It's coming from both groups, the ones from the east and the west. As for these two dead pig farmers! It only proves that the enemy is not spread out in a line as we thought. They must be moving in pairs and maybe in little groups. There isn't any other answer."

O'Malley stroked his chin. "Why should the Russians choose such bloody rotten tactics? Or maybe they have little Dutch boys in their brains who let the water go?"

"What did you mean by *evidence* that the ivans are after us?" demanded Quinlan. "I fail to see the connection."

"Ask yourself, Mike, why didn't the Russians bring more men up here? They didn't because they couldn't land enough Hook carriers on these mountains. The space to put down on is very limited. Another factor is that it's only a short distance from the west end to the Spetsnaz base. They could have sent 700 men, or a thousand, from the base. All they would have had to do is climb the west-side slope. The Russian command at the base didn't because they assumed we'd be watching through night-

[3]. A lot of Red Army communications has been stolen from American industry. The Ladko D-6 walkie-talkie is almost an exact copy of the RCA UHF or VHF Tactec series.

sight scopes and see the men approaching. The kind of operation they mounted was the best they could do on short notice."

"Short notice?" from a confused Bruckner.

"Either by accident or design, the Russians somehow got their hands on Shotit Pushko-Mialat," Camellion said coldly.

"They could not seize him!" Biho Tozmo'qu said angrily. "He would kill himself. He would never let himself become a prisoner of the devils from the north."

"Maybe he didn't have a choice," Camellion said. "They could have gotten to him from behind. I don't think they trapped him until late this afternoon or this evening, or they would have had time to have Spetsnaz waiting for us up here, or stationed at the various trails on the south slopes."

"Let's assume you're right." Quinlan sounded calculating. "If you are, there's no way of knowing how many Russian sons of bitches are to the east and the west of us—behind us and in front of us—right?"

"Dimo shuma la Allah," murmured Nemattulah i-Nan. "It is in the hands of Allah."

He might be right! "We'll find out soon enough," Camellion said in reply to Quinlan.

They found out twelve minutes later. They were moving over potholes and tangled masses of large rocks that had once been part of a monadhock. It was in this area that the Death Merchant heard voices on PISS, a lot of voices.

"I can't be sure," he whispered to Bruckner. "It's more than half a dozen men, southwest of us, and coming our way." The thought stabbed at him. Was it possible that there had been Spetsnaz in the two Russian trucks that passed them on the road? *Yeah! And virgin wool comes from ugly sheep!* What's the difference? The grim reality was that there definitely were Russians close by.

Damn the PISS. *Magic, huh? Only by half.* The trouble with PISS was that it only amplified voices. Directions, ditto. You had to listen to the intensity of the voices to know whether the enemy was coming at you or moving in a direction from you. Good enough. But it was a flaw. You could have a half-dozen groups coming at you from all directions, and yet remain confused. With only one enemy group, an operator would have little difficulty. With more than one group—difficulty, lots of it.

Behind rocks almost large enough to conceal them, Camellion

and his men waited, the voices coming though PISS growing stronger, a constant babble, yet the Death Merchant detected a strange quality to the sounds, as if they were coming from every direction.

He had first heards the voices and had assumed that the Russians were ahead of him. Accordingly, he had passed the word and the men were on watch. Presently, listening to more gunfire far to the east and one of the gunships moving back and forth over the west slopes, he and Bruckner spotted the first enemy, fifty feet in front of them. Then a second and a third. Camellion and Bruckner waited, not wanting to fire their silenced Rugers until they knew how many of the Russians were out front.

Jonhor Gonsuf, looking through the Chonna night viewer, saw the Russians, who had now grown to four. All the men, save Gonsuf, were concentrating on the southwest. For him, the Chonna was a marvelous new toy, a miracle toy. Why it could turn night into day!

Gonsuf was staring all around the area. He even turned around to scan the area behind him. He was turning around to stare at the Russians approaching from the southeast when he saw five of them—only twenty-five feet to the *northeast*. Two of them were holding Chonna scopes to their faces and staring directly at him.

The need for caution was over. ''Russian dogs! To our right!'' yelled Gonsuf, so excited that he had shouted the warning in the Pak language. It didn't matter. Luck had dropped to a pocketful of poor and a heartful of empty.

Gonsuf dropped the Chonna scope and reached for his MAT SMG, but it was too late. Three of the Spetsnaz opened fire with AKR submachine guns, a hail of 5.45 × 39-mm full metal-jacket projectiles raining all over Gonsuf and Biho Tozmo'qu, who was trying to swing his AKR to the right. Three slugs turned Gonsuf's face into bloody mush. More tore into his chest and left arm, tearing him apart with such speed that the echo of his warning words was still tumbling over in the tunnel of his throat.

Two 5.45mm slugs tore off Biho Tozmo'qu's right hand as one hit the underside of the short barrel of the AKR and slammed the weapon back. Four more made-in-Russia slugs exploded his skull and made bits of flesh and pieces of bone fly outward, along with tiny parts of his *toba* as slugs butchered his chest and shoulders.

Due to the rocks, the five Russians to the northeast could not see the other six men. Thinking that they had only discovered two Afghans, they charged ahead, reacting almost automatically. As Spestnaz, all their instincts were geared to take the offensive, never the defensive. They soon found out there were more than two "Afghans"! They detected the Death Merchant and Willy Bruckner at the same instant that the comrades to the northeast opened fire and wasted Jonhor Gonsuf and Biho Tozmo'qu.

Old pros that they were, Camellion and Bruckner jerked back when they heard the firing, jerked back, went flat, shoved their Rugers into holsters and reached for their Galil assault rifles. To their left, Mike Quinlan and the Peppermint Kid were safe for the moment, protected by rocks as long as they remained perfectly prone. They too prepared to fire, waiting for lag time on the part of the Russians.

It was Jaiiah Talequn and Nemattulah i-Nan who let emotion overrule common sense; they did not have the experience of the other four, whose entire lives were a chess game with the Cosmic Lord of Death. Enraged, Talequn and i-Nan rolled to their left, reared up and swung their weapons to the northeast.

Six automatic weapons roared, the four AKRs of the Russians to the southwest and the AKR of i-Nan and the MAT SMG of Talequn.

Projectiles popped the rocks in front of the Death Merchant and the three Thunderbolt Unit Omega mercs, the whines and shrieks of ricochets a riot of sound that tore at reason and stabbed at sanity. It was as close to sitting in the lap of the Cosmic Lord of Death as Camellion and the three others wanted to come. Five slugs ripped silently over Camellion's back, one tearing a cut to the depth of fifteen millimeters in the heel of his boot. Enemy slugs also passed close to Quinlan and his two men. Bruckner let out a rapid stream of German expletives when a cloud of granite chips stung him in the face.

Jaiiah Talequn and Nemattulah might have killed all five Russians charging from the northeast if the pig farmers racing in from the southwest hadn't fired at the same time. Talequn and i-Nan dusted off two of the surprised five with long bursts that performed an autopsy on the two Spetsnaz. Before the remaining and astonished three Russians could fire, i-Nan was stone dead, killed by four slugs from the other group of five Spetsnaz, and Talequn was wounded.

Oddly enough, only one 5.45mm projectile had found Talequn, and it had caused only a deep flesh wound in his right shoulder, the FMJ slug fracturing the end of the humerus in its passage.

Talequn cried out in pain, jerked, let the SMG fall from his hands and dropped with the dead i-Nan. With his shoulderbone cracked, he was out of action, his right arm as useless as sunglasses on an oyster.

The three other Spetsnaz from the northeast had no choice but to contain the attack. By now they were so close to the Death Merchant and his whittled-down force that they couldn't have retreated if they had wanted to.

It was darkness and the two NVDs, worn by Camellion and Bruckner, that prevented the Death Merchant and his four men from being slug-cut to bloody pieces. To the northeast, the two pig farmers with the handheld Chonna night-sight instruments had not hooked the devices to their equipment belts. They had only lowered the scopes and, with drawn Vitmorkin machine pistols, charged with Pavel Toompu, the third man still alive.

To the southwest, the ivan with the Chonna nightscope had hooked the instrument to his equipment belt and was getting to his feet when Camellion, sensing lag time in his favor, reared up and got off a long burst with his Galil, moving the assault rifle from right to left. Only an eyeblink behind him, Bruckner fired from a prone position on the ground, his Galil spitting out a dozen 5.56mm slugs.

Ten feet away from Camellion and Bruckner, Dmitri Pozhidayev gave a short, choked scream and dropped, six of Camellion's slugs having chopped him across the waist. Viacheslav, the goof with the Chonna scope, didn't make a sound as he fell sideways to the granite. Camellion's slugs had torn away his face and butchered his brain before he could even feel pain. It was the same with Yuri Utemov. Bruckner's projectiles had torn a hole in his chest the size of a baseball, and what was left of his heart wouldn't have been recognizable except to an experienced medical examiner.

Darkness now came to the aid of Camellion and his four men. Only he and Bruckner could see clearly in the "twilight." Quinlan and O'Malley couldn't. Neither could Jaiiah Talequn, who was lying flat and awkwardly trying to pull his .38 British Enfield Mark I revolver from its holster. The remaining five pig farmers were also severely limited by the darkness—the two who had been coming in from the southwest and the three from the northeast. All five were now right smack in the middle of Camellion and his men. Three of the Russians and Camellion and his men were weighed down with still another disadvantage—all seven were using assault rifles—a hindrance in an eyeball-to-eyeball firefight. Only Anatol Prikhodda and Vadim Liktov, the two Spetsnaz with the Vitmorkin machine pistols had an advantage. Unfortunately, the two Russian yahoos didn't have the experience to know that staying alive, under such conditions, was a craft that had to be learned.

Vadim Liktov—so close to Mad Mike Quinlan that if he had taken five more long steps he could have kissed him—opened fire with his Vitmorkin. Having anticipating this, Quinlan jerked to one side and cut loose with his Galil, the muzzle of the AR only several feet from Liktov's lower chest. Liktov's three 9mm slugs sliced by Quinlan, the third bullet leaving a long bloody line on his left rib cage. By then it was too late for Liktov, who did not have time to realign his machine pistol and was learning—the hard way—that when you tango with the Devil, it is wise to know the tunes in advance. Quinlan's burst of slugs knocked him backward, with his chest looking as though it had been hit by a buzz saw with very dull teeth, some of the blood even splattering over Mad Mike, who was still having better luck than one James Victorio O'Malley.

The Peppermint Kid came so close to Buying the Farm, he almost heard angels singing. He was turning to meet the charge of Pavel Toompu, who had chosen to attack the Kid because he was the closest to him. Concurrently with Toompu's charge, the big Anatol Prikhodda began to zero in on O'Malley with his Vitmorkin. O'Malley, seeing the move, did his best to twist away as he was swinging to his right to meet Toompu's attack. He didn't twist far enough. Forgetting to set the firing lever of his Vitmorkin to three-round bursts, Prikhodda pulled the trigger, the weapon firing on full automatic, eighteen 9mm round-nosed projectiles spitting out of the hot muzzle. Five ripped through the Kid's clothing at the hip. Four didn't count. One did. It tore through the flesh at a depth of a shave less than half an inch. Only a bit more and the slug would have scraped the top of the pelvic bone. The pain wasn't agonizing any more than the wound was life threatening; however, it did throw the Peppermint Kid off balance and, if only momentarily, leave him defenseless against Pavel Toompu, who was moving the barrel of his AKR toward the Kid, his finger only a micro-instant away from squeezing the trigger. It was the last second of Toompu's life and the last few moments in the twenty-six years of Anatol Prikhodda, who suddenly found himself with an empty machine pistol.

Frantically—he could see Quinlan's AKR coming toward him—he attempted to reach out, grab the forward end of the AKR and push the deadly muzzle away from him. He was too late with too little. Those seconds were the difference between life and death, life for Quinlan and the Peppermint Kid, death for the two Russians.

At the same time that Vlad Zhikin let out an agonized howl, Quinlan executed Prikhodda with six Galil slugs that made six holes in the pig farmer's chest, lungs and back and sent him into that country whose inhabitants have no memories. Quinlan, however, didn't have time to save O'Malley. He didn't have to.

There was the loud report of a single shot close to the ground. Pavel Toompu's mouth opened and his eyes went wide; then his eyes closed. The empty Vitmorkin slid from his hands, his knees folded and he started to go down to the granite.

Jaiiah Talequn had shot Toompu with his Enfield revolver. The lead bullet had hit the Russian low in the gut, zipped through his lower intestine, moved upward and come within an inch of going out his back. His hands pressed to his stomach, Toompu fell forward, almost crashing into O'Malley who shoved the dying man to one side.

Vlad Zhikin and Georgi Guchin, the last two Spetsnaz alive, had made the always fatal mistake of attacking the Death Merchant and Willy Bruckner. Doing his best to thrust the muzzle of his AKR into Camellion's stomach, Zhikin was confident that he would make short work of the enemy with the strange device over his face. Suddenly, he found Camellion expertly blocking the thrust with his Galil and shoving the AKR to one side. The Russian didn't have time to become worried. The Death Merchant let him have a lightning-fast snap kick in the scrotum. A world of pain and hurt exploded in Zhikin, his shriek automatic. Total blackness was dropping over his consciousness as Camellion put three Galil projectiles into his body.

Georgi Guchin was next to get a surprise. Bruckner did not attempt to push away the Russian's assault rifle with his Galil. He merely let it fall from his hands, sticking out his left foot to break its fall, grabbed Guchin's AKR with both hands and jerked the weapon from the now-worried Russian who tried to knee him in the groin. He failed. Bruckner sidestepped, slammed him across the jaw with the butt of the weapon, then jabbed him in the solar plexus with the barrel. Even more contemptuous of the Russians than the Death Merchant, Bruckner didn't intend to waste ammunition on the *Schweinerei*. As the tormented Russian gagged and doubled over from the blow to his solar plexus, Bruckner tripped him, slammed him in the right kidney with a left elbow stab and knocked the pig farmer to the ground, the dazed man falling on his face. Moving very fast, Bruckner didn't give him time to even partially recover his senses. He jumped on Guchin's back with both feet, all 240 pounds of him, his heels crashing into the lower part of the man's spine. There was a snapping sound, as though a twig had been broken. Guchin shuddered and lay still. He was dead, his back broken, the spinal cord severed.

A pleased Burckner looked at the Death Merchant, who was studying the entire area over which silence now reigned, except for the low rustling of the wind. It was the stillness that made the signal beep of the Ladko on Vadim Liktov's belt appear to be extra loud. Camellion tore across the area, almost tripping over a pothole. Reaching the corpse of Liktov, he pulled the Ladko walkie-talkie from its leather holder, turned it on and said excitedly in the Russian language, "There were maybe twenty of them. It was difficult to tell. We have killed half of the savages. The rest have retreated. They're fleeing toward the southeast."

A voice, speaking Russian, popped out of the Ladko. "Did you notice any white men among the Afghans?"

"None that we could see. We were too busy. We didn't suffer any casualties." Camellion hoped that whoever had contacted the Spetsnaz group would not ask his name. *And have I said the wrong thing. Suppose there was some kind of built-in code?*

Apparently, whoever the Russian was, he was satisfied. He wished him good luck and signed off.

The Death Merchant shut off the walkie-talkie, tossed it down on the corpse of its former owner and translated the conversation for the other men. Quinlan, Bruckner and O'Malley had picked up their Galil assault rifles, and Jaiiah Talequn, holding his Enfield revolver in his left hand, had gotten to his feet.

"We had better hope that whoever it was believed you," Quinlan said to Camellion. "We have to be within 500 feet of those three choppers. There's already one gunship patrolling the west side of these mountains. If that second gunship takes off . . ."

"It was Gonsuf who saved our lives," O'Malley said soberly, feeling a trickle of blood running down the outside of his right leg and the right side of his pants soggy with blood. "If he 'adn't seen those blighters to the right of us, they might 'ave wasted us, and if Jaiiah 'adn't shot that one bloody Russian, the son of a bitch would 'ave killed me." He regarded Talequn solemnly. "I thank you, my blood-brother, and I'm sorry your friends were not as lucky as I was."

"And as fortunate as myself, Kir O'Malley," Talequn said stoically. "Our lives are in the hands of Allah. *La ilah illa Allah.*"

As usual, Mad Mike Quinlan was all business. After learning from O'Malley that his hip wound was only "bloody but not serious" and that Talequn could use his left hand and arm but not his right arm, he turned to the Death Merchant, who was listening in on PISS, turning one way and then another. The whispers were the loudest when he was facing the southwest and, hunched over.

"We're going to have to move fast, Richard," Quinlan said. "Even if every pig farmer is moving southeast, they're going to get wise to the trick, sooner or later—probably sooner. You know those three choppers will be protected. There—"

"Two birds on the ground," Camellion said. "From the sound of the rotor we're hearing, one of the gunships is moving back and forth over the west slopes."

Quinlan refused to become irritated. "There'll be guards around the entire perimeter."

"I know. Here's how we'll play it."

It was easy to believe that there was an Allah and that He draped His protection over the Death Merchant and his pathetic squad of four. Even Camellion was privately amazed that they were able to get within 110 feet of the southwest perimeter of the flat area where the three Soviet helicopters had put down. Flat on their bellies, they could see everything, that is, Camellion and Bruckner could; they were wearing NVDs. And so could Quinlan, O'Malley and Talequn; they were using handheld Chonnas taken from the dead Spetsnaz.

There was something very quiet, yet very deadly, about what they saw. The Mi-6 Hook troop transport was sitting there like a large gray spider with its legs folded underneath its body. Its crew was kneeling on the ground to the starboard side of the craft. Evidently, they were playing some sort of game with dice, their light coming from a small battery-powered lantern.

One of the Mi-8 Hind-Ds was sixty to sixty-five feet southwest of the Hook, its crew of four standing in the dark by the side of the bird, drinking hot tea and smoking cigarettes. Camellion and his men could see the Spetsnaz, who, stationed around the perimeter, were guarding the two birds. Down on his haunches, the first guard was fifty feet to the northeast of the Hind-D. Another guard was to the south. Two more were to the east. Still another to the south and two to the north. The Death Merchant and his men could only see partially one of the Spetsnaz north of the two choppers, some of his body hidden by the tail rotor of the Hook.

"Mike, are you positive you can do it?" asked Camellion, his voice just above a whisper. "Hitting targets while looking through a nightscope you have to hold can be tricky."

Quinlan was clearly miffed. "If you think I can't, give me the Cyclops and you use a Chonna NVD to waste the crew by the gunship."

It required two hands to fire a Galil assault rifle or a AKR submachine gun. But a man could do the same job with only one hand if he used an RST-4 Ruger.

Camellion ignored Quinlan's insulted tone. "If I didn't think you could do it, I wouldn't have suggested it in the first place." He looked around him. Mad Mike held a Chonna night-sight scope in his left hand and a silenced Ruger in his right hand. Next to Quinlan was Jaiiah Talequn, ready to hand him the second Ruger if it were needed. Lying between Quinlan and Bruckner was O'Malley. He was the custodian of two fully loaded Galils. But it wasn't likely that Camellion and Bruckner would need the Galils any more than Mad Mike would need the second Ruger.

"Let me know when you're ready, Mike," Camellion said. "You too Willy." He wished that the crew of the Hind-D could have been scratched with the Galils. They couldn't. If the crew wasn't wearing soft body armory, the powerful 5.56mm slugs could go all the way through their bodies and harm the chopper. It was particularly risky since the crew was standing near the pilot control compartment.

"Let's kill the Russian bastards and fly the hell out of here," Quinlan whispered. "I'm going to catch a cold on these damned mountains."

"*Ja, lassen uns doch gehen,*" Bruckner said.

"On the count of five." The Death Merchant raised his Galil, saw that the dependable Bruckner was ready and that Quinlan had lifted his nightscope and Ruger. He began counting. Four seconds later, he came to "five" and squeezed the trigger of his Galil.

The Spetsnaz around the perimeter and the crew of the Mi-6 Hook all had the same chance for life—none! Hit in seconds by Camellion and Bruckner's slugs, they jerked, died and dropped. Only Bruckner and Quinlan has some difficulty—Bruckner with the joker half hidden by the tail rotor of the Hook. Willy solved the slight problem by shooting the man's legs out from under him, then exploding his skull with slugs after he fell.

Quinlan made his kills as expertly as a hawk swoops down and grabs a field mouse. *Zip-zip-zip-zip!* The four Russians fell like pins in a bowling alley and with the same speed. One man thrashed about but lay still after Quinlan put another .22 bullet into him. A second man, the pilot, managed to get to his hands and knees in an effort to raise himself. Quinlan placed two more slugs into his body, this time in the side of his head. This time the Russian stayed down.

"Reload these," Camellion said to O'Malley, and handed him the almost empty Galil as Bruckner placed his empty AR next to the Peppermint Kid. Picking up the fully loaded Galils, the Death Merchant and Bruckner started toward the clearing that had been turned into an instant morgue. Quinlan, who had pulled a Glock autopistol, was moving as rapidly—almost. He had to hold the Chonna scope in front of his eyes. Talequn followed, and soon O'Malley was heading west, a Galil in each hand.

Camellion and Bruckner were halfway to the gunship when they heard the second Hind-D. It had finished its last patrol over the west-end slopes and was coming in.

"Christ on a pink pony!" said Quinlan. Turning, he motioned frantically to O'Malley. "If the pilot spots his dead comrades, it's going to be worse for us than a dozen possums fighting over the same gum bush!"

"Get to the side of the gunship," Camellion ordered. "We still have time."

Camellion and his men had a slight advantage in that they could hear the chopper minutes before it could reach the clearing, the *thub-thub-thub* of its rotor growing louder.

By the time they reached the side of the Hind-D, they could see the other chopper. At an altitude of several hundred feet, it was moving in from the west. Camellion knew it would have to come down north of them because there wasn't room anywhere else. This was it: life or death. The odds were that the pilot and the rest of the crew would feel secure and not be looking for trouble, but if they spotted the corpses and the pilot took the bird up . . . *then our show goes off the road and closes forever*.

The gunship reached the clearing and began to descend, a hundred feet northwest of the Hook helicopter, its nose pointed straight north.

"We won't be able to hit the cockpit," said Quinlan in disgust. By then he was staring at the chopper through a Russian Chonna. He turned, reached out and took one of the Galils from O'Malley. He would have to fire blind. So would O'Malley.

"Willy, aim for the rotor hub," Camellion said. "There's too much armor plate around the engines."

"The hub is too small," Bruckner replied. "I take the engines; you fire at the hub."

The Death Merchant—he could see that the pods and auxiliary wings were empty of bombs and missiles—didn't answer. He knew he wouldn't be able to change Bruckner's mind on such short notice.

At sixty feet, the copilot spotted the corpses to the north and yelled at the pilot, who started to rev up. A second later, Camellion, Bruckner, Quinlan and O'Malley opened fire. The Hind-D didn't explode. It did go up another sixty-one feet and only then start to wobble and careen wildly to the northeast. Not a single one of Bruckner's projectile had been able to penetrate the Ynolskoy armor plate protecting the two Isotov TV-2-117-A turboshafts, and Quinlan's slugs had gone wild. So had O'Malley's, save two. But they also hit Ynolskoy armor plate.

Only seven of the Death Merchant's 5.56mm projectiles hit the hub. They stabbed into the friction dampers and the rotor bevel drive of the rotor's hub. There was a loud grinding sound, the same kind of tearing that a garbage disposal would make if someone dumped in a small sack of ball bearings.

Instant rotor decay. As the Hind-D shook and shuddered and began moving northeast, then north, finally northwest, Serge Mozikil, the pilot, tried feathering—increasing and decreasing the pitch of the blades in cycles as they turned. He couldn't. His efforts were useless. The helicopter was out of control.

The Death Merchant and his men didn't see the crash. They did hear the explosion when the Hind slammed onto the rocks of the north slopes and exploded.

"Allah is still protecting us," Jaiiah said emphatically.

"Maybe so," said Camellion. "But we did the shooting. Let's get in the chopper and grab sky."

"Why not?" said O'Malley. "I'm only waiting for something better to come along—like death!"

A Soviet Hind-D (originally designed as an air ambulance) is an awkward helicopter, even if it is one of the best gunships in the world. The rotor is naturally its highest point, followed by the two turboshafts in the center. In front of and below the two air intakes of the Isotovs is the first "hump," the first compartment. This is the main control center and belongs to the pilot and copilot. This compartment is reached by a door on the starboard side, the top half of the door forming the starboard side of the compartment. The second "hump" is in front of the pilot's compartment. This is the domain of the radioman/navigator and forward gunner who manually fires a 12.7mm gun.

There is a third door—several feet to the rear of the pilot compartment door. This door opens to the space forward and below the two free-turbine turboshafts, a small area easily accessible to mechanics. In flight, this area can also be reached by a "tunnel" from the pilot's compartment.

It was into this "dead" space that the Death Merchant had Jaiiah Talequn crawl, reassuring the Pathan that it was the best place available and that with his shattered shoulder, he would be in pain in the nose compartment. He could lie down on his good side in the dead space.

Bruckner and O'Malley climbed aboard via the pilot's compartment door and moved down to the radioman and gunner's places in the nose. Mad Mike Quinlan settled down in the pilot's seat and Camellion sat down next to him, watching the Thunderbird chief scan the control panel. Quinlan couldn't read the Russian lettering, but he had flown Hinds twice before, once in Africa and once in Syria, and was familiar with the controls and various dials and gauges.

Quinlan started the engines and began flipping switches. "Did you ever see so damned much ECM?"[4] he said to the Death Merchant. "Radar, all-weather monitoring and complete NV with broadview monitoring."

"How do I fire the gatling?" Camellion tapped a lighted Russian word on the panel. Over the word was the lettering,

4. Electronic countermeasures.

23mm ratio. "This must be the gatling ammo readout. It says 'full.' "

Watching the rotor tachometer, his hands on the throttle and cyclic controls, a look of triumph spread across Quinlan's face. "I was going to ask you the readout. It means the ammo-feed boxes for the gatling are full—and you don't fire the cannon. I do. We don't have time for a lesson."

"It makes sense about the ammo boxes being full," Camellion mused. "Almost none of the Afghans up here tried to escape on the west slopes, or else this bird never left the ground after it got here."

"Hold on. We're taking off."

The gunship soared up and to the southeast. In the nose compartment, Bruckner and O'Malley were very uncomfortable. O'Malley had always been afraid of airplanes (but wouldn't have admitted it even on his deathbed), and Bruckner had almost a phobia about heights. But only in an aircraft. On the ground, he could climb like a mountain goat and think nothing of it.

In the "dead space," Jaiiah Talequn prayed to Allah.

The Death Merchant and Mike Quinlan had a big edge on the rest of the Spetsnaz on the east end of the mountains. Although the other Russians to the east must have heard the Hind-D explode, they wouldn't know why. None of the west-end Spetsnaz had had time to radio a warning, and neither had the pilot or copilot of the destroyed gunship.

Mike Quinlan saw the remaining Hind when he was only a kilometer west of the area where the third gunship and the second Hook had put down. The Hind was to his port, several thousand feet away

"We have the son of a bitch," Quinlan said to Camellion. "I'm going to scatter him all over the sky. Then we'll go after the Hook."

"Why bother with it?" Camellion enjoyed the way Mike handled a chopper.

"Because I'm out to get every Russian I can," Quinlan said firmly. "This is one time I'm insisting. Don't argue."

The Death Merchant didn't, thinking that while Quinlan was a good man, he did have his faults. His extreme hatred of all Russians caused him to run serious risks on occasion.

Quinlan swung the bird to port and started to close in on the other gunship. The Russian pilot, thinking that Quinlan's Hind had also come to investigate the crash, did not suspect that all the milk of human kindness was about to curdle. By the time he and his copilot did begin to feel uneasy about the other gunship, it was far too late. Quinlan had him on the automatic sight and pressed the button.

Bbbrrrrrrrrrrrrrrr! The gatling-type electric cannon roared, a thousand 23mm projectiles raking the side of the enemy Hind, exploding the gunship into a ball of fire and smoke.

Quinlan swung back to the east and in only minutes was closing in on the area where the Hook sat defenseless and Spetsnaz were running frantically for cover. Only a few escaped.

The kill sweep required only one run, Quinlan then heading southeast by south. At 170 mph it would take less than a hour to reach Sirzihil. "If we can find Sirzihil," Camellion said. "These maps might help. I found them in the map compartment."

"What does the fuel guage read?"

"The tanks are half full."

"More than enough." Quinlan looked at the compass and altered his heading slightly. "All we have to do now is figure out how to land without the Paks using us for targets before they know who we are."

BOOK THREE

CHAPTER THIRTEEN

General Saha I'Zada's wife had once told him that he should be thankful for problems within the Pakistan security police. "My husband," she had said, "if problems within the Chanwiri-lu-Shabudar were less difficult, someone with less ability might have your position."

At the time, I'Zada had considered her remark amusing. Since then, he had changed his opinion, especially during the past week. His problems were mounting and becoming more complicated. Lieutenant Moukarim and his report weren't helping the situation.

"Lieutenant, you are positive that Lukriz Au-mumin didn't say anything of importance before he was murdered?" I'Zada leaned back in the Tripos Balans lounge chair and studied and young intelligence agent whose left arm was in a sling. He was very resourceful or he would not be alive.

Lieutenant General Yahya Si'Quetta said evenly, "Tell us again what happened, every detail."

"I can only repeat what I have said," Moukarim said, shifting about in his chair. "Lukriz Au-mumin didn't want to discuss any matters where he was living. He suggested that he and I and Hawaji—agent Gulaka—go to a teahouse. We were on the street, only a block from the teahouse when we were attacked from a passing car. Our attackers used pistols. Gulaka and Au-mumin were killed almost instantly. I was hit in the left arm. I escaped by dropping and rolling into a doorway. The car continued on its way."

"The three of you must have discussed matters on the way to

the teahouse," I'Zada said. "I'm sure you discussed more than the weather."

"Yes sir. It's like I told you, my general. Au-mumin said he could not understand how the four foreign agents could have escaped the trap set for them at the shrine of Abdul Bu-I-Zum. He also said he had heard that Chief Mirza-Khan was in Gubukil. We told him of the rumor that Banwad Girnayl had related to us. Au-mumin said he had not heard anything about the Russians flying across the border and attacking Chief Mirza-Khan's winter camp."

"You are positive that he didn't say anything about the various Pathan and Garukal clans being on the move—thousands of them?" said General I'Zada. He leaned forward and put his hands on the arms of the chair.

"No sir. He didn't. He didn't say anything about movement of any of the clans in the northwest frontier." He shifted again in the chair. The seat was hard and he hated being in a building that had formerly been a Christian church.

"You did talk to Lukriz Au-mumin two days ago," I'Zada persisted.

"Two days ago—yes, sir. It was in the afternoon. After the gunmen attacked us, I went straight to our local headquarters in Peshawar. I assumed our cover—Gulaka's and mine—was blown. After I received medical treatment, I made arrangements to fly straight to the capital. After I arrived, I turned in my report. I'm sorry. There isn't anything I can add."

Si'Quetta said gently, "Relax, Lieutenant. You haven't done anything wrong. It's only that we had to be sure."

"Yes sir, I understand. I—I was surprised when I was summoned to make my report again. May I ask a question?"

Si'Quetta and I'Zada nodded.

"Why all the concern with the movements of the Pathans and the Garukals? They never leave their winter headquarters, not until middle or late spring, depending on the weather."

The expression of concern on General I'Zada's face deepened. "For the past week, we've been getting reports, mostly from our recon planes, that large numbers of tribesmen in the northwest frontier have been on the move. This morning we received confirmation."

"Not toward the capital?" Moukarim said in alarm. "Those Pathans have always been against our president and his politics. They're still living in the lawlessness of the nineteenth century!"

"West," I'Zada said in a firm tone. "We are of the opinion that they're moving toward the Khyber."

Moukarim's lips parted in surprise. "Toward the Khyber Pass! But why? There can be no logical reason for such a migration, even if it were the middle of summer. It doesn't make sense."

"It is not logical to us." I'Zada sighed deeply. "It does make sense to the Pathans. We will have to find out the reason. We must also ascertain how the Pathans deduced that Lukriz Au-mumin was our agent. None of this is your concern, Lieutenant Moukarim. You may go. We hope there are no complications with your wound."

Lieutenant Mohammed Moukarim stood up, saluted and turned smartly on his heel. After he had left the building, Lieutenant General Si'Quetta got up and went over to a table on which a metal teapot was sitting on a warmer.

"General, we must face the possibility that our agent in Mirza-Khan's camp is dead." He picked up a cup and reached for the teapot. "It's been almost a month and we have not had a single report from him. Surely within that length of time, he could have sent a runner."

General I'Zada didn't answer. He had another problem that was annoying him. President Mohammed Zia ul-Haq had called him into the presidential office and had ordered him to stop using the Methodist church building as a "second headquarters."

"Saha, how does it look?" President Zia had said politely but very firmly, with just a slight edge to his voice. "A good Moslem, such as yourself, spending so much of your time in a building that was formerly a sacred place of Christians! There has been some talk among the ministers. I'm sorry, Saha. You will have to stop using the building. In another week, I shall have it torn down."

I'Zada became aware that Si'Quetta was speaking to him.

"Would you care for a cup of tea, General?"

CHAPTER FOURTEEN

The Death Merchant had the philosophy that the acid test of intelligence was the ability to cope with stupidity. This was the main reason why he and Mike Quinlan worked so well together. Camellion did not have to cope with Mike because he was highly intelligent and always knew what he was doing, even when drunk.

Quinlan flew the Hind-D straight to Sirzihil and began to hover at an altitude of 3000 feet. It was dawn—05.22 hours.

"Directly below is Sirzihil; I'm positive," Mike said. "Now you tell me how we're supposed to land without getting our peckers shot off?"

The Death Merchant solved the problem using a scratch pad he had found in the map compartment. He printed ten different notes and, with wire found in a toolbox behind the copilot's seat, secured each note to a small tool. On each piece of paper he had printed the word *friends* in Urdu, one of the few words in that language he knew. In other English letters he printed: *Do not fire. We have escaped in this Russian bird without wings from Afghanistan. Kir Camellion.*

Quinlan was highly skeptical of the plan. "All I can say is that somebody down there had better be able to read English. How do you figure on dropping the messages?"

He was even more dubious when Camellion told him that they would fly over the village at 500 feet "and I'll open a window and toss out the tools. All they have to find is one. With the sun coming up, they'll see more than one object falling from the chopper."

Quinlan glanced at Camellion, who had the tools and notes in his lap, and shook his head—then suddenly laughed.

"Yeah, I know," Camellion said. "Our almost getting wasted back in Afghanistan is hilarious!"

"Sorry," Quinlan said, and laughed again. "I was thinking of something else."

This was the second time that Mad Mike had laughed at a crucial moment and Camellion didn't intend to let him get away with it—not this time.

"Give! I want to know what's so damned funny. And this time, don't give me any 'I'll tell you later.' "

Still chuckling, Quinlan explained that he was thinking of a joke he had heard in Cairo, a few months previously. "You see, there was this dumb-ass Englishman. We'll call him John Bull. He was in the States, and a callgirl told him the following limerick. *There was a young man named Skinner, who took his girl out to dinner. They sat down to dine at a quarter of nine; at a quarter of ten it was in her—not the dinner—Skinner!*

"Bull goes back to England and tells the deal at his club. Having the mentality of a retarded sponge, he told it this way: *There was a young man named Tupper, who took his girl out to supper. They sat down to dine at a quarter of nine, at a quarter of ten it was up her—not the supper or even Tupper! It was some chap named Skinner!*"

Now it was the Death Merchant who shook his head. "Take the chopper down, Mike. I'm a little anxious to confront Chaudhriy."

Quinlan began to rev down. "We don't have any actual proof against the son of a bitch. We'll have to play it damned careful."

"We have to get down first." Once more Camellion toyed with the scheme he was evolving for the attack on the Spetsnaz base. It could work. *If Grojean will drop what I need. If he won't, forget it!*

Down went the Hind gunship, Quinlan expertly swinging it to the west and Camellion cranking down the starboard window of the main control compartment; and when Mad Mike had the bird at 500 feet and began the "scim across" to the east, both he and the Death Merchant could see scores of Pathans firing at the Hind-D, thinking it was the Russian enemy. They did hear several *ping-ping-pings* as they flew over the village. However, the slugs did not do any damage.

It took only seconds for the Death Merchant to toss out the

message-wrapped tools, after which Quinlan took the Hind-D up to a thousand feet and began to hover.

"We'll give them ten minutes," Camellion said. "Then you can take her down. Either it will work or they'll blast us."

"It has to work," Quinlan said. "Can you feature us blowing up in a pig-farmer chopper in the middle of Pakistan?"

"Yes, I can. But I don't think we're going to—I hope!"

It was a very slow 600 seconds—not only for Camellion and Quinlan, but for Bruckner, O'Malley and Jaiiah Talequn. Quinlan had tried to contact O'Malley and Bruckner in the nose cockpit, but both men had neglected to put on headphones of the intercom/radio.

Expecting the worst, Mad Mike took the chopper down, centering it over a clearing around which were three stone houses. Down: 700 feet . . . 600 . . . 400 . . . 325.

Not a shot was fired.

One hundred feet . . . fifty . . . and then the tricycle landing gear was touching ground. Quinlan switched off the two Isotov turboshafts and, with the Death Merchant, looked out the window. The Pathans had read the message but were not taking one chance. They circled the gunship, standing fifty feet away, pointing assault rifles and submachine guns at the craft.

"Don't even sneeze," Camellion joked, and reached for the handle of the door.

Ten minutes later, with revolvers shoved in their backs and surrounded by hard-faced Pathans, the Death Merchant and the three members of Thunderbolt Unit: Omega were being escorted toward one of the larger stone houses in Sirzihil.

After getting out of the chopper, his hands in the air, Camellion had asked if anyone among the suspicious Pathans spoke English. Several said that they did. He had then told them about Jaiiah Talequn in the dead space, and had warned, "He has a broken shoulder. Be careful with him."

They crossed the *hurja*—the "sitting and talking place" of the porch—and one of the Pathans opened the door and motioned Camellion and the others inside. Once inside, Camellion and his companions found themselves facing a smiling Chief Mujibur Ali Mirza-Khan. With him were five other men, two of whom were very familiar: Iskander Chaudhriy, looking as choleric as ever, and the impassive-faced Jiko Krim-Lizak.

Mirza-Khan rose from his *bodza*, walked over to Camellion, and shook his hand with surprising vigor. "Allah has been merciful, Kir Camellion. Not only did you and your men return ahead of schedule, but you came back in a Russian bird without wings."

"We were lucky, Malik-Sahib Mirza-Khan," Camellion said calmly. "It was not our time to die." He turned and looked at Iskander Chaudhriy. "We do have much to tell you."

Mirza-Khan shook the hands of Quinlan and Bruckner and O'Malley, and when he saw the caked blood on O'Malley's side, he inquired of the wound. O'Malley told him the cut was deep and "something of a pain. But I'll live."

Mirza-Khan turned, spoke in Urdu to several of the *badragga*, and the two men hurried forward. "They will see that your wound has the proper ointments and is dressed," he told O'Malley. "With rest you will recover."

As Mirza-Khan spoke to the Peppermint Kid, one of the other men sitting on the rug turned and spoke loudly in Urdu, obviously to someone outside the sitting room. The Death Merchant surmised that he was ordering the women of the household to prepare the morning meal and to "put out our best china for our guests."

After O'Malley and the two bodyguards left, Mirza-Khan introduced Camellion, Quinlan and Bruckner to the three men on the rug. The man who had spoken to the women was Finar Lachok. In his early fifties, he was of medium height and stocky, clean-shaven and intelligent looking. He wore an old blue suit, a black turtleneck sweater and short brown leather boots. Mirza-Khan explained that "We are in his house" and that Lachok was the *cinork* of the village, the elder of Sirzihil.

The other two men were Laski Shamspir and Fazal Qayyumkor. In his early twenties, Shamspir was slightly cross-eyed, with a face that was one big mess of ugly. Looking at him made Camellion think that Shamspir's mother had conceived him during a nightmare and had lived in a state of constant terror all the time she had carried him.

The first thing that one noticed about Fazal Qayyumkor was his blond hair, very thick and the color of wheat ready to be cut. About the same age as Finar Lachok, Qayyumkor was tall and broad and wore two German PO8 Lugers in shoulder holsters.

Mirza-Khan waved a hand toward the rug. "Be seated, my *baya-darkas*," he said to Camellion, Quinlan and Bruckner. "We are anxious to hear of your adventure in Afghanistan."

Only then did Iskander Chaudhriy speak up. "Kir Camellion,

you have not mentioned Asad Dizakan and the three other guides who were with you. Are we to assume that they are dead?"

Tugging at his heavy black beard, Jiko Krim-Lizak said, "The man you brought out with you from Afghanistan. He is Pathan. But he was not one of the guides. How did you meet him?"

"*Ched*, the four guides are dead," Camellion said sincerely, answering Chaudhriy. Watching the handsome Chaudhriy, the Death Merchant couldn't detect the least trace of disappointment—or fear.

Michael Quinlan and Willy Bruckner, sitting down cross-legged on the rug, remained silent. They were leaving the play—and the explanation—up to the Death Merchant, who sat down and waited as two women, both veiled, came out from behind a curtain. One carried a small table, the other, a large teapot, cups and sweet *mucha* cakes on a large wooden platter. He waited until after the two women had set up the table and poured hot tea for everyone to begin his report, starting with "after we had crossed the border into Afghanistan." As he told the story, not once did he mention the names of the four guides. Not once did he even use the word *guide*!

He finished with "after we destroyed the last two Soviet birds without wings Kir Quinlan brought our craft straight to this village. With the help and grace of Allah, we are safe."

"I congratulate the three of you, and your friend who was wounded," Finar Lachok said solemnly, his voice as deep as a bass drum. "Malik-Mullah Mirza-Khan told us that Allah must have given you special powers. I feel that he was correct."

Laski Shamspir said, "It will be a blessed day for all of us when that Russian base in Afghanistan is destroyed . . . *ched* . . . a blessed day."

"There is only one way we can attack the base and hope to win," Camellion said, tossing out the bait. All the while he could see, from the sly expression in Mirza-Khan's eyes, that the old man was doing some hard and furious brainwork. Mirza-Khan was old, but his mind was as clear as spring water. As *Mullah*, his position was similar to the pope's. Whatever he said was law. *Which is why he's top dog in Finar Lachok's house. But why hasn't he said anything about the guides?*

Mirza-Khan fixed his eyes on the Death Merchant. "Kir Camellion, not once have you told us about the fate of the guides who led you into Afghanistan. You have not told us how they died."

"I killed them," Camellion said matter-of-factly, picking up his cup. "I personally killed the four of them when they tried to kill us during the middle of the night."

In detail, he proceeded to explain what had taken place on the hilltop, noticing as he spoke that only the three Pathans who lived in Sirzihil seemed surprised. As far as Mirza-Khan and Chaudhriy and Krim-Lizak were concerned . . . *I might as well have said that I blew my nose!*

Mirza-Khan folded his hands in his lap. "Kir Camellion, you have proof that Asad Dizakan and the three others were treacherous in their actions?"

"We found a special kind of transmitter, a radio, on Syed Serneabiz," Camellion said, a sharp overtone to his voice. "The radio was a tracking device. If we had not found it, the Russians would have known the second we left your nation and crossed into Afghanistan. They could have reached out and touched us."

Iskander Chaudhriy spoke up, sounding not the least bit nervous. "Why would the guides need a tracking signal radio if they had intended to kill you? I don't think they would have carried four dead men all the way into Afghanistan."

A smile—or was it a sneer?—crossed the face of Jiko Krim-Lizak. "Iskander is right, Kir Camellion. The Russian dogs have no need of dead bodies. They have turned all of Afghanistan into one vast graveyard."

"I don't think that Dizakan and Serneabiz and the other two wanted to kill us," Camellion said. "If all they had wanted was to kill us, they could have sprayed us with slugs. They intended to take our weapons, make us prisoners and turn us over to the Russians. The tracking transmitter was to help the Russians pinpoint us the instant we reached Chagasar. As it turned out, Jaiiah Talequn and his four friends led us to Sylhet Pass and got us through Chagasar and to the mountains close to the Spetsnaz base."

Mike Quinlan leaned forward and stared at Mirza-Khan. "For all we know, it's possible that the guides had made other arrangements for meeting the Russians. It could be that the plan was for them to remain stationary for a certain length of time. That would have been the signal for the Russians to send a helicopter across the border and pick us up."

"Michael, tell Malik Mirza-Khan how we met Nelkik Farah-Rinrooz and his band," Camellion said, feeling more relaxed.

At the mention of Nelkik Farah-Rinrooz, Mirza-Khan's wrinkled face glowed with intense interest. "You met my old friend Farah-Rinrooz? Ah . . . Allah is good. What did he say? How did he look?"

The Death Merchant told him how they had met Farah-Rinrooz on the trail and what had taken place. "By now, he and his small group have reached Tigmal. He and many many Pathans are afraid of the Russians. There are rumors of a Russian invasion."

Mike Quinlan continued with the story, telling how five of Nelkik Farah-Rinrooz's band had led them to Sylhet Pass, and how they had left the tracking transmitter with Shotit Pushko-Mialat and why. "We know that three of them are dead. They were killed in the mountains in Afghanistan. We have no way of knowing what happened to Shotit Pushko-Mialat. The plan was to go back and meet him, but after the Russians attacked we knew we either had to fly out in a bird without wings—or die!"

Willy Bruckner said in his stilted English, "We think the Russians became suspicious of the transmitter signals moving back and forth. The Russians sent over the chopper and they captured Pushko-Mialat."

"Our concern is that the four guards were working for the Russians," the Death Merchant said, "or else they were working for some individual who is in the employ of the KGB or the GRU." His eyes searched the faces of the Pathans, his intuition telling him that Mirza-Khan and Iskander Chaudhriy were waiting. *But waiting for what?*

Camellion stabbed an accusing stare at Chaudhriy. "Four guides you found for us," he said vehemently.

Chaudhriy's expression didn't change, his demeanor one of total confidence. There was only a new shrewdness in his eyes and a faint curl of a smile on his twisted mouth. "*Kir* Camellion, you should say what you are thinking," he said briskly. "You should say what you believe that I am an agent of the Russians."

Without direct proof, the Death Merchant knew he was on dangerous ground, and he wondered if there were anything in the Pathan code of *Pukhtunwali* to cover accusing a man without having substantial evidence.

The Death Merchant went the rest of the way. "Kir Chaudhriy, it was you who found the guides."

"I did not supply the guides!" Amusement flowed all over Chaudhriy's good-looking face, a jocularity that instantly changed to cold fury as he turned to Jiko Krim-Lizak. "It was this traitor who found Dizakan and the other three."

Krim-Lizak, more shaken than Camellion and his men were surprised, drew back, fear leaping into his eyes.

"And it is this traitor, Kir Camellion, who is working for two masters: the Russians and General I'Zada's Chanwiri-lu-Shabudar!"

Chief Mirza-Khan raised a hand in a signal. At once, two of the *badragga* stepped forward, one calmly shoving the muzzle of a .44 Charter Arms revolver against the back of Jiko Krim-Lizak's head.

"There has been a mistake." In panic, Krim-Lizak turned and looked pleadingly at Mirza-Khan. "I . . ." He didn't complete the sentence. He knew he was speaking to the wind and that Mirza-Khan and the other Pathans had trapped him. How they had accomplished it didn't matter, not now. He only wondered how he would be executed. He was certain it would be slow and unpleasant.

"Take him from our sight," Mirza-Khan ordered the two bodyguards. "We will question him at length this afternoon and hold his trial."

"I'll be damned!" muttered Quinlan, who was sitting next to the Death Merchant. "The box of Crackerjacks is full of surprises!"

While Quinlan and Bruckner were startled by the sudden turn of events, Richard Camellion was dumbfounded and rapidly beginning to suspect that he and the three Thunderbolts had been set up, not only by Jiko Krim-Lizak but, in another sense, by Chaudhriy and Mirza-Khan.

As the two bodyguards escorted Jiko Krim-Lizak from the room, Iskander Chaudhriy looked for a moment at the Death Merchant, smiled slightly, then said that for over a year he and Mirza-Khan had suspected that Krim-Lizak was a traitor.

"We did not have anything definite against him," Chaudhriy explained. "It was little things that made us wonder about him. All we could do was watch him. At times this was most difficult. We didn't dare risk his becoming aware that we suspected him."

Malik Mirza-Khan said patiently, "When you and your people were ambushed at the shrine of the saint, we were certain that we were correct. It was then we became positive that he was working for either the dogs from the north or General I'Zada."

His expression not revealing the intensity of his inner anger, Camellion frowned. "Krim-Lizak supplied Likstom, Sorhib and the two guides who led Kirs O'Malley and Bruckner to the shrine?"

"I chose the four." Chaudhriy answered the question in a polite tone. "One of them became ill. He died overnight. We think he was poisoned. We will know after we question Krim-Lizak later this day. It was Krim-Lizak who found a replacement. The man's name was Lukriz Au-mumin. It was Lukriz Au-mumin who tipped off General I'Zada's security police and helped arrange the ambush at the Shrine of Abdul Bu-I-Zum. But Allah protected the four of you.

"Allah assisted us also in dealing, only recently, with Lukriz Au-mumin and the two agents of the Chanwiri-lu-Shabudar who were with him at the time. One did manage to escape. We are told he was wounded."

"*Wunderbar!*" exclaimed Bruckner, forgetting himself and speaking in German.

Tiny muscles twitched in Camellion's neck. He gave Chaudhriy a long, sweeping look, then sent visual daggers in Mirza-Khan's direction. Camellion didn't like being set up. "Are we to understand that the two of you suspected that the four guides, the four who were supposed to take us to Sylhet Pass, would try to kill us?"

Quinlan added, sounding angry, "You did know it was Krim-Lizak who supplied the guides?"

"We knew," Mirza-Khan admitted calmly. "We had to—as you would say in the West—force Jiko Krim-Lizak to expose his hand."

"I stalled, pretending I could not find guides with the courage to take you into Afghanistan," Chaudhriy said. "I turned the problem over to Krim-Lizak. He sent a runner to another village. We hoped the men he obtained would intercept you. They did."

"We suspected that they might try to kill you," Mirza-Khan said. "But we were not worried about your safety. We knew that men of your ability would not place yourselves in a position by which the guides could accomplish your murders."

Bruckner turned to Camellion and Quinlan and said in German, "We thought they were dumb! It's the other way around. But the sons of bitches still made targets of us."

"Forget it, Willy," Quinlan said. "The way they figure it, it was for a good cause."

The only thing that Camellion was enjoying was the anticipation on the faces of Finar Lachok and the other Pathans. They were like people watching a murder-mystery movie, waiting for the name of the killer to be revealed. What bothered him was that Mirza-Khan and Chaudhriy were acting as though they had obtained proof positive against Jiko Krim-Lizak. And Krim-Lizak was working for both General I'Zada *and* the Russians! Where was the proof? Yet neither Mujibur Ali Mirza-Khan nor Iskander Chaudhriy would accuse a fellow Pathan without proof!

The Death Merchant rubbed his upper lip with a forefinger. "Malik-Sahib Mirza-Khan, where is your proof against Jiko Krim-Lizak?"

Chaudhriy put down his cup and dabbed at his lips with a handkerchief. He looked at Camellion and said in a steady voice, "I chose the eleven men who would go to the various *Maliks* with Malik Mirza-Khan's message. I chose eleven trusted men. Conveniently one of the men became 'ill.' I told Jiko Krim-Lizak to replace him with another man."

"You knew that Krim-Lizak would choose a man in his network," the Death Merchant finished.

Chaudhriy nodded in agreement. "Understand, we did not have any actual proof against Krim-Lizak until four of our trusted men following Al Seiffi Banrizm, the man chosen by Krim-Lizak, took him prisoner and threatened to put out his eyes and castrate him if he did not tell them the full truth."

"Al Seiffi Banrizm decided that telling the truth was preferable to living in darkness the rest of his life." Mirza-Khan's voice, no longer soft, was cold and contemptuous. "Banrizm confessed that after he delivered my message to Malik Daoud Abdul Ellah, he was to proceed to Peshawar and contact a maker of guns by the name of Banwad Girnayl. He was to do that on the direct orders of Jiko Krim-Lizak. He was to tell Banwad Girnayl that I was preparing to attack the special Russian base in Afghanistan and was asking the other chiefs for their help. Banrizm confessed that while he had no proof, he felt that Banwad Girnayl was either a private informer or an agent of the Chanwiri-lu-Shabudar."

"How does all this tie in with Krim-Lizak's being a Soviet agent?" Camellion asked.

"Al Seiffi Banrizm also admitted that he had done other work for Krim-Lizak," Chaudhriy said. "During the last eight months, Banrizm has delivered sealed envelopes from Krim-Lizak to a non-Pakistani in Islamabad. Sometimes he would meet the recipient of the envelope in Zia Park. At other times, there were other locations. But always they were never far from the Soviet embassy."

"Later during this day, we will get all the truth from Jiko Krim-Lizak," intoned Mirza-Khan. Abruptly then he changed the subject. "The various Pathan and Garukal clans are giving us their full cooperation. To the number of 9000 they are moving slowly toward the Khyber, taking their time." He spread his arms in a gesture of helplessness. "But we cannot attack until the American CIA sends us more weapons, lots of weapons."

"We must have ground-to-air and ground-to-ground missiles, and half a dozen heavy machine guns, Kir Camellion." Finar Lachok peered closely at the Death Merchant and tugged at the thickly rolled collar of his turtleneck sweater.

Short of being flabbergasted, Quinlan and Bruckner glanced at Camellion. The Pathans certainly didn't want much—only missiles! Why not heavy armor, such as tanks. Why not toss in a dozen squadrons of jet fighter–bombers!

Moving toward the Khyber Pass! *Insanity!*

There were times when Colonel Mike Quinlan ignored protocol, especially when he was confronted with what he considered stupidity. Now was one of those times. "Any attack through the Khyber Pass is pure nonsense," he said, sounding disgusted. "The Russians would kill every one of you. Why we never even discussed the Khyber with you!"

Quinlan was even more annoyed when Mirza-Khan answered, speaking to him as though he were chastising a small child. "Surely you are familiar with a diversionary tactic? We have no intention of mounting an attack through the Khyber. I should think you would have guessed as much, being an ex-military man."

"It doesn't make any difference," Camellion said quickly, seeing that Mad Mike was losing his Irish temper. "It's impossible to attack the Spetsnaz base from the east, in the manner we previously discussed. From the west end of the mountains to the base the distance is only a little over a *serai*. The distance is far greater from Chagasar to the Russian base. We'd be massacred."

Laski Shamspir turned his unsightly face toward the Death Merchant. "You did say there was one way we could attack the Russians and win."

"By moving in small groups, and with luck, we could reach Sylhet Pass," Quinlan inserted. "Beyond the pass, the Russians would be waiting. It would be sheer suicide."

Camellion glanced at Shamspir, who was waiting for an answer. Intuitively, he sensed that Mirza-Khan and the other Pathans agreed with him and Quinlan. How then did they expect the attack to succeed? Not even they would expect that kind of miracle from their Allah. . . .

"That's correct," Camellion admitted. "I did say there was only one way the base could be attacked."

"From the north!" Chaudhriy said hastily, not giving Camellion time to finish. "The only logical approach is from the north. The distance to the base from the mountains to the north is only half a *serai*. We can reach those mountains from our own land as they are part of a chain that stretches across the border."

Mirza-Khan said politely, "It is the plan we decided on while you gentlemen were on your way to inspect the Soviet base. We do realize that moving our men into those mountains will be difficult."

"Difficult!" The word exploded from Mike Quinlan's mouth. "You mean impossible! Have you forgotten Russian and President Zia's recon planes? President Zia and the Soviet command in Kabul will know at once what we were trying to do. And that's only half of it!" Quinlan turned and looked the Death Merchant in the eye. "Even if the CIA would agree to sending missiles and God only knows what else, how in blazes do you expect a couple of Galaxies or Cargomasters to fly the length of Pakistan, then out again, without being spotted on radar and intercepted by Pak fighters?"

"We cannot attack the Spetsnaz base," said Bruckner. "We would be committing suicide."

Camellion sighed. Life could be trying at times, and it was almost always boring. "Mike, they've come up with the same plan I had. As for the cargo planes, they'll be protected by a 'magic box' that will render them invisible." Camellion spoke as well for the benefit of the Pathans, knowing that "magic box" to Quinlan and Bruckner would indicate stealth aircraft.

Mike was fast on the uptake. "Oh, the magic box! I see. OK, so the planes could get in and out without being seen. That still does not solve the problem of how thousands of men could move through the mountains without being detected by the Pakistani air force and Soviet agents."

"I was thinking along the lines of 500 men—500 to 600," Camellion said. "There can't be more than 2000 Spetsnaz at the base." He assessed the Pathans as he spoke and got what he wanted: satisfaction showing in their expressions. The Pathans had formulated the same kind of plan: a diversionary force that would move toward the Khyber Pass while the actual attack group would come in from another direction—from the north.

Quinlan eyed Camellion suspiciously. "Five hundred against 2000. Those are some odds."

"You and your Thunderbolts have taken on worse odds and won!"

"Yeah, but most of our assignments were against sloppy, poorly trained troops. We're talking about Soviet Spetsnaz—among the most disciplined fighters in the world. You're talking lunch meat! I'm talking prime rib!"

Fazal Qayyumkor said smugly, "Five hundred of our number could easily handle 2000 of the Russian dogs, easily. . . ."

Quinlan let him have a another-fool-heard-from look. "You mean if the land mines don't kill all of you!" Again he turned to the Death Merchant, who was thinking of the Antarctica and what Grojean had confided to him months earlier.[1]

Quinlan said wearily, "As close as the mountains are to the base, you know the Spetsnaz will have the area heavily mined and guarded in other ways."

"Naturally." Camellion shrugged. "Still another reason why we'll need G-to-G missiles and heavy mortars. Moving the attack force will be risky. We can move the men in groups of fifty—hide in the daytime and travel as much as we can at night. It's still a chance. Zia's planes and the Soviet aircraft have infrared and other man-detecting sensors."

"And a lot of sensors in the mountains north of their base," Quinlan said tonelessly. "Even if we could knock out whatever they might have, when the equipment went dead, it would be a tipoff—and don't tell me about any 'magic' black box that can cover an area that large for a bypass. There isn't any."

"No, there isn't," Camellion said. "We'll have to play some of it by ear."

"If—and only if—we get the ordnance!"

Mirza-Khan asked in a very polite voice, "This 'ordnance.' Do you mean the weapons we need?"

"*Ched,*" said Camellion, "and the sooner I get on the radio

[1] See Death Merchant number 62, *The Soul Search Project*, and the forthcoming number 64, *The Atlantean Horror*.

and contact my *Malik*, the sooner we'll know if we're going to get heavy stuff."

Finar Lachok, all smiles, got to his feet. "Come, I shall escort you to the house that has been reserved for you. Your radio is there, being guarded by some of the men of the village."

He walked toward the door. The Death Merchant and Quinlan and Bruckner followed. Behind them came five *badragga*—not for protection, but as an honor guard for honored guests.

The instant that Camellion and the two Thunderbolts were alone in the house, Quinlan lit a cigarette and gazed at the Death Merchant fiercely. "What's all the crap about a magic box that will make an aircraft invisible? I know it wasn't all pigeon poop—but invisible! That was really stretching it, Richard."

"I meant *invisible* in the fullest sense of the word," Camellion said. "The device can render an airplane or surface vessel or submarine—whatever—totally invisible to people outside the craft."

"*Mein Gott! Das ist unmoglich*," exclaimed Bruckner.

"*Nein*, Willy. It is not impossible. It is. The device exists. It's called a Gf Mechanism and it's ultra-ultra secret. Don't ask me how it works. I honestly don't know. I only know that somehow it uses electromagnetic waves to make the object invisible. I've been within ten feet of a sub using the Gf Mechanism and couldn't see the hull.[2] I do know that the actual device is no larger than a footlocker."

Quinlan was still as skeptical as a farmboy from the middle of China who was seeing New York City for the first time. How could building be so tall!

How could any device make any object totally invisible?

"Then if each plane has one of these Gf deals, no one could see it," Quinlan said at length.

"Or hear the engines," finished the Death Merchant. "Radar would be useless, both primary and secondary."

"Ach, the Philadelphia Experiment," Bruckner said, switching back to English. "That was the beginning for the Americans."

"You got it, Willy." Camellion laughed. "We Americans can't make a decent automobile but we can make ships and planes invisible. Now, let's get out the radio and contact the Fox."

Moving behind Camellion who was walking across the room,

[2] See Death Merchant number 37, *The Bermuda Triangle Action*.

Quinlan chuckled. "You'll always find me where there's cheap booze and loose women. So why am I here in Pakistan where there are neither and where people belive that 'War is the Man, Motherhood the Woman.' And that reminds me—"

"I'm way ahead of you, Mike. I won't forget your Scotch when I talk with the Fox." Camellion opened the lid of the shockproof case in which rested the AN/URC 101 Satcom Tactical Transceiver.

Courtland Grojean was in a good mood. His frame of mind didn't have anything to do with the project. Grojean was limited in what he could do, his actions depending on his bosses and what their boss would permit. Their boss was the Very Highest Authority in the United States.

Camellion told Grojean what he needed and what had to be done.

"There is no other way it can be done," Camellion concluded.

Grojean's reply was to the point. "I'll get back to you by 16.00 hours. Stay close to the radio."

Camellion switched off the set. "Now we wait," he said to Quinlan and Bruckner.

"Have you considered the logistics and communications involved in such an operation?" Quinlan stared at him.

"Yep. It's going to be trickier than a coon dog tiptoeing away from a skunk."

The Fox made contact at 13.00 hours. The Very Highest Authority had authorized the mission. *Give them anything they need.*

In spite of all the radio security—frequency hopping and triple scrambling—Grojean and Camellion resorted to certain key words, code phrases, agreed upon between them before the mission had begun.

Courtland Grojean said: "We have more than enough supplies in King David (*Israel*) to give you what you need. It will take a day to make all the necessary arrangements and iron out the details for the High Line (*the airdrop*), and then get the matériel to the Point (*Sirzihil*) in Highland (*Pakistan*). First, we'll have to clear everything with King David's NS1.[3] The Highline will be at night and the Storks (*planes*) will have Little Marys (*Gf Mechanisms*). I'll get back to you at 12.00 hours tomorrow—12.00 your time. I repeat: 12.00 hours your time over there."

[3] This is the Israeli National Security Institute, or as it is more familiarly known, the Mossad.

Grojean was prompt the next day. It was 12.04.6 hours when he voice came through the telephone handset of the AN/URC 101.

The airdrop would take place at 03.00 hours in the morning.

The Death Merchant, a stickler for each tiny detail, was concerned. "Are you certain that the pilots know the location of the Point in Highland. They must be absolutely certain. They have only half a klick square in which to drop the stuff."

"Don't worry about it," Grojean replied. "We have maps that show us where the Clown (*President Zia*) pats his mistresses on the butt. There is just one more thing: tell that goofball Mr. Q. to watch it with his drinking. I had to pull a lot of wires to get his Scotch. How would it have looked if I had put a couple of fifths on the list? He's getting an entire case. His name will be on the case for ID. I told Upstairs that I needed a whole case for a bribe, that one of the *Maliks* was a drunk. Tell that screwball he had better not get stoned out of his skull and goof up the operation, or he'll have to find refuge in the middle of the Soviet Union."

"I'll tell him. How about the escape route out of Highland. I've calculated another six weeks—by the time our force gets to Moonstone (*Afghanistan*) and we get back and are able to get out of Highland. I don't intend to spend my old age in Highland."

"The Diamond Route (*India*) is still open. It will remain open for the next three months. You know the details. . . ."

Making a great pretense of solemnity, Camellion did convey Grojean's message to Quinlan, whose only comment was, "The son of a bitch!" But he said it with a special fondness, for he knew that the Fox had gone out of his way to do him a favor, and he knew too that should he ever meet Grojean and thank him for it, the Fox would act insulted and probably tell him to go to hell. That was Courtland Grojean's way. He was a man who had a lot in common with Richard Camellion. Grojean didn't want friends and never really let anyone get close to him.

"The drop will be at three o'clock tomorrow morning," the Death Merchant told the three Thunderbolts and Mirza-Khan and his Pathans.

"I'll have to see it to belive it," Quinlan said, referring to the aircraft that would be invisible.

Mad Mike did see. They all saw, twelve hours and fifteen minutes later. They waited, in the darkness . . . the Death

Merchant, the three Thunderbolts, Mirza-Khan and several hundred Pathans scattered about the large area, many with gasoline lanterns or tar torches. Among them was Jaiiah Talequn, who was now considered a *rito'k*, a hero, his arm and shoulder in a leather and wooden "cast."

There were long strings of scattered clouds in the sky, some playing tag with a new moon. The night itself was calm and quiet, the wind down to a soft breeze.

Very suddenly, very unexpectedly—it happened. Hundreds of flares began bursting into bright light at an altitude of 500 feet. There wasn't even the whisper of an engine.

No one could see them, but there were two Lockheed Galaxy C-5A transports. The largest airplane in the world, a Galaxy could carry 443,760 pounds of freight and, fully loaded, fly at a maximum speed of 571 mph.

One Galaxy could have easily handled the fifteen tons—30,000 pounds—of cargo to be dropped. One Galaxy did. The second Galaxy had not, however, come along "for the ride." It was there to test highly secret electronic gear and to photograph Pakistani air bases and other vital areas along the route after it was inside Pakistan airspace. The CIA was especially interested in any site that could possibly be assembling a nuclear weapon. For any number of years the rumor was that President Zia was about to make an H-Bomb.

The Pathans were amazed at the magnesium flares. They were astonished when, a few minutes later as the flares drifted slowly to the ground, the high sky gave birth to dozens of blossoming cargo shutes. At the end of each parachute was a wooden pallet, cases of weapons wired tightly to each platform.

"*La ilah illa Allah!*" Mirza-Khan said in awe, staring upward at the gifts. "And we are seeing proof of His goodness."

Richard Camellion glanced at the "Jerry Falwell" of the Pathans.

You are also seeing the "goodness" of the poor American taxpayer!

CHAPTER FIFTEEN

Communications and logistics. Now that the matériel had been dropped, numerous problems had to be resolved, the first of which was how to obtain a force of 600 men without letting any secrets slip to Pathan traitors in the employ of the KGB and/or the GRU or the Chanwiri-lu-Shabudar. Each man would have to be strong and tough and willing to die for his homeland

Malik Mirza-Khan could supply 192 first-class fighters, Finar Lachok 176 men; 232 more men were needed.

"Wrong," the Death Merchant said. "We need 282 men. I'll tell you why. All the weapons are here in Sirzihil. The 368 men already here could carry everything; yet it would be difficult. The extra fifty men could be older men. They wouldn't have to fight. They could help us carry the matériel. We'd make better time."

Mirza-Khan spoke in Urdu to Finar Lachok, who considered for a moment. Finally he replied to Mirza-Khan in Urdu, then said to the Death Merchant, "Fifty more men from this village will not be a problem."

"The only problem will be the number," Iskander Chaudhriy said; 418 men. I think we should leave in groups of fifty, five to six hours apart."

"It's as good a way as any," Camellion said. "We could leave in pairs and it would still be a risk."

"It's getting the rest of the men that troubles me," Mirza-Khan said. "Which towns should we choose?"

It was Richard Camellion and Iskander Chaudhriy who suggested that Mirza-Khan and Pinar Lochok send runners, trusted men, to the six closest settlements with a message: would each *cinork*, each elder, supply thirty fighters. Mirza-Khan would explain in the message that he could not give the reasons why he needed the men—it was a matter of security—but that they would be used to help preserve the freedoms of their homeland.

Mirza-Khan stroked his long beard for several moments. "*Ched,* Kir Camellion. I think your idea is a good one."

The next problem was where the six individual groups would be gathered into one united strike force

Mike Quinlan was quick to point out that they'd lose valuable time if the various groups first came to Sirzihil. "We've already agreed that we're going to make the journey north in groups of fifty. If we sit around and wait until the other six groups get here, we'll simply waste time—and then more time when all 650 of us split up into groups and leave one after the other."

The Death Merchant and the Pathans agreed. "I feel that each group should start from its own village and go to an assembly point in the north." On his knees, he leaned over the map on the rug.

"These mountains here"—he traced a six-inch line with his finger, from east to west—"are part of the same chain that crosses the border into Afghanistan, the same mountains that are only a bit more than a *serai* from the Spetsnaz base. Why couldn't the other six groups meet up with ours in these mountains? The location would have to be no less than thirty *serais* from the border. That would be about thirty-two kilometers."

For a time, Mirza-Khan, Chaudhriy, Lachok and the other Pathans consulted the map, now and then commenting in Urdu among themselves. At length, Chaudhriy looked across at Camellion and his tiny group, a hint of a smile forming on the corners of his mouth. "We have found a place. I will show you on the map. Right here." He drew an imaginary circle on the map with his thumb and forefinger.

The Death Merchant, Quinlan, Bruckner and O'Malley couldn't read the Urdu script; however, they could see the numerous red squares with a space that was an inch in diameter.

"This place is about twenty-eight of your kilometers from the border," Chaudhriy said. "It is the ruins of the ancient city of Cesmorius. Even the great grandfathers of our great grandfathers cannot remember when it was built, and we know its name only from the legends of our people. It is said that the one we call Alexander *Kumilaaz zum i'Abrul* built the city—Alexander the Conqueror. The history books of your West call him Alexander the Great."

"Cesmorius is an ideal place for our purpose," said Fazal Qayyumkor, sounding pleased with himself. He hooked a thumb on the narrow strap of his shoulder holsters. "Our *baya-darkas* from the six villages can go straight to Cesmorius. We can travel there from here in Sirzilhil."

The Death Merchant did some rapid calculating. *Twenty-eight kilometers is only eighteen miles. There are those rare times when the pig farmers have more nerve than sense*. Just the same, opportunities multiply as they are seized, and die quickly when neglected. Using the Pathans to smash the Spetsnaz base was the only opportunity that he and Quinlan were going to get. If Cesmorius was to be a part of the deal, so be it. *Yeah—Inshallah* . . .

Could the Soviet GRU know what was being planned? This was the unknown factor that kept nagging at Camellion. GRU—Soviet military intelligence—was a past master in operating in a labyrinth of mirrors. No, the GRU did not know—if one wanted to believe Jiko Krim-Lizak.

Several days ago he had confessed. Fatalistic, as were all Pathans, Krim-Lizak had known he was trapped and would be executed. He did have a choice. He could refuse to tell what he knew and be hideously tortured until he begged to confess. (One favorite method of the Pathans is roasting a victim's feet over red-hot coals.) He would then be executed, and because he had been stubborn, his death would be slow and agonizing. A cord would be knotted around his penis, making it impossible for him to urinate. Gallons of water would then be forced down his throat. Unable to urinate he would have died from a burst bladder.

Or he could cooperate and tell what he knew. In return, he would be executed quickly—a bullet in the head.

Jiko Krim-Lizak had chosen the easy and the less painful way. He had talked without coercion, confessing that he had been an agent of the Russians for nine months. He had sent his reports to the GRU at the Soviet embassy in Islamabad by personal messenger—Al Seiffi Banrizm! In return for information, the Russians had promised to make him the president of the Independent Republic of Baluchistan after the Red Army invaded and conquered Pakistan. Krim-Lizak was simply a case of desire for power being stronger than love of nation and loyalty to tribe.

He swore over and over that the GRU did not know of the plan to attack the Spetsnaz base in Afghanistan—not that he hadn't intended to report that vital piece of information. He hadn't because he had not had the opportunity to send Al Seiffi Banrizm on any errand that would have given the man a chance to go into Islamabad, phone the Soviet embassy and make contact with the GRU—not one opportunity since the very first time the Death Merchant and the three Thunderbolt Unit Omega men had met with Chief Mirza-Khan.

Krim-Lizak's first and only chance to warn the Russians had been when Iskander Chaudhriy had asked him to find a man to replace the messenger who had become "ill."

There were four other traitors in Mirza-Khan's group, the four men who were supposed to have taken the Death Merchant and his group into Afghanistan to reconnoiter the Spetsnaz complex. Krim-Lizak could not use them. The cautious GRU would only deal through Al Seiffi Banrizm.

The Death Merchant had been right. Krim-Lizak had ordered Asad Dizakan to take Camellion and the other three men prisoners and turn them over to the Russians. Although Krim-Lizak had not exchanged messages with the GRU for many weeks, he did have the tracking transmitter in his possession and instructions on its use and operation. He had obtained the transmitter when he had gone to Peshawar four months earlier to buy supplies for the winter.

The transmitter was a kind of security to ensure the success of any possible kidnapping. The GRU agent had told Krim-Lizak: *Should anyone of importance ever have to be guided any distance and you can arrange men of your network to act as guides, all one of them has to do is turn on the transmitter. When your men are close to the border, they should remain in one spot for ten hours. That will enable our technicians in Afghanistan to get a positive fix. We'll then send over a helicopter to pick up the important person.*

Asad Dizakan and the three other "guides" were to have retraced their steps, go to Sirzihil and report that Camellion and Quinlan, O'Malley and Bruckner had been killed in a rock slide.

To compound Krim-Lizak's treason and forever damn his soul in the eyes of Allah, he was a double agent, also giving information (for 4000 rupees a month) to the Pakistan Chanwiri-lu-Shabudar, a fact not known to the GRU (then again, perhaps the GRU did know and was using Krim-Lizak for its own purposes!) any more than General I'Zada and his "Protectors of the People" suspected that Krim-Lizak was passing secrets to the Russians.

Krim-Lizak readily admitted that he had been responsible for the ambush of Camellion & Co. at the tomb of the Moslem saint. He had passed the details of the rendezvous to Abdus Powidi, who, having had occasion to go into Peshawar, had passed it on to Lukriz Au-mumin.

Camellion, who had been present during Krim-Lizak's interrogation, had asked, "Why didn't you have Powidi inform Au-mumin of our plans to attack the Spetsnaz base?"

Krim-Lizak had been prompt in answering. "I was never given any information by the Chanwiri-lu-Shabudar; yet I suspected that President Zia and his government were planning some kind of strike against our people. I was afraid that if I revealed your and Malik Mirza-Khan's plan against the Russians, Zia might decide that would be a good opportunity to strike. Should our people have been placed under the iron thumb of President Zia, I would no longer be in a position to report anything of value to the Russians."

"Well, you can't blame a spy for not wanting to lose his job," Quinlan had cracked. No one laughed. . . .

The Pathans executed Krim-Lizak the night of the same day that he had been exposed as a traitor and a double agent. He limped to the side of a stone house and turned his face toward the wall. He was still wearing his gun belt, only the holsters did not contain their Sig Sauer autopistols.

Iskander Chaudhriy had killed him with one shot in the back of the head.

That same night, the Pathans executed the seven captured Septsnaz—prisoners taken from the attack on Gubukil. The terrified Russians had been brought from Gubukil, one even on a stretcher. During the battle, the Death Merchant kicked him in the testicles and the man was unable to walk.

The Pathans took the Russians—two of the captives carrying Albert Visko, the man who couldn't walk—several *serais* south of town and shot them.

Later, Quinlan remarked laconically to Laski Shamspir, "I trust you gave those Russians time to pray?"

A direct, simple man, Shamspir took Quinlan seriously.

"Of course not, Kir Quinlan. They were not Moslem. They knew not Allah. If we had let them pray, they would have prayed to the god of the infidels. Since the god of the infidels is a false god and does not answer prayers, it would have been a waste of time to have permitted them to pray."

* * *

During the seventeen days following the airdrop, the Death Merchant, Quinlan and Bruckner, and the Pathans who had left Serzihil learned the full meaning of hardship. It took a day to open the wooden crates and prepare the weapons for the journey. Leather carrying-slings had to be made for the 110 hollow-charge warheads that would be fired from the forty MILAN launchers. Then there were the 200 82mm HE projectiles, each weighing 7.27 pounds, that would be fired from the five 82mm mortars. Each mortar weighed 121.3 pounds.

The airdrop had included 400 Colt CAR-15 submachine guns and six magazines for each SMG. There were also 100 Colt AR-15 assault rifles with six magazines for each. All these had to be carried. How else could they have been distributed to the other groups when all the Pathans met in Cesmorius?

The journey was a hardship for O'Malley as well. His wound excluded him from the actual attack on the base, but he was needed to direct mortar fire. Without the mortars there could not be an attack. Without the mortars, the force would not even be able to reach the Spetsnaz base.

Added to all the weapons was the food and the *ti'rusis* each man had to carry. The hundreds of men who had left Sirzihil had been weighed down like mules, in spite of the extra men helping carry the loads.

"A fool's journey!" Quinlan had remarked to the Death Merchant. "We're going on a fool's journey. We don't even know if the Pathans from the other villages will come to Cesmorius, especially under such conditions."

Those conditions were the security that had been imposed by Mirza-Khan and Richard Camellion. The trusted messengers sent to the different villages had been ordered not to reveal the destination of the groups. Instead, each messenger would act as a guide and lead each group to Cesmorius. The *cinorks* were expected to cooperate on the word of each messenger that he was a personal representative of Malik-Mullah Mujibur Ali Mirza-Khan.

"Suppose Krim-Lizak lied?" Quinlan had said to Camellion. "Suppose he did report the attack plan to the GRU and the Spetsnaz are waiting for us on their side of the mountains in Afghanistan?"

Quinlan had a valid point, although Mirza-Khan and the other Pathans had reassured the Death Merchant and his group that Jiko Krim-Lizak would not have had any reason to lie.

Iskander Chaudhriy had explained. "Krim-Lizak knew he was

going to die. He would not lie to protect the Russians, and he would not have lied to seek revenge against us. You would have to be a Pathan to understand, Kir Camellion. Krim-Lizak knew he had betrayed us. He knew the sin was on his head. As you would say, he gambled and lost. He accepted his fate. He did not hate us because we outsmarted him. To him . . . it was the will of Allah."

There was still President Zia to worry about. If Zia wanted to smash the Pathans in the northwest frontier, especially Malik Mirza-Khan, who was known to be the head of *Quiddin Azi-Hulam'ki*, the "Circle of Pure Blood" (which O'Malley said sounded like a Nazi organization for racial purity!) he might decide that now was his chance. Pak air-force planes and General I'Zada's agents and informers had to have noticed the thousands of Pathans and Garukals moving toward the Khyber Pass. The only certainty was that the groups from the other villages would arrive at Cesmorius—if they came—before the fighters of Mirza-Khan and Finar Lachok. The men from the other villages did not have fifteen tons of weapons and missiles to carry.

Only twice during the seventeen days did the fighters from Sirzihil spot aircraft. Each time the men had been in a very rocky area and had been able to hide, in spite of the planes being on a course far in the distance.

Mike Quinlan continued to voice his doubts, his main worry being that the force would be detected by the Russians before it could even get close to the Spetsnaz base.

"Hell, Richard. You know the pig farmers. There have to be Spetsnaz listening posts and patrols in those mountains on the Russian side of the border," Quinlan said when they were only a few hours from Cesmorius. "If we miss just one pig farmer, he could get off a warning and we'd never be able to climb down the south slopes and get into position to use either the missiles or the mortars."

Bone-tired, Camellion glanced up at the sun. They would reach the outskirts of Cesmorius by sunset.

"Well, the Company dropped three more 'magic ears' and several dozen night-sight scopes," he replied. "With them and silenced weapons we should be able to take out any Spetsnaz guards."

"And with luck," Quinlan said.

"We'll make it, Mike. Some things have to be believed to be seen—and believed in order to succeed. . . ."

* * *

Much to the relief of the Death Merchant, the three Thunderbolts and the hundreds of Pathans who had made the journey with them, the fighters from the other villages—180 of them—were waiting in Cesmorius, the ruins of which stunned Camellion, who, with his archaeologist's mentality, saw the richness of history in the large stone buildings fronted with tall columns. The long-dead past became alive in the semicircular theater that must have seated several thousand people and in the large square and what had been the opulent baths.

Gazing upon the parade of public edifices, honey-hued in the warming sun, Camellion let his imagination quicken the porticoes and plazas with the silent shades of people who had lived and loved here thousands of years ago. In his mind he could hear various sounds—the clink of the sculptor's chisel, the loud clanging of the smith's hammer on the anvil. He could see cloth merchants, potters, money changers, perfumers and crowds of shoppers in the *agora*, the central marketplace. And there, just outside the gates of the city, were peasants shouldering their produce. Again that very intense sensation . . . *I have seen all this before! I have been here before!*

He became aware of a voice far in the distance, a voice growing louder and getting closer, and of a hand on his arm.

"Kir Camellion, are you all right?" Iskander Chaudhriy looked concerned. There were four other Pathans with him and they too, along with Quinlan, Bruckner and O'Malley, were regarding the Death Merchant with a strange curiosity.

"Can you hear me?" Chaudhriy shook his arm.

"I was only thinking." Very quickly, Camellion reorganized his thoughts and came back completely into the present. "I was thinking of the border only twenty-eight kilometers from here. We have a long way to go and a lot to do."

"You acted as though you were in never-never land," joked Quinlan. He finished lighting a cigarette. "If the attack fails, I guess we'll all go to the Twilight Zone."

Chaudhriy introduced the four Paks with him and explained that they represented the fighters from the other villages. He said, "Every man has firearms, but nothing they have can match the submachine guns and assault rifles your friends so generously dropped from invisible airplanes. I was—"

"Invisible airplanes?" Josiki Kowir, who was actually a member of the Garukal tribe, drew back and turned to Chaudhriy in skepticism.

"The airplanes were invisible, my brother," Chaudhriy said seriously. "The Americans have devices that make objects invisible to all eyes."

"Except to the eyes of Allah," the Death Merchant said diplomatically. "We also have devices that can see in the dark, and magic ears that can hear a whisper half a *serai* away. Soon it will be darkness. I will show you and the other men that I speak the truth."

"Could we not then also distribute the weapons, Kir Camellion?" Chaudhriy said anxiously, then in a sly tone, "A fine weapon gives a man more confidence."

The Death Merchant agreed with a large nod. "A splended idea. "We'll give each man a submachine gun or an assault rifle. With the leaders, we'll then plan the move westward. The closer we get to the border, the more danger we'll be in. After we cross the border and are in Afganistan . . . I hope you've told the men what our mission is and what we are going to do?"

"They know. They are willing," said Chaudhriy. "They hate the Russian dogs as much as we do."

Kargath Kuuls, who did not speak English, spoke furiously to Chaudhriy in Urdu, pointing up at the darkening sky several times.

"Our brother is concerned about Russian warplanes," Chaudhriy translated. "He wants to know how we will defend ourselves against Russian planes when we attack. He said he knows there are aircraft at the base, including birds without wings."

"Tell your brother that we have ten launchers that will fire what are called Redeye missiles. They're ground-to-air missiles and will destroy the Russian planes."

"That's another thing we have to do before we get to the border," said Quinlan. He sounded like a businessman about to close a deal. "We'll have to show these guys how to fire the Redeyes and the MILANS."

It happened. Very suddenly, while Chaudhriy was explaining to Kuuls and the three other men, it happened. Bright green auras radiated from Kuuls and Chaudhriy's faces. Slowly the green changed to a dark brown, then to black.

I'm looking at dead men!

CHAPTER SIXTEEN

Science fiction is the probable made possible. Fantasy is the impossible made possible. In only one area of life and social existence does the possible, the probable and the impossible merge into a united front: in communism, in the Soviet Union where often the impossible is deemed probable. Once it is probable, it is therefore possible.

Immediately after the Spetsnaz had been beaten by Mirza-Khan's fighters, the second Directorate[1] of the Soviet general staff had demanded a full explanation from Lieutenant General Gregor Kerchenko and from Colonel Josef Arbikochek. Moscow reasoned that since it was impossible for any group of Spetsnaz to lose any battle, why then had the Spetsnaz been slaughtered?

General Kerchenko and Colonel Arbikochek had to make the "impossible" very possible. Unable to deny the reality of what had happened, they told the truth, emphasizing in their individual reports that the Spetsnaz had been ambushed by a "force of savages that greatly outnumbered our brave fighting men."

For a time, Moscow had seemed satisfied.

Until last night! This time, Moscow did not contact the Soviet Central Occupational Command in Kabul. The Second Directorate made contact directly with *Mogilki* on the shortwave. The order was to the point: Lieutenant General Gregor Kerchenko was to leave "Little Graves" the next morning, fly straight to Moscow and report—the instant he landed—to General Leonid Nikolaevich Klymov at GRU headquarters.

General Kerchenko knew why he had been ordered home.

[1]This is the GRU Central Apparatus.

Colonel Josef Arbikochek also knew why. There was to be an investigation. The old generals would want definite answers to certain questions. Why had not reconnaissance revealed any sign of an ambush? Why had assessment and information processing failed? To tell the truth, that assessment and information processing had been done and that Mirza-Khan and his people had outsmarted the GRU and the Spetsnaz would not be possible.

The old generals would not accept such "impossibilities."

Lieutenant General Gregor Kerchenko got little sleep that night. He knew what he had to do—turn the impossible into an acceptable explanation or suffer the consequences.

Colonel Josef Vadim Arbikochek slept even more fitfully, his dreams consisting of seeing himself as commander of some peasant militia in some tiny town beyond the Arctic Circle. Someone would have to take the blame and he was afraid it would be he. Why not. He was the field commander of the Spetsnaz at Little Graves.

Early the next morning, both men were deeply worried as they left the administration building and walked toward the GAZ-69 field car that would take them to the airstrip of the base, to the Ilyushin 11-18 transport that would fly General Kerchenko and other officers from Kabul to Moscow. Both, however, pretended that nothing was wrong, neither wanting the other to see how worried he was.

Snug in his greatcoat, Lieutenant General Kerchenko glanced toward the east. Dawn was more than traces of light. The rim of the sun had already risen. "It's warmer this morning," he said, trying to sound unconcerned. "I think we will have an early spring."

Colonel Arbikochek stared ahead, his eyes on the enclosed field car by the side of the concrete road, its driver sitting ramrod straight. Arbikochek was about to reply that he too felt that there would be an early spring when he saw Captain Stefan Belous running toward them. Belous was waving his arms and shouting, "Wait! Wait!"

Colonel Arbikochek and General Kerchenko stopped and stared at Belous. Something had to be wrong. Belous had thrown his greatcoat on over his pajamas, the bottoms thrust into boots. Panting from exertion, Belous explained that for the past hour the main watch in the radio center had not been able to make contact with the three patrol posts in the mountains to the north.

"Main Watch said that the last report they received was at 0.400 hours." Belous said anxiously.

"It can't be anything serious," General Kerchenko said quickly. "Those mountains are not even a full kilometer from here. How far to the north are the three posts?"

"All three are close to the end of the mountains," Colonel Arbikochek told him, a worried frown creasing his forehead. "Captain Belous, take a dozen men, go up there and see what the trouble is. It's possible that the problem lies in radio transmission. The three radios up there are—"

Blammmmm! The explosion came from the north, its suddenness making the three officers jump in astonishment.

"That was a mortar shell!" Arbikochek said in alarm.

In quick succession there were five more explosions from the north.

Berrrroooommmm! The detonation came from the west, several hundred feet to the right of the three men. Turning, they were in time to see one of the barracks dissolving in a cloud of smoke and boards and other material shooting upward and outward. With the debris were the crushed, torn bodies of men—Spetsnaz still asleep and who would now never awaken.

"We're—we're under attack!" gasped Lieutenant General Kerchenko.

Another impossibility . . .

At least this beats being in Los Angeles or Mexico City! Pleased with how the attack had begun, the Death Merchant, hands on his hips, studied the area at the south end of the mountains. Beyond the slopes there was a level area 400 feet long, 600 feet wide and filled with boulders of all sizes. It was in this area that he had stationed the men with the missiles and the mortars. He and Chaudhriy and Josiki Kowir had placed the forty men with the MILAN launchers out front, behind the first line of boulders facing the open area between the mountains and the north side of the Spetsnaz base.

Fifty feet behind the men with the MILANS were the five men with the mortars and their helpers. The Peppermint Kid and Wanja Likstom were in charge of the mortar crews, O'Malley constantly resetting the range of the mortars so that the 82mm HE shells would saturate the area between the first line of boulders and the north side of the base. Camellion and everyone else had assumed that the space—500 feet wide and slightly over half a mile long—would be filled with land mines. They had been right. Bursting 82mm mortar shells were exploding mine after mine, the whole area erupting with geysers of dirt.

Fifty feet behind the mortars waited the men with the launchers and the Redeye missiles.

Camellion was particularly pleased with the swift elimination of the *Spetsnaz* guards, which had been accomplished by slipping up on each group of five and shooting them with silenced AR-15 assault rifles. With the aid of night vision scopes and magic ears, the task had been fairly easy. That the Spetsnaz, in spite of their training, had been lax, not expecting anyone to dare attack them, had also helped.

The Death Merchant turned back to Mike Quinlan, who was observing, through binoculars, the mine field that continued to explode.

"You know, Richard, we might just pull this off," Quinlan said in German, sensing that Camellion was beside him. "By now, Willy and Seif-Bualy have everyone ready to charge across the area. We'll have it made if the pig farmers don't get any of their armor against us. Remember all those T-10 and T-54 main battle tanks we saw, and the BTR carriers and those line of armored cars?"

"I doubt if any of that armor is even gassed up," Camellion said. "So far we've done what we set out to do. We caught the pig farmers with their pants down. By the time they do get organized, we'll be in the base. See for yourself: the mine field is about cleared. The area looks like a field that's just been plowed by a drunken farmer."

Quinlan moved behind the giant boulder, put away the binoculars, looked around, saw that no one was watching him and pulled a bottle of Scotch from the medium gear bag whose long strap was over his left shoulder. He had brought three quarts of Scotch with him, carrying one and giving the other two to Bruckner and O'Malley. He had drunk only half of the quart in his bag. Now, seeing that no one was watching, he opened the bottle, took several very long swallows and licked his lips. He quickly capped the bottle and shoved it into his bag.

"We're not going to be able to grab any of the big shots," he said to Camellion, "Unless you and I and Willy do it ourselves and get lucky. Once the Pathans reach that complex, they'll slaughter every Russian in sight."

The Death Merchant, listening with pleasure to MILAN warheads exploding inside the Soviet base, gave a loud chuckle. "I certainly hope they kill every Russian in sight. That's why we're here. It's difficult to tell where the high-ranking officers will be. They might even fly out before we get there."

"We can charge anytime," Quinlan said, and belched. "You saw the space in front of us. Those shells have churned up every foot. Hell, I doubt if the mortar boys have fifty shells left."

"I'm going to talk to O'Malley and see what the score is. You keep an eye on the base. If you see any vehicles coming our way, yell out."

Camellion turned and started north, picking his way through the rocks. He was soon approaching the five mortars that were spread out in a sixty-foot line.

Voof! Voof! Voof! Three more 82mm shells had left the firing tubes by the time Camellion reached O'Malley and Wanja Likstom and told Likstom to order a halt to the firing.

"How many shells are left?" Camellion asked. "The mine field is clear."

Likstom called out to the five Pathans, and one by one they answered. There were twenty-four shells left.

"Jimmy, what's the maximum range of these babies?" asked Camellion.

A weapons expert, the Peppermint Kid replied instantly. "Approximately 3500 yards. That's 10,500 feet. What do you have in mind?"

Camellion did some rapid calculating. "Extend the range 1500 feet beyond what you now have and get off twelve rounds. Then extend to 1800 and get off the other twelve. We might just blow hell out of some planes at the airport side."

"It's as good as done," O'Malley said, and started toward the closest mortar.

"Kir Camellion, I am not staying here," said Wanja Likstom in a tone that sounded as though he were prepared to argue. "I am making the charge with the other men, with my blood-brothers."

"Of course you are," Camellion said. "Who said you had to remain here. Once the twenty-four shells are gone, the mortars will be useless. O'Malley's only remaining here because of his hip."

The RCA Tactec UHF/VHF walkie-talkie on his belt made a buzzing sound. At the other end was Bruckner, who, speaking German, wanted to know when they would make the charge.

"Chaudhriy, Kuuls, Shamspir and the other group leaders are having a difficult time holding them back. When do we go?"

"I'm with the mortars," Camellion said. "Give me five minutes to make sure the boys with the MILANs quit firing, then give the word GO. Willy, Mike and I are close to the MILANs. You stop when you get to us. The three of us will go in together."

"Good. See you shortly."

"I will go with you, Kir Camellion," said the fierce-looking Likstom. "When we reach the nest of Russian curs, it will be like it was weeks ago at the Shrine of Abdul-I-Zum."

"Be my guest." Camellion grinned.

The Death Merchant and Wanja Likstom were soon at the front line by the edge of the boulders, close to a Garukal tribesman using a MILAN launcher and the Pathan who was shoving in the projectiles.

It was clear why the CIA had sent Colt CAR-15 SMG and Colt-15 assault rifles. The Corporation knew a lot of the weapons would be dropped and found by the Russians. The CIA was sending the Soviet Union a message: *This is our work. We destroyed your base. Stay out of Pakistan.*

But why the Company had chosen MILAN[2] missiles was anybody's guess. Essentially a large tube, the launcher had a firing mechanism, an optical sight with X7 magnification and an infrared goniometer. All one had to do was load, take aim and fire the high-speed weapon. The two-foot-long, wire-guide hollow-charge projectile would then be on its way, traveling at 132 meters per second and carrying two pounds of TNT.

Slightly over half a mile to the south, the Spetsnaz base was being blown apart. Camellion could see that half of the buildings had been wrecked and were burning, flames and black smoke crawling up to the clear, morning sky. Yet many targets remained. To the southwest, he could see nine fuel tanks, each one twenty-five feet tall and sixty feet in diameter.

Those tanks gotta go! "Likstom, my friend, tell some of the men to send missiles at those fuel tanks," Camellion said. "Then they can gather their weapons and get ready to move out."

Likstom rattled off a stream of Urdu. Within a minute and half a dozen MILAN missiles were stabbing into the steel tanks of gasoline and exploding. The destruction of the fuel tanks had to be seen and heard to be believed, the concussions so tremendous

[2]MILAN = *M*issile d'*I*nfanterie *L*éger *AN*titank.

that at even this distance one could feel pressure in one's eardrums. Rolling balls of fire and long streamers of orange flame shot 150 feet into the sky and mushroomed outward for 300 feet. It was a minihell.

The tribesmen put down their launchers and began to prepare for the charge. Hurriedly they took off their long and heavy *chudkis*. Not only did the heavy coats inhibit movement, but they wouldn't be needed as protection against the cold. By the time the attack force reached the burning Spetsnaz base, exertion alone would have made their underclothes heavy with sweat. They would pick up their coats on the return trip—those who were still alive.

The Death Merchant and Likstom hurried to Mike Quinlan, who had taken off his *chudki* and was checking his weapons. He and Camellion and the two Thunderbolts were dressed in Pathan clothes. The airdrop had included a dozen SWAT heavy-duty, cold-weather coveralls. To have worn the black coveralls would have set Camellion and his men apart and made them special targets for Spetsnaz slugs. However, the four men had decided to wear the Corcoran paratrooper boots and use the Lo-Rider Holster Systems, the black nylon holsters riding low on the thigh and double-strapped to the leg.

The Death Merchant had inspected his two Bren Ten autoloaders, and Quinlan was securing the Glock[3] pistols in their low-hung nylon holsters when the Pathan and Garukal fighters, led by Iskander Chaudhriy, Fazal Qayyumkor, Kargath Kuuls and a dozen other Pathans, poured from the rocks and with loud war cries left the first line of boulders and started across the open space toward the Spetsnaz base, all of them racing past Camellion, Quinlan and Likstom as though they didn't exist. And then Willy Bruckner had stopped and joined the three men.

The Death Merchant picked up his Galil assault rifle and checked to make sure that the cover of his shoulder bag, filled with explosives, was buckled. He and Quinlan and Bruckner were each carrying twenty pounds of RDX in half-pound blocks, and forty timing/detonators for each block—very effective against

[3] The inventor of the Glock-17 9mm autopistol, Gaston Glock, would not permit his military pistol to be entered in the 1984 XM9 Personal Defense Weapon trials. Used by the Austrian army, the Glock-17 has a plastic frame, with four steel rails integrated into the molding to accommodate the slide. The staggered box-type magazine, also made of plastic, holds seventeen rounds. Some experts rate the Glock-17 as the finest military pistol in the world today.

tanks and other heavy armor. Antitank missiles would have been even more effective. But they would have been too difficult to carry. It was a matter of weight. The MILAN and Redeye missiles and the mortar shells had been more important.

"What's our first objective?" asked Quinlan. "I should think it would be the administration building."

"You guessed it." Camellion switched off the safety of his Galil AR. "Let's go out there and do it."

Considering that the mind set of the ivans in the Spetsnaz Little Graves base was geared to attack and not defense, the Russians organized with amazing rapidity. Training didn't have anything to do with it. It was sheer stress, and the suddenness and violence of the attack that made them fight back. Also, the Spetsnaz were different from the ordinary Red Army soldier who was trained not to think for himself but to follow the orders of his superiors. The Spetsnaz had been taught to think for themselves during emergencies—another reason why some of the Russians who had survived the missile bombardment rushed to the wreckage and to buildings still intact and prepared a defense.

Except at the airstrip! Here was only confusion. The pilot of the Ilyushin 11-18 transport that had flown from Kabul took off the instant he realized the base was under attack. In the cargo section were sixteen officers, some of very high rank. Sixteen officers were more important than any single officer at the base. Lieutenant General Gregor Kerchenko was on his own. . . .

There were six Sukhoi-9 fighters on the airstrip in front of the hangar. By the time four of the pilots—they hadn't even suited up—got to the SU-9s, the hundreds of Pakistanis, already kill-crazy, were halfway to the north perimeter of Little Graves.

The twenty-four 82mm HE shells from the mortars had done little damage. Only nine had fallen on the airport section of the base and had succeeded merely in digging small craters in the concrete runway.

The four SU-9s took off, one right after the other, their Lyulka single-shaft turbojets thundering. It was partially a ridiculous effort on the part of the pilots. A SU-9 could carry only four AA-1 "Alkali" air-to-air missiles. The Afghan rebels didn't possess an air force, so the pods in the SU-9s had been modified to carry eight GZ GA-6 air-to-surface missiles. Only one of the SUs had eight of the GA-6 "Spicer" missiles. Another fighter had six. Two of the SU-9s had only their pilots, who intended to buzz the attackers and disorganize them.

For four hours, Mike Quinlan had instructed the ten men with the Redeyes how to aim and fire the missiles, which technically were FIM-43A surface-to-air missiles. Mad Mike had been a good instructor and the men had been attentive pupils. Now they were ready for the Soviet fighter planes.

Two of the SU-9s came in low from the west, the third from the east. The fourth fighter, the one that carried eight Spicer missiles, made a five-mile turn and started to roar in from the north.

Very knowledgeable about how deadly any missile could be—Soviet missiles had turned whole sections of Afghanistan into wastelands—the ten Paks were very careful in aiming, following Kir Quinlan's instructions scrupulously. Almost as one finger, the ten men fired.

The two SU-9s in the west were turned into pure fire and smoke.

The SU-9 to the east exploded at an altitude of only 200 feet, as its pilot was starting his "buzz-and-confuse" run.

The Sukhoi-9, coming in from the north, was luckier, but for only several seconds. During those 1000 and 1s the pilot shot off three of the laser-guided Spicers, almost at the same moment that three of the Paks sent infrared terminal-homing Redeyes at his plane.

Trailing thin gases from the exhaust of its rocket engine, the first Spicer hit the flat area of boulders and exploded, killing fourteen of the older men who had acted as carriers. Seven others were wounded by flying rocks.

The second Spicer missile exploded in the rear of the force racing toward Little Graves and tore apart twenty-one men, while the third Spicer became a part of those rare million-to-one happenings. It was hit by a Redeye, both exploding in a brief big ball of fire. A moment later the other two Redeyes found the SU-9 and turned it and its pilot into almost nothingness.

Suicide can be deliberate self-murder or a result of the stupidity of placing oneself in a position in which the odds of surviving are one in 500. During war, soldiers in the front lines do not have a choice. The Death Merchant and the three Thunderbolts, as well as Iskander Chaudhriy and the other group leaders, did have a choice. Just as a general staff does not lead soldiers into battle, neither did Camellion and his three men place themselves in the front of the charging force. Nor did Chaudhriy and the other Pak leaders. Such self-sacrifice would have been counterproductive. Who would have led the force?

By the time the SU-9 shot off its three Spicer missiles, the first wave of Pakistani fighters was only eighty feet from where the two chain-link fences had stood on the north side of the Soviet base. Entire sections had been ripped out by exploding mortar shells and the way into the base was open.

There were several hundred men ahead of Chaudhriy and the other leaders, who, although they had led the charge, had then hung back, realizing that there were scores of men in the front lines who would be cut down by enemy fire once they were inside the base.

Forty feet behind Chaudhriy were the Death Merchant, Quinlan, Bruckner and Likstom, all five of whom had narrowly missed being hit by flaming wrecking of the SU-9 that had come in from the east. Pieces of wreckage did kill seven Pathans. Four minutes earlier, another thirteen Paks had been killed by two MON-50 *Miny ye Oskolochonym Napravleniem*[4] mines that, somehow, the 82mm mortar shells had failed to explode.

The first wave of Pàk fighters, racing over the torn-up ground where the two fences had been, were met with a deadly crisscross fire from Spetsnaz, many of whom were only half dressed. Russians were to the right of the Pakistanis, down in the wreckage of what had been food storage buildings before MILAN HC warheads had demolished them. Other Spetsnaz were to the left, amid the wreckage of a former recreation hall, both groups of pig farmers opening fire with AKR submachine guns and AKS-74 assault rifles, the streams of 5.45 × 39mm FMJ projectiles cutting ruthlessly into the first ranks of Paks.

The dead didn't stop those Paks who were still alive. They were used to seeing corpses, even bodies chopped apart by *kaurangs*. The Pathans and the Garukals in the northwest frontier led harsh, brutal lives in which blood feuds were common and justice right out of the Middle Ages; and being right next door to Afghanistan—turned into a hell on earth by the Soviet Union—they were used to violence of the worst kind. Their capacity for horror had become blunted. No longer could the Pakistanis *see* blood or *smell* the sweet stench of death or *feel* the results of pure evil.

[4] Antipersonnel mine with directional fragments.

Like battle-hardened veterans in any long war, they were anesthetized to the hideousness of the Cosmic Lord of Death.

The first wave of Pathans and Garukals fell beneath the onslaught of Russian slugs, but the second and third waves pushed on, firing and pitilessly trampling over their dead brothers, some even picking up the riddled corpses and using them as shields.

Hundreds of projectiles from Colt CAR-15 SMGs, Colt AR-15s, Galils and dozens of other makes of automatic weapons—even captured AKRs and AKS 74s, taken from dead Spetsnaz who had attacked Gubukil—chopped into the Spetsnaz on both sides and into other groups of Russians rushing in to help their hard-pressed comrades.

The Paks moved very fast. Yelling and shouting, they poured inside the base and quickly reached the pig farmers who had been firing from the wreckages of the food stores and the recreation hall. Face-to-face with the cruel-eyed tribesmen from Pakistan, the Russians could not have surrendered even if they had been so inclined, although two attempted to do so—the Pathans chopped off their hands with razor-sharp *kaurangs* and left the victims to bleed to death.

Human beings, even the "nice" people, are inclined to be more ruthless in the face of stress, and certainly the Pakistanis killed every Russian they found alive. Why not? As far as the Pathans and Garukals were concerned, the Russians were not even human beings. They were only a kind of disease that looked and walked and talked like men.

Now inside Little Graves, the Paks fanned out and began attacking those buildings that, untouched by MILAN missiles, offered refuge for the 714 Spetsnaz still alive. More Paks were cut down by streams of slugs before they could reach the first structures toward the center of the large area. But when the living jumped over the dead and closed in, the end came quickly for the frantic Spetsnaz, who were used to fighting on their terms—which meant infiltration, sneak attacks and other methods that come naturally to the Russian character. But here they were, cornered and actually defending themselves against *ne kul'turno* savages, *chernozhopski* fit to be only the sweepers of side streets and back alleys.

The Pathans and Garukals may have been "uncultured savages," but they knew what to do when they reached the sides of the wooden buildings that had not been constructed with defense in mind. Bent on revenge for the deaths of their Moslem brothers in

Afghanistan, they tossed West German Zeldt-14C grenades through windows and, after the explosions (which in some cases even injured the overanxious Paks) charged in before the survivors could recover their senses, their automatic weapons roaring. But not in every case. There were a few times when Spetsnaz survivors were so dazed that the Paks didn't even bother to slice them with slugs. Instead they chopped off arms and hands and split open skulls with their deadly *kaurangs*.

Iskander Chaudhriy and his group of eighteen fighters were very cautious. They remained down in a pile of rubble—splintered boards, overturned tables and chairs. Included in the mess were five Russian cooks and their helpers—killed by concussion or crushed to death by falling timbers.

"What is our next objective?" asked Laski Shamspir, who was next to Chaudhriy. "And where are the foreigners?"

"Do not concern yourself about Kir Camellion and his people," advised Chaudhriy. "They are experts. It is they who planned this strike against the Russian dogs. We are going to get to the tanks and destroy them—what's left of them."

Shamspir's expression indicated skepticism. Fazal Qayyumkor, on the other side of Chaudhriy, was not enthused either.

"How can we destroy those metal monsters?" asked Qayyumkor. "Grenades will not do it."

"I have nine kilograms of a powerful explosive that Kir Camellion gave me. It was contained in little bars that weigh very little. And he gave me the electrical devices that can make the bars explode. We will move out in a short while."

If Laski Shamspir had been psychic, he would have known that the Death Merchant, Quinlan, Bruckner, Likstrom and five other Pathans were in a half-wrecked garage only fifty feet from the mess hall. Some of the vehicles had been wrecked, but six GAZ-69 field cars and two huge MAZ-543 eight-wheeled heavy-duty trucks were still intact.

From their positions, Camellion and the rest of the men could see that much of the area was littered with dead—Pakistanis cut down by Russian slugs and Spetsnaz who had been killed not only by Pak projectiles but by concussion from exploding MILAN missiles and rubble.

"It smells like a barbeque with the meat burned," remarked Quinlan, referring to the inferno created when nine storage tanks, filled with gasoline, had exploded. The mushroomlike fire had roasted seventeen pig farmers running from one of the barracks toward the rows of main battle tanks, troop carriers, armored cars and other vehicles. The seventeen had been crew members of T-10 and T-54/55 heavy tanks and had been trying to reach the vehicles. The Spetsnaz had been preparing for the invasion of Pakistan and many of the main battle tanks were ready to roll—with full racks of shells for the 100mm and 120mm guns. The seventeen Russians had made a brave but useless effort. The rolling sea of fire from the nine exploded diesel-gasoline storage tanks had not only fried them to a crisp but had washed over many of the tanks and other vehicles parked in the vicinity of the fuel dump. In the open, diesel fuel will burn longer than gasoline, and now many of the vehicles began to explode from the sheer heat, fuel tanks and 100mm and 120mm shells bursting with giant thunderclaps of sound that made the ground and the buildings shake.

The crashing blasts were also sources of exaltation to the Pakistanis and also a message to Iskander Chaudhriy, telling him that he could forget his scheme to destroy the Soviet armor. He now debated what to do. From the position of his group, he could see, far to the west, a large two-story building shaped like a fat T, its south end partially destroyed by a MILAN missile. The concussion had also toppled the three-legged radio tower that lay crumpled over the foresection of the building. There were Russian dogs firing from the numerous windows on both floors, and Chaudhriy was positive that the building was the heart of the nest of Russian vipers.

How to reach that building was now the problem.

The Death Merchant was tearing apart the very same problem.

CHAPTER SEVENTEEN

Michael Quinlan was certain that a man with a mind as logical as the Death Merchant's would swarm all over the Spetsnaz administration building. It was only a matter of balancing maximum effort against minimum losses.

Camellion took the Tactec walkie-talkie from his belt but did not turn it on. "What we need to reach the headquarters building is some kind of gimmick," he speculated.

"Sure—and traveling nuns are roamin' Catholics," Quinlan said. He was playing the role of Devil's advocate. "That building is 250 feet from here. We'd be cut down before we got a third of the way."

Bruckner said in German, "There's also a lot of firing coming from those two buildings northwest of the administration building. See for yourself."

The Death Merchant was seeing—and doing some very rapid calculating. A hundred or so feet northwest of the main Spetsnaz building had stood four structures, two of which had been used to store medicine and uniforms. They had been obliterated by MILAN missiles. The other two buildings, the officers' mess and the officers' recreation hall, were under heavy attack by the Pakistanis, who were pinned down by furious firing coming not only from the two buildings but also from the main headquarters and administration building.

Due north of the half-demolished garage, in which Camellion and his group were hidden, had been two barracks. Now there were only wooden floors and piles of splintered boards, torn blankets, pillows and crushed bunks. The Russians who had occupied the bunks had been lucky. They had left the barracks before they had been hit by missles.

Fifty feet southwest of the garage was another mess hall, this one eighty percent destroyed. South of the mess hall was the blown-apart base "post office" and the dispensary.

Quinlan finished lighting a cigarette. "However we do it, we'll need help. Nine of us do not an army make."

Listening to Camellion and Quinlan, Likstom and the five other Pathans began to feel uneasy. It was so: the three foreigners were very brave, but to sneer in the face of death! Were they not also a little crazy?

"Affirmative, Mike," agreed the Death Merchant. "We'll need a lot of help when we boldly go where no man has gone before—where non–pig farmers have never gone before!"

"Like maybe a couple of dozen 'Spocks'!" Quinlan joked.

Camellion turned on the Tactec and held the walkie-talkie close to his mouth. "Kir Chaudhriy, come in. What is your position?"

Iskander Chaudhriy's voice was soon coming out of the walkie-talkie, explaining what he had intended to do until the armor had begun blowing up. Further conversation between him and the Death Merchant revealed that Chaudhriy and his group were only fifty feet southwest of Camellion and his knot of men.

"Kir Chaudhriy, come on over to us," Camellion said pleasantly. "I have a plan for attacking the headquarters building. I'm sure the method will work. I'll tell you about it after you get here."

"Very well. I will not shut off this radio device."

Camellion switched off his own RCA Tactec and shoved it into its holder, a kind of smirk on his smoke-smudged face.

"I'd like to know what you have in mind?" This time Quinlan was in earnest. "We haven't any tanks, no protection of any kind. You should have asked the Company to drop some one-man Gf Mechanisms!"

Kunar Rahm-Vavin said in a loud voice and in very broken English. "We do have the protection of Allah."

The Death Merchant didn't bother to give Rahm-Vavin a don't-be-an-idiot look. If Mike only knew the truth! The last Camellion had heard, through Courtland Grojean, American scientists were experimenting with a SUMC—Single Unit Man Carried—Gf-M. "The trouble is," Grojean had said, "that an individual needs a 'ton' of metal around him in order to make a SUMC work."

"We can use two of the MAZ trucks, if they're fueled up," Camellion told Quinlan. He added with a perfectly straight face, "And as our *baya-darka* here said"—he indicated Kunar Rahm-Vavin—"we do have the protection of Allah."

Both Quinlan and Bruckner knew better than to make any cute remarks about dear Allah around the Pathans, who loved their god better than the pope loved his.

An expression of new found enthusiasm spread over Quinlan's face. Old Blue Eyes—and Quinlan wasn't thinking of Frank Sinatra either—had done it again. He had come up with an answer.

Quinlan, Bruckner and the six Pathans stared at the six MAZ general heavy-cargo trucks. They were monsters. Each cab resembled the kind that would pull a trailer carrying an SS-1 (Scud-B) medium-range missile. Eight feet wide, the entire cab assembly rested on four large self-sealing tires that were fifty-two inches in diameter, with the enclosed driver's compartment on the left. On the right was the powerful diesel engine.

A four-wheel-drive truck with a payload of nine tons, the cargo section, or bed, was made of steel, the sides four feet high, the floor steel-ribbed and wooden. The high tailgate was of metal. Fifty men could hide in the bed. In the driver's compartment there was room for the driver and his relief.

"Well, Richard, if the Kid were here, he'd call you a twit," Quinlan said, looking at the large trucks which reminded him of a Roland mobile unit.[1] "The men in the rear would be safe, but what about the drivers? That cab will be shot to pieces before the truck is fifty feet from the garage—listen!"

The firing came from the west and from the southwest. The replies were much closer, coming from men who were running, darting and weaving to duck Spetsnaz slugs.

Iskander Chaudhriy and the fourteen men with him reached the garage. The race from the ruins of the mess hall to the garage had cost the lives of two men. A third was wounded, a bullet tearing through his left arm, barely clipping one of the collateral arteries. In spite of a tourniquet, he would slowly and quietly bleed to death.

The Death Merchant quickly revealed his plan to Chaudhriy

[1] The Roland Mobile Low-Level Air Defense System is a self-contined unit—tractor and trailer—that can be adapted to twin launchers with up to four missiles in ready-to-fire status, plus an additional eight missiles in automatic magazines to counter saturation attacks.

. . . a daring plan that would enable them not only to crash inside the Russian headquarters building but also to silence the guns of the Spetsnaz firing from the officers' mess and the officers' recreation hall.

Although pleased with the Death Merchant's plan, Iskander Chaudhriy was not bent on suicide, and he was an intelligent man, certainly a cut far above the average Pathan. Normal enough. He was not only Baluch, but was also educated in the fullest sense of the word. He was even likable, now that he had gotten over his suspicions of Camellion and the Thunderbolts.

Chaudhriy studied the closest MAZ truck, considering all factors. "Kir Camellion, tell me, what is to prevent enemy bullets from exploding the fuel tank of the truck?"

Camellion smiled. "A good question. The answer is that these trucks were designed to operate close behind front lines. The cab, the engine—and that includes the fuel tank—are heavily armored. The only flaw—"

"The only thing that could stop us is an RPG projectile," finished Quinlan soberly. "We don't have to worry about RPGs, not in my opinion. Our only worry will—"

"The trash in the headquarters building and in the other two shacks don't have anything but automatic weapons," Camellion cut him off, a new ruthlessness in his eyes. "The missiles probably blew up their RPG warehouse. If they had launchers, they would have used them against us by now." His smile became sinister, his eyes hooded. "But we have the trucks and plenty of grenades and more than enough RDX for what we have to do."

"Granted, but there's a matter of the windshields in the cabs," said Quinlan, not liking the way Camellion had interrupted him. "So the windows are bulletproof. That doesn't mean they'll hold up against sustained, concentrated firing. They'll be shattered by the time we're halfway there. How do we drive then? Those steering wheels are set up high. Sure, sure, I know the answer. I only wanted to mention it."

The peculiar blend of roasted flesh[2] and burning rubber drifted to Camellion. He looked first at Quinlan, then let his eyes sweep Chaudhriy and the rest of the Pakistanis. "With all the splintered wood and other junk in this garage, we can easily find something to brace the steering wheels when we are down on the floor. The

[2] Smells like pork roast, but sweeter.

difficulty will be with the truck that first passes in front of those two other buildings—I mean the two buildings a hundred feet northwest of the main headquarters deal. After the driver passes those two buildings, he will have to sit up for a moment to sight in on the headquarters building. That will be as dangerous as riding a motorbike in Tel Aviv. He'll also have to work fast rebracing the steering wheel—all the while holding down on the gas pedal."

"I will drive the truck," volunteered Bruckner. "The odds are with me. But I will drive only if you, Richard, are in the back tossing the RDX at the swine in those two buildings."

"I'll drive the other truck," offered Quinlan. A slight laugh jumped from his mouth. "What the hell! We could be worse off. We could have nagging backaches and nagging wives."

"What do you mean by nagging wives?" Jailan Dakhteri, one of the Pakistanis in the group that had entered the garage with Camellion, was puzzled.

"Bossy broads," explained Quinlan. "Women who try to tell their husbands what to do . . . who order them around."

Dakhteri shook his head. "Our women know better. They do what we tell them to do. That is the way Allah wants it."

Quinlan didn't answer. With Camellion, Bruckner, Chaudhriy and two other men, he started toward the trucks.

"How do we know the keys will be in the ignitions?" asked Wanja Likstom, tagging along. He had once hauled goods through the Khyber Pass.

The Death Merchant explained: "All Soviet trucks have the keys attached to chains fastened to the dash. The chains can be unlocked. But why should they be? The Spetsnaz felt safe in this base."

Reaching one of the big trucks, the Death Merchant looked at the cab. Yes, sir—big! The top of the cab was eleven feet above the ground. He grabbed the handholds, stepped up on the five-rung ladder, opened the door and looked inside. The key was there, on a chain and in the ignition.

Bruckner moved on to the next MAZ, and Quinlan called up to Camellion who was settling down in the driver's seat. *Suppose the fuel tank is empty?*

"We could ignore those other two buildings, but strategically we'd be taking a risk. We have another thirty to forty minutes, then we have to get lost in the mountains. The Ilyushin we saw taking off had to have made radio contact with Kabul."

Camellion turned and looked at Mad Mike, who had climbed up and was standing on the top rung of the short ladder. "Once we snuff the pig farmers in the two buildings and are in Spetsnaz headquarters, that will free the rest of the force to mop up. Eighty percent of the resistance is coming from those three buildings."

He turned the key in the ignition, fed fuel to the V-6 six-in-line water-cooled diesel and looked at the gauge. The tank was half full.

Ah yes . . . God is still in His heaven. "Michael, me boy," he quipped, "we're as good as inside the administration building. I'll tell you something else, my Irish lad—we're going to take two or three prisoners."

"You hope!"

"We will!"

CHAPTER EIGHTEEN

Toss down your dreams and gamble them on the dice table of life, but don't expect life to be fair. Even a piggybank full of pennies—rubles in this case—and a big potful of prayers would not have helped the Russians, who were determined to fight to the last man should reinforcements not arrive in time from Kabul.

A hundred and ten men were in the administration building; another sixty-two were defending themselves with AKRs and AKSs in the officers' mess and in the officers' recreation hall. Both groups were running low on ammunition and not a single Russian hoped to survive. Surrender? *Nyet!* Better to die fighting than to be hacked to death on one's knees.

At the south end of the administration building were Lieutenant General Gregor Kerchenko, Colonel Josef Arbikochek and Captain Stefan Belous. Major Petry Ukormidev was upstairs, directing the fire from what was left of the second floor. There had been three two-room apartments on the north end. A missile had left nothing but a gaping hole, with the splintered ends of framework and flooring sticking out into space.

It was falling into the hands of the Afghanistans that worried Major Ukormidev, who had not gotten out of bed to escort Lieutenant General Kerchenko to the plane. Colonel Arbikochek had told him it wasn't necessary. "Go ahead and sleep," Arbikochek had told him. Ukormidev now wished he had been ordered to escort Kerchenko. At least, he would have been dressed. As it was, he was wearing only trousers, slippers and a greatcoat. It wasn't that he was cold. Sweat rolled down his back and chest. It didn't seem right for a soldier to die half dressed—half naked. The thought continued to bother him.

Kerchenko and Arbikochek had more to worry about than staying alive. Even if help from Kabul did arrive in time, how could they possibly explain the cause of the disaster to Moscow. The base was wrecked, heavy and light armor destroyed, fuel storage tanks erased from the face of the earth. Over 1000 good and brave Spetsnaz were dead—and every bit of this destruction had been caused by either Afghan rebels or Pakistanis. It was impossible, yet it had happened. *It was*. There wasn't any explanation that Kerchenko and Arbikochek could give a board of inquiry.

During a short lull in the firing, Colonel Arbikochek remarked to a frantic-faced General Kerchenko, "Those four foreign agents we never found. They are responsible for this. Don't ask me how I know. Call it a hunch. But I'm certain. Somehow those four arranged for missiles to be dropped to the rebels."

"What difference does it make?" Gregor Kerchenko said bitterly. He shoved a full magazine of 5.45mm cartridges into an AKR submachine gun. "If help arrives, we'll live—probably to face a firing squad back home . . . shot for incompetence. I—"

"Look! The garage!" A dozen men, watching at the windows, shouted at once.

Kerchenko and Arbikochek hurried to a window and peered around each side. A MAZ truck was coming out of the garage to the northeast.

A highly experienced strategist, Colonel Arbikochek became even more of one when confronted with the fragility of his own mortality. He knew why the enemy was using one of the giant trucks.

"They are going to ram us," he said dully.

It had to be a matter of timing, of Mike Quinlan's being able to steer his MAZ toward the administration building and crash it through the front entrance, on the east, at the same time that Wilhelm Bruckner slammed his vehicle into the southwest corner of the building. Such synchronization would be extremely difficult.

Quinlan would have a straight shot. Bruckner's route would be far more complicated. After leaving the garage, he would have to drive west, then turn and go north and drive the truck only ten feet in front of the officers' mess and the officers' recreation hall. After going by the two buildings, Bruckner would make a left turn, go west for a short distance, then make another left and proceed south. The final turn would be slightly to the southeast and Bruckner would crash the front of the truck into either the middle of the building or its southwest corner. Or maybe even into the northwest corner, such as it was. It all depended on how many men would be firing down at the truck from the second floor of the administration building. The high steel sides and the tailgate would protect the men from slugs on ground level. From Spetsnaz firing downward was a different matter.

"Calculate it all on a speed of twenty miles per hour," Camellion had said.

Quinlan waited impatiently in his truck inside the garage while Bruckner, driving the other MAZ, took his vehicle out. The Death Merchant and ten Pathans were lying on the bed. Iskander Chaudhriy and eight fighters were in the rear of Quinlan's MAZ. The ninth man, Laski Shamspir, was watching through a crack in the west end of the garage. After Bruckner had passed the two buildings, Shamspir would race back to Quinlan's truck, yell "go," and climb into the rear with Chaudhriy and the other men. Quinlan would then drive his truck from the garage. The two vehicles, it was hoped, would crash into the headquarters building at the same time.

Only moments after Bruckner had driven the truck from the garage and had turned west, 5.45-mm projectiles began hitting the windshield, so that by the time the big MAZ had moved forty feet, Bruckner was forced to get down on the floor and, in an octopuslike position, hold the steering wheel by means of a chain, the ends of which he had tightly wired to the wheel. By pulling on each side of the chain, he could turn the steering wheel. The truly difficult part involved twisting his left leg so that his heel could press down on the gas pedal. The only way he could guess his speed was by the movement of the large truck.

Scores of FMJ projectiles from the headquarters building, the officers' mess and the officers' recreation hall struck the cab, windshield and doors, where bulletproof glass hung in grotesque patterns of tatters. Slugs tore into the seats, zipping through the leather and losing themselves in the padding, the ricocheting metal whining, shrieking, and howling. Other projectiles whizzed through the shattered rear window and buzzed over the bed where the Death Merchant and the men with him waited, most of them full of fear they didn't dare show. Only Camellion, lying on his back, seemed so nonchalant that Wanja Likstom felt as if this strange man from the West was actually enjoying himself; and thinking such thoughts made him afraid. The Pathans were an uncomplicated people and feared what they didn't comprehend, unless the mystery was explicable as the work of Allah. Mere mortals were not meant to understand the ways of Allah. *Inshallah* . . .

The Death Merchant had taken out seven half-pound blocks of RDX and had inserted the Mertex timer/detonators. All he had to do was turn the tiny knobs, toss them over the side and wait for the big bang—after, and only after, Bruckner turned the truck and was moving past the officers' mess and the officers' recreation hall. Camellion would partially use intuition and the sounds of enemy fire to judge when he should toss the packages of RDX from the truck.

Bruckner, however, would have to use far more than intuition to avoid crashing into the officers' mess, driving too far from the buildings for the RDX to be effective. He had no choice but to wriggle himself into a position by means of which he could take a quick look over the top of the dash, see his location and measure the distance. With effort, he managed to do so, his left foot having to ease off slightly on the gas pedal.

Mein Gott! He saw that he was only thirty feet from the two buildings, and also in a position that made it possible for the Russians on the north side of the headquarters building to fire at the left side of the big truck.

During those few seconds as Bruckner looked up and assessed his position, sixty slugs whined off the armor around the engine. Projectiles tore into the tires and against the truck bed. Three bullets also came close to his head. Two were even closer, the first only nine millimeters from his right ear, the second three millimeters from his left temple.

Donnerwetter! Then he was down on the floor, pushing against the gas pedal and frantically pulling on the chain to *his* left. A man of lesser strength couldn't have done it. But Bruckner had the strength of a baby bull; he succeeded in turning the big truck and heading it north.

The left side of the MAZ was eighteen feet from the east side of the officers' mess and the officers' recreation hall. Now the Spetsnaz on the north side of the administration building began firing at the rear tires and the tailgate of the truck. At the same time, confused Spetsnaz in the two buildings, wondering what the truck was trying to do, tossed a hundred or more projectiles at the left side of the vehicle.

It wasn't difficult for a man of the Death Merchant's experience to know when to throw the packages of RDX. To him, the Spetsnaz were the same as those "medical researchers" who sew the eyes of cats shut (to study "sight deprivation") and smash dogs in the head (to study "brain damage") and he was going to enjoy killing the trash. Rapidly he turned the knob of the first detonator to 15S—fifteen seconds—and tossed it over the left side of the truck. One after another, three more followed. He didn't throw them as hard as he could. He didn't want any of the half-pound packets bouncing back from a wall.

They didn't. The rear end of the truck was twenty feet north of the second building when the four packets of RDX began to explode. *Blammmm-blammmm-blammmm-blammmm.*

Bruckner had done a fine job and so had the Death Merchant. The four half-pound blocks of RDX had landed in front of the two buildings. The closest had been only a foot from the wall of the first building, the farthest five feet from the wall of the second building.

When the smoke cleared the fronts of the two buildings had disappeared and thirty-one Spetsnaz were dead. The survivors—twenty had been wounded and were unconscious—were dazed, many even unaware that they had been splattered with blood and pieces of flesh and bone and cloth from their ripped-apart comrades. A slaughterhouse would have looked more tidy.

The four concussions hadn't helped the health and welfare of the Death Merchant and the men lying on the bed of the truck. Most had tiny trickles of blood running from their ears and noses, including the Death Merchant—and weren't bells ringing in the center of their brains?

Down on the floor in the cab, Bruckner had been protected—up to a point—from the concussions, although there was a loud ringing in his ears. As he looked up over the dash to get his bearings, then ducked down and pulled on the chain to turn the truck to the west, Mad Mike Quinlan pulled out of the garage in his MAZ. Quinlan turned, aimed the large cab at the main entrance door of the administration building and ducked down, to the tune of a dozen AKR projectiles hitting the windshield and generating hundreds of spider webs in the bulletproof glass. Wishing he were fighting anyone in Angola instead of pig farmers in Afghanistan, Mike Quinlan shoved two pieces of wood under the horizontal spokes of the steering wheel and eased up on the gas by shifting his right buttock. Now the whole nine yards was in the hands of—why not Allah? Canary crap . . .

It was the intense cramping in his legs that forced Bruckner to make the decision, pain and the very real possibility that the Russians on the second floor might be able to fire down into the truck bed. Should that happen, Old Blue Eyes and the other men wouldn't have chance one.

After Bruckner had made another turn and was headed south, he looked up once more over the dash and through the shot-out windshield, saw that he was on course and made up his mind to slam the cab into the northwest corner of the building. Not that there was actually any northwest corner! There wasn't even a north end. There was only a gaping maw surrounded by a tilting second floor and on both sides the splintered ends of framework that had buckled and then broken. Overhead, the ends of joists protruded and furniture was tilted precariously. Joists also stuck out from underneath the bottom floor that was littered with broken furniture, smashed metal desks and metal files half buried in rubble.

So much the better! thought Bruckner. He would take the big truck all the way into the damned building.

On the east, the Russians around the main entrance of the building (at the very bottom of the fat T leg) were horrified when they saw that Quinlan's MAZ was roaring straight for the door. They weren't any more astonished than the Spetsnaz on both floors of the open north end who, when they saw Bruckner's truck, ran back to the stairs in the center of the building. The only weapons the Russians possessed were submachine guns, assault rifles and pistols, and they knew there wasn't anything they could do until the two large vehicles came to a halt and the attackers jumped from the trucks. Grudgingly, the Spetsnaz were forced to admire the rebels for their insane bravery, at the same time regarding them as suicidal fools. Every Russian was afraid, including Colonel Josef Arbikochek and Lieutenant General Kerchenko. Both men had hurried from the south end of the building and had been in time to see explosives, tossed from one of the trucks destroy half of the officers' mess and half of the officers' recreation hall. Both buildings had vanished in clouds of fire and smoke. Arbikochek, Kerchenko and Captain Belous had then hurried to the west side of the building. Their main fear now was that the two trucks were on a suicide mission, that the crazy *chernozhopy* would explode forty or fifty kilograms of explosives and destroy the entire building and everyone in it. The frustrating part, was that there wasn't a damned thing Colonel Arbikochek could do about it. Nothing but wait and see what would happen.

"Get down!" shouted Arbikochek. "Get behind anything you can find, and don't fire until they're out of the trucks."

Lieutenant General Gregor Kerchenko, his uniform filthy, turned angrily on Arbikochek. "Down here? Why not the second floor? The stairs are still intact."

"One of the trucks might come so far in it'll take the stairs with it," Arbikochek snapped. "We don't dare be trapped upstairs." He turned to Stefan Belous, who was still wearing his greatcoat, pajamas and boots. He was armed with a PPS-43 SMG and had a bag of magazines slung over one shoulder. "Go upstairs and tell Major Ukormidev to—never mind. I see that he and his men are already coming down the stairs."

"Here comes one of them!" yelled one of the Spetsnaz. *"Get down!"*

A few moments later the cab of Mad Mike Quinlan's truck crashed through the main front entrance of the headquarters building, pulverizing the door and its framework with the ease of a T-64 main battle tank rolling over a hedgerow. Sections of walls on both sides of the entrance fell inward and part of the ceiling fell, most of it on the cab, but some of it tumbling down on Iskander Chaudhriy and the nine men with him in the bed of the truck. The weight of the monster caused the front tires to break the wooden flooring, with the result that very quickly the entire cab had dropped two feet and all four tires were rolling over bare ground. Yet while the truck was slowing, its momentum continued to carry it forward, the wooden floor buckling in front of the big bumper. The truck, now completely inside the building, would have stopped anyhow, for right after Quinlan felt the front of the cab batter down the door and parts of the wall, he twisted around and pushed down on the brake pedal with both hands. Gradually, the truck came to a stop. At once, he twisted around, pulled his two 8mm Glock autopistols, switched off each safety and waited. Now everything *was* in the hands of whatever God existed—and where in hell was Willy and Camellion?

Iskander Chaudhriy, Laski Shamspir and the other men in the rear were not concerned about Bruckner and Camellion. They couldn't afford to be. They pushed aside the boards that had fallen on them, took out Zeldt 14-C grenades, pulled the pins and tossed them over the cab of the truck.

Developed to kill terrorists, a Z-14-C *Besonder Zweck Granate* is a special-purpose grenade. With a six-second fuse and 226.8 grams of TNT, the body is composed of thousands of needles, each 9.53 millimeters long, all held together by a special substance. When the grenade explodes, the needles fly outward with the force of .22-caliber bullets.

The seven grenades thrown by Iskander Chaudhriy and his group killed eighteen Russians and wounded ten more, the casualties minimal only because the majority of Spetsnaz had gotten down flat behind various pieces of furniture and the force of any grenade is always up and outward.

The Spetsnaz still alive would have slug-riddled Chaudhriy and his small group as they leaped from the rear of the truck if Willy Bruckner and his truck hadn't roared through the open north end, the large tires of the cab repeating the performance of the first MAZ and breaking through the wooden floor. The entire truck "dug" its way inside the building for twenty feet and finally came to a stop, the framework of a metal chair popping as the right front tire of the wide cab squeezed it between the hard rubber and a broken joist of the floor. Instantly, Darham Poldo and Sarvin Castikol reared up and began to sweep the forward area with CAR-15 5.56mm projectiles, firing over the rim of the bed and over the big diesel engine that was next to the cab. Their hail of slugs stung nine more Russians to death and chopped through metal desks, files and other items of office furniture.

Afraid of more grenades, the Russians were at a disadvantage, since by now, Iskander Chaudhriy and his group had jumped from the truck and were hosing the entire area with slugs and the Death Merchant and his men were racing in from the north, and with them Bruckner, who had crawled from the cab. Mike Quinlan had also gotten out of his tractor and was moving forward like a man undergoing a violent epileptic seizure while remaining on his feet—jerking first one way and then another.

The first floor of the building became an arena of pure racket, of roaring AKRs, AKSs, some PPS-43s, Colt CAR-15s, Galils and Colt AR-15 assault rifles; and there were cries and yells, shouts and screams of agony. It was a battle in which only the most experienced killers and the luckiest would survive.

For several minutes the firing from the Spetsnaz and from the Death Merchant and his people was almost at point-blank range, with Camellion and his men closing in and the Russians charging forward to stop them, the progress of both groups hampered by fumes that stung the eyes, and by bodies and other litter on the floor. Yet it was the inexperience of the Pakistanis that was responsible for the Spetsnaz losing. While the Russians were brave and more than willing to die in battle, their training did not permit hatred to overcome common sense. One does not win battles by being a fool and taking suicidal risks. In contrast, the Pakistanis were convinced that if they died in battle, they would go straight to heaven and see Allah face-to-face. Also, in contrast to the Russians who were only doing a job, the Pakistanis harbored a burning hatred of anything Soviet and were determined to take as many Russians with them as possible. The Russians would drop straight into hell. The result was that the Paks charged forward, firing short bursts, and were often face-to-face with Russians, down behind overturned furniture, before the ivans could realize what was happening and swing up their weapons.

The Death Merchant and the two Thunderbolts were also well-trained fighting machines who relied not only on experience but on the practical aspects of survival. All three were facing the Russians for only one reason: money. They were being well paid to do a specific job, and they intended to live in order to see those nice fat bank accounts get even fatter.

Iskander Chaudhriy was also a logical man, being a Moslem in name only and feeling that it was highly improbable that he would see anyone or anything after death, certainly not Allah.

Consequently, Camellion, Quinlan, Bruckner and Chaudhriy did not charge ahead like maniacs but waited until what remained of the force was almost clashing with what remained of the Russians—face-to-face.

What remained of the Death Merchant's group was thirteen men, including Camellion, Chaudhriy and the two Thunderbolts. Of the Russians, Lieutenant General Gregor Kerchenko, Colonel Arbikochek and his three main staff officers were very much alive, hidden behind filing cabinets. The cabinets had been hit scores of times, but always the yards of paper, from front to back, had absorbed the 5.56mm projectiles.

However, the four Soviet officers could no longer remain concealed behind the six cabinets. The Pakistanis had closed with the Russians in bitter hand-to-hand combat, and although outnumbered, the Paks were winning. Colonel Arbikochek, Major Ukormidev and Captain Belous rushed out with drawn Vitmorkin machine pistols.

Not Lieutenant General Gregor Kerchenko. He was not a

coward. But he was not a fighting man. He was in his fifties and, while in good health, out of condition. He knew he was not a match for any blood-crazed *chernozhopki*! Should the Spetsnaz win—fine. Should they lose, Kerchenko would lie facedown on the floor behind the filing cabinets and pretend to be dead. The chances were that the enemy would not even see him. They would be anxious to lose themselves in the mountains before reinforcements arrived from Kabul.

It was pure savagery. It was kill or be killed. The Death Merchant wasted six Spetsnaz with the two Bren Ten autopistols, the big 10mm slugs smashing into the pig farmers with the force of sledgehammers. All too soon, he found himself right in the thick of the fighting, with Chaudhriy to his left and Quinlan and Bruckner to his right. At point-blank range, he killed two Spetsnaz rushing at him with AKR Shinkov SMGs that no longer had ammo in their magazines, the two Russians making an attempt to smash the Bren Tens from his hands before he could waste them. They failed. It was their time to Go West. They did—10mm projectiles in their chests.

Sensing a pig farmer trying to come in behind him—Andrei Lipusnik had a *pastavilki*, a combat trench knife—the Death Merchant killed another man with a round from the left Bren Ten, then turned to the left and stopped Lipusnik with a powerhouse kick, the bottom of his boot sinking into the pit of the joker's stomach. Lipusnik's eyes popped, his mouth opened and a strangled cry jumped from his mouth. Down he went. Camellion could easily have put him to sleep forever with a 10mm bullet, but why waste ammo on an adversary whose fighting ability had ended?

Fazal Qayyumkor thought otherwise. As the angonized Lipusnik was going down, Qayyumkor chopped him across the back of the neck with his *kaurang*, the heavy blade almost decapitating the pig farmer.

Fazal Qayyumkor, swinging blood and gore from his *kaurang*, never realized what hit him when Captain Belous, only seven feet away, put three 9mm projectiles into his body, one in his left side, one in the neck and one in his head. But Belous had made a fatal mistake. He had not considered Iskander Chaudhriy, who reached him before he could swing the long barrel of his Vitmorkin machine pistol around. Chaudhriy was grabbing Belous' right wrist at the same time that Vasil Erzin, using an empty AKS-74 assault rifle as a club, aimed at the Death Merchant's left wrist with the underside of the barrel, his intention to knock the Bren Ten from Camellion's left hand. Simultaneously, Pavovich Tsymbal came in from the right, an AKS-74 in his hands, a deadly *pastavilki* attached to the barrel. Camellion suddenly had the feeling that he had the Cosmic Lord of Death perched on his shoulders!

Yet he wasn't in any worse fix than Mad Mike Quinlan, who had exhausted the ammo in his two Glock pistols and was about to tangle with three of Mama Russia's "best." In his left hand, Quinlan had a 2-S survival knife; a *kaurang* was in his right hand.

Two of the Spetsnaz had trench knives, the third man an empty AKR Shinkov submachine gun that he intended to use as a baseball bat, with Quinlan's head the baseball. To Quinlan's left, the Russian came in fast with a low, intended upper thrust—only moments before the man in front of Quinlan charged. Concurrently, the third man swung the AKR.

Quinlan barely managed to twist from the first man's knife, the blade of the *pastavilki* slicing through his heavy shirt. The Russian had left himself wide open with the miss. Quinlan promptly stabbed him in the stomach with the 2-S survival knife, the thirteen-inch blade almost tickling the slob's spine. Practically in the same microsecond, Quinlan ducked the blade of the second Slavic sap and managed to jerk his head down to dodge the arcing swing of the AKR.

Mad Mike was far more than highly experienced; he was also very fast. Surprising Pavel Kiktev and Maksut Ryzhkov, he dropped the 2-S knife and the *kaurang*, grabbed Kiktev's right wrist with both hands and called the man a son of a bitch in Russian. Pulling on Kiktev's right arm, he jerked the man closer to him and let him have a short but very powerful snap kick to the testicles. Kiktev couldn't even howl. He could only make animal sounds as he dropped his trench knife and started to fall, his entire body in a purgatory of pain.

This time, Mad Mike easily ducked the AKR swung viciously by Maksut Ryzhkov. And this time he did something about it. He struck the muzzle away with his left hand, stepped forward and grabbed the upper part of the weapon's hand guard with his right hand and the small of the stock with his left hand. Very fast,

Quinlan pulled with his left hand, pushed with his right hand and stepped to the right of Ryzhkov with his right foot, the entire movement knocking the Spetsnaz off balance and enabling Quinlan to slam him on the head with the barrel—a short but powerful blow. Half dazed, Ryzhkov didn't have much of a chance. Mad Mike twisted the AKR from the Russian's hands, broke his left instep with a right-heel stomp, and then, when Ryzhkov yelled in pain and bent over, stabbed him mightily in the stomach with the barrel of the AKR. Ryzhkov was finished. And in another few seconds, Mike Quinlan would have been. But he stepped to one side in time to prevent another Russian from bayoneting him in the gut with a *pastavilki* on the end of an AKS-14. The Russian screamed shrilly when Kunar Rahm-Vavin chopped him in the shoulder with a *kaurang*, then turned and grinned at Quinlan. He didn't have time to smile very long. More Spetsnaz were coming at him and Mad Mike.

The Death Merchant, although managing to jerk back his left hand and prevent Vasil Erzin from breaking his wrist, had not been fast enough. The end of Erzin's gun barrel came down on the slide of the Bren Ten with such force that if Camellion had not opened his hand and released the autoloader, his trigger finger could easily have been broken. The Bren Ten fell to the floor, but before Erzin could make another move, Camellion swung the Bren Ten in his right hand to the left and put a 10mm slug into the Russian's chest, knocking him all the way back to a Spetsnaz who was struggling with Wanja Likstom. Camellion then turned the Bren Ten back to the right, toward Pavovich Tsymbal—and tripped! With his lower right leg, he tripped over a metal chair and fell backward, landing heavily on his back. No fool, Tsymbal was very much aware that Camellion still had possession of the one Bren Ten. He rushed in faster, knowing he would have to kill the enemy before the tall man blew him away. Tsymbal lost. He was stabbing downward with the AKS-74, aiming the blade of the *pastavilki* at Camellion's midsection, when the Death Merchant raised the big weapon and pulled the trigger, the big bullet hitting Pavovich Tsymbal in the center of the nose. In the process the slug erased most of his face and blew out most of the rear of his skull. Instantly, Camellion rolled to his right, for the weight of the dead Tsymbal kept the deadly trench knife moving downward. Camellion had not had one second to spare. The blade barely touched the side of his *toba*, then buried itself an inch and a half in the wooden floor. The dead Pavovich Tsymbal, his face a big maw of emptiness dripping blood, crashed to the floor beside Camellion, who was getting to his feet.

Iskander Chaudhriy almost broke Captain Belous' right arm, so savagely did he tear the Vitmorkin machine pistol from the Spetsnaz officer's hand. Belous, however, was an expert in Sambo, the Russian martial-art form, and he did not intend to go down easily. With his left hand, he chopped Chaudhriy viciously on the right side of the neck, a blow that staggered Chaudhriy and made him even more angry. With a cry of rage, he slammed the long barrel of the Vitmorkin against the side of Belous' head, but not with all his strength. He wanted the man to know what was going to happen. The blow did make Belous stagger, cry out with pain and half sink to his knees. Watching with satisfaction, Chaudhriy could have killed him then and there with a bullet from the machine pistol. Instead he dropped the Vitmorkin, grabbed Captain Belous' right hand with his left hand and pulled a *kaurang* from his belt. There was a loud swishing sound and a high-pitched scream from Belous, whose right wrist, no longer attached to a hand, was spurting blood from severed digital veins and metacarpal veins and metacarpal arteries. Cursing Belous in Urdu, Chaudhriy tossed away the man's hand and watched the bleeding-to-death Russian, who had fainted from shock and was falling to the floor.

It took only a few seconds, and Iskander Chaudhriy was a corpse. Colonel Josef Arbikochek had put six 9mm Vitmorkin projectiles into his chest. His mouth slack, his eyes closed, blood oozing from six different holes, Chaudhriy crashed to the floor. Yet Arbikochek had made a serious error in killing Chaudhriy. He had permitted hatred and a desire for revenge to supersede common sense. He had pushed the firing lever of the Vitmorkin from semi-automatic to three-round burst, determined that the damned savage who had just killed Captain Belous would die. One 9mm hollow-point bullet could have done the job. Certainly three would have scratched Chaudhriy. Instead, Colonel Arbikochek had pumped *two* three-round bursts into Mirza-Khan's right-hand man.

Arbikochek soon realized his mistake. He saw a tall, blue-eyed man rushing toward him, two large pistols in his hands, and suddenly sensed that this man was neither Afghan nor Pakistani. As he raised the Vitmorkin, he knew that the man was one of the four elusive foreign agents. For a hundredth of a second, he felt intense satisfaction in that he had been right. He had said those four intelligence agents were responsible for the attack on Little Graves. And now, at least one of the son of a bitches would pay for it!

Arbikochek pulled the trigger of the Vitmorkin.

Click! The firng pin fell on an empty breech. The machine pistol was empty.

Major Petyr Ukormidev, twenty feet away toward the stairs, had also spotted the Death Merchant rushing at Colonel Arbikochek and, sensing that Arbikochek's machine pistol was empty, raised his own Vitmorkin. The scar-faced Ukormidev was too late. A very big man and a group of Pathans were rushing at him and the other four Spetsnaz around him. Only one of the Russians had a spare magazine left for his PPS-43 submachine gun and was now desperately trying to reload the weapon.

Major Ukormidev raised the Vitmorkin that was set to semi-automatic fire and pulled the trigger. The weapon roared and Jailan Dakhteri went down. Again the Vitmorkin snarled, this time the slug hitting Kargath Kuuls in the midriff. And then the machine pistol was empty and time had run out for Ukormidev and the rest of the Russians. Wilhelm Bruckner and the remaining three Pathans closed in on the group of Spetsnaz.

Reaching Major Petyr Ukormidev, who was trying to pull a 9mm Makarov from his greatcoat pocket, Bruckner let him have a dynamite right-legged kick in the groin, and when the man screamed and started to go down, Bruckner kneed him in the face, breaking his nose and half a dozen front teeth. The big German mercenary took time out to jerk a PPS-43 submachine gun from the hands of another pig farmer and then, after Ukormidev had fallen in agony on his face, Bruckner killed him by stamping on the back of his neck with his right foot.

The five other Russians fought with fury, but they were not a match for Bruckner and the three blood-crazed Pathans. *Kaurangs* sang in the air and chopped into Russian flesh, thick blood spraying from the blades. The slaughter took only a few minutes, and when it was over, Bruckner and the other men were splattered with blood. On the floor lay the butchered Russians, large pools of red spreading underneath them.

"*Zdravstvuite!*" the Death Merchant said pleasantly to an astonished Colonel Josef Arbikochek, the word being the Russian equivalent of "Howdy." Since Camellion had one cartridge in one Bren Ten and three in the second autopistol, he could easily have killed Arbikochek on the spot. He would have liked to. He had seen the Russian officer kill Iskander Chaudhriy. He didn't blame him. The Spetsnaz officer was only doing his duty. *We attacked his base. He was defending himself.*

Even so, the Death Merchant was not the type to let personal feelings interfere with logic. The battle was over, although scattered gunfire from outside indicated the Pathans were still mopping up. The man in front of the Death Merchant was an officer. He would have valuable secrets to tell.

Camellion was half right. Josef Vadim Arbikochek did have secrets, but he would never tell them. He was staring at the tall, blue-eyed man and wondering why Camellion did not pull the trigger of one of the Bren Tens when Laski Shamspir, one of the men with Bruckner, threw the *kaurang*, the blade burying itself right up to the crossguard in Arbikochek's right side, just above the belt.

Angry, Camellion looked at Shamspir, Bruckner and the other two Pathans as Colonel Arbikochek, blood trickling from one side of his mouth, sank to his knees, a hurt expression on his face, as though he were trying to say, "Why? Why did you do this to me? I was already your prisoner. . . ."

The dying man wobbled from side to side, the final darkness pulling itself down over his mind. Finally, he fell forward on his face and lay still.

Michael Quinlan and three other men, who by now had reached the Death Merchant, looked in disbelief around the large area. There were far more than a hundred corpses on the floor. No one could see him, but he was there, laughing his eternal insane laugh—the Cosmic Lord of Death. He had laughed in 1917 when the Bolsheviks came into power in Russia. He had laughed in 1933 when Adolf Hitler had become chancellor of Germany. During the 1990s he would laugh hardest of all. What a joke would be played on humanity. . . .

"The man you just killed was an officer," Camellion said firmly to Laski Shamspir, who was leaning down and pulling the bloody *kaurang* from the corpse of Colonel Arbikochek. "He could have told us many things about the setup here."

Wiping the blood from both sides of the blade on the back of the corpse's greatcoat, Shamspir looked up at the Death Merchant, resentment in his dark eyes. "He killed our *baya-darka* Iskander Chaudhriy. I executed him for his crime. What I did was pleasing in the eyes of Allah."

"Kir Camellion, you can have the next Russian officer we find," said Kunar Rahm-Vavin, amusement in his voice. "Some of the dogs might still be alive."

Mike Quinlan shoved a magazine into his Galil AR. He was covered with blood, his clothing ripped in many places. But once more he had survived. "Well, well, I haven't seen so much dead meat since Angola. And to think we did it all without any EMs or SITREPS."[1]

"Nein, mein Standartenfuhrer," Bruckner said. "Do not forget Ethiopia. We killed over 600 at Dire Dawa—and how many of their Russian friends. We made believers of those bastards."

"We'll have a quick check, then get out of here," the Death Merchant said, looking at the Paks. "I gave Kir Chaudhriy a dozen walkie-talkies to distribute, but I don't know who he gave them to."

Wanja Likstom cocked his head to one side. "Why is that so important, Kir Camellion?"

"Because we have to signal the men to retreat and get to the mountains," Camellion explained. "Should Soviet gunships get here before we reach the mountains, we'll all end up dead—and we won't be all that safe in the mountains, not until nightfall."

"Having our brothers return to the mountains is not difficult," Likstom said, laughing. "We have a special yell we use. Once we are out of this house of evil and death, we shall give the call and the men will know it is time to go to the mountains with all speed that is possible."

"Don't forget the poor guy in the garage," Camellion said. He looked down at his equipment belt, frowned, and then started looking around on the floor.

"The man in the garage is wounded," Likstom said in a simple voice. "We cannot lose time taking care of any wounded. Do not concern yourself. He will commit suicide and not let himself be captured."

Camellion glanced at Likstom but didn't comment. Why argue

[1] Enlisted men; situation report.

with a thousand-year-old custom, with a culture that was ancient before Chris Columbus' great-grandfather had been born?

Quinlan and Bruckner stared down at the body. The man lay on his belly, his head turned to one side, three bullet holes in the back of his dark green greatcoat. Quinlan poked at the hip of the body with the barrel of the Galil, then winked at Bruckner, who grinned. They had seen the trick tried before, and if it ever worked, they had never known about it. They never could have known because they would have thought the body to be an honest-to-goodness dead man. This body was not a corpse. There wasn't even a tiny drop of blood around any of the three bullet holes in the greatcoat. During the fighting, the noise and confusion, this officer had removed his greatcoat, fired three slugs into the back, had gotten back into the coat and had lain down.

"He's dead too," Quinlan said, noticing that while the left hand of the "corpse" was in plain view, the right forearm was underneath the man. "Just the same"—he placed the muzzle of the Galil against the back of Lieutenant General Gregor Kerchenko's head—"I'm going to blow his damned head off. I never did like pig farmers."

Miracle! Miracle! The "corpse" became alive! It spoke—a frightened Kerchenko saying in fairly good English, "Don't shoot. I surrender."

Forever cautious, Mad Mike kept the muzzle of the Galil pressed against the rear of Kerchenko's head. "Bring out your right hand, very slowly. If there's a weapon in it, you're dead."

Kerchenko's right hand was empty, and Bruckner jerked him roughly to his feet. While Kerchenko stood with his hands on his head, Bruckner began searching the stone-faced but frightened officer

"Camellion, come over here," yelled Quinlan. As soon as the Death Merchant was behind the filing cabinets and saw Kerchenko, Quinlan said, "Look what we done got us—a gen-u-wine Rooshun big shot. Those gold and red shoulder boards with the stars indicate he's a damned general. How about that?"

"He'll sing an entire opera, provided we can keep the Pathans from turning him into chopped liver," Camellion said, eyeing General Kerchenko, who stared straight ahead as Bruckner removed a small weapon from his left pocket in his uniform coat and handed it to Quinlan. Mad Mike briefly inspected the pistol and gave it to the Death Merchant.

"Ever see one like this?"

Camellion had. The small handgun was a Soviet GRU-Spetsnaz PSM (*Pistolet Samozaryadniy Malogabaritniy*) assassination semi-automatic pistol that resembled a Walther PPK and fired a 5.45 × 18 bottlenecked rimless cartridge.

Camellion returned the PSM to Quinlan. "Keep it as a souvenir."

Quinlan shoved the weapon into a pocket. "Here comes trouble and maybe bye-bye general!"

The trouble was Kunar Rahm-Vavin and Nangarhar Yagum'qi who had stepped behind the filing cabinets, their eyes becoming cruel and hard when they saw General Kerchenko.

"This one is mine," Camellion said coldly. "He's not wounded, can run with us if he has to, and he's going back. If there are any objections spit 'em out now."

"Give us one good reason why this son of a whore should not die?" demanded Seif-Bualy.

"The best reason in the world. He has valuable information that could possibly save the lives of hundreds of Pakistinis and Afghans. And I don't want him getting a *kaurang* in the back when we're on the trail. Understand that—now!"

There was a certain quality about the Death Merchant's voice, a high strangeness in his eyes, that warned the Pathans that he meant exactly what he said; and very suddenly, they were slightly afraid.

"The cur is your responsibility, Kir Camellion," Seif-Bualy said slowly, and turned away with the other two Paks.

The Death Merchant turned his attention to the prize. "You're a lucky man, General. What is your name?"

"I am Lieutenant General Gregor Ivanovich Kerchenko," the Russian responded stiffly.

"Attached to what—the Spetsnaz here in Afghanistan? That means you're Soviet army."

Kerchenko didn't answer

"There's still time to turn you over to the Paks." When Camellion saw Kerchenko's eyes widen at the mention of the Pakistanis, he said, "That's right. They're Pakistanis, not Afghan *Mujahideen*."

"You could turn me over to those savages, but you wouldn't. A dead man cannot give information."

"How right you are." Camellion's voice was sickeningly

sweet. "Dead men can only howl in hell or sing forever in heaven—"

"Or they don't even know they're dead!" interjected Quinlan.

"But before a man dies, he can talk his head right off his neck, if his feet are being roasted over hot coals, or his head is in a bird cage with hungry rats nibbling away at his flesh. What's your office?"

"I'm in the *Glavnoye Razvedyvatelnoye Upravleniye,* if that means anything to you?"

"Come, come, General. I'm very familiar with the chief intelligence directorate of the Soviet general staff," Camellion said in perfect Russian, enjoying the surprise in Kerchenko's eyes. "Before I'm dead, I'll see the Soviet general staff and your precious Moscow turned into radioactive dust." *And Paris, Rome, London, Berlin, Tokyo, New York, Chicago, Los Angeles, Rio, and a thousand other targets . . .*

Mad Mike Quinlan's laugh was mocking. "We done grabbed us a real big fish out of the red pond. We done got us a GRU general."

The Death Merchant said, "For now, Gregor Ivanovich Kerchenko, here are the facts of life. Try to escape if you want. When you do, these two jolly fellows will kill you."

"And take the greatest pleasure in doing it," Quinlan said in Russian. He was no longer in the mood to clown around. "We'll chop your legs off with slugs and leave you to bleed to death—believe it!"

The Pakistani signal cry was a cross between a yodel and a Rebel battle yell. It worked. Five hundred and forty men had charged across the open space and had attacked the Spetsnaz base. Only seventy-two were now running back toward the relative security of the mountains—including the Peppermint Kid and the men in the rocks who had survived the Spicer missile attack, 109 men would take to the mountains and try to get back to Pakistan—110, when one included General Kerchenko.

The Spetsnaz base, over which hung a cloud of smoke and stink, was far behind them, the boulders just ahead. The Death Merchant, however, was not a happy man. Somewhere back at the Soviet base, he had lost the *jambiya* he had taken weeks ago from the corpse of Asad Dizakan.

How cruel and unfair life could be.

Fudge . . .

EPILOGUE

14.00 hours.
The embassy of the United States in New Delhi, India.
Twenty-one days after the successful attack on the Soviet Spetsnaz base in Afghanistan.

Richard Camellion, dressed in a blue all wool worsted Glen-plaid suit, stood by the window of the third-story conference room and idly surveyed part of the embassy compound. There was a soft breeze blowing through the tall deodar and cinchona trees. Nice. However, after sunset it was still a shave too chilly to walk in the garden.

Camellion contemplated the time factor. The operation had eaten into his busy schedule, gobbling up three months and seventeen days.

It could have been more time-consuming. . . .

It could even have been fatal. . . .

Traces of faint laughter sparkled in his eyes. After you've broken your legs three times, you become damned cautious about taking that first step. Yet sometimes you have to ignore that first timid, hesitant step and go right into a high jump, the way he and the three Thunderbolts had. *By now, Mike and Willy and the Peppermint Kid are back at their headquarters in Sardinia. Mad Mike will be juiced for a week. . . .*

The "high jump" into Afghanistan had worked beautifully; the Spetsnaz base had been destroyed, its destruction worth every life lost. The escape had been difficult. Soviet Hind-Ds had harassed the survivors for days, even after the Paks had crossed the border and were ten klicks into Pakistan.

Thirty-four Pakistanis, two Americans, one German, one Englishman, and one pig farmer had finally reached Sirzihil. The next problem was how to get out of Pakistan, Lieutenant General Gregor Kerchenko complicating the riddle. Worse, the "Sapphire Route" had been closed. That had been the underground from Pakistan to Bikarner, India. The Indian intelligence service had been getting too close.

Courtland Grojean had done the unexpected and, the Death Merchant suspected, without proper authorization. From some secret take-off base in India—he had not told Camellion the location, nor had the Death Merchant asked—he had sent two Kaman SH-2 Seasprite helicopters to Sirzihil, each chopper carrying a Gf Mechanism and each having extra-large fuel tanks—two in case one developed engine trouble and had to land. Both birds had been sanitized; neither had had a single marking or number. The crews had been equally enigmatic; they hadn't spoken thirty-nine words.

From Sirzihil, the two "invisible" choppers had flown back into India, one going to the United States embassy in New Delhi and landing in the large compound, in a small, open area beside the garden. The craft had then refueled, turned on the Gf Mechanism and taken off to . . .

A dumbfounded Lieutenant General Gregor Kerchenko had been immediately whisked to one of the VS rooms in the Company station at the embassy, stripped and handcuffed. He was worth more than triple his weight in solid gold and the CIA didn't intend for him to have a change of heart and commit suicide.

Thinking about Kerchenko, Camellion had to smile. The GRU officer had not been able to understand how two helicopters could openly fly from India into Pakistan and back again without being challenged by either Indian or Pakistani ground control or Indian or Pakistani aircraft. Curiosity had finally gotten the better of Kerchenko and he had asked Camellion for an explanation.

"Oh, that's easy, General. We're invisible," Camellion had told the Russian with a straight face. "We can neither be seen nor heard."

"You see, General, the Central Intelligence Agency has 'dark powers,' powers from hell," Quinlan said with a sincerity that qualified him for an Academy Award. "The Company made a pact with the Devil."

General Kerchenko had sneered at Quinlan and Camellion.

Both knew that he hadn't believed a word about the two birds being unseen and unheard. How could he? It was too ridiculous. Why, everything appeared "normal." And why not? Kerchenko was *inside* the chopper.

Camellion and Quinlan could almost hear him thinking: that the CIA had made some kind of secret agreement with the Indian and the Pakistani governments and that the two helicopters had some kind of ident code the pilots were using with Pak and Indian ground control.

The Death Merchant had been present at the first five questioning sessions of Kerchenko, much to the annoyance of Jonas Hightower, the chief of station and the other professional career "government employees." All of them considered themselves far superior to a "mercenary" (even if they couldn't change a light bulb with printed directions and a trial run), to an on-contract agent (who wasn't a right-wing fanatic). There hadn't been anything they could do to keep Camellion away. Grojean had given his permission for the Death Merchant to be present.

General Kerchenko, anxious now to get to the United States, had explained that he wanted to defect. To prove it, he would give only a tiny bit of the valuable information he possessed. Some of the intelligence he revealed was as fantastic as screen doors on a submarine. For example, Lieutenant General Yahya Si'Quetta was an agent of the GRU. Yahya Si'Quetta was the assistant of General Saha I'Zada, the director of the Pakistan security police and intelligence service. There were four other GRU agents—Pak traitors—in the Pakistani Ministry of the Interior. None of the men were aware of the other agents.

"Do not ask me about the Pakistani traitors working for the *Kah Gay Beh*. As you know, the *Geh Eh Ru* is a separate service and does not have any connection with the *Kah Gay Beh*."

The Death Merchant turned from the window and sat down in one of the leather chairs at the conference table. He would be happy to be leaving the embassy, even happier to be getting out of India. Yes, sir, he would be glad to be on his way, not that he minded the stiff politeness of the professional CIA men. There was a single exception, one of the women in the station's code room. She was very friendly and, under different circumstances, could have given Camellion ideas. She looked like twenty million dollars with every cent invested in the right place.

Anyhow, it would all even out in the end, no matter what the

CIA or the GRU and the KGB might do. What none of the people in government realized—in both the United States and the Soviet Union—was that their respective nations were a part of a plan, of a cosmic scheme that mortal man was not meant to comprehend. The paradox was that if man could comprehend such power and even manage to get the barest glimpse of the hidden force motivating people and orchestrating world events, he would not be man! He would not stand on his crooked little legs and scream at the stars that *I am a special creation in this universe, I and I alone.*

Pathetic. If man were not man, he would realize that all he really had to lose was his ridiculous pride. He would realize that of all the creatures on the planet, he was the most cruel and the most immoral. He would also know that he was responsible for the world's mess because he had lost all sense of good and evil.

The Death Merchant was a realist. *What is to come will be. Italy will drop out of NATO after a severe economic crisis. Before that happens many problems will close in on the Vatican. The pope will reveal the third secret of Fatima, and even the "good people" will refuse to believe him. Much worse will be the decline of U.S. prestige in the world and the political and military pressure that the Soviet Union will exert upon Europe. The USSR will become more of an open partner of the Arabs in their hatred of Israel, and this alliance will lead to a further deterioration of East-West relations. He will be assassinated and the world will be astonished. Some will be happy. Many will be sad and accuse the wrong people. . . .*

Camellion emerged from his reverie when the door opened and Dane Bachalor, the assistant chief of station, came into the conference room, carrying a large brown envelope. He closed the door, walked across the room, pulled out a chair and sat down next to the Death Merchant.

Bachalor was one of those young men who age before their time. Thirty-six years old, he looked forty-five, and by the time he reached forty-five, he would appear ready for Medicare. The Death Merchant, with his keen eye for disguises and other facades, detected that the AC/S was wearing an expensive toupee, which made him look like a mole with mange.

Bachalor's strong voice did not match his sagging face. "We have everything you need in the envelope, Mr. Camellion: British passport . . ." Opening the envelope, he paused to give a rapid series of tiny laughs. "I was about to ask you if you spoke

English. How ridiculous. I was thinking of another agent we sent out last week. We had a Spanish passport ready for him. Unfortunately, he didn't speak Spanish. As I was saying, here's your British passport, your Indian visa and several letters of credit drawn on London banking institutions. The letters of credit are genuine. You are to turn them over to one of our people in London. It is our understanding that you already know how to contact our street man in London."

"Yes, that was arranged with Mr. G. before I left the States." Camellion carefully and methodically checked the passport and the visa. Both were in the name of James Glen Sherman. Both were beautiful jobs of forgery.

Bachalor handed Camellion a long white envelope bulging with currency. "And here is $3000 American and the equivalent of $2000 in rupees. Remember, you are James Glen Sherman. In the envelope, you will also find your original ticket, the one you had when you landed in India months ago."

Camellion found the ticket and examined it. The ticket was genuine. "I see. The Company used a *doppelgänger*."

"Yes. The same day that you and Colonel Quinlan landed in Pakistan, your doubles landed in India. It was the same with Colonel Quinlan's two men. We would have gotten you out of India with them, four days ago, but yours is a special case that requires special handling; and three men departing are less conspicuous and less suspicious than four. By the way, we heard by radio this morning that Colonel Quinlan and his two men arrived safely at their final destination." Bachalor peered closely at Camellion. "From here you will fly to Paris. After six days in Paris, you will proceed to London. I assume you know how to handle customs and immigration at Orly and Heathrow?"

"Why the stopover in Paris? Why not a straight shot to London?" The Death Merchant knew it was Courtland Grojean's fanatical preoccupation with security, but he wanted to hear Bachalor's answer.

"I don't know. We are only following precise instructions." Bachalor took another envelope from the much larger one on the table. "But you do know how to deal with customs and immigration, don't you?"

Camellion felt sorry for the man. Did Adolf Hitler know how to stir the emotions of the German people?

"I've used the 'in transit' dodge[1] numerous times," Camellion said lazily. "I will need a list of departures from Orly Airport, those that will be leaving for other countries within three to five hours after I land at Paris—flight time, the whole nine yards."

"I have the list here." Bachalor handed the envelope to the Death Merchant. "Your ticket to Paris is also in the envelope. Take-off time is at 6:10 tonight. Uh . . . you know how to make contact with our man in Paris?"

"I know." Camellion looked inside the envelope, making sure that everything was in order and thinking of Courtland Grojean. He knew that the Fox knew that a bluff was as good as a full house—depending. To be on the safe side, Grojean was even fooling his own people at the Company station in the U.S. embassy in India. Camellion was almost positive that he would not be flying from Paris to London. He would meet the contact in Paris and from Paris go to—where? Whatever the arrangements might be, the Death Merchant knew his final destination would be far far to the south: Antarctica . . .

"We are calling it Operation Blowpipe," Grojean had told him, "and believe me, this mission is extremely important, not only to us but to the entire world."

Camellion recalled other information that Grojean had divulged about the mission. In Camellion's opinion, the operation had been misnamed.

It should be called the Atlantean Horror. . . .

[1] On the landing card one writes "in transit" and lists a flight to another city in another country and states he will be departing in a few hours. Any passenger who makes such a declaration does not have to go through immigration; however, a "watch book" at the customs desk will contain his name, or it should. But customs and immigration people are so busy that they seldom bother to check the book. In recent years there has been a stricter control, due to the international drug traffic.

WHERE THEY ARE NOW

Chief Mujibur Ali Mirza-Khan died during March of 1985. From the rumors that have floated out of Pakistan, he was murdered—poisoned.

Lieutenant General Gregor Kerchenko is still in custody of the Central Intelligence Agency and acting as a "Special Consultant in Intelligence" to the Agency. He gave the CIA enough inside information to fill 7,413 typewritten pages—not only about GRU operations in Pakistan, Afghanistan, India and other nations, but also about special GRU *otdels* in the United States.

Kerchenko's capture and revelations were a major setback for the GRU, one that caused the downfall of scores of Soviet agents and forced a general reorganization of foreign GRU cells and channels of information. Lieutenant General Kerchenko's capture and the destruction of the Spetsnaz base in Afghanistan also caused a shake-up in the Soviet GOU, the Main Operations Directorate *(Glavnoye Operavnoye Upravleniye)*, under the first deputy chief of the general staff, General Varennikov. Six officers were replaced. General I. K. Varennikov came very close to demotion.

Colonel Michael Wade Quinlan is rumored to be in Bolivia with nine of his Thunderbolt Unit Omega men.

Mohammed Zia ul-Haq remains the president of Pakistan. He is still playing the Soviet Union and India against the United States and Israel, and is very successful at it. The Soviet Union was enraged when, in 1985, Pakistan and Romania concluded an agreement to increase mutual cooperation in international affairs. After Romanian President Nicolae Ceausescu's visit to Islamabad,

President Zia said that the two nations "hold similar views or very similar views on most contemporary world issues."

General Saha I'Zada, the chief of Pakistan intelligence and internal security, was replaced by President Zia, who stated to the national assembly and the senate that I'Zada "is too preoccupied with ideas foreign to our national beliefs to be effective as director of the Chanwiri-lu-Shabudar. I am, therefore, giving the post of director to Lieutenant General Yahya Si'Quetta and promoting him to general."

In January of 1985, Saha I'Zada committed suicide by shooting himself through the roof of the mouth. He was buried with full military honors. President Zia himself gave the eulogy. Plans are now under way for Saha I'Zada Square, to be built in Islamabad.

The Soviet Spetsnaz base in Afghanistan has not been rebuilt.